CATS NEVER FLY

Willow Lake Supernaturals

Book 4

LORI AMES

Cats Never Fly by Lori Ames

Published by November Snow
Copyright © 2024 by S.L. Paton. All rights reserved.

Digital edition / 2024 - ISBN 978-1-989764-75-6
Print edition / 2024 - ISBN 978-1-989764-76-3
Large Print edition / 2025 - ISBN 978-1-989764-88-6

Cover by: S.L. Paton
Beta Reading by: Kirk Waite at Rare Bird Beta Reading & Courtney Bassett

Content Warning

Generally, I would not characterize my books as the kind that will rip your heart out and stomp on it until you cry, however they do have some content that people may find uncomfortable or triggering.

Note: This list contains spoilers.

Content warnings include: swearing, violence, unexpected bond created between main characters due to an external force, sexual content, abduction, fall from a great height, one mention of suicides of unnamed characters, injuries, trafficking of supernatural people, supernatural people in cages, bad guy loses his hand in fight, death (not of main characters).

Chapter One

SIMON

Earlier in the Summer, During the Heat Wave (takes place just before Hellhounds Never Lie*)*

I'd always been comforted by the knowledge I had nine lives.

That was particularly true now when things in Willow Lake were getting a little tense. Mama said this tension in the air was nothing new, that things had been like this since the wolf pack split in two, but that made little sense to me—although I'd never ever tell her that. I mean, sure, I'd grown up thinking of one as good and the other as evil, but the pack broke apart *years* and *years* ago. Why would something that happened when I was a kid bother me now?

Maybe this crazy heat wave was messing with me. The longer it lasted, the more people got antsy. But whatever was causing it, I'd be okay. I was still on life number one, after all. And Mama always said Mother Magic, who almost everyone else called the Eternal Magic, liked cats, which was another blessing in my favor.

Really, who wouldn't want to be a cat shifter?

Sure, the three wolves I was observing—from a safe distance and downwind—would likely disagree, but they weren't the nice wolves. They might smell a bit like our alpha Hayden, but they weren't our wolves. No, these could only be from the half that'd broken away from the Willow Lake pack, the ones who were a bunch of jerks. So what would they know?

At least they hadn't noticed me.

I wasn't keen on losing one of my nine just yet, and I didn't like my odds if they discovered me out here on my own. They'd think I was spying on them. I wasn't. Not really. It was an accident that I'd seen them at all.

My brothers would call them prickholes or something like that, but I tried to keep the language, even in my head, to a PG rating. When I remembered, anyway. Mama was merciless about pinching our ears whenever we swore. It didn't matter that we were all adults now. I didn't know how the others could stand it.

Which is one of the many reasons they called me a mama's kitten or a scaredy cat.

Whatever.

I was just smarter than the rest of my brothers.

Take now, for instance. It made sense to stay hidden and safe. Anyone with half a brain would do the same if they saw the scruffy trio who had appeared out of nowhere a few minutes ago.

Although, I doubted my brothers would hide like me. Did that mean they had less than half a brain?

Mama would disagree with that conclusion. She was ridiculously proud and protective of all her kittens, even the reckless ones who refused to protect their nine.

The wolves were in their human form, but that didn't stop one of them from tipping his head back and howling at the night sky. The noise was meant to intimidate, and it was doing an excellent job. Icy fear skated down my spine. I held my breath and prayed they wouldn't find me.

Not for the first time, I was thankful for my black fur. It was perfect camouflage on nights like this. And right now, I was banking on my coloring to keep me concealed in the shadows of the leafy tree branches. We were far enough from the lake here that the trees were further apart and more aspen than pine. Mama always complained that this area looked grubby and untidy with all the scrubby bushes, but I liked it.

Really.

It was… um… pretty. Sure.

I sighed.

Okay, fine. It *might* be because large predators often stalked their prey closer to the water, but no one needed to know that.

"That was too easy," one wolf said to his buddies. His gruff voice carried across the sleepy landscape. Apparently, he didn't see the need to whisper, even though it looked like he'd been up to no good, as Mama liked to say.

"They say Ulric's grandkid ain't a supe. Don't even know about us. Wouldn't think to watch his shit or have

3

wards or nothing," another wolf said as he lumbered toward an old clunker of a pickup truck hiding behind a scrubby shrub.

The truck was more rust than anything else. I bet even a human with their weak eyesight could see how bad it was. But that wasn't what caught my attention. Nope. It was the bag—its bulging sides and contents clanging and clinking with each step he took—that one wolf had hoisted over his shoulder. My ears twitched and my nose wiggled as I tried to figure out what they were hauling.

The scene reminded me of those old cartoons with a robber and his cloth bag of stolen stuff I used to watch as a kid. The only things missing were the dollar sign painted on the side of the bag and black masks covering the top part of their faces.

And yes, maybe I *still* enjoyed cartoons on Saturday mornings. Cats needed time to relax and chill. It was a thing. But that wasn't what was important right now.

I watched, unblinking, as the guy lifted the bag higher to toss it in the back of the truck. And—

Oh!

What was that?

My breath caught.

Something dropped out of the bag. It caught the moonlight on the way down, looking all shiny and golden. I didn't know what it was, but it was pretty. Even from this distance, I could tell that much.

I know, I know. That dead human poet talked about glittering things not always being gold or whatever... but I didn't need gold. I just needed that thing, whatever it was. Something in my gut said *mine, mine, mine*. My tail trembled, and I clenched my teeth to keep from chirping at my prey... my prize.

Please, please, please... Don't let them see it.

I desperately wanted to know what had dropped out of that bag, but it would be stupid to look right now. Particularly when these three looked hyped up on adrenaline from their heist of the Willow Lake Inn—because that was the only place they could be talking about.

I should report the robbery to the police.

It was the right thing to do.

Probably.

Although, after growing up in a houseful of cats, all of whom, except maybe Mama, saw the world in varying shades of gray—not the fifty sexy ones, but the morally ambiguous kind—I had a bit of an aversion to snitching on anyone or anything. I might work in security, but when I wasn't at work, I kept my whiskers out of other people's business. My brothers taught me being a tattletale was asking for trouble.

And would it actually harm anyone if the wolves got away with whatever they were doing?

Ulric, the former owner of the inn, had been a mage of some kind and had collected all kinds of magical junk. He died almost a year ago and left the place to his grandkid, so it wasn't like anyone was using the stuff.

I'd always found him creepy—Ulric, not the grandkid. The grandkid, Jake, was weird, but kind of cute too. If Jake was the least bit supernatural, I might have asked him out. Or, rather, I would have daydreamed about asking him out. I hadn't ever been on a date, and I couldn't imagine starting with a guy like Jake. He was out of my league, like every guy in town. Because Ash was pretty cute too—and he *was* supernatural, so he fit my hypothetical dating criteria—and I hadn't asked him out either.

Being a scaredy cat might protect my nine lives, but it could also make life pretty boring. It was worth it though. My nine weren't going anywhere if I could help it.

But coming back to Ulric, the grandfather, now he had been creepy, like a fictional wizard brought to life with scraggly gray hair, wire-rimmed glasses, and grotesquely long and thick hairs protruding from his nose and ears. I swear those things—the hairs coming out of his orifices, not the rest—twitched and writhed around like skinny little worms with every breath he took. It was disturbing.

I'd had nightmares about those worm hairs... or would they be hair worms?

Whatever.

Mama always said I was being silly when I told her about them, but that hadn't stopped me from avoiding the man when he'd been alive, which meant I didn't know much about Ulric except what the town gossips said. For years, there'd been rumors about all the creepy things he had squirreled away in his private chambers at the inn. And now it looked like the wolves had stolen them. But how? Willow Lake Inn was miles away, and I hadn't seen or heard them walking through the woods until now.

"What about the cat?"

I froze. Had they found me? Did they know I was watching and listening?

"I didn't see it."

"Me neither."

They shrugged in unison.

"Whatever. We did it once, we can do it again."

Phew. Okay. They weren't talking about me, although my heart felt ready to pound itself to freedom outside my body anyway.

And the cat they *were* talking about wasn't any normal cat shifter.

Paws lived at the inn and had been there ever since the werewolf pack had abandoned it years ago. Some people thought he was a god doing penance for some mischief he'd caused. Others speculated he was a plain old cat shifter who'd been cursed by a mage to never change out of his cat form. There were also the people who believed he was once a beloved pet who belonged to a Norwegian goddess. And then there was the theory about him being a Scottish fairy creature.

Speculating about their neighbors was the one thing the people in Willow Lake liked to do. Honestly, why hadn't someone asked the cat what he was?

Well. Not me. I wouldn't ask. That cat was almost as freaky as old Ulric's hair worms. But someone else could have and probably should have.

Anyway, it didn't matter if I didn't know exactly who the cat was or where he'd come from. What I *did* know was that being near him made my tail puff up and twitch like the inflatable tube man thing my boss Levi had installed outside the Tarbeck Motel last week.

Each time the tube man collapsed down, it reached right for me before the air filled it and it went shooting up again. Just thinking about it made my fur puff up more. The thing was freaky. I swore it spied on me as I did my rounds every night.

Now, you might think working security at the motel was a bad career choice for a scaredy cat like me, but no one ever did anything in Willow Lake, especially not to a place that a minotaur owned. The job was boring, like me. Just the way I liked it.

I never expected to come across a robbery like this before.

Without another word, the trio of bandits hopped into their old truck. The engine started with a cough and a sputter, then the truck peeled out of sight, leaving behind a cloud of dust that settled quickly in the still night.

My claws dug into the tree branch I was clinging to. I itched to jump down and go for my treasure, but were they really gone? I didn't see another truck, so I figured it was a pretty safe bet that no one else would pop up out of nowhere, but what if those wolves realized they'd dropped something? What if they came back to get more stuff from the inn tonight?

No. It was too risky to act too quickly.

My mama always told me the best way to live was to treat each of my lives like it was precious. "*You might have nine, but that doesn't mean you should squander them.*"

I didn't know how many times she'd told my brothers and me that when we were growing up. It was usually after one of them did something stupid, like when Clive jumped off the roof of the house, convinced he could leap farther than a flying squirrel could fly.

Yeah, that brother wasn't the smartest kitten in the litter.

Cats were not meant to fly.

Mama said he might have been okay if he'd stayed in

his cat form the whole time, but for some crazy reason he shifted into his human form when he realized he wouldn't make it. But even after breaking both his legs and losing one of his nine, he hadn't learned his lesson about what cats should or shouldn't do. I was pretty sure he was down to about five lives now, although Mama thought he still had seven.

I'd found the whole thing educational, though. I'd written an essay about cats and their ability to survive falls for one of my biology classes in high school and everything.

If I was ever in that situation, I wouldn't make the same mistake as Clive. Of course, I never ever planned to be in that situation, so there was that. I was the only one of my brothers who still had all nine. And yep, you guessed it. I'd been called a scaredy cat my whole entire life.

It was fine. Really. There were worse things.

And I wasn't about to rush over to that shiny bit of temptation and risk losing one of my nine now.

I was patient. I could wait.

As pinks and oranges streaked across the eastern sky hours later, I cautiously descended from the tree branch I'd perched on for most of the night. My cat form was small, so I was pretty agile, even if I was a little on the chunky side. As soon as my paws hit dirt, I paused again and listened. Nothing. I inhaled and found no fresh scents in the air.

I slunk toward the treasure, my furry belly close to the ground.

My ears swiveled with each sound. My muscles coiled,

ready to sprint if I needed to make a quick getaway. My steps were silent.

As I neared the place where the wolves had been, the scent of wet wolves grew stronger. Disgusting. My nose twitched and threatened to sneeze. How was that smell possible when it hadn't rained in at least a week?

I inched forward.

There, glinting under the new day's warm rays of sunlight, was a shiny lump on the dusty ground. I padded a little closer. It looked like a whistle made of some kind of gold-like metal. Ornate curls and swirls, which reminded me a little of both fire and waves on the water, covered the surface.

It was wonderful.

It was mine.

I pounced and covered it with my body.

The smells of ozone and lightning and licorice, all mashed together in a distinctive blend, hit my nose. The sneeze that threatened to come a moment ago exploded out of me. Once. Twice. Three times. Mama said sneezing three times in a row was lucky. I hoped she was right because that smell could only be one thing: magic.

My brand-new little whistle was drenched in it.

What did that mean? What did it do? Was this a trap?

Normally, I'd have abandoned the prize at the first hint of magic, but… I just couldn't. If I didn't know better, I'd swear Mother Magic herself was screaming at me to take the whistle. Hide it. Protect it. As long as I didn't start calling it *my precious* I'd be okay, right?

Mama always said we should trust our instincts. And I trusted my mama.

I looked left. Then right. Then over my shoulder.

Nothing seemed out of place. No one jumped out at me.

I shifted into my human form, my clothes reappearing with the magic of my shift. When I'd left home last night I hadn't known I'd need pockets, but I was glad I'd worn my hoodie with the zippered pockets now.

I reached for my whistle.

Then I froze before my human-shaped fingers touched it.

Would the magic hurt me?

Nah. It wouldn't, right? I'd touched it as a cat, and it hadn't bothered me. Although, a shifter was always stronger and more immune to magic in their alternate form. But those wolves had all seemed okay. One of them had to have touched it when they put it in the bag, right?

Decision made; I plucked the whistle from the dirt.

It was lighter than I'd expected. Dust dropped away from its surface without me having to do a thing. The whistle was the length of my hand, from the tip of my middle finger to the bottom of my palm. Cradling it like a newborn kitten, I turned it to get a better look at the etchings. I still didn't know if the marks were supposed to be waves or flames, but it didn't matter. I loved it.

I curled my fingers around it as I looked around to see if anything else had dropped out of the bag. Nothing but faint footprints and tire tracks marked the dirt. That was okay. My prize was enough. I tucked the whistle into my pocket and zipped it up. My hand wrapped around it through the fabric. Just to make sure it was still there. Safe and secure.

And then, because I couldn't curb all my cat-like impulses, I let my curiosity take the lead. Those wolves didn't have the magic to create portals, like some of the supernatural beings did, so they had to have done something else to get to the inn from here. I sniffed and followed the trail.

A few steps away, concealed by more scrubby shrubs, was a disguised doorway of old weathered wood and rusted hinges. The wolves had left it slightly ajar. I peered through the crack and found a tunnel. I bet it led right to the inn. That place had been an old pack house once upon a time. This had to be a secret escape tunnel from way back, likely built during the Shifter Wars.

So freaking cool.

I stepped toward it, ready to explore it for myself.

But then the whistle shifted in my pocket.

Right.

The tunnel opening was tempting, but I already had a prize from tonight. I'd come back and explore the curious passage later, after I knew the wolves were done with it. There was no reason to go in there, especially when the wolves might come back. I would be trapped inside. I doubted there'd be an escape route from the tunnel since it *was* the escape route.

I was too protective of my nine to risk it.

I tightened my grip on the whistle and turned away from the intriguing door.

As soon as I moved away from the tunnel, the whistle filled my thoughts again. I wished I could ask someone about it, but what if someone recognized it as something belonging to the inn? I mean, yes, I probably should return it to Ulric's grandkid, but he hadn't been using it, I was sure of that. Like the wolves said, everyone knew Jake wasn't a supe.

The other locals found it strange he wasn't a supernatural being considering who his grandfather was—they even had a bet going at his pub about when his magic would show up and he finally discovered magic was real—but I figured strange things happened every day. Why couldn't a non-supe be born in a supe family?

According to my high school biology teacher, genetics did weird things sometimes. Of course, that didn't mean I hadn't put some money down on the bet. The chances of winning were much higher compared to the human-run lottery.

And wasn't finding the whistle almost like winning the lottery too?

Yes. The more I thought about it, the more I was sure the whistle was better off with a supe—me specifically—than with Ulric's mundane grandkid.

But was it weird to feel a connection to the pretty whistle? I hoped it hadn't cursed me. Mama would have my hide if I let something like that happen. Still, I knew, right down to my polydactyl toe, I couldn't give the whistle over to someone who wouldn't appreciate it.

No. I'd figure out what the whistle did all on my own. Because this was no ordinary whistle. Magic wouldn't cling to it like it did if it was no different from the shrill whistles police constables used in those historical mysteries Mama liked to watch on Netflix.

First, though, I had to get back to the house before Mama threw my breakfast in the garbage because I was late. Since neither my siblings nor I were kittens anymore, we didn't live with her and Pops, but she still insisted we all come for breakfast every day. She called it family bonding time and the most important meal of the day. The time when we all talked about our lives and what we'd gotten up to during the night.

Today was the first time I wouldn't be completely honest with my family as we chatted over bacon, eggs, and smoked kippers.

I didn't want to tell anyone about my whistle, not even my mama. Not yet anyway.

Chapter Two

SIMON

After possessing the whistle for approximately twenty-one hours, thirty-seven minutes, and forty-three seconds, I was a mess. I jumped and hissed at every little sound. Guilt ate at me like those caterpillars who infiltrated Mama's garden every year and gnawed on her cabbages. Every time footsteps headed in my direction, I was sure the police were coming to arrest me. Nothing calmed my nerves, not even holding my precious new whistle.

My concentration was non-existent, but at least my job was boring and predictable, so I didn't need a lot of brain power to get through my shift. I stomped along my usual route at the perimeter of the property, more out of muscle memory than from an actual conscious decision.

When I was rounding the corner, a shadow jumped toward me. I leaped away, darting in the opposite direction to return to the narrow walkway along the side of the property. Leaning against the wall, I gasped for breath. I swore my heart stopped beating as my ears strained for any sound of someone pursuing me. Then there was a sound like fabric snapping. What was that? I peered around the corner. The shadow bounced out of sight.

My hand trembled as I reached for my phone.

I swallowed hard.

This wasn't good. I couldn't remember anything. What was I supposed to do? Call someone? The police? Levi? My hands shook so hard I couldn't get the screen unlocked. I messed up the pattern every time I tried to drag my finger across the screen.

That wasn't working.

I gulped as I shoved the phone back in my pocket.

I needed to get help the old-fashioned way. If I shifted, I could run to the police station.

The transition to my cat form slipped over me. Then I crept around the building, hugging the shadows. My tail was all puffed up. I didn't dare blink.

The shadow swept over the ground again in an erratic, jerky motion. What was that?

I inched forward.

Then I saw it. The inflatable tube man.

I gasped for breath. How had I forgotten about that thing in the one hour since my last round? Yes, anxiety had muddled my thoughts, but I was worse off than I had thought.

But was something else there too?

I held my breath and watched.

The shadows swept over the ground again and again as the inflatable man waved around. Nothing was there but that stupid tube man thing.

I let out the breath with a gusty exhale.

It hadn't felt like it at the time, but my phone not working had been a stroke of luck. The whole town would have laughed at me if I'd made that call.

The thing collapsed down, coming right for me, before the air filled it and it went shooting up again. Then it did the same thing again. And again. Coming straight at me every single time.

Was the thing possessed?

The way its wide, unblinking eyes stared at me made my fur stand on end. It shot down toward me again, its big eerie smile coming right at me, as if it meant to eat me.

It mocked me. I swore it screamed at me every time it flew down toward me. *I know what you did. Those wolves are going to make trouble and you aren't doing anything. Thief! Lazy! Scaredy cat!*

I arched my back. I hissed. No way!

I wasn't letting it taunt me like that. It came at me again.

With a screech, I leaped. My claws tore at the slippery fabric, slicing the tube into ribbons that flapped and slapped at me. I doubled my efforts.

Die, you blasted thing! Die!

I didn't stop until the thing lay limply across the ground. I panted and stared at it, daring it to come after me again.

It didn't.

Eventually, my breathing slowed, and my heart rate returned to normal.

I surveyed the mess I'd made. Bits of fabric covered the sidewalk, the road, and the lawn. The air blower still hummed as usual, but only a sliver of fabric still wiggled in its breeze.

Uh oh.

What had I done?

I didn't think anyone would be too upset about the inflatable man being gone. Getting rid of the thing was a community service, right? Except I doubted Levi would see it that way.

I tiptoed back to the shadows and looked up and down the street. Nothing moved, but that was normal. Willow Lake was a small town. There usually wasn't much activity on the streets in the middle of the night.

I prayed to the Eternal Magic no one had seen me. Maybe I should call her Mother Magic like Mama did. Would that help me gain her goodwill?

Then I sent out a second prayer that no one ever found out I'd destroyed the inflatable tube man, particularly Levi. As a minotaur, Levi could be a bit bullish. I doubted he'd see the humor in the situation, at least not before firing my furry butt.

And what would people think?

Everyone in town already gave me strange looks. I didn't need them finding out I'd lost control and attacked the tube man like a kitten high on catnip for the first time. Not only would it make me more of a weirdo in everyone's eyes, it might even cost me my job, and then what would I do? Job opportunities were scarce for a regular cat shifter like me. I'd never survive picking up odd jobs here and there like my brothers Clive and Warren did. I liked the routine of steady employment. Knowing I'd get paid each month helped me sleep like a kitten each night.

I sighed as I crept around the building toward the front office again. As I shifted into my human form, I sucked in a couple of deep breaths. All I wanted to do was run home and hide under my bed, but I liked my job and if I wanted to keep it, I couldn't abandon the motel.

How could I explain this? And more importantly, what had come over me?

It almost made me suspect the whistle was bad luck.

Almost.

Except it was too shiny and pretty to be bad luck.

No. I knew what this greasy, slimy, heavy feeling was. It was guilt. My brothers always called me a sucker for falling for Mama's guilt trips, but it was what it was. I was who I was.

That inflatable tube man's death was all about my guilt.

I sighed.

I had to tell the police what those wolves had said. Jake was too nice. I couldn't sit back and let someone rob him again. Although... Had he even noticed being robbed the first time? The robbery should have been the talk of the town today, but no one had said a peep.

No. Jake's ignorance didn't justify the robbery.

I needed to go to the police station and tell them what I knew. It was the right thing to do. In the meantime, I had to write up an incident report about the tube man and hope I still had a job. My brothers didn't have trouble telling a few white lies here and there, so maybe I could do it too.

Of course, their lies usually sounded like:

Have I eaten? No, of course not, I'm starving.

Do I want my belly rubbed? Sure.

Of course I didn't turn up my nose at this same dish the last time you gave it to me.

Huh. Now that I thought about it, maybe gaslighting was a better way of describing what they did. Unlike them, I only lied when it was absolutely necessary. I was always too scared of getting found out.

After I fudged my way through the report, I heaved out a sigh and went hunting for a rake and some garbage bags. The front desk clerk offered to help clean everything up, but I had to do this myself. I'd made this mess; I needed to clean it up. It took longer than I thought to pick up all the little pieces. A few fine threads of fabric still clung to the grass when I was finished, but I'd done the best I could. I wheeled the air blower over to the maintenance shed and shoved it inside.

Then all I had left to do was wait for Levi to get there in the morning.

The minotaur stomped into the office at seven with a large, insulated cup of coffee in his hand. The side of the cup read *Half of what I say is bull*. He always used it when he bought coffee from the Flying Rowan Café. The way he flaunted things like that suggested he wanted Parker, the human owner of the café, to discover he was a minotaur. I'd seen them flirt, so maybe he did.

I couldn't imagine trying to have a relationship with someone who knew nothing about supernatural beings. The guilt over keeping quiet about the wolves stealing from the inn overwhelmed me; I couldn't imagine what it would be like trying to keep the Eternal Magic a secret from someone I dated.

Levi's drink smelled strong, like he didn't have a drop

of cream in it. How anyone could drink coffee without cream was a mystery to me, but Levi smiled when he took a sip. Then he spotted me, and his broad forehead furrowed.

"What's the matter, Simon?"

"There… uh… was a… situation…" I stuttered. He was totally going to know I was lying.

"Hey, it's okay." Levi clapped his large hand over my shoulder and gave it a little squeeze. "Calm down. Tell me what happened."

I shoved the incident report at him. He set down his coffee and took the form. As he read over my report, his face flushed, his nostrils flared, and he tilted his head down like he was ready to charge after someone and ram into them.

If I'd been in my cat form, I'd have ducked under the desk.

"Damn kids," he muttered and shook his head in disgust.

I kept my mouth shut. Sweat beaded along my brow.

"Hey, don't blame yourself," Levi said when he glanced at me. I could only imagine what I looked like. I was terrible at hiding my emotions. "You can't be everywhere at once."

Guilt clawed at my throat.

"And thanks for cleaning up the mess. I wouldn't want anyone to trip over that stuff."

Not trusting myself to speak yet, I nodded.

"I hope you didn't worry about this all night. You look shattered," Levi said with a soft voice.

I bit my tongue.

"Go home and get some rest."

I left work feeling guiltier than I had when I started. But, by some quirk of fate—or perhaps with the Eternal Magic's help—I left the Tarbeck Motel still employed. But how was I going to make it up to Levi? I sighed.

I didn't go to Mama's for breakfast.

She would have sniffed out my lies the second I walked through the door. Instead, I went home and climbed into bed. I tried to sleep but I couldn't. By the time the sun went down, I knew it was time to act. My shift at the motel started at midnight, so I had a deadline.

Still, I didn't rush to the police station right away. It took most of the evening to work up the courage to go over there. Then I meandered over to the building, where I sat in front of the station for a bit until I finally sucked in a deep breath and accepted that I couldn't put it off any longer. I only had an hour left before my shift started.

I'd heard police stations in human towns weren't open all night, but luckily a supe ran our police department. His name was Van. He was a hellhound and someone I usually tried to avoid. I prayed I wouldn't have to talk to him. I could still remember when he came to talk to my class in elementary school. He'd looked at me with his eyes all lit up like fire and I swore I didn't breathe again until he left. I was ready to confess to anything and everything that'd ever happened in Willow Lake, regardless of whether or not I was involved. As soon as I got home, I slipped into my cat form and hid under my bed for the rest of the day.

I looked over my shoulder and scanned the sidewalk and the road up and down before I climbed the steps to the front door. I didn't see anyone watching me, but I knew

Mama would hear about it anyway. She always knew where her kittens were and what we did.

I pulled open the door and forced myself to take those last few steps to the front desk. A scary looking woman looked up from whatever paperwork she was doing and glared at me from behind a barrier of protective glass. I swear her pale green eyes were almost cat-like with their thin, vertical, slit-shaped pupils as she stared at me. Except one whiff told me she was no cat shifter. She was an alligator or a crocodile or something like that. She could probably devour me in one bite if she shifted completely. I took a step back.

"How can I help you?" Her tone suggested helping me was the last thing she wanted to do.

"I… I need to report… uh, something…" I croaked out. Then I swallowed. My mouth had never been so dry.

"What is the nature of the incident?"

I gulped. "I… uh…"

Another woman I recognized approached the window and looked at me. This one was wearing a uniform. She eyed me curiously.

"I can handle this, Sandra," the newcomer said. "I know you're ready for your break."

"Thanks, Dot." Sandra nodded as she stood. "It's been crazy in here tonight. I can't believe they found that hellhound guy out in the woods. It's like half the town was out looking for him after that bartender had that vision and now everyone and their dog wants to know what's going on." The woman frowned at me. "That's not why you're here, is it? I've heard about you cats and your curiosity."

I shook my head.

"Good, then," the woman nodded. "Constable Hubert will take your statement."

Dot—or I guess she was Constable Hubert now—and I went to school together. She was a year older than me and my littermates. She'd always struck me as a timid person, ready to bolt at the first whiff of trouble. It may feed into a stereotype, but law enforcement seemed like a strange profession for a deer shifter. Their kind was known for running from trouble rather than tackling it to the ground and going for the jugular. I'd always thought that if I was into girls, she would be a perfect choice for me. I couldn't believe she'd become a police officer. I respected the heck out of her for overcoming all her challenges to go for the job she wanted. Obviously, she'd gotten over her scaredy cat tendencies better than I had.

She looked at me with her big brown eyes, assessing me. "You're one of the Rivers boys, aren't you?"

I nodded. It didn't surprise me she didn't remember my name. No one ever did. Littermates like mine usually attracted all the attention, and I was *the other one*.

"You said you had something to report?"

I nodded again. "I overheard some supes talking about something... Something, uh, criminal, I guess."

She blinked at me, then nodded slowly. "Okay. Stay here for a minute. I'll let Chief Clark know. Okay?"

She wasn't gone but a moment. When she returned, her cheeks were a little flushed. She opened the door to the office area of the police station and motioned me inside.

"He's, uh, busy at the moment. I'll take your statement and if he has questions, he'll follow up with you. Sound good?"

She led me to a messy desk and motioned for me to sit on a chair beside it.

"Normally we'd do this in a meeting room, but... uh... not tonight." She pulled out a form from a pile and then took a minute to unearth a pen from the heaps of things on her desk. "Okay. Tell me what happened."

I told her about everything except the whistle and the inflatable tube man. She didn't need to know about those things. No one needed to know about them but me.

Chapter Three

OGDEN

Present Day

The crate was too small. I couldn't stand. I couldn't stretch. I definitely couldn't shift into my dragon form without harming myself.

So I sat in my bare-assed human form on the floor.

Normally, a crate like this wouldn't be able to hold me, but magic had been used to reinforce the thick metal bars on this one. Unlike other shifters, dragons kept the full capacity of their magic, superior senses and strength included, even in their human forms, so whatever magic my captors had used was impressive. Those bars weren't budging until my abductors decided they wanted me out.

None of that explained why I was naked, though. Fucking perverts.

What else had they done to me when I was unconscious? I hated that I didn't know. I remembered nothing between the time I stuck my toes in the water for my late-night swim and waking up here.

Wherever here was.

To top it all off, some little bastard mosquito must have bitten me too, because a bump on my forearm itched like crazy. Usually, I healed too quickly to be irritated by little bites like that, so the fact I wasn't was another cause for concern. What if it wasn't a bug bite? What if they'd injected me with something?

Did I mention how much I hated this?

I scratched my arm as I took in my surroundings, looking for clues about how to get out of here. What I saw was alarming, but not especially useful.

Stacks of crates, like the one I'd woken in, filled the nondescript, concrete-walled room. Each cage contained a naked person. My senses identified each of them as a supernatural being.

You know that saying about misery loving company? That's a damn lie. Because every single supe here was miserable and no one was loving the company. I knew I didn't wish to share this experience with anyone. We were being held like this for one reason: We were merchandise in a trafficking scheme.

Fucking assholes.

A whole host of supernatural products, the rarer the better, showed up on the magical black market from time to time, or so the headlines on Supenet claimed. Dragon scales were, unfortunately, always popular, but flaming phoenix feathers and shavings from unicorn horns were the most coveted because of how scarce they were.

None of those headlines ever mentioned someone selling a whole supernatural being. Supes were full of magic, so we were usually too difficult to contain. I hadn't worried about personal security for years, possibly centuries, not since the Supernatural Council had seized and destroyed those heinous summoning spells and talismans.

Honestly, I hadn't worried about it much before then either. Why worry about something before it happened?

But I didn't think anyone had summoned me to this cage. No, this was more like a prison. Apparently, I was naïve for believing a dragon at the peak of his power would be safe. What was the world coming to? I sighed.

Change sucked.

You'd think that after all this time of being alive on this earth, I'd be a bit more accustomed to change. And usually, I was. When cars replaced horses, I was good. When the first vinyl record released, I was happy. When I could listen to music on my cell phone, I was even happier. And central heating was a luxury I thoroughly enjoyed; it didn't matter that my natural body temperature negated the need for it. But when someone discovered a way to kidnap and cage supes? Well, there were limits to what I was willing to accept.

The silence from all the other people in cages around me was eerily unsettling. A few sniffles, a groan or two, and the soft hush of breathing broke the quiet, but nothing else. Our captors, whoever they were, hadn't made an appearance since I woke.

"Hey," I said with a smile to the monkey shifter to my left.

He shuddered, shook his head, and cringed away from me. Several people hushed me.

Well… okay, then.

I leaned to the right.

"Hi, there," I whispered to my other neighbor.

The guy to my right looked at me with big, wide eyes. His hair was a mop of chaotic curls, making him look rather cherubic. Oh. He was adorable. I wanted to take his cute little cheeks in my hands and give them a squeeze. I always felt that way about unicorns, and based on the iridescent shimmer to his curls, I figured that was what he was. His gaze darted to the far end of the room, to where I imagined the door was, even though I couldn't see it.

"My name is Ogden," I said.

The guy's mouth opened and closed twice before he swallowed. "Umm… Morgan. Morgan Russell."

His voice sounded hoarse, like he didn't speak much. If he'd been here a long time and his other neighbors were like the guy to my left—too scared to even whisper hello —he might be a little rusty.

"Hey, Morgan, do you know what's going on here?"

Someone across the aisle hushed us.

"Shut up," a woman whisper-shouted as she glared at me. "Shut up or you'll make it worse."

I frowned.

We were already in cages. What could be worse?

Although… I supposed things could *always* get worse. Damn it. I hated when I jinxed myself. Because now that I thought about it, I realized there were dozens of ways to make this worse. The place could catch on fire, and we'd never be able to escape. Our captors could deny us food.

They could slaughter us and harvest bits of our bodies to sell.

That last one made me pause.

I may have lived for a long time already, but I had no intention of dying now. Not like this.

They wouldn't be that short-sighted or dumb, would they?

After all, if they kept us alive, they could harvest our scales or our feathers or whatever else again and again. Not that I was knowledgeable about animal husbandry or the agricultural industry—that was more my parents' purview—but I figured that was the difference between shearing sheep for their wool and butchering them to eat them. You could shear a sheep repeatedly, but you could only eat it once. Although I was definitely too pretty to be compared with any type of livestock.

Still, if I was going to accept that someone had tricked me and captured me, I would prefer that they at least be a bit clever.

I needed more information. It usually required a lot of powerful mages in a stable coven to maintain the Supernatural Council's prisons—complaints about the cost of hiring covens to do that had been all over the Supenet news articles a few years ago when they changed the correctional system from execution to imprisonment. I glanced around. No one was in the concrete room except the prisoners.

"How many people are in the coven?" I asked.

Morgan's forehead squished up in confusion. "What coven?"

Now it was my turn to be confused. "If it isn't a coven, who is keeping us here?"

He lifted one of his thin shoulders in a small shrug. "A troll comes in and checks on us."

A troll. A single troll. That made no sense whatsoever.

"Why don't we have our clothing?" Okay. That wasn't the most important question I could have asked, but sitting here with all my bits on display was annoying. Not to mention that I wasn't all that eager to see all these strangers' bits either.

"We used to…" Morgan's face paled. "But a few of the others used their clothes to hang themselves…" He shivered as he spoke.

I was sorry I'd asked.

"Shut up," the woman demanded again.

Morgan's cheeks darkened at the angry woman's reprimand, which at least brought a bit of color back into his cheeks.

"It's okay, Tammy, we'll be quiet," the unicorn said. He shot me an apologetic smile and stared ahead again.

Fine.

Maybe Ms. Angry Ass across the way would fall asleep soon and we could chat then.

I drew in a deep breath and closed my eyes, suddenly wishing I'd learned to meditate. I could use some Zen in my life about now.

Who was I kidding?

Being mellow was not my thing.

Maybe a little pick-me-up would be better. Yeah, that was the answer. I never left the house without doing a little shimmy to a good song. "Great Balls of Fire" was my favorite because I could punctuate the verses with blasts of actual fire. When that song was first released, every dragon I knew, me included, picked up the single. It set my mood for the rest of the day. I couldn't dance in the cage, but there had to be something we could do.

Frowning, I scanned the room again. No one succeeded in this morose atmosphere. It looked like it was time for a little sing-along.

I hummed as I filtered through the songs in my head until one made me smile. Perfect. The '50s were a fantastic era for music. Seriously. Like what's not to love about "Lollipop" or "The Purple People Eater."

I sat up, crossed my legs—since that's the only way I could fit them in here even though I was a little on the, ahem, petit side—and leaned against the bars. The magic on the crate tingled along my spine, but I ignored it. True performers didn't let a minor discomfort interfere with pleasing their audiences.

My fingers snapped four quick beats into the oppressive quiet to get the timing. Someone cried out.

Across the aisle from me and beside the angry lady, a phoenix went up in flames. Oops. I waited for the smoke and flames to die down before doing anything more. Well, that was one way to find out there weren't any fire alarms or sprinklers in here.

When a mature human figure emerged from the ashes in the other cage, I waved at them. Their skin was rosy from regeneration, which made their scowl look fierce. They definitely didn't look like someone who would have a heart attack and die so easily. And if they were, the regeneration probably did them a world of good. Clear out the arteries. Start fresh. All that.

"Sorry," I called out. "Didn't mean to startle you. Just thought we could all use a few tunes."

The phoenix muttered angrily, but I ignored their complaints. I hadn't scared them on purpose, and I'd already apologized. What more did they want from me?

"Okay, folks, let's try this again," I announced loudly. I didn't need anyone else to freak out.

I snapped my fingers again in a quick one, two, three, four... Then I belted out the opening lines of "All Shook Up."

By the time I was on my sixth tune, the mood had improved a lot.

The adorable, dark-haired unicorn in the crate beside mine was happily singing with me in all his rainbow glory. When he forgot a line, he laughed freely, sending little iridescent bubbles shooting out his mouth. Unicorns were strange little creatures, but his happiness was infectious. Several people were bobbing their heads now and joining in on the choruses. It was great. Of course, I stayed away from the somber tunes like "Leader of the Pack" and "Tell Laura I Love Her", so that helped. No one needed morbid ballads right now.

"What the fuck is that noise?"

The shout came from a troll of shockingly diminutive size. She lumbered across the room toward me. Well, to clarify, she wasn't smaller than me, but compared to other trolls, she was tiny. This must have been the troll Morgan had mentioned.

Instead of showing my fury at my situation, I beamed at the newcomer and waved. My unicorn buddy wasn't laughing now, and that made me want to hurt the intruder. Something about the little guy made me want to protect him.

Actually, now that I thought about it, I realized most of the beings in the crates were smaller than what was typical of their species. Had our kidnappers intentionally chosen the smallest of our kind to nab? Did they think we were weaker because of our size? If that was the case, I looked forward to proving them wrong.

"Oh, hello," I said as I wiggled my fingers at the troll. "We're singing a few songs to pass the time. Do you want to join in? I think everyone knows the lyrics to 'Splish Splash'. If you don't, I think you'll pick them up quickly." I started the song, ignoring how my fellow prisoners gaped at me and pushed themselves up against the backs of their cages, away from the troll as she stalked toward me. A cattle prod dangled from one of her long arms.

"Shut up." The troll glared at me.

"Oh, don't be rude." I shook my finger at her. "You know that's not nice. Now where was I?" I cleared my throat.

"No more songs."

"Oh, honey, don't clench your teeth like that. You'll hurt yourself." I leaned forward. "You seem a little stressed. I once dated a troll, so I understand about troll families. I love my mom, but you trolls are next level. You are all about your strong matriarchs. It is truly impressive. I'm guessing you don't have your own clan yet, hey? Are you still living with dear old Mom? Do you want to talk about it?"

Most of that was true. Sort of. I hadn't actually dated Wendell, but he'd come into my old bar all the time and cry in his ale while I served him. For the record, trolls don't tip well, but they can drink a lot. It kind of worked out at the end of the night. As long as he sat at the bar and didn't take up a table where the staff had to deal with him, I was happy to pour his drinks and listen to him.

"Oh, I know… it's the '50s you're not fond of. How about 'Dancing Queen'?" Every troll I'd ever met had a thing for ABBA. When *Mamma Mia!* came out, the trolls had been the first ones through the door.

The troll's face softened in interest for a moment before she scowled again. "No songs. No singing."

She hit the side of my crate with her plump palm. The magic on the bars hummed but didn't zap her or me. The cage itself jostled a bit, but I wasn't worried. Trolls didn't have magic, at least not the kind that could do anything to the crate. No, whoever had put the spells on the metal bars, it hadn't been a troll.

"Are you sure? It doesn't have to be 'Dancing Queen'. What about 'Take a Chance on Me'? That's always a crowd favorite."

"Stop talking. Stop singing. Stop it all."

"Or what?" Okay. Most people wouldn't goad their captor—at least that's what I was sensing from my fellow prisoners, based on the way they were cowering—but I was a dragon. I didn't have to listen to anyone.

The troll's bulbous nose crinkled as she sneered. "I will come in there and—"

"Oh? You're going to open the crate? Honestly, that would be swell." I clapped my hands in delight and grinned as I twisted and made a half-assed attempt at stretching. "I'm getting stiff sitting like this. I would *love* to stretch my legs."

The troll snarled as she shoved a cattle prod through the bars. I snatched up the end of it, brought it toward my mouth. I inhaled sharply, then spewed a blast of fiery electricity along its length. The crackling current shot up the metal.

Contrary to what the prod's design specs undoubtedly said, the insulating protective grip wouldn't confine all electricity to the metal rod—at least not when a dragon produced the electricity. My fiery electricity zinged over the surface of the prod until it reached her hand, then continued up her arm. It only stopped when she dropped to her knees in pain and pulled the prod out of my crate.

Apparently, no one told her my species of water dragon had not only fire, like other dragons, but also power surges like electric eels. Some people were victims of their own ignorance.

The reek of burning flesh made me cough. I waved my hand in front of my face. I hated when that happened. It was such an unpleasant smell.

She shrieked, cradled her hand, and sprinted for the door. Well, given her size, it was more like a clunky trot than a sprint.

"Bye." I waved cheerily at her retreating back.

I smiled at my fellow prisoners, who were now looking at me with the same wariness they'd shown the troll when she first arrived.

"Okay, now, where were we? Oh, yes, we left off at 'Splish Splash.' I want to hear the people in the back, so remember to sit up straight and smile. Alright, everyone, I'll count us in. And a one, two, three, four…"

Chapter Four

SIMON

It'd been months since I found the whistle, and I still had told no one about it. Mama suspected I was keeping a secret, but she didn't press me for details. Not yet. But I doubted her restraint would last long. She'd heard about my visit to the police station all those months ago. I hadn't even finished giving my statement when she blew up my cell phone.

At that time, she'd accepted the same story I told the police, but she was getting suspicious now. Even when she was in her human form, I swore I could envision her tail twitching back and forth as she studied me. It wouldn't be long before she pinned me down about it.

Her curiosity was legendary. That she hadn't found out about the whistle already was surprising. It felt like a lifetime had passed since I found it by the tunnel entrance.

So much had happened since then.

Not only had the wolves gone back to the inn to steal

more things, they'd gone on to blow up the tunnel. I'd heard some awful things had happened out at their pack lands too. Clive, Warren, and our younger twins had gone out there to snoop and scavenge after the police had finished their investigation. They said the place reeked of blood. I shuddered at the thought. I hadn't gone out with them, but I still had nightmares about it.

But I was losing more sleep over my whistle than my nightmares.

And Mama had noticed the bags under my eyes.

At breakfast this morning, she'd asked me over for supper, claiming it was to make sure I had a hearty meal before heading out for the night. That was a lie. We both knew it. She wanted to corner me and unravel my secrets without my brothers around to distract her. So I made up an excuse. I felt guilty for lying to her, but... I wasn't ready to say anything yet.

And worse? She knew I was lying because she knew my schedule better than I did. She kept better tabs on all her kittens than the paparazzi did on those famous humans in Hollywood.

But now that I'd told her I was busy, I felt like I needed to go do something. My guilt was almost a living, breathing entity. What was I going to do?

Despite not having a shift at the motel until tomorrow night, I still attempted to maintain a nocturnal schedule during my free time. I had been raised that way, and breaking those habits was hard. Years ago, I'd tried to question Mama about our nighttime lifestyle after my high school biology teacher taught us cats were crepuscular, not nocturnal. Mama hadn't been impressed, nor had she felt inclined to change how we lived.

When we were in grade school, our schedule was more nocturnal than most of my classmates. We slept as soon as we were home from school so we could be up all night. It'd made making friends difficult, since we couldn't join most extracurricular activities. Not that I would have been very good at team sports—the very idea of participating in a game where you had to perform while everyone stared at you was horrifying—but something else might have been nice.

I'd been off work the night I found the whistle too. That was why I'd been out roaming. But I didn't want to roam too far tonight. Going out and hunting held no appeal. All I wanted—this was going to sound crazy—all I wanted to do was hang out with the whistle.

But my guilt over lying to my mama meant I had a heck of a time falling asleep after breakfast and it didn't get any better throughout the day. A series of catnaps broken up by staring at my whistle wasn't helping me think any more clearly.

Finally, I gave up around dusk and wandered over to the Willow Lake Inn. My mama would at least hear I'd gone out tonight, and I could pretend that had been my plan all along. Besides, I hadn't eaten since breakfast, so dinner at the pub sounded like just the thing.

I debated leaving the whistle in my apartment, but the thought of leaving it behind made me queasy. Like every time I went out with the whistle in my pocket, I prayed Paws and all the other supes who hung out at the inn wouldn't sense its magic on me. I wasn't a thief—me keeping the whistle was more of a finders-keepers situation—and I didn't want to be blamed for its theft.

Yes. I know. My reasoning was a little suspect. I could hear my mama's voice in my head saying that I needed to return the whistle to Jake, but... Not yet, okay?

Soon.

Pinky promise.

Worries and hopes whirled through me by the time I arrived at the door to the pub. What if this time someone talked about a missing whistle? Or, better yet, what if someone mentioned what it did? I braced my shoulders and kept my hand in my pocket with my fingers tight on the whistle as I pushed open the door to the pub.

The Willow Lake Pub was attached to one end of the Willow Lake Inn. The building used to be the old were-wolf pack house back in the day, but the wolf pack had broken up when I was a kid. Hayden had sold the building to wormy nosed Ulric, who'd still owned it when I'd gone to the pub for the first time as an adult.

The place still stank of wolves on an average day, but it was worse on muggy days. And everything was old, not the fancy old things that rich people liked to buy, but this-should-be-thrown-away old.

The inn was changing now, though. The bombing hadn't given Jake any other choice but to renovate.

Hmm... How was Jake paying for all those changes? It wasn't any of my business, but it still made me curious. Because if he was selling some of his grandfather's things to pay for the repairs, then maybe I didn't need to feel so guilty about keeping the whistle. Maybe I'd start leaving

him some bigger than normal tips, kind of like an install-
ment payment plan for the whistle.

The smell of new paint and sawdust assaulted me when
I walked into the pub. I sneezed. Every head in the place
turned toward me.

I cringed and thought about shifting and hiding to
escape their stares. Luckily, when they saw it was me, the
regulars all turned back to whatever they'd been doing. I
crept forward, trying to avoid catching anyone else's
attention.

Through the corridor that connected the pub to the inn
came the sounds of hammers and saws. It was already
evening, so I was surprised there was still construction
happening. At least the pub was still open while they reno-
vated the rest of the inn.

The pub itself had sustained minor damage in the
bombing. The biggest problem was the lingering smell of
smoke. Jake had tried to fix that by painting the walls and
putting new fabric on the chairs. The result wasn't perfect,
but I thought it was enough. I hated change. The pub's
familiar atmosphere was comforting.

Half the tables were empty, which made sense since it
was a weeknight. I recognized everyone, and all of them
were supes. To my right sat the pool table, and just like
every other time I'd been in here, Carter Jones was leaning
over the pool table, displaying his muscular behind, with
his big beefy hand wrapped around a long, sturdy pool cue.
If he wasn't such a big bear of a man—even in his human
form—you'd think he was compensating for something,
given the way he was always fondling that big stick. Old
Thom, a grumpy ancient-looking troll, was in his usual

spot in the corner. Sally the Succubus, with her tight pink jeans and puffy platinum blond hair, sat on her usual barstool, watching Jake mix a drink.

Mama had said something about Sally now being in a relationship with the couple who owned the bakery, so she didn't need to find partners at the pub anymore. But she had decided she needed to watch over Jake, so she still came in here regularly. At least that's what Mama figured. I didn't know why Jake needed a surrogate mother since he was a grown man and was mates with one of the most powerful supes I'd ever met, but Mama still ruled my world, so I wasn't one to argue about mothers or mother figures.

Should I go over there or sit at the bar?

Unlike when I first found the whistle months ago, Jake knew about supes now. He even had his own supernatural abilities. If I was going to hear anything juicy, I'd need to be close to him. After all, it was his stuff that had been stolen. If anyone was going to talk about what was still missing, it'd be him, right?

Except I never sat up there.

People would wonder what I was doing if I switched things up now. That's how people got caught, right? They started acting out of character. That's what Mama's mystery shows said.

Okay, sitting at the bar was out of the question.

Or maybe I was overthinking it.

Wait… Jake was an oracle. What if he'd had a vision about me and the whistle? What would his demon boyfriend do to me if he thought I stole from Jake?

My stomach felt like it dropped about five inches. Fur

sprouted along the back of my neck just so it could stand up and quiver. My gaze darted to Jake. He wasn't looking at me. Would he look at me if he'd had a vision about me? Would he keep an eye on me until someone took me into custody? He still wasn't looking at me. Did that mean I was safe?

I let out a shaky breath. *Relax. It's fine.* Except it didn't feel fine.

I really wasn't cut out for a life of crime.

I should give the whistle back.

My fingers tightened on the whistle in my pocket. At this point, I'd probably have the engravings embedded in my hand for the rest of my life.

"I'll be over in a minute to get your order, Simon," Jake called out.

Everyone looked in my direction. I gulped.

Sally turned on her stool and tapped her bottom lip with her finger. The shiny bright pink polish on her fingernail glittered under the lights. Mama always told me to stand at least six feet away from the succubus. Something about pheromones or something. I hadn't paid much attention. Women weren't my thing, especially not a woman who was older than my mama and looked like an extra in the movie Grease. Her gaze grew assessing as I squirmed under her attention. What was she thinking?

Did she know I had the whistle?

Alice rushed in, with flushed cheeks and red, wet lips, as if she had just been thoroughly kissed. The sexual energy around her distracted the succubus and drew Sally's gaze from me.

"Sorry I'm late," the brownie said as she threw her purse behind the counter.

"How long were you sitting outside making out with Buddy?" Jake teased.

"Shut up." She laughed and punched him lightly on the arm. "Like you don't get distracted by your mate."

As if her words summoned him, Jake's boyfriend walked through the door leading to the inn. Before the renovation, the demon had always been ridiculously clean in pressed shirts and trousers, so I almost didn't recognize him in stained and sweaty construction clothes. Sawdust covered him all the way up to the tips of the horns protruding from his dark hair.

"See? I have perfect timing," Alice said as she shooed Jake away. "Go sit with your mate."

Jake grinned and hurried around the bar to Gage. Their kiss was almost X-rated. You'd think they hadn't seen one another for months. They were oblivious to everyone else. No one had ever kissed me like that. I couldn't imagine being so lost in someone's mouth that I forgot everything else. Losing awareness like that was just asking to lose one of your nine.

Of course, I wouldn't want to kiss Gage—not only was he Jake's mate, but he freaked me out almost as much as old Ulric had. At least now I didn't have to worry about where to sit. I wasn't getting any closer to the demon than I had to. People said he was nice and all—some amazing protector for Willow Lake or whatever—but Clive and Warren had forced me to watch too many horror movies when we were kittens. The demons in those movies might have been fictional, but I didn't care. I didn't need to find out the difference between fiction and reality for myself. And wasn't Van supposed to be our protector? He was a hellhound *and* a police officer. Why were people letting this new guy come in and take over?

I'd never ask those questions though. Not out loud.

I didn't want that demon looking at me, wondering why I was stirring up trouble for him.

I chose a small empty table within hearing distance of the bar and sank into a chair. My gaze darted around the room. No one was paying any attention to me. Not that I could see. But what if they were being sneaky about it and I didn't notice? My leg bobbed up and down. My free hand rapped a chaotic rhythm on the scarred wooden surface of the table. My other hand remained wrapped around my whistle.

When Jake and Gage separated, Jake's lips and cheeks were as red as Alice's had been. He glanced around the room, as if suddenly remembering where they were. His gaze landed on me. I ducked my head, but I was too slow. Jake was already dragging his boyfriend to my table.

"Hey, Simon," he said. "Can we join you?"

I wanted to hiss and hide, but all I could do was nod. Once they took their seats, the creepy cat-like creature Paws joined my table as well. Mama would have been thrilled to know I was sitting with so many influential Willow Lakers, but all I could think about was escaping. My whole body was numb.

Was this an intervention? Had they found out about the whistle? Were they going to corner me and demand it back?

The demon narrowed his eyes at me. I hunched. Jake swatted his boyfriend playfully.

"Quit that," Jake admonished. Then he looked at me. "Crap. I forgot to take your order, didn't I?"

"It's fine." My voice cracked, betraying my nerves.

"You were too busy sucking on Gage's tongue," Paws muttered.

Jake's cheeks darkened as he waved Alice over. The blush stretched down his neck and seeped into the strange tattoo he had that matched his mate's. I knew those marks were given to fated mates, but if I ever found my fated mate—not that I was looking—I hoped I got a bit of color in my hair like Mercer and Oak. I didn't want a tattoo-like mark like these two or like Ash and Dillon. I was not a tattoo kind of person. Once we ordered our drinks, silence fell over the table. Awkward.

"What is the matter with you people? Why aren't you talking?" Paws asked. His black, white, and orange tail flicked back and forth across the table. Mama would have skinned us alive if we ever dared jump on the table in our cat forms.

"Paws," Jake admonished. "Be nice." I'd heard that tone before. The *don't scare away Simon* was implied.

"You disrupted my afternoon nap again," Paws said. He was staring at the demon.

"Construction is noisy," Gage said, not at all bothered by the complaint.

Paws harrumphed. "And what about my food dishes? Who moved those? They were in the perfect place. Out in the open. Away from the smelly garbage. Now some asshole's moved them over in a corner by the garbage can. I'd like to see you assholes eat in those conditions."

Gage lifted one of his eyebrows. "Did you want them filled with sawdust and drywall dust? I can move them back where they were."

Paws, somehow, scowled. I didn't think I'd even seen Mama scowl in her cat form the way Paws was scowling right now. I didn't think cats' faces did that. Sure, they could look unimpressed or pleased or content, but this look was next level. It was one more sign of how freaky the strange creature was.

"So, Simon," Jake said, leaning forward, abandoning his boyfriend to Paws and his complaints. The oracle smiled widely. It was the smile I'd seen him use when he served drinks at the bar. The smile was friendly, but it lacked the happy energy he showed when hanging out with his friends. "Jeremy keeps including you on his group texts, but I feel like I haven't truly gotten to know you."

His words surprised me. He wanted to get to know me. Why? "Uh… Okay?"

"I know your mom," he said. "She's in my painting group. She talks about you and your brothers a lot."

I squirmed. I could only imagine what Mama would have said. Her pride in us was legendary… and a bit misplaced. Well, it might have been appropriate for Justin. I wasn't sure what he'd done since he moved away, but it involved a lot of secrets, which made it seem important.

"How is the renovation going?" I threw out the random question like a smoke bomb. Anything to steer the attention away from me.

"Good," Jake said, gracefully accepting my change of

subject. "The upper floors need a lot of work, not just because of the recent damage, so we've been concentrating on the main floor and the common areas first while we come up with a plan for the rest. We've put plywood over the broken windows and that's about all so far on the top two floors."

"Makes sense," I agreed. I knew nothing about construction.

Jake nodded. "It's hard to remember we need to space out the repairs. I want to do it all. We had to prioritize the dining room because it sustained the most damage and couldn't be sealed up with a few pieces of plywood, like the broken windows."

While we were talking, Van—the freaking head of the local police department—arrived and sat down with us. Once Mama had realized most—if not all—of her sons were gay, she'd turned her eyes to the eligible bachelors in town and, in her opinion, Van was the most eligible one around. I agreed with Mama that he was handsome and successful and had a steady job. That his job was being a police officer didn't even deter her, although Pops always looked like he had indigestion when she talked about the hellhound dating one of her kittens.

Mama would vibrate if she saw me sitting with him. If she were here, she'd be kicking me under the table, trying to get me to flirt with him. Yeah. I wouldn't do that. Besides, I suspected he had feelings for Doctor Roberts. He'd never be interested in a simple cat shifter like me when he had eyes for a successful doctor who was also a sphinx.

Van settled into a conversation with Gage and Paws.

No one was paying much attention to me, except Jake. I prayed to the Eternal Magic it would stay that way.

At least Alice had brought our drinks over so I could take a deep gulp of my cream ale. It didn't taste like cream, which was unfortunate. Still, I hoped it would help me get through this.

I reached down and felt for my whistle. It was still in my pocket. At least that was something.

Maybe I could guzzle my ale and get out of here.

A few minutes later, I chugged the last of my pint and was ready to bolt when the woman on Gage's team swept into the pub like a modern-day Marlene Dietrich, complete with wide-legged trousers, a matching fitted jacket, a tie, and a cap. She styled her hair with tight waves, resembling a character from a period drama. I only knew about shows like that because Mama loved them. She hated watching them alone and I could never figure out how to escape like Pops or my brothers.

"Gage, we need to talk," she said as she elegantly slipped into the last empty chair at the table.

The air in the pub grew heavy the minute she said those words.

The demon looked around the pub, as if hunting for threats. "What's happened, Davina?"

"Stand down, big guy," she said as she waved a folder at him. "I've been re-checking everything in Ulric's room with him. He's remembered a few more things. Things that are still missing."

Ulric was dead. How could she…? Oh. She must be able to see ghosts. I shivered and looked around for signs of invisible beings, not that I'd ever been able to see ghosts before. Although I knew some cats could, like my brother Justin. I found it unsettling how his gaze tracked things I couldn't perceive. Now I wished I'd asked him more questions. Like, how far could a ghost move? Could Ulric have been there when I picked up the whistle? Did he know?

"We suspected there was more out there that we haven't found yet," Gage said, like he wasn't worried.

Davina tapped on the folder with a very shiny, very pointy red fingernail. "Except we didn't know the damn mage had kept such dangerous shit. That gramophone thing wasn't the worst of it."

"What?" Gage demanded. His skin turned a strange red color. Uh oh. That was his demon side coming to the surface.

Van's had gone all fiery like his hellhound was ready to burst free too. The flames were bright against his dark skin. Everything that made an eye look like an eye—his dark brown irises, his pupils, and the whites of his eyes—had disappeared. That was freaky. I'd never get used to that. Eyes were supposed to look like eyes, not bonfires.

I sank down in my seat.

I wanted to run, except… what if they talked about the whistle? I wanted to know what they knew. Based on how quiet the room had gotten, everyone else in Willow Lake wanted to know too. Davina glanced around the room, as if suddenly realizing that everyone was eavesdropping.

"Should we talk about this somewhere else?"

Van glanced around at the pub's patrons. "They're all local supes. Ones I trust and who've been called on in the past when things have gone to shit. You might as well say what you have to say."

Davina pursed her lips.

"It's better if they can prepare in case we need their help," Van continued when Davina didn't say anything.

"Fine," Davina agreed with a scowl. She flipped open the folder and shoved it between Van and Gage. Paws stepped closer to read the page too. She tapped aggressively at what appeared to be a list. I waited to hear her describe my whistle. I tightened my fingers around it. "Look there."

"A Coven of One ring?" Gage looked up sharply. "Are you sure?"

Van cursed and rubbed the back of his neck.

I huffed out a relieved breath, but I was the only one who did. Around the room, people gasped.

"What is it?" Jake asked.

"It's a ring that multiplies the power of one mage until it equals that of an entire coven," Davina explained. Then she turned to her left, where no one was standing, and frowned. "Oh, don't start making excuses. You knew it was dangerous. You should have destroyed it as soon as you acquired it."

She was talking to a ghost, probably Ulric.

"Holy Michelangelo," Jake muttered. "I wish I hadn't asked."

"That would explain the cages we found in Babette's warehouse," Gage said.

I didn't know what they were talking about, but I wasn't about to ask questions.

"Exactly," Davina agreed. "We thought there was a coven involved, given the amount of magic needed to trap so many supes, but we might just be looking for a single mage with that damn ring."

"So maybe we aren't looking for a rogue demon?" Van asked.

No one seemed to know what to say to that, but I really wished they'd say *something* about it. They couldn't toss out a phrase like *a rogue demon* without causing panic. Then again, no one in the pub looked panicked. Except me. I was panicked. Very, very panicked.

Rogue demons were scary. Dangerous. Murderous. Powerful.

Why in all Magic was I the only one worried about this?

"What else is missing? Anything dangerous?" Gage asked as he scanned the list.

Davina pointed out a handful of other things. Right in the middle of the list were two whistles. One of those had to be mine. I wanted to ask about them, but that'd bring unwanted attention my way. If I had to lie, the hellhound would know. And why would Davina describe the whistle as dangerous? It was a whistle, not a sword. She'd obviously made a mistake.

"We need to get this information to the SC," Van said. "Do you want to do it, Gage, or do you want me to?"

The SC? As in the Supernatural Council? I gulped. I knew Gage and his team had connections with the SC, but would this bring more teams to Willow Lake? Would they conduct door-to-door searches? Would they demand people empty their pockets to see if they were hiding anything?

I couldn't go to a supernatural prison. I wasn't cut out

for a life like that. I was a simple cat shifter. More domesticated than most.

Fudgesicle.

I couldn't do this.

I stood abruptly. The chair tumbled back. Everyone in the entire place turned to stare at me again. If I'd suspected people were looking at me earlier, I *knew* they were now. Drat. Drat, drat, drat.

"Simon? Are you okay?" Jake asked.

"Fine," I wheezed, barely able to get enough air in my lungs to push out the single syllable.

"It's okay." Jake tried to use a soothing tone. "These guys know what they're doing. They're good at their jobs. There isn't anything to be worried about."

If only this was about my normal scaredy-cat impulses.

"I gotta go." I yanked out a handful of bills and tossed them on the table. That should be more than enough to pay for the pint.

My hand shook as I scrambled to fix the stupid chair. Then I ran out the door without any thought for my previous hunger. The cream ale was churning in my empty stomach, and I hoped I'd make it outside before I lost it. I may enjoy pampering myself like a house cat with regular meals, but I'd survive without eating tonight.

Across the street from the inn, Willow Lake glittered under the setting sun. The days were getting shorter as fall approached, but tonight the late summer's heat lingered in the air. Light bounced off the undulating water and seemed to call me to it. I'd never liked big bodies of water all that much. I pretended it was a cat thing, but my brother Warren loved swimming, so I knew it wasn't really that.

But tonight, for some reason, the water captivated me. Maybe because the undulating surface reminded me of the etchings on my whistle.

The lake was large enough that the water lapped at the shore. The sound was sort of soothing. If you liked that kind of thing. I climbed onto a large boulder that sat right where the water met the land and stared at the water.

My phone pinged, announcing a text message. Dread coiled in my belly. I hoped it wasn't Jake or Gage or worse —Van—demanding answers for my weird behavior. With a trembling hand, I pulled it from my pocket and found a text from Jeremy.

Jeremy had recently started texting me. One day, he'd asked me to feed his cat. I'd said yes, mostly to get away from him so he wouldn't ask me a bunch of questions. I'd seen him working his way through the supes around town. He asked a lot of questions. He was more curious than a cat, and that was saying something.

Then he'd asked to exchange numbers. I didn't know how to say no, not after I'd agreed to feed his cat. If some-thing went wrong with the cat, I'd need to phone him. He'd tried to convince me to put his contact information in my phone under some weird name. I hadn't.

After that, things got weird.

I should have known he'd use it for more than just checking in about his cat, but I hadn't expected the guy to be addicted to texting. And the stuff he asked? It was super strange. Most of the time, I didn't answer him, but I still opened every message. Like now…

Jeremy: We're getting together Saturday

night to watch "The Lord of the Rings" movies at the inn. Have you seen them? It'll only be you, me, Ash, and Jake, so I need you there to help answer questions Jake and I might have about the magic in the show. Like, do you think a magical ring could make you invisible? Do you think actual supes inspired the species in the show? Oh… and one elf can sense the future, so I thought Jake would appreciate that. But mostly we're watching because Jake needs to have more pop culture in his life and it's our job to help him. Anyway, don't worry about bringing anything, but if you really want to, a bag of chips would be great.

"Huh?" I blinked at the message.

I hadn't agreed to any of that, had I? I ignored the message and shoved my phone back in my pocket. My fingers brushed against the whistle, and I forgot all about Jeremy.

I pulled the whistle from my pocket and stared at it.

It was too pretty to be dangerous.

Maybe if I blew on it once, it'd satisfy my curiosity enough that I could give it back. Then the SC wouldn't have any reason to come after me. My mouth went dry at the thought of putting my lips on it. Who knew where the whistle had been? Should I wash it first?

I dunked the whistle in the lake water, then dried it off

with the sleeve of my hoodie. Then I stared at it some more.

My heart pounded as I lifted it to my lips.

My hand trembled. Was I really doing this? I pulled it away before the metal touched my mouth. Why did this seem so important? It was just a whistle, right? Right.

I brought it to my mouth again. This time, I wrapped my lips around the cool metal mouthpiece without yanking it away.

I blew softly.

A faint noise came out, but it was hardly noteworthy. I frowned. Was it a fancy dog whistle or something? No, I would have heard that, even in my human form. I hoped it wasn't broken. Maybe if I blew on it harder, it'd sound better. I licked my lips, sucked in a deep breath, then blew into the whistle with everything I had.

I wanted this to work. I wanted to know what it could do. I wanted…

Chapter Five

OGDEN

My throat was getting sore, but I'd be damned if I stopped singing now. I was a supernatural fucking being and I could do this. My magic would repair any damage I did to my vocal cords, so I was going to keep singing my fucking heart out, damn it. They might have put me in a cage, but they couldn't lock down my spirit.

I was bellowing loud enough to wake up Little Susie when the door at the end of the room clanged again. The little troll was back. She dragged the end of her cattle prod along the concrete floor. The hand and arm I'd zapped were wrapped in bandages. The thing about supernatural healing was that it worked great until a dragon attacked you. Our magic had a way of changing things. I grinned. It'd take her a while to heal.

"I've thought of a way to shut you up." The troll grinned evilly at me as she banged her weapon against the cage next to mine. The cute little unicorn jumped. His curls jolted and bobbed around his face. The happy little rainbow bubbles the unicorn had giggled into existence a mere moment ago were all burst and gone now.

"See this?" The troll held my gaze as she wiggled the prod between the bars of the unicorn's cage. "Shut up or I'll start poking your neighbors with my little toy."

"Oh, that sounds rather dirty. I didn't know you were kinky," I said with a grin. If I didn't get upset at her threat, maybe she'd leave him alone. I doubted that ruse would last for long, though. I needed to save my little unicorn friend, but how?

He was too sweet to torture. He didn't whimper or cringe like most of the other creatures. He just slumped in his cage and stared at the troll like getting tortured was nothing new for him. And I wanted to destroy whoever had taught him that.

I'd start with this troll.

If only I could figure out what to do.

As if anticipating my plan, the troll stood close to the other cages instead of in the middle of the aisle like she had last time. I didn't have a clear shot at her. Damn it all anyway. If I blasted electricity at her from here, I'd hit another cage. The last thing I wanted to do was electrocute the poor unicorn. The electrical currents would zip over the bars and zap him, because he didn't have a choice but to sit on the crate with his bare ass like me.

Wait. I think I'd read about a kink like that. Hmm... Maybe shooting an electrical current through his balls wouldn't be so bad. Maybe the little unicorn would be into something like that.

Then I remembered the smell of flesh burning when

I'd zapped the troll earlier and changed my mind. If too much of my electricity ran through the cage and hit the unicorn, things would be bad. No one wanted their family jewels cooked.

But I still had my fire. Could I send it, without its electric sidekick, through the bars in both our cages without hitting the unicorn?

I opened my mouth to try it, when a tingling sensation rolled over me. My toes curled. The hair lifted from my nape. My fingers twitched.

Then the air shimmered and twisted.

What was happening? This was not normal. Was the troll a distraction? Were they piping in poisonous gas?

Oohh.

Could a person feel squishy? Because I felt squishy and rubbery and light. Too light. I hadn't tried drugs since the '60s. They hadn't done much to me, probably because I was a supe, so it'd been a rather blah experience. But this was what I'd always imagined it would be. Psychedelic swirls wrapped around me in a way that suggested colors could be tangible. Bright rainbows spun hypnotically in front of me, making me dizzy.

Ooh... I totally understood the word groovy now. Totally groovy. Far out. Ten out of ten. Would recommend.

Then my vision whited out for one long moment before everything—my sight, the weight of my body, everything—rushed back. A tingling sensation coursed through me. I gasped, only to have water rush into my mouth and nose. Water dragons couldn't drown, but inhaling water unexpectedly still made me choke for a moment before instinct took over. My body shifted into my dragon form.

All those happy, pretty, swirling colors vanished. I was one hundred percent sober now. Instantly. How disappointing.

My dragon undulated and whirled through the water. An indistinct tugging sensation dragged me upward to the surface. I erupted out of the water and gulped in the sweet tasting air, letting it fill my lungs. My wings snapped open, and I lifted myself upward into the air, swimming as easily in the air currents as I had through the water.

I didn't understand what had happened, but I was free. No crate. No troll. No cattle prod. It was time to fucking celebrate.

But first, I had to find out why I was here and where *here* was. The air reeked of magic and after being held in a magically reinforced cage, I doubted this change heralded anything good. As I rose higher, some invisible tether latched on and tugged me back down. I flapped my wings harder, but it didn't work. I couldn't go any further.

What the fuck was going on now?

Chapter Six

SIMON

A little shock of electricity zinged over me. My skin vibrated until every little hair on my body stood on end and my hands trembled. I lowered the whistle.

What was that? I scanned the shoreline but didn't see a mage practicing magic out there tonight.

A thick ripple rolled over the calm surface of the lake. It started way out in the middle. Was it Weston? The local merman swam in the lake a lot. Or maybe it was—

Whatever I'd been thinking dropped out of my head like a bowling ball through tissue paper as a large shimmering creature breached the surface of the lake in an explosion of water. It shot straight up into the air. Water glistened over its body before the droplets fell like a fine mist to the lake below as the creature went higher and higher into the air.

That was not Weston. Or a fish. Or a tentacled supe like the couple who owned the bakery.

I gaped.

It was a dragon of some kind. Or a basilisk?

No, I was right the first time. It had to be a dragon.

The creature wasn't big and bulky like I'd always envisioned a dragon would look. You know the image: curved horns protruding from its head, sharp-looking spikes along its back, thick reptile-like legs, and gigantic wings. Yeah, well, this creature was nothing like that. This creature was sleek and lean and long, with surprisingly small wings on its back. Its whole body was more snake-like than not.

Its body undulated through the air, surfing the air currents the same as fish swam along the currents in the water.

Then the creature's body jackknifed. Now, rather than shooting up, it blasted back to the ground or the water or...

Oh...

Oh no...

It wasn't heading for either of those. The creature was coming straight for me.

Uh oh.

What had I done?

I was definitely losing one of my nine lives tonight.

Hovering over the middle of the lake, the creature hadn't seemed too big. But my eyes must be broken because as the thing came closer, it appeared more and more enormous.

I gulped down a breath and prayed it wasn't going to eat me.

In my shifted form, I was on the smaller side—more house cat than lion—but right now? In my human form? I was big enough I'd catch in the creature's throat, and that didn't sound pleasant. For either of us.

"Hi, nice dragon-y person," I choked out as I raised my hands in surrender. "I'm pretty sure I'd taste awful. I eat too much processed meat and sodium and sugar—no, forget I said sugar—I meant... uh... artificial coloring... So, yeah, you definitely don't want to eat me."

The dragon was close now. Every undulation of its long body mesmerized me as it glided toward me. Was that how it incapacitated its victims? The glow from the town's evening lights caught on its scales, which appeared to glitter and glisten as it moved. I swallowed hard. The creature was beautiful and utterly terrifying all at once.

The part of my brain that loved having all its nine lives, which until this moment had always been the most dominant part of my psyche, couldn't even motivate me to move. I had to see what was going to happen next. I had to know more.

And then it was too late.

The creature was on me. Its long, thick body whipped around me, encircling me, until I couldn't budge if I wanted to. Its coils squeezed my soft belly, making me keenly aware that I wasn't super fit like my brothers. I wasn't beer-belly fat, but I'd never seen my Adonis belt either. Of all the ways to lose one of my nine, I'd never imagined being crushed to death. This was the worst moment of my life... even worse than when I'd coughed up a hairball on my biology exam in high school and made the girl next to me throw up. It'd been awful. My classmates—especially my brothers—never let me forget it.

But this? This was awful in a different way.

What if the creature took more than one of my nine? What if it took all nine? Wiped them out? Gone. Kablooey. Poofed into thin air.

I started counting down to my impending death.

I would be down to eight lives in three… two… one…

My lungs sucked a breath in and let it out. And again. The creature wasn't crushing me. It hadn't bitten me yet either. Hope surged through me.

"I'm sorry." The words rushed out. "I'm sorry. I don't know why you are mad at me. I didn't mean to do anything. Please don't hurt me."

"Who are you?" A drawn-out hiss punctuated the dragon's question as its long, thin, forked tongue curled through the air in front of my face. A slight English accent coated the words. I usually found accents sexy, but not this time, not when spoken by an angry dragon.

"S… Simon…" I stammered. "Simon Rivers."

"Simon the Cat." That tongue hissed the "s" before it unrolled and drew a long lick up my cheek.

I shivered. "J… Just Simon is fine."

"How am I here, Just Simon?" The tail tightened around my body. If it wanted, the creature could kill me. We both knew it. I really didn't need the demonstration.

"I… I…"

Suddenly I knew the whistle was no ordinary whistle. I'd always suspected it was special, but… Davina was right, unfortunately. The whistle was dangerous.

I gulped. I couldn't lie my way out of this. With the way I lied—or rather *couldn't* lie—I'd just anger the dragon if I tried. I had to be smart about this, except I wasn't the smart one in the family. That was my brother Justin. My heart pounded faster. But I did have the whistle still. If I surrendered it to the dragon, maybe that'd be enough. Holy Magic, I hoped so.

Only because the creature allowed it was I able to move my arm and free it from the dragon's coils. I presented the whistle to the dragon.

"I think this did it."

The creature's electric blue eyes narrowed at the whistle. I'd never seen eyes that color. They were shockingly bright and vivid and very pretty.

And wasn't that a stupid thought to entertain as I was about to be eaten? Weren't you supposed to have your life flash before your eyes or something? I shouldn't be mooning over a dragon's pretty eyes.

"You are a dragon summoner," the dragon spat the words at me. "How many of my kind have you captured? Who else is here with you? Where is your coven? Are they hiding as they perform the spell to capture me? Do you plan to hold me down? Torture me until I submit? You might have been told I'd be weak and vulnerable after being summoned, but you can see you are wrong." The creature swung its massive head around with its long tongue fluttering through the air, as if searching for more threats.

"Uh. No. I mean I don't think so? Just a cat, remember? Not a summoner. No coven. Shifters don't form covens. And I haven't captured anything. Or I mean anyone." Although was that technically true? "I mean I guess I've hunted for mice. That's what I was doing when I found the whistle. Just a bit of hunting. But, uh, no supes. Just field mice. Really. Promise. And definitely no torture. I don't even play with the mice I catch. Nope. None of that."

"Well, Just Simon, Just a Cat, if you aren't a dragon summoner, why do you have that whistle?"

"I… I found it?"

"Are you asking me?"

"No?"

Its eyes narrowed again.

I cleared my throat. "No. Definitely not asking a question."

"Any dragon worth his gold would eat the person who dared to blow a whistle like that." The tip of the dragon's long, long tail brushed my cheek again, then it followed the same route with its tongue. Was it sampling me? Checking to see if I was tender or if I'd taste good?

"Did I mention how much processed meat I eat?"

The dragon laughed, tilting its head from side to side as if it didn't know what to do with me. "But you are too adorable to eat, aren't you? I can think of all kinds of other things to do with you instead."

My mouth went dry. Was that an improvement? What kinds of things did he want to do? They wouldn't be sexy things, would they? No. Of course not. Why had my brain gone there?

"I am inclined to trust you," the dragon said.

"Oh, thank Magic," I gasped.

The coils unwound, leaving me quivering on my own

two feet again. I slumped in relief. Then the dragon's body started to glow. It grew brighter and brighter until a blast of white light blinded me. I lifted my hands to my eyes with a cry.

When I shifted into my cat form, the process was a lot less dramatic. There were no bright lights. Nothing glowed. Truthfully, I'd never considered the ability to shift forms to be particularly magical before. It was just something all the other shifters in Willow Lake did. There was nothing overtly special about shifting, except this guy's change had been beautiful and strange and, yes, definitely magical.

In the next moment, everything was dark again. I drew my hand from my face and blinked. When my eyes cleared, I blinked again. There, standing in the dragon's place, was the most beautiful man I'd ever seen.

And he was completely naked.

The man's blue eyes sparkled as he smiled at me. His dark brown hair was short, and he had a scruffy sort of beard on his jaw like he'd forgotten to shave this morning. Although, honestly, it would take me at least three weeks to grow that much, so it was hard to tell. I gauged him to be older than me, but with supes you could never really tell how old someone was based on their appearance alone. He could have anywhere from five years to decades or even centuries on me.

Despite sensing he was older, I felt an instant sort of connection to him… like he was a homeless puppy I'd found in an alley. I wanted to take him home. Except he was no puppy. He was a strikingly handsome man, one that was way out of my league. I knew that at just one glance.

His lean frame was smaller than mine, which probably contributed to why I felt a little protective of him. Not that he needed my protection. When he'd had me wrapped in his coils, he could have ended me. But he hadn't. I still had my nine, which was more than I thought I'd have when he burst out of the water and swooped toward me. But despite his obvious strength and abilities, my burgeoning and misguided protective instincts weren't going away.

And he was naked.

Did I mention he was naked?

Like all of him. Right there. Hanging out. In front of me.

I tried desperately not to look.

But he was right there.

Did I say that already?

There was absolutely no reason for him to be naked. Every single shifter I knew kept their clothes when shifting. Unless he was doing something that required him to be sans clothes when I'd whistled. Oh! Sweet mother of kittens. Had he been in bed with someone? And why had my brain gone straight to sex? I mean, sure, he could have been having a shower or something… But this guy oozed sex appeal. He probably didn't sleep alone very often. Heck, maybe he didn't shower alone either.

I'd never understood the appeal of showering with someone else. I showered to get clean in the fastest way possible. Showering was a functional necessity. But… Maybe if I was in a shower with a guy like him, I might consider ways to draw it out just to be close to him naked.

Great. Now I was picturing his very naked body glistening and wet.

It was so wrong to get a boner right now, but my body was doing its own thing without consulting my brain.

"Hello, Just Simon, Just a Cat. My name is Ogden Walsh." His English accent was stronger than it had been when he was in his dragon form. And this time, it was definitely sexy, which was wildly confusing. I'd spent my whole life protecting my nine, only to suddenly discover my libido had no sense of self-preservation. What was even happening right now?

The dragon extended his hand toward me. I stared at it for a long moment before I realized he meant for me to shake it. I put my palm against his. His firm grip made me shudder and suddenly I was imagining all kinds of ways he could use that grip on my body.

A rumbling noise rolled out of me. I didn't know if I was trying to purr or growl, but whatever my body was doing, it needed to be shut down. Fast. I tightened my control.

The guy's eyes crinkled at the sides, like smiling and laughing were common things for him. It looked so natural and good on him.

"Hello?" The word I said was only two syllables, but my voice cracked anyway. It hadn't done that since I was going through puberty. How embarrassing. Heat shot over my face, and I hoped Ogden couldn't see my blush in the dark.

"So, Simon Rivers, Dragon Summoner, we need to have a chat."

"Oh?" I glanced down at the whistle in my hand, then I thrust it toward him, even though some part of me still wanted to keep the pretty whistle. I'd been carrying it around for months now. I wasn't sure what I'd do without it. But this obviously wasn't any normal whistle, and I really shouldn't go about summoning dragons. Sadly, it would probably be better if a dragon had it. "I think this is yours."

Ogden shook his head. "It doesn't work that way, I'm afraid."

I stared at him.

"You don't know what's going on, do you?"

I shook my head.

He reached out, as if to take the whistle, but his fingers passed right through the metal. He looked at me like that explained everything. But it didn't. It really didn't. He huffed out a breath and rolled his eyes.

"For better or worse, you've activated an ancient magic and summoned a dragon."

"Okay." I nodded like an attentive student. "I, uh, got that. Now what?"

"Summoners usually try to control my kind, try to make us call them master and that kind of ridiculousness." Except he didn't sound like he was laughing. He sounded dead serious and rather angry about the whole thing. "Whistles like that have been banned for a long time." He narrowed his eyes at me again. "But here you are with one. Do you think I'll call you master, little kitty cat?"

I jerked my hand back and dropped the whistle like it'd burned me. I rubbed my hands on my jeans. The possessive thoughts I had about the whistle and how I'd just ogled the poor naked dragon caught in its magic made me feel dirty. My stomach turned. "No, that'd can't be. I'm no one's master. Definitely not a dragon's."

Ogden scowled and crossed his arms over his chest. "I'm not all that fond of the idea either, believe me." He pointed his bare toe at the whistle on the ground between us. "But let's not leave that lying about, m'kay? The last thing we need is for someone else to come along and blow on it."

"Are you sure that's what it is?" This had to be a mistake.

Ogden shrugged. "I'm sure you've heard the stories of witches summoning demons. There are always memes like that floating around on social media, like it's some joke." He scowled. "Anyway, it's like that. There have always been people who want to control other supernaturals. This particular whistle is for dragons, but there are others for different shifters or… well… you name any kind of supe and there will have been people who tried to enslave it."

"I've enslaved you?" My stomach rolled again, and I was suddenly thankful I hadn't eaten at the pub earlier. I doubted the dragon would appreciate me throwing up on his bare feet.

Ogden tipped his hand back and forth. "Not exactly. Now we negotiate."

Okay. That didn't sound so bad. "Okay. I'll start. You are free to do what you want. I don't want anything in return."

He looked like he would accept, but then he shook his head. "As much as I want to agree to those terms, I don't think I should. Not yet."

"No? I don't understand."

"If you'd listen for a minute, you might." The dragon shook his head at me like I was the ridiculous one.

If I was in my shifted form, my tail would be twitching like crazy about now.

"If I agreed to your terms now, the magic might sense we are done and send me back before I could finish the first line of 'Tutti Frutti' and I'd be no further ahead than I was before. I can't risk that. Not yet."

"But—"

"I can't return there empty-handed. I was running out of my regular repertoire of upbeat songs, and the '80s hair bands and ballads have never been my jam, you know? And as much as I hate to admit it, music can only do so much." Ogden shivered. "Honestly, I'd prefer to stay here, but that can't happen either. I need supplies and a plan."

"I don't understand." Was he trying to confuse me? Or had the summoning magic broken his brain somehow?

"We don't have long. From what I remember..." Ogden tilted his head to the side and stroked his chin. "I think most summoning magics stay active for about three, four, or seven hours, depending on the strength of the coven."

"Without a coven?" I asked, although I wasn't sure I believed any of this. And yet, what other explanation for his sudden appearance could there be?

He eyed me and nodded like I'd said something important. "A bit of an unknown, isn't it?"

A bright beam of light flashed over us.

"What in the name of Magic is going on, Simon?"

"Oh, uh, hey, Van... Uh, I mean, Chief Clark." I squinted into the light and inched away from Ogden. Could I make it to the tree line before Van caught me? Probably not. The guy was a hellhound. His job was all about policing everyone in town and catching people who ran, particularly if they were doing something wrong. I hadn't meant to enslave a dragon, but would Van see it the same way? My scalp tingled as panic screeched up and down my spine. I swallowed hard. "Uh... How's it going?"

"Who is the naked guy?"

"Uh, this is Ogden." I glanced at the dragon. "Ogden, this is Van Clark. He's the hellhound in charge of our local police."

Ogden inhaled, as if to confirm Van was a hellhound, then his eyes lit up. "Perfect. I would like to report a crime. Oh, and I need to make a call."

Drat.

"I didn't mean to do it. I swear," I blurted.

Fur sprouted all over my body. I was seconds away from bolting, but running away wasn't a long-term solution. I'd never been more than a few miles from Willow Lake. It was all I knew. I couldn't imagine trying to make it out there in the world on my own. Cats were supposedly independent creatures, but this cat shifter liked the comforts of home.

I was no alley cat. I'd never survive.

Even now, my instincts told me to run back to my apartment... or to my parent's place. Ugh. I was so predictable. If I escaped Van now, he'd know how to find me. In fact, all the hellhound would need to do was phone my mama. She'd turn me in with a slap on the back of my head for her troubles. Pops wouldn't snitch on me, but Mama held us kittens to higher standards.

Ogden cast a confused look in my direction.

"Someone better start talking." Van's words sounded more like a growl. His fiery gaze, betraying how close his hellhound was to the surface, peered at me from his shadow-covered face.

"I was kidnapped," Ogden said.

"I didn't know. Please. Believe me. I didn't know." My heart was beating so fast. Too fast probably. Like a ticking bomb counting down to detonation.

"Simon? Are you saying you abducted this man? Did you take his clothes too? And here I always thought you were the best of your litter." Van tsked like I'd disappointed him.

Ogden huffed and clapped his hands twice to get our attention. "Quit talking. Both of you. This is important. I was kidnapped and held in a place with a bunch of other supes. Simon saved me by summoning me. Now we need to get to work. Preparations need to be made. I have until the summoning magic time runs out to do that, so I'll need your help. I can't leave everyone there either."

I gaped. "Someone kidnapped you? Besides me?"

"It surprised me too."

"Okay. We're going back to the office. All of us," Van said, pointing at me. "That means you too, Simon Rivers." Then Van pointed at Ogden. "And I'm finding you some clothes." The hellhound shifted his flashlight. Little blobs of color danced over my eyes as they adjusted to the dark again.

What would my mama say when she found out I'd been dragged into the police station alongside a naked man?

Because she would hear.

She knew everything that happened in Willow Lake—from the current odds on when Hayden would step up as our alpha to the latest fad pastry at the bakery. Knowing which of her children was being escorted to the police station for questioning was kitten's play for her.

This would be almost as bad as losing one of my nine.

Chapter Seven

OGDEN

"Come along, kitty cat." I waved Simon closer. "It's time to go with the nice Officer Hellhound."

The hellhound rolled his eyes.

Simon's eyes, on the other hand, were wide as his gaze bounced between me and the police officer before darting to the nearby trees and shrubs. I knew he wanted to run. Anyone with eyes would have known that. But I couldn't let him get away yet. If he walked away now, the magic that brought me here might decide we were done and send me back before I was ready.

I set my hand on his forearm. I didn't grab him, but I could if he tried to bolt. Okay. I might have given it a little squeeze. He wore a jacket so I couldn't get a good feel, but his forearm was nice and thick. I liked it.

I was also half tempted to put my hand to his cheek and reassure him everything would be okay, but I didn't think he was ready for that. I couldn't risk scaring him so much that he ran off. Then I'd have to go hunting for him and that'd just waste precious time. And I didn't have time to waste right now.

At least that's what I'd heard.

Polite company never discussed summoning, not that I ever worried too much about being polite. The mere idea of being transported somewhere against your will and tortured until you submitted to the summoner's will and agreed to serve them forevermore made people antsy. Nowadays, summoning someone just wasn't done. I wasn't aware of anyone being summoned in the last hundred years or so. Although, when you were as old as me, time blurred, so that timeline might not be entirely accurate.

The Supernatural Council, for all its flaws, had been remarkably effective at eradicating the spells and talismans used in a summoning. Apparently, I was naïve to think that, since they'd obviously missed at least one. And where there was one, there would always be more.

I hated it when the world tried to make me cynical.

Still, if anyone *had* to be summoned, it was better for it to be me than someone else—not because I was self-sacrificing. Nope. I had no interest in such a defeatist attitude. But I'd been around long enough to know things many younger supes didn't, like how to navigate my way through a summoning without losing my autonomy.

At least I hoped I did.

The first step was to secure a hostage as quickly as possible. The best hostage was one who held a position of power, but any hostage was better than no hostage. Okay. I'd done that. Although… I'd since let them go because of what had happened during step two. I hoped that wouldn't come back to bite me in the ass.

I liked a bit of a nip on the ass now and again, but not like this.

Step two was all about interrogation. The goal was to discover who had used the magic and why. This was where things usually got dicey, because how could anyone summon another supe and have honorable intentions?

Well, except maybe Simon.

But this was an unusual summoning.

There was no coven, no mob of power-hungry assholes trying to make me submit to them. I didn't need to eliminate the hostage to prove my point. Keeping hold of the hostage in this case would have been pointless, regardless of how much I enjoyed having the cute little cat shifter in my coils.

I also didn't think you were supposed to find your summoner adorable, but here we were.

Step three was tricky because it involved biding your time. If the summoned supe agreed to any terms offered by their summoner, the magical trap would snap shut and bind them to the summoner.

However, if they avoided agreeing to anything, the magic that had pulled the supe to the summoner would eventually collapse and set everything back to how it was. The summoned supe would return to where they had been, and both continued with their lives. That was usually the goal. Every survival story was adamant about needing to bluff at this stage, pretend you still had full access to every bit of power and magic that you normally had.

Why not fight for your freedom? Well, because the other thing about being summoned? It made you weaker than a hatchling who'd just popped out of its shell.

Any sane supe would think I'd lost my mind, having already released my hostage and not having agreed to Simon's generous offer as soon as he presented it. Except this whole situation demanded the rules be broken. Simon had unintentionally summoned me, which meant he didn't plan on keeping me. With that sorted, I needed to capitalize on the time I had. I refused to return to that blasted cage without weapons, armor, and a way to break out.

Nope. No thank you.

I didn't want to go back there at all, but needs must and all that. No one should lock up and threaten an average law-abiding supe with a cattle prod.

My hasty plan had a lot of problems. The most challenging obstacle was the magic reinforcing those cages. I did not know how to overcome it. It'd been tough enough to fight the troll when I had full access to my magic, but the summoning had thoroughly fucked that up. My fire wasn't responding. My electricity wasn't working. I doubted I'd be able to do anything but shift, which wouldn't do me much good without my fire and my electricity. Stupid summoning spells.

At least I hadn't needed to defend myself against Simon. I wouldn't have been able to do anything but squeeze him to death and, frankly, that sounded horrible. Can you imagine the viscera and other goop that would have gotten on my scales when his body burst like an over-filled water balloon? So unhygienic.

"Simon, give your friend your jacket," the police officer said. "Last thing we need is for someone to post on social media about skinny dippers at the lake. Whenever that happens, we end up with a bunch of perverts with binoculars hiding in the bushes."

Simon's gaze darted down to my junk and back up again, as if he'd forgotten I was naked until the hellhound reminded him. He shucked his jacket and flung it at me. Truthfully, I'd kind of forgotten about being naked too after having been without clothes for most of the day. It wasn't like dragons ever felt cold. Although, admittedly, being without clothes when the others were dressed was a little weird. I didn't mind a bit of kink, but being naked in a crowd of fully dressed people had never interested me. Bondage, though, might be fun to do with the kitty cat. I'd rather enjoyed having him at my mercy in my coils.

Of course, my arm chose that moment to start itching again, distracting me from imagining the sexy cat shifter tied to my bed. I rubbed at that irksome little bite quickly before pulling on the jacket.

Simon's body heat lingered in the lining in the most delicious way. I wasn't cold, but like most of my kind, I loved heat. My sister had thought I was crazy for moving so far from the equator and its blistering year-round sun. I doubted I'd ever convince her of the merits of cuddling with someone under a cozy blanket in front of a roaring fire. She preferred her solitude too much. Her favorite way to spend her afternoons was napping in her enclosed courtyard, where the tiles were hot enough to fry an egg on. No, she wouldn't like it here. At all.

I pulled Simon's jacket tighter around me and reveled in the warmth. The cat shifter wasn't a big guy like the hellhound, but he was still larger than I was. His jacket, which fit over wider shoulders and thicker arms, was too big for me, and it wasn't something I would have chosen for myself, but it'd do. The hem fell to mid-thigh, so it covered my twig and berries, which was the hellhound's goal.

Although dragons didn't have as strong a sense of smell as some supes, enough of Simon's scent infused the jacket that even I could enjoy it. It was all freshly mown grass and wildflowers, and I wanted to push my face into the fabric and close my eyes. It reminded me of home and safety and hope—things I wasn't sure I'd ever experience again after waking up in that stupid cage.

I swallowed down the lump in my throat and blinked away the burning in my eyes. Simon didn't realize it yet, but he'd saved me. And I was going to reward him. On my terms. After we saved those other supes.

Of course, my brain conjured all kinds of delightfully decadent ways to reward him, but I wasn't sure the cat would be onboard with any of those. I was sure he was an adult—because ew, I could *not* be attracted to someone underaged—but he seemed a bit young. A little naïve. I'd hate to shock him so much I scared him away. But, if I had my way, I would have fun teaching him a few things as a thank you.

I let my gaze wander down his body again. I'd already felt the bit of softness around his middle and the sturdy thickness of his thighs when I wrapped him in my coils earlier, and now I regretted letting him go as quickly as I had.

He was stocky with nice husky arms—perfect, I was sure, for holding his lover tight... or, better yet, bracing himself to be taken on all fours. His face was a little too broad to be considered classically handsome and his nose a little too round and cute to be elegant, but the gentleness in his eyes reminded me of how I imagined a romantic poet might look when eyeing his love.

I could easily imagine this cat shifter sprawled across the fainting couch in the vault where I kept my hoard. He would be naked, of course, wearing only a gem-encrusted crown nestled in his dark brown hair. Divine. It was a shame he didn't wear any jewelry because his skin would be lovely adorned with gold. And his pale eyes... I was sure I had a gemstone that precise color. But if I didn't, I could always buy more until I found the perfect match. And then I'd cover him with them.

Were his eyes in his shifted form the same color? If they weren't, I'd collect that color too. My chest warmed at the idea of adding to my hoard. There was nothing I enjoyed more.

But first things first. The hellhound was right. I had things I needed to say. People to save. Et cetera. Et cetera.

I wouldn't have been so quick to talk about the cages to just anyone, but hellhounds were remarkable creatures. There were fewer around than there used to be, but that was true for all supes. Magic was fading, and as far as I could see, no one was fixing it. I hoped the SC held think tanks on how to save magic, even if no one thought to invite me, a lowly bartender and entertainer. That didn't stop me, though, from philosophizing with my regulars when it got close to last call on quiet nights. That was when thoughts turned to all those big life questions. Those were always the best conversations.

The fact there was a hellhound here now, just when I needed one, when there were so few in the world, felt like a sign. Hellhounds were inherently trustworthy. And they could be deadly if you broke any of the big supernatural laws. Or so I'd heard. I'd never actually seen one mete out justice. But hellhounds were the stuff of legends. They inspired countless stories, which were usually told to baby supes to make them behave.

I grabbed Simon's hand and pulled him along as we followed the hellhound away from the lake. Which reminded me...

"Where are we?" My senses picked up all kinds of magic in the air and in the earth beneath my feet too. What a strange sensation.

"Willow Lake," Simon said.

I knew where that was, which meant I hadn't gone too far from my home in Aspen Bay. I'd never been to Willow Lake, though, so everything was unfamiliar, particularly all that magic. The town must sit over a nexus of ley lines. It would explain why other supes were drawn here, because there were a lot of supes here. I could tell that much. The strange mishmash of their magic washed over me, colliding and dancing and shimmering together to form a heady and delightful cocktail.

I partially shifted my feet when we arrived at a gravel road. I sighed. My dragon feet weren't a good look at the end of my human legs, but without shoes, it couldn't be helped. This would at least help save the pedicure on my human-shaped feet. Luckily, the pedicure on my paws wasn't as susceptible to damage. Had Simon noticed my neatly trimmed and shaped claws with their glossy coat of clear polish?

When we arrived at a parking lot in front of a large old building with a sign that read *Willow Lake Inn*, Van guided us to a police vehicle. He glanced down at my dragon paws at the end of my legs when he opened the passenger door for me.

"Sorry, I didn't think about your feet," he said, and it sounded like he meant it. Wait, of course he did. Hellhounds couldn't lie.

"It's fine, Officer Hellhound."

"You can call me Chief Clark or Van," the hellhound said, but we both knew that wouldn't happen.

I patted him on his chest before I climbed into the front seat of the SUV. It wasn't the most graceful of movements, but I made the most of it. Okay, I may have bent over a bit more than necessary as I crawled into the seat and maybe I extended my legs one at a time as I let my feet take on their human shape again. I had great legs. I knew it and I didn't see any reason not to show them off a little.

Behind me, Simon purred. The kitty cat liked what he saw.

Then he abruptly stopped, coughing as if to cover up his reaction. But it was too late, I'd already heard. Apparently Van had too, since the hellhound chuckled as I plopped my bottom onto the seat and situated myself. I caught Van patting a blushing Simon on the back. I took that as a good sign for my plans to reward Simon for saving me, even though the cat shifter was currently looking anywhere but at me.

"Why don't you take the back seat, Simon?"

Simon swallowed and did as the hellhound suggested. I wouldn't have minded sitting on his lap in the front seat, but Simon had jumped into the back before I could suggest it.

"When we get to the office, I'll grab you some clothes. We've started keeping a few things on hand, just in case. They won't be pretty, but they'll be better than what you have," Office Hellhound said as he drove us through town.

The police department filled a boring little one-story building close to what appeared to be the town's main commercial district. True to his word, soon after Van ushered us inside a little meeting room, he disappeared, only to return a few minutes later with a dreary looking set of clothes and an equally awful pair of paper-like slippers for my feet. I sighed as I accepted them, knowing I wasn't in any position to be picky. Van and Simon left the room long enough for me to change.

The bland gray T-shirt and generic gray sweatpants were hardly my style. Not only that, the shirt was way too big for me. I tugged on the bottom hem of the shirt and tied it into a knot. That helped a bit. But there was nothing to be done about the pants. When the two returned, Simon gulped. His eyes widened as he eyed me from top to bottom. His pupils changed, taking on the slitted appearance of his feline form, which suggested he liked what he saw. I looked at the travesty I was wearing, and I didn't understand his reaction.

Simon's gaze darted to Van with an accusatory scowl on his face.

Van chuckled again as he patted Simon's shoulder. "Sorry, kid, that's the best we have."

That just made Simon's scowl deepen.

Chapter Eight

SIMON

Ogden was gloriously gorgeous.

I kind of noticed that when we were down by the lake, but I'd tried my best not to look at him too much. I mean he was naked, and my mama had drilled it into me that ogling was bad manners.

But he wasn't naked now.

Instead, he was wearing gray freaking sweatpants that revealed things I had trouble ignoring. And the way he tied up the T-shirt to reveal that sliver of skin along his tight abdomen? My tongue nearly fell out of my mouth, but I wasn't a disgusting dog. We cats didn't let our tongues loll out of our mouths.

Cats purred.

But I shouldn't do that either. He was a stranger, and I'd seen him naked, and I'd summoned him, and… The whole situation was messy. I didn't want him to feel uncomfortable. Except my chest kept rumbling and vibrating and... I needed it to stop. I thumped my chest a few times to interrupt the purring before things got out of hand.

I was making a mess of this. Did he think I was channeling some latent caveman impulse by hitting my chest like that? And if he did, would he be wrong? After all, I *was* itching to throw him over my shoulder and haul him off to my apartment, where no one else could see him in those stupid sweatpants.

How could anyone look as good as him with so little effort?

Ogden didn't look like he'd been dunked in water earlier. Every hair was in place. And he didn't smell like the lake either. Not really. Sure, there was a bit of a lake scent about him, but under that was the most delicious scent I'd ever smelled. It was like catnip, only a thousand times better. My body rippled, and I fought back the urge to shift. I couldn't let that happen. If I did, I would probably end up in his lap, rolling around on him like a weirdo, rubbing my scent all over him.

"Thank you, kitty cat," Ogden said as he returned my jacket. The same jacket he'd been naked in.

I took it from him, barely resisting the urge to push my face into the lining and inhale his scent.

"Let's sit and you can tell me what happened tonight." Van waved to the cushioned chairs around a shiny wooden table. Unlike some of my rowdy brothers, I'd never been to the police station before reporting the wolves all those months ago. That time, I'd sat beside Dot's desk while she made some notes. This time, we were in a separate room, but I doubted this was the interrogation room. It was too nice.

Van and Ogden sat down at the table like normal people, but I didn't move from the doorway. I wanted nothing more than to sit beside the dragon, but would that be weird? I didn't know him. He'd probably want a bit of space. It sounded like he'd had a pretty awful day, and part of that was my fault.

"I'm not sure I should be here," I said, my gaze darting over my shoulder to the hallway.

"Come here, Simon." Ogden patted the chair beside him. "You can't leave me yet."

I jumped forward and sat in the chair he indicated, like an obedient dog. Thank the Eternal Magic that my brothers weren't here to see that. They'd never let me hear the end of it. Across the table, Van lifted one eyebrow.

I didn't want to know what he was thinking.

"Okay, I need to tell you what happened. I know that," Ogden said, meeting Van's eyes steadily. "But I need your help first. When the time for our negotiating expires, I can't go back without gear. The only way I'll stand a chance of escaping again is if I'm armed from head to tail. Something magical would work best, I think, but something mundane might work in a pinch, like a blowtorch." He nodded. "Yeah. That might work. But not one of those wimpy ones used for crème brûlée. I'm talking a powerful one, like something a bank robber would use to break into a safe."

"I know you believe what you are saying to be true, but I'm going to need more information." Van eyed the dragon. "Let's start with your name."

"Ogden Walsh," he said with a resigned sigh.

"Okay, Mr. Walsh. What can you tell me about how you came to be in Willow Lake?"

Ogden smiled, and it lit up his face. His laugh lines crinkled, and his pretty blue eyes sparkled and… Ugh. I bit back a groan. Seriously, no one should be that attractive. "Please, call me Ogden. Even my lawyers don't call me Mr. Walsh."

Van nodded and made a note. I wanted to ask why Ogden needed lawyers, but I didn't. Maybe he was a criminal mastermind, and if he was, I felt a strange compulsion not to get him into trouble with Van. I probably watched too much TV if that was my first thought, but whatever.

"Last night, after I closed up the bar for the night, I went to the lake for a little dip."

"Do you do that often?"

"Almost every night. No matter the weather."

Van made another note.

"And then…" Ogden frowned. "Actually, I'm not sure what happened. I remember changing into my bathing suit." He turned to face me with a sexy smirk. "It's a tight little number I got in Monaco the last time I was there."

A *tight little number… Meow.*

My cheeks burned. I tried to swallow so I wouldn't drool. Ogden grinned as if he knew exactly what he was doing to me. When a little purr squeaked free, he winked at me.

Van cleared his throat. Right. He needed answers. "So you changed. Then what?"

"I went down to the water…" His words trailed off and his forehead furrowed. "Huh…"

"You don't remember?" Van asked.

I reached for the dragon's hand, needing to offer some sort of comfort. Why I thought he'd find comfort in holding my hand, I didn't know. His face didn't register any obvious distress, but his fingers tightened around mine.

"No… I don't remember what happened next." He frowned. "I woke up, naked as the day I hatched, in a large-ish crate or cage thing. It wasn't super big. I couldn't stand or stretch out my legs, but I could sit up in it. Magic coated the cage, reinforcing the bars enough that I couldn't bend them or break the lock."

"A cage?" Van's face contorted like he'd tasted something vile.

Ogden nodded. "That's why the blowtorch might work. The magic on the cage will probably repel other magic, but they might not have protected against a mundane approach."

Van leaned forward. "What else did you see?"

"A bunch more cages, all filled with other supes." Ogden stared at the wall behind Van, as if envisioning the scene in his head.

Van's body went eerily still. The only movement was the creepy fire dancing in his eyes. "What can you tell me about where you were being held?"

Ogden's hand squeezed mine. "The walls were concrete and so was the floor. I couldn't see the ceiling because the top of the cage was solid, but I know the lights were fluorescent. They hummed and gave off that awful glow that makes everyone look sickly."

"You didn't recognize it?"

Ogden shook his head.

"Shit," the hellhound muttered. "Okay. I'm going to call in a few other people to hear this, okay?"

"Whatever you think is best," Ogden agreed. "But hurry. We need to get everything sorted before my time runs out. Do you have a gun I could borrow?"

"I can't give out guns, but we'll figure out something. Do you think you could pull another person with you going back?"

Ogden considered the question, then shook his head. "I don't know, but it seems unlikely. The way the magic felt when it pulled me through... It seemed specific to me."

"Good to know. Okay. I'll be right back," the hellhound said as he left the room.

"I can't believe you were in a cage." I wanted to cling to Ogden and make sure he never went back there again. "What if I hadn't blown on that whistle tonight? I've had it for months without doing that. What If I'd waited another few months or years or...?"

Ogden peered into my eyes. "But you did."

"But what if—?"

"Don't think of that," he said. "I'm beginning to suspect the Eternal Magic had a hand in this."

"You think so?" My eyes widened. I couldn't imagine the Eternal Magic taking an interest in me.

But I was wondering if perhaps she had even bigger plans for the two of us. This connection between us might be just a product of the summoning magic, but what if it was more?

Before we could say any more, Van returned with a large box filled with a variety of strange looking gadgets.

The ozone-licorice scent emanating from the contents suggested that at least some were magical. "The others will be here soon. In the meantime..." He pulled a small device from the box and presented it to Ogden. It was the size of a fly and looked like a bit of circuitry. "This is a tracker. Keep it on you just in case things change before we have a new plan. It'll let us track you down to wherever they're keeping you."

"Where am I going to stick that? Based on what happened last time—you know, the whole naked part— there aren't a lot of places to hide something like that. Even if it is small." Ogden poked at the tracking device. "Can I swallow it?"

Van lifted an eyebrow and looked at the device. "I've never been asked that before, so I don't know. Put it in this pouch for now." He plucked up the device and tucked it into a small pouch with a long string loop before offering it to Ogden again.

Ogden put it around his neck and tucked it under his borrowed shirt.

"Okay, now try this," Van said. He held out a belt made of thick leather with pouches hanging off it.

Ogden squished up his nose. "What's that?"

"Put it on and we'll fill it with supplies."

"Fine," he muttered. As soon as he fastened it around his hips, Ogden let out a long and soul deep sigh. "Does it have to be so... utilitarian?"

Van ignored Ogden's complaint and presented him with a wide assortment of both magical and mundane weapons, including wire cutters, screwdrivers, a magical pocketknife capable of slicing through spells, and a spray that when deployed could temporarily suppress magic in anyone it hit. Being so close to all those dangerous implements made my skin crawl, but I couldn't make myself leave.

I didn't understand it. At all. I should have shifted and ducked out of the room as soon as Ogden put the tracker on. He didn't need me anymore.

"That's all I have here that I can give you," Van said.

Ogden adjusted the belt. The contents of his pouches rattled against one another. "This is a start."

"Just don't take off the tracking device. We'll need it to find you." Then Van eyed Ogden's forearm, which he'd been scratching while we talked. "What's the matter with your arm?"

"Just a bite, I guess."

"When did you get it?"

"When I woke up this morning."

I leaned over to see the spot he'd been itching. Red, irritated skin surrounded a little mound on Ogden's forearm.

Van tilted his head. "We should get it looked at. Most insect bites don't bother supes for so long."

Ogden and I both looked at the bump a little closer.

"Yeah. I'd wondered about that. If I'm still here in the morning, I'll go then. Is there a supernatural doctor in town?"

I hated the reminder that he expected to be returned to that cage soon.

"Yep. I'll phone and make sure they see you. If you aren't here, we'll sort it out after we find you and have dealt with those bastards." Van left to make the call.

"Do you really think it is a bite?" I asked as I brushed my thumb over the bump.

Ogden shuddered. "I hope that's all it is."

Mama always said cats were excellent judges of character and I trusted my instincts. Ogden didn't deserve any of this, of that I was sure. The idea of someone experimenting on him was driving me nearly feral.

Van returned with a group of people. Willow Lake was small enough that I knew almost everyone, but I hadn't been prepared for the demon and his team to walk in. I don't know who I expected… Maybe Hayden?

Gage's face didn't reveal any emotion, but I still got the sense he was surprised to see me here. It wasn't that long ago that I'd been sitting with him at the pub… you know, right before I bolted and made everyone wonder what was wrong with me. Since Gage and his team had moved to town, some locals tried ingratiating themselves with the demon, including Mama. Not me, though. I'd done my best to stay under their radar.

It looked like I was fully on his radar now, with a big neon arrow pointing right at me.

Could this day get any worse?

I shrank down in my seat. My gaze darted to the door. Could I shift and run? Could I get out the door before anyone stopped me?

No. I couldn't leave Ogden.

Hairballs and rocking chairs! How was I going to survive this?

The demon's horns glinted under the office lights as he sat across from me. When his gaze met mine, I swallowed and managed a brief nod in acknowledgement. The others followed in behind him and sat down at the table with a familiarity that suggested this wasn't the first time they'd all gathered here.

"Let me introduce everyone," Van said. He nodded toward Gage first. The horned demon radiated power from the far side of the table. "The demon is Gage. He's recently bonded to Willow Lake, so he's stable. He leads an investigative team sanctioned by the Supernatural Council. I invited him and his team here because they found a warehouse with a bunch of caged supes recently during another investigation. Around that same time, our local oracle had a vision of more imprisoned supes. And now, here you are, talking about exactly that. It seems highly probable this is all connected with the SC's ongoing investigation."

Ogden glanced at the others. "And who are the rest of these people?"

"The wolf is Adrian." Van waved toward the muscular blond man with a very defined jaw line. The first time I'd ever seen Adrian, a strange wolf shifter, I'd run away. Okay. I ran away from a lot of situations, but it was better to be safe than sorry, as Mama said. But except for Hayden and Oak, wolf shifters didn't have a great reputation. Adrian was okay, though, I guessed. Although a lot of that had to do with my opinion of Jeremy. Jeremy was quirky and weird, but I couldn't see him putting up with a nasty mate. The wolf was also a lot less intimidating with a pale green batch of hair and skin along his temple that marked him as Jeremy's fated mate. The color and pattern almost made him look approachable. "He's mated to Jeremy, who is sitting beside him."

"Hi! I guess I know why Simon didn't reply to my text earlier," the smaller man said with a wide grin as he waved enthusiastically at us. Jeremy's pale green markings matched Adrian's, but I thought they suited him better.

And for the record, Jeremy's implication that I usually replied was a lie. Today had not been the exception.

"Is it true you're a dragon?" Jeremy wiggled in his seat. He held a pen against a pad of paper, ready to take notes.

"Yes."

"Do you have a hoard? Can you really breathe fire? Does your—?"

"Save your questions for later, Jer," Adrian whispered in his mate's ear, cutting off his questions.

Jeremy pouted, but everyone ignored him.

"Beside Jeremy is Davina. She's a medium and Gage's second." She still reminded me of an old-time movie star, except she was all sharp angles, narrowed eyes, and pursed lips. "Then, on the other side of the table, we have Teague, who is a death mage."

I squirmed as the mage's eyes went to Ogden and then to me. He might look nice and innocent like the stereotypical guy next door, complete with freckles and all, but I wanted nothing to do with a death mage, thank you very much. I didn't know what his magic did, and I didn't want to know. The word *death* said it all. I was glad he was sitting far, far away from me. My nine lives were precious. I didn't need to think about death for a long, long time.

"The centaur is Isaac."

Isaac lifted his hand in a wide, sweeping motion like his

big body couldn't do small gestures. His long bleached blond hair and bright smiling face always struck me as strange. It wasn't natural for someone to smile that much. It just wasn't.

"And the shadow jumper beside him is Nelson."

The dark-haired man scowled at the mention of his name. Not too friendly, that one. I didn't know what a shadow jumper was any more than I knew what a death mage was, but Ogden's eyebrows lifted at the mention of Nelson's magic.

"There are a few others we'll be bringing in to help us too, but this is the core team." Then Van nodded at Ogden. "Could you repeat what you told me earlier about the room with the cages?"

"Wait. What about Hayden?" I asked. "Shouldn't he be here?" I trusted the alpha wolf more than I trusted anyone else at this table... well, except maybe Van.

"I texted him. He didn't respond," Van said.

"But we all know he doesn't check his messages," I argued. Heat rushed over my face as I struggled to stand up to Van. Everyone was watching me, but I didn't back down. Ogden needed help, and getting the best help around was the least I could do for him. Hayden was second to none when it came to helping people, ask anyone in Willow Lake. I lifted my chin and met Van's fire-filled eyes. Hellhounds were so freaky when they did that.

Normally, I'd have slipped under the table and shifted under the intensity of Van's stare, but I didn't this time. Oh, how I wanted to, though! My hair felt all puffed up, the back of my neck tingled, and my claws poked out through the ends of my fingers and toes. My socks would be ruined. But I didn't back down.

Finally, Van sighed and pulled out his phone. Hayden picked up on the second ring. The hellhound explained the situation and Hayden's curse, even over the phone, was loud enough to fill the room.

Ogden leaned toward me. "Who is Hayden?"

"Our alpha."

Hayden must have heard my whispered response because he proclaimed he wasn't "the fucking alpha" loud enough even the mage and the medium flinched. That said something because their kind didn't have great hearing. Then he said he'd be right over, just like an alpha would.

While we waited for Hayden, I tucked Ogden as close to me as I could. I wanted to pull him into my lap, but I talked myself out of it. I didn't understand my need to touch him. I didn't understand my desire to put myself between him and the rest of the world.

For one thing, he was a dragon. He didn't need me to fight his battles. And more importantly, I was so far outside my norm that I could have been on Pluto. This was not like me. At all. But I couldn't stop.

Ogden didn't seem to mind. He wasn't huddling at my side like a frightened kitten, but he also hadn't moved away from me either. In fact, I suspected he was enjoying my attention based on the way his hand kept stroking my leg.

His one foot swung back and forth like a metronome, brushing my leg with each swing. Jeremy tried asking a few questions, but he stopped after getting *the look* from Gage. I recognized that type of look; Mama had used it a lot on us when we were younger. It meant *quit talking and behave.*

After that, we all waited in awkward silence. My phone pinged, announcing a message. Then it pinged two more times. With my free hand, I pulled out my phone, convinced I would find a bunch of messages from my mama asking why I was at the police station again. Instead, a series of texts from Jeremy filled the screen. I glanced over at him, but he was pretending to whistle while doing his best to look anywhere except at me or the dragon at my side. I opened my app.

Jeremy: Is he really a dragon? That's amazing. I didn't know dragons existed. So freaking cool. Where did you meet? Did he tell you about his hoard? Is it something random, like scratch and sniff stickers from the '80s? Can he fly? What color are his scales? Does he have scales? I bet he does. What do they feel like? Are they soft? Leathery? Like a fish's scales? If he flies, do you think he could carry someone? Did he grow up in a castle? Or a cave? Can he breathe fire?

Jeremy: Shoot. I hit send before I meant to.

Jeremy: Crap. Adrian is getting suspicious. I'll ask more questions later. Oh! Maybe this weekend when we meet up to watch

"Lord of the Rings" you can bring him too. Do you think he would want to come? Can you imagine talking about Smaug with a real live dragon? Amazing! *thumbs up emoji* *high five emoji*

Another ping. Another message.

Jeremy: Wait… Is Smaug in LOTR? Or am I confusing things with *The Hobbit*? I'm so freaking excited about meeting a dragon IRL that I'm losing my mind. Either way, ask him if he wants to join us!

I blinked at the messages, then looked up at Jeremy again. Ogden looked at my screen and snorted.

"Jeremy?" Adrian, catching the exchange, frowned at his mate. "What did you do?"

"Nothing," Jeremy said quickly. His fingers were crossed as he scratched his temple.

Van sighed. "I know when people lie. You know I do."

"Come on! There's a dragon. Right there!" Jeremy waved his hand toward Ogden. "Of course I have questions."

Ogden smiled indulgently at Jeremy. It was the same expression old people used when talking to precocious children. "Perhaps we can talk later."

"Yes!" Jeremy did a fist pump before he turned to his

mate. "See? If I hadn't done anything, I wouldn't get to talk to a dragon later."

Adrian narrowed his eyes and growled at Ogden. The hairs on the back of my neck bristled, and I hissed loudly. My claws pushed free. If Adrian was closer to me, I would have swatted him. A few claws across his nose would do the trick.

Jeremy brushed a light kiss over his wolf's cheek. "There, there. You'll always be my favorite. You know that."

The tension disappeared as Adrian's wolf preened under his mate's attention. Ogden smiled at me, obviously delighted by my reaction. Then I realized what I'd done.

Holy, holy, holy.

What had come over me? I couldn't challenge a werewolf! Things like that cost cat shifters their nine.

Chapter Nine

SIMON

Before anything else could happen, Hayden burst through the door, bringing with him the smell of oil and grease. Those were the smells I always associated with him, but under those was something else. It reminded me of ash at the bottom of a firepit. His dirty blond hair was a wild mess. His eyes flashed with the golden color of his wolf as he glanced around the room.

"I'm the last one to arrive?"

Van nodded sharply. "Sit. We need answers."

Hayden found an armless chair in the corner of the room and hauled it to the table. He swung it around, so he was sitting with the back of the chair against his chest. He motioned for things to start. Van introduced Ogden and Hayden, then asked Ogden to tell his story again.

Everyone listened. Jeremy's pen scraped over his paper as he took copious notes. Other than that, no one else made a sound. They were all fixated on my dragon.

"What else did you see in the room?" Gage asked, leaning forward. The motion made the light catch on his horns again. I shuddered. I'd never get used to seeing horns on someone's head.

"There were... I want to say... like... twenty or thirty other crates, stacked two high. Maybe more. I couldn't really tell from where I was. Each crate held a supernatural. Everyone was my size or smaller. I don't know if our sizes are important, but it seemed odd to me. I saw a unicorn, a phoenix, and a few other shifters of various kinds. Based on the scents, which I'm not the best at, I think maybe there was a vampire and perhaps a yeti in there too. Maybe. I'm not sure about the rest."

I sucked in a breath. That was a lot of supes to hold captive.

"Do you think it's the same trafficking ring?" Van's gaze caught on Gage's.

My ears started ringing. A trafficking ring? Of supes? How was that possible? One of the best things about being a supe, even a little cat shifter like me, was that Mother Magic blessed us and took care of us. It was just the way it was. No one could keep a supernatural being contained for long without a lot of effort. And the only ones I knew of who had that kind of ability were working under contract for the Supernatural Council, imprisoning criminals. And even then, Mama and Pops said that it wouldn't be long before the SC returned to the old ways again and executed their criminals because the effort of keeping them locked up was a waste of magic.

I shuddered. I couldn't imagine being imprisoned like that. There was a reason I acted like a tamed kitten instead of a wild one. Well, that and the fact that I really did like having my nine lives. Those two things went hand in hand.

Wait. When we were at the pub earlier, someone had mentioned something about cages. Was this what they were talking about?

"I don't think it could be anything else," Gage agreed. "It seems like a smaller operation though. The warehouse we found had a lot more supes. So either they think that keeping things small will help them avoid detection longer and they are still recovering from the blow we dealt them last time, or—"

"Or this is a smaller branch of a larger operation," Nelson finished for him.

"Exactly," Gage agreed.

Holy Magic, I hoped it wasn't that last one.

"Did anyone mention a goblin named Babette?" Gage asked.

Ogden shook his head. "No one said much of anything. No one mentioned a goblin, but a troll came in at one point. I didn't see anyone else, which was strange considering the amount of magic needed to contain me. I would have expected a coven of mages at the very least."

We all considered the implications for a minute. "The troll was small for her species. I had a feeling she wasn't a matriarch yet." He grinned a little viciously. "She tried to poke me with a cattle prod, but I zapped her."

"She tried to do what?" My claws, which had been poking through the tips of my fingers for most of the conversation, broke through completely on my free hand. At least they hadn't sliced through the hand holding Ogden's, but my control was shaky at best. I pulled my other hand out of his so I didn't scratch him if I couldn't contain my shift. The impulse to go after this troll and shred her was almost too strong. I wasn't a big creature, but I could do some damage.

Then I froze.

I'd never, ever in my life wanted to take my claws to someone before and here I'd wanted to do exactly that twice in the last few minutes. Some cats might like to fight, defend their territory, let fur fly. Before now, that'd never been me. I preferred to run and hide. I didn't like this change.

"Don't worry, kitty cat," Ogden patted my arm, oblivious to my scary thoughts. "She got what was coming to her. She'll have those injuries for a few days at least."

"So you shifted?" I asked. "I thought you said the cage was small and that you couldn't break out. There is no way your dragon form could fit in the cage you described."

"I don't need to shift to access my powers. Dragons aren't like other shifters. The only thing that changes when I shift into my dragon form is my body. Everything else— my senses, my strength, my magic—stays the same regardless of which form I'm in. I don't have to do a partial shift."

I blinked. Wow. That was... amazing. Van and Gage didn't look surprised by this information. Jeremy squealed in delight and scribbled in his notebook. And me? I was blown away.

Gage looked at Hayden. "Are you still in touch with those wolves from Robbie's pack?"

Hayden's face turned stoney and his eyes flashed, showing his wolf. "Why?"

"We should ask them if they remember a troll. They might know her name."

Hayden clenched his teeth so hard I thought he'd break a tooth. Then he slowly nodded. "I'll ask."

"I can, if you don't want to," Van offered.

"I said I'd do it," Hayden snapped.

"Creating a spell that could keep so many supes, including a dragon, contained. That's a lot," Davina said. "They have to be using the Coven of One ring."

"Those only exist in fairy tales," Ogden scoffed.

"Ulric had been collecting magical artifacts for a long time. He owned a lot of things that shouldn't exist," Van said, sounding tired. "We discovered tonight that he had one of those rings along with a lot of other dangerous artifacts that were stolen."

"Well, fuck," Ogden said, summing up what everyone was thinking.

"It always comes back to Robbie," Hayden muttered.

"Who is Robbie?" Ogden whispered to me.

"Hayden's brother," I explained. "He did some… uh… not great stuff. He's missing now. No one knows where he is. The SC is looking for him."

Upon hearing my description, Hayden's eyes turned golden, suggesting his wolf was close to the surface. He gritted his teeth and shook his head to get control. A moment later, he cleared his throat, looking more like his usual self. "Are you sure he stole it?"

"That's what Ulric said." Davina nodded.

I squirmed, because I had one of those missing artifacts too. I swallowed hard and slid down in my chair. Everyone else let that bit of news sit for a minute before Van turned back to Ogden.

"Then what?" Van prodded. "What happened next?"

"Not much really." Ogden tilted his head as he went back through his memories. "The troll came back just before I came here, but otherwise no one else came into the room while I was there."

"How long were you held there?" Van asked.

The dragon tapped on the table as if he was counting something. "I finished about seven sets." We must have all looked confused, because he shrugged again. "I sometimes perform at my bar. I thought some songs might help lift people's spirits. It certainly couldn't hurt."

"How long is a set? An hour?"

Ogden nodded. "Thereabouts."

"So you sang for seven hours?" Van asked.

Ogden rolled an elegant shoulder. "I took a few breaks between sets so magic could soothe my vocal cords, but none of them were too long. The morale really dropped quickly when I stopped singing."

Both Van and Jeremy added more notes to their books.

"I'd like to show you a picture of a message from our oracle," Gage said as he leaned forward.

Ogden's eyebrows rose. "You have a hellhound, a demon, and an oracle here? That's... surprising."

Gage inclined his head in acknowledgement.

I hadn't ever thought about Willow Lake being special or unusual. It was just my home. But maybe it was strange to have all these powerful and unusual supes living here.

"Okay. Let's see your oracle's message." Ogden nodded.

Davina tapped on her tablet a few times before turning it toward Ogden. I leaned over and looked at the image too. It showed people in cages. Oh, right. I remembered something about that now. Mama had been there when Jake painted it. But I'd been so caught up in my whistle that I hadn't paid much attention to it. It had just been so… separate from me and my world. It hadn't meant much. Sure, I felt for the people, but what could I do about it?

But now that I knew Ogden had been there…

Ogden swallowed as he took the tablet and zoomed in on it.

"Yeah," he said with a dry sounding voice. "Yeah. That's it. That's where I woke up. That's the view from the cage I was in." His voice cracked, the first obvious sign that he might not be as calm about the situation as he seemed.

He was handling everything so much better than I would have. Just listening to him talk about what happened made my anxiety grow. My skin felt too tight for my body and my stomach churned.

I desperately wanted to comfort him. But how? Mama would know what to do. Should I hug him? Mama's hugs usually helped me. I wrapped my arm around the dragon's slim shoulders.

"The middle-aged guy is a phoenix," he continued. "The woman there? Her name is Tammy. You can't see him in this picture, but the guy to my left was a monkey shifter. And that guy on the right side, he's a unicorn. His name is Morgan. Morgan Russell, I think he said."

"A unicorn?" Nelson asked as he jolted upright. I wouldn't have said he was slouching before, but he looked ready to spring from his seat now. The edges of his body seemed to dissipate, then solidify again.

Ogden nodded. "He is a sweet man. I haven't seen a unicorn in… It must be centuries. I didn't think their kind were still around anymore. His energy felt… innocent. That might not be the right word, but I'm not sure how else to describe him. It made him seem young. It's always difficult to tell with supes, though."

The shadow jumper was usually on the pale side, but his face looked ghostly white now against his black hair and his black clothes.

Hayden's hand shot out and covered Nelson's, as if he couldn't stop himself from trying to help the guy. I'd seen Hayden try to help people he considered his pack, even if he refused to believe he was the alpha. So I guessed that meant Nelson and the rest of Gage's team were part of the pack now too. "You okay?"

Nelson blinked at Hayden, then turned his attention to Gage. "Can I see the picture again?"

Gage passed the tablet over. The shadow jumper swallowed hard as he stared at the image.

"You know him?" Van asked Nelson.

"Not yet," the shadow jumper answered, without looking away from the screen.

Gage caught Van's eye and shook his head. A wordless message to back off.

"Oracle business?" Van asked.

Gage pressed his lips together and inclined his head in acknowledgement.

Van frowned.

"And how did you end up here?" Gage asked Ogden

before Van could press Nelson harder about his reaction to finding out about the unicorn.

I glanced at Ogden, who nodded at me. He reached over and rested his hand on my leg under the table, and that light touch helped me rally my courage. I swallowed hard. I pulled out the whistle and dropped it on the table. It clattered as it tumbled before coming to rest in front of Van.

Everyone stared at the whistle.

"I found it. I blew on it. Then the dragon… Ogden… He, uh, came shooting out of the middle of Willow Lake."

Van moved to poke at the whistle with the tip of his pen, but before he could, Ogden's hand shot out across the table and swatted Van's hand away.

"Don't."

"Is that what I think it is?" Van asked.

"Probably." Ogden nodded and licked his lips. "If anyone but Simon touches it, they might disrupt the magic that summoned me here. I expect to be sent back to the cage when we don't succumb to the whistle's magic, but let's not hurry things along, m'kay? Yes, Officer Hellhound here has hooked me up with some interesting goodies to stuff into this monstrosity." Ogden jiggled the belt Van had given him. "But I'd rather not return sooner than necessary."

The idea of him going back to that place made me queasy.

"That's one of Ulric's whistles, isn't it?" I was lucky that Davina was a medium and not a mage with the way she scowled at me.

I nodded quickly. My stomach flipped and flopped even more under her disapproval.

Van's gaze softened as he eyed Ogden. "Are you sure you want to return? My job is to protect civilians, not send them into danger. What if you work something out with Simon instead? He's a good kid, and we can ensure the connection between you is balanced. If you finish what the summoning started, you would stay here. You'd be safe."

"Could we?" That sounded like the perfect solution. Why hadn't I thought of that before? We could negotiate and Ogden would stay here where he was safe. "Maybe we should do that."

The dragon pursed his lips but didn't jump on the suggestion like I'd expected.

"What aren't you saying?" I asked. That same queasiness I'd experienced earlier reared up again. "You said it wasn't slavery."

"But it could be if you don't handle things properly. The magic evoked during a summoning has the power to bind you together. For life." Van rubbed his forehead. "I could call the Supernatural Council and arrange a representative for you. No one would blame you, Ogden, if you didn't want to return there. We will try our best to get to you as quickly as possible, but I can't guarantee your safety."

My chest tightened. I couldn't send Ogden back to a cage Magic only knew where, for people to do Magic only knew what to him. We should do everything we could to keep him away from that cage. But how could I forge a lifelong bond with someone I'd only just met? That was so not good. Mama was going to be so pissed at me when she heard about this.

What would I tell her? I doubted saying "So, Mama, it looks like I've adopted a dragon" would go over very well. She was going to pinch my ear for this. I just knew it.

Although, given that Ogden was older than me, maybe I wouldn't be the one being adopted. Would he want me to call him Daddy? No. I couldn't. That wasn't for me. I had Pops; I didn't need a daddy. Ogden would understand, right?

"I'll be fine," Ogden said firmly. "I need to get those people out. This is the best way to do that."

I slumped. He didn't want to bond with me. That was understandable. He was magnificent, while I was just a simple cat shifter. I prayed to the Eternal Magic for his plan to succeed. I'd only known him for a few hours, but I couldn't imagine a world without Ogden in it.

The very idea of it made my chest feel like it was imploding.

Chapter Ten

SIMON

A knock on the meeting room door interrupted my panic attack before it could truly take hold. Dillon, another hellhound, opened the door and peered inside. Like Gage and his team, he was new to town, but he had been working to become a police officer since the robbery at the inn a few months back. He wore a uniform, so maybe he had finished his training now.

"I'm done now," the new guy said. "You wanted me to do something?"

"Simon," Van said as he pointed his pen at me, "go with Dillon. He'll take your statement about the whistle. I have a few more details I need to review with Ogden here."

Ogden's hand shot out and wrapped around my wrist before I could stand. "He needs to stay."

The sudden scent of his fear stopped me from leaving

as much as his surprisingly tight grip. There'd been signs he wasn't as relaxed about everything as he appeared, but this was the first time fear shattered his calm façade.

Fear was something I understood all too well.

"Simon won't leave the station." Van swung his gaze over to me. "Will you?"

I looked at Ogden. I swore the irises in his vibrant blue eyes sparked and shimmered like they each held little electrical storms. His fear was palpable. As much as I had been panicking a few minutes ago, my fears and worries faded with the realization of what he was facing. I wanted to help him. I wanted to be the one who wiped away the furrows in his forehead. I wanted to be the one who would save him.

I may have only known him for a few hours, but I'd do anything to protect him. Me. A little scaredy cat. And him, a fierce dragon. To even pretend I could protect him better than he could protect himself was ridiculous. But I couldn't help the way I felt. It was startling.

But there was also a rightness to it.

My free hand slipped over his as I met his gaze steadily. "I will not leave you and I won't let you go back there any sooner than necessary." I didn't want him to go back there at all.

He nodded. Just once. His eyes blinked rapidly for a moment, and I realized he was fighting back tears. My chest tightened. Nothing should make this man feel so vulnerable. I wouldn't allow it. I wrapped my arm around him and pulled him close. Only then did I feel the almost imperceptible tremble coursing through him. He shoved his face into my neck and took a deep breath. I squeezed him tighter.

"It's okay," I murmured. "I've got you. We're going to make sure you're safe, you have a plan, and we're going to get all those other supes too."

As soon as I spoke, I knew those words would haunt me when I tried to sleep later. Because who was I to make such promises? I was simply Simon. I wasn't a tiger or a cheetah or a cougar. Even with a little extra weight around my middle, I was still small enough to hide behind the geraniums in Mama's garden.

Still, when he nodded, I felt like a lion.

When he finally pulled back from my embrace, he straightened his shoulders. He'd pushed his fear down again, but I sensed it was still close. It was strange how I could see under his mask now.

"The magic could send me back any time now," he said. "Before that happens, I wanted to make sure you know how thankful I am that you summoned me. I know it was an accident, but I can't help but feel the Eternal Magic had a hand in bringing us together today."

"Should I wait to talk to Dillon?" I'd never be able to live with myself if Ogden disappeared while I was away from him. I couldn't do anything, but the least I could do was be there with him.

"It'll be fine for a few minutes." Ogden glanced at Van. "But I think my time will be up soon."

I hated the way he'd phrased that.

"Understood," Van said. "You can still negotiate, you know. Should I call the SC?"

I wanted to say yes. One hundred percent. Ogden needed to negotiate. He needed to stay. Here. With me. Instead, I said, "Ogden made his choice."

"I'll be okay. This is what I want. Don't worry about me, Officer Hellhound." When Ogden said his nickname for Van, the somber mood in the room eased. Jeremy snorted and scribbled in his notebook.

"I've told you that's not my name," Van said with a smile that showed he wasn't all that bothered.

"Oh?" Ogden grinned a little wickedly at the hellhound.

I felt the start of a growl vibrating along the back of my throat. I didn't like Ogden looking at Van like that… Like he was flirting with him. When everyone turned to look at me, embarrassment heated my cheeks, and I cleared my throat.

Jeremy laughed and glanced at his mate. I guess the big werewolf and I had something in common. Both of us got growly when our mates—

Nope, Ogden wasn't my mate.

I needed to shut down any thoughts like that. I was just trying to help. That's all. Whatever connection we had was artificial, a product of the whistle's magic. Why did that make me sad?

Ogden's mouth softened into a smile. "Don't worry, kitty cat. I'm teasing the hellhound. It means nothing, and he knows that. You have nothing to worry about." Then he leaned forward until his lips brushed my ear. I shivered at the intimacy. Okay. Maybe this thing between us really was something more than one guy helping another. "You are the only one I'm dreaming about getting naked with.

When this is all over and done, I'm coming back here to find you and thank you properly for everything you've done today."

I sucked in a sharp breath and choked on my own spit. I coughed and coughed and coughed. My eyes watered. Snot clogged my nose.

Ogden pulled back a little but patted my back in what was likely meant to be a soothing gesture. The amusement in his bright blue eyes didn't ease my embarrassment, though. At least his fear had subsided. Maybe my dignity was an acceptable sacrifice if it took his mind off everything else.

When my coughing subsided, I ran to the door to escape. But I couldn't let Ogden think I was leaving him. I swung back around.

"I'll come right back," I said. My voice sounded croaky and rough.

Ogden winked at me and opened his mouth as if to say something. I fled from the room before he could utter a word, knowing whatever he'd say would likely make me embarrass myself all over again.

As soon as I was free of the room and away from where Ogden could see me, I stopped and closed my eyes. What was it about this dragon that made me act like such an idiot? Or, worse, believe I could be some kind of hero? I was the scaredy cat of my mama's kittens. Literally anyone else in Willow Lake would be better at protecting Ogden. If it were up to me, I would have allowed the summoning magic to bind us and left the rescue plan to someone else.

Most importantly, Ogden would be safe.

Was I feeling this way because of the whistle?

Beside me, someone cleared their throat. My eyes snapped open again, and I found Dillon staring at me with an amused glint in his eye. Perfect. Everyone was laughing at me and my obvious reaction to the sexy dragon. Har freaking har.

"Come on," he said, beckoning me to follow him down the hallway. I sucked in a breath and did as he asked.

Once again, I found myself seated beside a desk in the main part of the station. I glanced around for Dot as Dillon settled in his chair. I didn't see her.

"I'm out here because Van wants to ask Ogden some questions without me being there, aren't I?"

Dillon shrugged. "I'm not gonna lie, that's probably part of it. But we also need to get some more information on that whistle."

Why hadn't I grabbed it off the table? Was this a ploy to get me away from it? Were Van and the others planning to steal it? What would happen to Ogden if that happened? He thought if anyone interfered, the magic might return him to that cage. Van wouldn't do that, would he? I needed to see Ogden again before that happened.

"Hey," Dillon said. "It's okay. The whole situation is sketchy as fuck, but we will not endanger the dragon any sooner than necessary. And if there is a way to avoid that altogether, we will do that instead."

"Promise?" I swallowed hard. My eyes burned.

"I'm a hellhound," he said, like that meant something. When I didn't respond, he added, "I can't lie."

Right. I knew that… Did that make him a good guy? I wasn't sure, but I trusted Van, and Van trusted Dillon. My gaze went back to the hallway that led to the room where Ogden was still sitting with Van and the others. As much as I wasn't loving being trapped in a room with all those people, I wished I was still in there with my dragon.

"Let's finish this quickly, then you can go back in there. Okay?"

"Okay."

"So, tell me about the whistle. Where did you acquire it?"

"I found it. I didn't steal it," I blurted.

"And…?"

"I don't remember when exactly I *found* it." Yes, I emphasized the word found again. "Can you look it up in the report I made? It was right around then."

Dillon frowned. "You made a report?"

"Yeah." I scratched my head. "It was right before the wolves in the hills tried to stage that big robbery. Now that I think about it, I made my report the same night Ash found you. That's why Van was busy that night. He was in talking to you."

Dillon's eyes widened and filled with flames for a moment before he cleared his throat and got control again. "Who took your statement?"

"Dot… I mean, Constable Hubert."

He clenched his teeth as he turned toward his computer and started typing. After a few moments, he sucked in a deep breath and let it out slowly, releasing a thin curl of smoke. "I don't see it here. So I would like you to go over everything again, if you could."

I glanced around the open room with all its desks again. "Can't we ask Dot? She took notes."

More smoke curled out from Dillon's nostrils as he shook his head.

"Dot is in custody for aiding and abetting the wolves in their robbery of the inn. She also shot…" His voice broke. He swallowed hard. "She also shot someone."

"What?" My mouth dropped open. "It was Dot who shot Ash?"

A pained look shot across Dillon's face, but he nodded. His throat convulsed like he was swallowing hard. The action made his mate mark—a tattoo-like mark that looked like fire—undulate. "We haven't released all the details to the public, since the internal investigation is still happening, but yes… Still, I'm surprised you haven't heard about all that. Everyone in this town seems to know everything, whether or not the information has been released."

I bet Mama knew all about this. Had she said something when I wasn't paying attention? The whistle had consumed so much of my attention I'd apparently missed a lot of conversations over the last few months. I slumped in my chair. This day kept bouncing from one surprise to the next.

"The faster you talk, the sooner we'll finish," Dillon reminded me.

Because, yes, as shocked as I was about Dot, I realized she wasn't the shifter I thought she was. And if she shot Ash, she didn't deserve my pity or concern. Still, I couldn't believe she'd done something like that. I'd known her all my life. How had I been so wrong about her? What if I just sucked at reading everyone? What if Ogden wasn't a good person either? Perhaps it was for the best that we weren't negotiating. I wouldn't want to end up tied to someone awful for the rest of my life.

And yet, even on the heels of that ominous thought, I knew I'd bind myself to Ogden in a heartbeat. For the first time in my life, my cat was determined to be brave, all because of that beautiful dragon Mother Magic had brought into my life.

Chapter Eleven

OGDEN

From the time Simon left my sight until he returned, I wore an indifferent mask. I'd had practice. I was a performer, after all. Mustering up a little fake courage wasn't so hard, particularly if it meant getting out of this room faster... and, of course, helping those poor people trapped in cages.

Honestly, it would have been fine except everyone kept looking between me and that stupid whistle with pity in their eyes.

Teague cleared his throat, drawing my attention. If I remembered correctly, he was the death mage. With a boyish face that made him seem trustworthy and sweet, he didn't look like the ancient and powerful death mages I'd known in the past. But old men would have been young once upon a time.

"I know this is a difficult situation, but I can help," the death mage said. "You don't have to go back there. You have options. I could help guide the connection between you and Simon, keep it fair. Although I haven't seen the type of bond created by a summoning before, I'm familiar with bonds between chosen mates and fated mates. I also have personal experience with bonds created by demons." He gestured toward Gage, who nodded in agreement.

"You think those bonds are like this?"

"Yes and no," Teague said. He narrowed his eyes as he studied me. Black bled over his irises and the whites of his eyes until nothing else remained and I knew he was accessing his magic. "This isn't equal like a mate bond, nor is it mutually beneficial like a bond with a demon. From what I can see, the summoner's magic dominates, making the other supe's magic subservient. It is like a parasite in some respects. Although energy can travel both ways along the bond, we know summoners historically pulled magic from the supes they summoned to make themselves more powerful. Archival records suggest a summoner may also command the other to do their bidding, but I suspect that isn't always the case. I can see the threads linking the two of you together already. The ones created by the summoning are obvious."

I didn't doubt he could do what he said and more. Death mages were blessed with a strange magic, seeing things others couldn't. But was that what I wanted?

I considered his offer.

My dragon's discontent rumbled through me at the thought of anyone interfering with this tenuous, unfinished link with Simon. I didn't intend to complete the connection created by the summoning, but I didn't want anyone messing with it either. I'd learned a long time ago to trust my dragon's instincts, since they were rooted in magic, and I trusted the Eternal Magic to steer me where I needed to be.

"As I've said, I'm doing what I want. No one is pressuring me," I said. "But thank you."

I wasn't lying, but I also wasn't an idiot. Going back to the cage worried me, more than I wanted to admit, but I needed to do this. I was the only one who could help those people.

Teague glanced at Gage, who shook his head. The death mage twisted his lips like he was trying to keep himself from arguing with me. As he sat back in his chair and folded his arms over his chest, the black drained from his eyes.

"Okay. Let's go over everything again," Van said.

Each moment Simon was out of my sight, though, was like an eternity. My unease unsettled me. It was disconcerting. I was always the person in control. I entertained and amused and put people at ease. These insecurities were unfamiliar and unwelcome. I was a dragon, for pity's sake. My kind were essentially supernatural royalty. I was never unsure. Never lacked confidence. Never overwhelmed with self-doubt.

Never.

With that word embedded in my thoughts, I shoved the strange feelings away.

I straightened my shoulders and prepared to answer all the same questions all over again.

Except... those feelings weren't so easy to dismiss, so I turned to songs again. Music had always been my companion. I filtered through the many, many songs in my repertoire. I decided some more feel-good tunes were in order. Needing a break from the '50's songs I'd been singing all day, I started humming "Happy" while they reviewed their notes.

"Oh! Good one, little dragon dude," the young inquisitive one—Jeremy, I thought his name was—said as he lifted his hand to fist-bump mine. The gesture felt refreshingly normal, so I tapped my knuckles to his. Then he jumped in to sing the lyrics, harmonizing with me. He had a decent voice. We finished the song, and I was about to transition to a new tune when Van cleared his throat, drawing everyone's attention. He seemed to do that a lot.

"We still have more questions," he said, punctuating his words with a frown.

"Oops," Jeremy said. "Sorry." He didn't look sorry; I wasn't either.

"Yes, yes, Officer Hellhound." I waved my hand, gesturing for him to continue.

This round of questions was much the same as before.

"Okay," Gage said finally when it was clear I wasn't offering any more new details. "I think we have a fair idea of what happened. My team and I will follow up with the Supernatural Council to see if there have been more missing persons reported."

Van nodded. "We'll touch base when we know more."

"Do you have a desk I can use?" Hayden asked as he stood. "I'll start calling people. Give them a heads-up so they're prepared to leave when we know where we're going."

It was such an alpha thing to do. I wondered why the guy fought against the title.

"Talk to Dillon," Van said.

Then Gage and his team followed Hayden out of the room—well, everyone except Jeremy.

"When can we meet?" Jeremy asked.

"Jer, not now," Adrian said.

"I know." Jeremy's cheeks darkened at the gentle reprimand. "I didn't mean like right now or later tonight, but soon? Oh, and you need to come to our next karaoke night. We can sing a duet like... Oh! I know, "Under Pressure." We'd be amazing. What do you think?"

"Later," Adrian said. He looked ready to scoop his mate up and haul him out of the room. "Let the dragon be. He's got other things on his mind."

Jeremy's eyes looked so damn hopeful, though.

"I'll get in touch when this is done," I promised.

I enjoyed chatting with people. Owning a bar gave me an opportunity to engage in superficial and easy conversations with lots of people while keeping my lair private. But all these promises tonight were starting to feel like something else. Something more... *personal*.

Jeremy's face lit up with an eager smile. At least I could make someone happy. Although, by the end of the night, I planned to make a lot more strangers even happier.

"Come on, Jeremy." This time, Jeremy let his mate drag him out of the room. Then I was alone with Officer Hellhound again.

"How are you holding up?" Van asked.

I shrugged. "Happy to be done with all those questions. This isn't how I like to spend my time."

"That's fair," the hellhound said. "I've contacted the Aspen Bay police. They're heading over to where you said you go swimming to see if they can find anything. In the meantime, is there anyone you need to call?"

"Yes. I should have called Wesley, my assistant manager, as soon as I popped up in Willow Lake."

"Okay. Let's make that happen."

The Great Blue Heron shifter would be beside himself with worry by now. Either that or they'd scooped him up too. Just because I hadn't seen him in the room didn't mean he wasn't there.

Van left the meeting room to give me a little privacy after showing me how to dial out on the landline. I called The Drunken Drake, the bar Wesley helped manage with me.

"Hello?" Wesley sounded tentative. He was probably confused about why the bar was getting a call from the police. Relief filled me at the sound of his voice.

"Wesley, thank Magic. You are okay."

Wesley didn't speak for a long beat. I imagined my little heron friend to be welling up with joy. "Hold on, let me get somewhere quieter," he said.

The loud and boisterous background noise suggested the bar was hopping. It was too bad I had to end it. A moment later, it was quieter on his end. He'd probably gone into the office.

"Ogden? Is that you?" Wesley asked.

"The one and only." I grinned.

"How…" He paused and cleared his throat. "Where are you?"

"I've had the strangest day. You won't believe what happened." I laughed.

"Oh?" It sounded more like a squeak or that *awk* sound

his kind usually made when they took on their shifted form.

"Are you okay, Wesley?"

"Me?" He squeaked again. "Yes. Yes. Of course. You were saying?"

"I'm at a police station of all places, can you believe it? I was abducted during my swim last night. It was the strangest thing. Are you okay? What about the rest of the staff? Is anyone else missing? Has anyone shady been hanging around today?"

"No. No one that I noticed," he said quickly.

"Are you sure you're okay? You sound a little breathless."

"Fine. Just fine. Busy night." I could hear him swallow. "You say someone abducted you?"

"Yes. But I'm free now. Obviously. I've made my statement to the police. They've already contacted the Aspen Bay Police, so someone will come poke around shortly. Don't worry. They have my blessing to do anything they like. Give them full access. I want these bastards found."

"Of course. Who would do such a thing?"

He sounded squeaky again. Herons didn't usually squeak. At least not in my experience. What was wrong with the guy? Unless…? No. Wesley couldn't be involved. Could he? In the past, my kind ate his kind. I hoped he hadn't done something stupid. He wouldn't want to earn my wrath.

If only I wasn't so damn blank about what had happened to me.

"Who indeed," I said.

Another long pause followed.

"What can I do?" Wesley asked eventually.

"We need to shut the pub down for a bit. Make apologies to the staff. Everyone will receive their full pay. But until we know what happened, I don't want to put anyone else at risk. I don't know how my abductors chose me, but if they used The Drunken Drake as a hunting ground, I refuse to let them do it again."

"Closed?" Wesley squawked. "We never close."

"Needs must, Wesley," I said firmly. His attitude was annoying me. "Close the doors."

"But… But…"

"Do it. It is my money and my business. I will return as soon as I can, but there are a few things I need to deal with first." What an understatement.

"Okay." Sullen and sulky didn't suit Wesley. Come to think of it, pouting didn't suit anyone.

"Good," I said.

After another few minutes of discussing logistics, I ended the call.

I waved Van back into the room. I considered letting my suspicions go until I knew for sure whether Wesley was involved or if he was just coming down with a throat infection that was making him sound weird, but too many other supes were at risk. If he was innocent, he had nothing to fear. And if he wasn't, well… I wasn't about to protect him. No matter how long I'd known him or how much I'd trusted him in the past.

After I explained my strange conversation to the hellhound, I asked to make another call. At the moment, my will listed Wesley as the recipient of The Drunken Drake if

I died. Most long-lived supes didn't worry about things like wills, but I liked to be prepared for all eventualities. Giving my business to an employee might seem bizarre to some, but neither my parents nor my sister would want it. The place wasn't particularly lucrative or worthy of adding to a hoard; it was simply something to keep me amused for a few years.

As soon as I'd met Simon, I had a niggling sensation that my life was going to change. My conversation with Wesley just solidified my decision. There were more legalities to sort through, of course, but for now, I needed my lawyer to draft up changes to remove Wesley from my will at the very least.

Van assured me Wesley, if he was involved, would not be rewarded by my death, but if Simon hadn't blown that whistle, who would have known to stop him? My parents' hoard kept them running. Our conversations were always short; they barely had more than a few minutes to spare whenever we spoke. Although my sister and I talked regularly, we commonly missed each other's calls as well. We were each busy with our own lives. How long would it have been before anyone realized I was missing? Would there have been any evidence left at that point? Was there any evidence even now?

I hoped I was mistaken about Wesley, but I was still going to make those changes.

It only took a few moments on the phone with my lawyer to set my request in motion. As I ended my call, Van reappeared to pepper me with more questions about Wesley.

By the time we finished, I was sure my paranoia was

making me see things that weren't there. Everything that'd happened over the last twenty-four hours or so had left me feeling upside down, and everyone knew dragons couldn't fly for long if they weren't right side up. The magic connected to the whistle wasn't helping. The longer we went without completing our bond, the more I felt the foreign magic urging me to fall in line.

Yes, Wesley was awkward. He always had been. All that squeaking and squawking probably didn't mean anything. But it was in Van's hands now. And I had other things to do, like spending my last few minutes of freedom with Simon before I went all Jack Reacher on a trafficking ring.

When Simon finally popped his head inside the meeting room again, I couldn't hide my relieved sigh. Was it because of the magic from the whistle or was something else going on? I didn't know. But I sprang out of my seat and glommed onto the cat shifter anyway. I didn't think he minded me clinging to him.

"You can stay here until you have to leave," Officer Hellhound said. "That way we'll know the moment you leave, and we can start tracing your location immediately."

Simon paled at the reminder of what was about to happen. I wasn't feeling so thrilled about it myself.

"Are you on shift all night?" I asked Van.

"I am tonight," he said.

I noticed how tired he looked. That was fair. None of us had planned to do this tonight. Then he left the room and shut the door. Finally, I was alone with my little kitty cat again.

I pulled Simon over to the chairs and pushed on his

shoulders until he sat. I took the seat next to him, although what I really wanted was to slip into his lap, but this wasn't the time or place. As soon as we were settled, my skin tingled. I recognized the sensation; it was exactly how I'd felt before everything went psychedelic, then a moment later I'd ended up in the lake.

"My time is running out," I admitted.

He sat up straighter. He looked like he wanted to lunge for me and hold me there with him forever. "I wish this didn't have to happen."

"As much as I appreciate the sentiment, that won't work." I wrapped my hands around his. "I must help those people. No one else can."

Simon stared at our linked hands and nodded. The tingling sensation was growing. Every hair on my body was quivering. Simon tipped his head forward and pressed his forehead to mine. My eyes closed as I savored the feel of him so close to me. His scent filled my senses. The soft brush of his breath fell against my mouth.

Unbidden, my magic swelled and streamed toward him. It undulated and zinged over me like electric waves. As it grew stronger, it began gathering at the spot where my skin touched Simon's. The tips of my fingers itched as my magic bridged our clasped hands and reached for him.

Suddenly a foreign magic—Simon's magic—surged up and greeted mine.

As a dragon, I was an ancient creature, filled with more magic than most. I was a creation of the Eternal Magic, built of water and air and fire. Three of the four elements were within my domain. But Simon's, his was different. Like most land-based shifters, his magic was earthy and solid and strong. A beautiful counterpoint to mine. It grounded me, like a firm foundation upon which I could build a life…

It almost felt like we could be mates. Almost.

After centuries of being alone, I'd never imagined a cat shifter from a small town in the middle of nowhere could be the answer to everything I'd ever dreamed, but maybe I should have. Or perhaps my heart was caught up in the moment and pretending to see things that weren't there.

"Wow," Simon whispered. "I love how I can feel your magic. I've never felt anyone's magic before."

"Hmm…" I agreed, not ready for words yet.

This was why I wanted to come back to Willow Lake. I needed to know I would see Simon again. I needed to know if any of this was real, because if it was…

"Ogden." He spoke my name so softly that it felt like a caress. I shivered and opened my eyes. He was staring back at me. "I want…"

He didn't finish his sentence, but those two words *I want* sounded sure and confident, so different from the stuttering, insecure shifter I'd found on the lakeshore a few hours ago. Then his magic rushed toward me, wrapping around me. Everything about it was perfect and comforting and beautiful. I wanted more. My magic leaped forward to greet it.

"Yes," I murmured, suddenly sure that whatever he wanted, I wanted it too.

With that one word, everything changed. He hadn't asked for anything, not with words, and yet I knew with my single syllable reply something powerful had been set in motion.

I sucked in a breath.

Okay, it probably sounded more like a gasp, but that would be a wrong conclusion. I did not gasp unless it was for dramatic effect.

I wasn't sure what Simon had wanted. He hadn't told me yet, but our magics weren't wasting time waiting for words. I could almost explain my own reaction—I tended to be decisive—but this was the most definitive action Simon had taken since I met him, but I wasn't sure he was aware of what he was doing.

And although I had impulsively agreed to Simon's unspoken invitation for more, it almost felt like my magic was surrendering. Why would it do that?

Before I could utter a word of protest, fence it in, or establish any limits, our magics collided. They rubbed up against one another in a bizarre way that reminded me of cats marking their territory. And apparently my territory now included Simon, and his included me.

Dragons were notoriously independent creatures. My clutch mate and I left our parents' nest as soon as we were able. We all still talked regularly, even doing video calls on holidays, but our lives were separate. My sister and I didn't even live on the same continent as each other or our parents. I'd lived alone for centuries, and I liked it that way. My home was my castle, and my hoard was mine and mine alone.

But this little cat had somehow breached my defenses.

His magic vibrated against mine like it was purring. Such a strange sensation. I wasn't sure what to think of it all. I wasn't disappointed, but it was… unusual. Yes, I'd wanted the cat shifter from the moment I had him in my coils by the lake, but this… this was something different. This wasn't lust. I wasn't merely seeking physical pleasure from him, nor was he just a means of keeping me out of that cage.

This was something else entirely.

Something intangible but powerful clicked into place between us, and I knew in that moment the summoning magic had won. The agreement was made. The contract was complete. Our lives were irrevocably locked together. And neither of us had discussed or agreed to the terms.

Our connection must have originated from whatever spell the whistle had evoked. A bond, but not a natural bond. Before I could retract my magic and extricate it from his, I swore the Eternal Magic herself wrapped around us and added another layer to our bond.

I gasped. This time I could have pretended it was for dramatic effect. The situation warranted a little drama. But the truth was, everything about this made me short of breath. I gasped again.

"Son of a fire breather." I choked out the curse.

My skin tingled with the strength of the newly forged connection. Could it really be so simple? Happen so quickly? Could his life become entwined with mine in one unguarded moment, an impulsive push of magic, and a nudge from the Eternal Magic?

His magic had decided what would happen, mine had submissively agreed, and boom it was done. Just like that?

I growled at the thought.

I did not submit. I was never the submissive one in any relationship. I was a dragon. I was always in control. What had my magic been thinking?

Except my magic hadn't acted alone, had it? Simon's had been right there too. We were in this together.

That damn whistle had fucked us both over. Although, based on the way our energies swirled and danced around us like this new arrangement warranted a joyous celebration, it was hard to tell. It almost felt like they were frolicking. And then our magics moved through one another, merging and blending until it was impossible to tell where his ended and mine started. But even now, it all felt hollow. Shallow. Not quite right.

And worse yet, there was no going back. I didn't know how I knew that, I just did.

Nausea roiled through me. This was not what I'd planned when I first realized I'd been summoned. But my magic—well, and Simon's too—had decided for us. And the connection was so much deeper than I could have imagined.

The power of the summoning magic overruled everything else. Now I was trapped here with Simon. I wouldn't be going back to that cage. Not tonight. I wasn't saving anyone. All those people would stay trapped because my magic selfishly chose to connect with Simon.

If my little kitty cat had been holding out hopes of finding his mate, I suspected this pseudo-bond of ours had just destroyed any chance of that happening. It was too deep and powerful to allow another between us. Once the bond formed, even as artificial as it was, it would eliminate the chance of anything else. I hadn't expected that from a summoning bond. Why would anyone perform a summoning if it meant they'd never find their mate?

I'd long ago given up on finding my fated mate, but I

wondered if Simon would resent this change. Would he be disappointed when he got to know me better? Of course, I knew I was fabulous, but I'd also never let anyone close enough for them to decide if they thought that was true or not. I prayed my timid little kitty wouldn't regret binding himself to me like this. It was all a little too much, a little too fast.

"What have we done?" I whispered.

Chapter Twelve

SIMON

"That was the bond, right?" I gasped as Ogden's magic flowed through me. "The one that started from the whistle?"

"Yes. It's done." Ogden sighed. "I won't return to the cage now. I can't because of the connection between us."

"I'm not your master," I said quickly. I never wanted him to believe that. But at the same time, selfishly, I wanted to rejoice. Ogden wouldn't be going back there. He was safe. Here. With me. If there was anything I knew about, it was how to stay safe. No one would cage him again.

His magic continued to rush over me. Until now, I didn't think anyone but mages could manifest external magic, but clearly Ogden could. And... maybe I could too? Because I was pretty sure that's what just happened.

"I feel your magic, like it's linked to mine. Like it's inside me," I whispered. I pushed my fingers into my chest where a knot of our combined magic seemed to be writhing within me. "How is that possible?"

"It's part of the summoning spell," Ogden said as he rubbed his own chest. Did he feel the same thing I did, or had my magic stolen his? I was too scared to ask.

Before today, I hadn't thought about how other supes' magic worked... or any magic at all, really. Magic and magical beings surrounded me all the time. It just was. I lived my life. I had my family. Mama always said Willow Lake was special, but what did that mean? I wished I'd paid more attention. Did that mean everyone could put their magic out there like that?

Ogden was a lot more worldly than I was—I'd known that even before he mentioned buying swimming gear from Monaco or having his own lawyer. I bet he'd know. Since we were tied together now, I should attempt to learn stuff too. I cringed. I didn't know where to begin. Except for biology class, I'd never really liked any of my school subjects. And I only liked biology because it was practical. Where else could you find out the answer to important questions like: Could cats survive falls from great heights?

Maybe I should start with learning more about summoning magic and the kinds of connections it forged. Huh. I bet some scientist out there had classified all the various bonds made between supes. Could I look that up on Supenet? Until today, I'd only known about bonds for mates, whether chosen or fated.

But this wasn't like that, was it?

I gulped for air.

"Are we mated? No, we can't be."

"No." Ogden shook his head. "But there is something connecting us."

"Holy hairballs, what have we done?"

Ogden didn't say anything.

My parents weren't fated mates; they'd chosen one another instead of having the Eternal Magic do it for them. With so many people finding their fated mates this past summer, Willow Lakers talked about bonds a lot, so I knew a tiny bit more about how fated and chosen bonds happened than I did before. It made me suspect something like that might have happened between Ogden and me, except... not?

"I might not be the smartest cat in town, but this..." I hit my chest where the magic was still tangled up inside me. "Whatever this is between us, it feels a lot like what I think a mating bond is supposed to feel like. So what does that make us? Companions? Chums? Comrades? Partners? And don't say I'm your master. Nope. Nuh-uh. Not happening."

"Partners?" The word resonated between us. "I could live with that." Ogden said.

"Sweet mother of kittens," I whispered as I rubbed my chest harder.

I was unprepared to be someone's partner. I was an unambitious night security guard at a motel where nothing ever happened. And if something ever did happen when I was on duty, it was a sure bet I'd run in the other direction as fast as I could. I wasn't exactly a prize. But, for Ogden, I suddenly wanted to do better, be more.

And what about the other magic I had sensed when we'd waited for the whistle to take him back to the cage?

For a moment, I'd almost thought it felt... I don't know. Real. Like a true connection. Except it wasn't. It was created by the magic in the whistle. False. Artificial. Fake. Counterfeit.

"This is all so very, very wrong, isn't it?" I asked. "You feel it too, don't you? How wrong it is?"

Once again, Ogden didn't speak.

I hated I could mistake such a manipulative spell for the real thing. Even for a minute. How was that possible?

It was something to think about later. Much later. Or never. Because did it matter now? The magic had joined us together. What use would it be to dissect the past?

For now, all I could do was try to relax as Ogden's magic pushed into all the gouges and crevices in my own. The strange magic should feel foreign and intrusive, but it didn't. It soothed me, even more than a hug from my mama. Ogden felt like home.

That stupid summoning spell was messing with me.

My heart pounded in my chest.

It was so wrong to crush on a stranger who'd been dragged into my life against his will. And yet I couldn't regret it too much, because where he'd been before I blew the whistle sounded horrible.

And... what if we tried to make the most of this situation? I'd never believed I'd find my fated mate. But Ogden and I were stuck together now, right? Maybe we could find a way to be companions. Lovers even? Or was that too ambitious? I mean, he could be attracted to me. He had flirted with me. But then again, he flirted with the others too. It might not mean much.

But if it did...

"Hush now, kitty cat," Ogden whispered. He rested his hand on my chest, right over my racing heart. "You're stressing yourself. Stress isn't good for anyone. What's done is done."

He was right. I nodded and sucked in a deep breath. Ogden stroked my chest, almost like he was petting me. Would he do that? If I shifted, would he pet me? I could remember my parents doing that for one another. It seemed... I don't know. It wasn't sexual, but it was nice. Soothing.

Then Ogden hummed. I didn't recognize the song, but it sounded like a lullaby. He smiled as my heart slowed to a normal rhythm and my whirling thoughts quieted.

"There you are," he whispered.

I stared into his bright blue eyes and leaned forward. Now that I was calmer, other feelings were getting stirred up. Sexy feelings. Then I remembered we were at the police station.

I pulled back. "We need to tell Van what happened."

Chapter Thirteen

OGDEN

Van and Hayden had been understanding, but I could sense their disappointment. Me? I wasn't sure what to feel. Relieved. Guilty. Selfish. Apprehensive. Most notably, I was strangely happy to be staying with my cute little kitty cat.

"Can we go?" I asked Officer Hellhound.

"Before you leave, can you take a look at something?" Van tapped something into a tablet, then turned it to face me. "Is this Wesley?"

I recognized the picture of Wesley sitting in a Bentley Bacalar. He'd gone to a car show in Vegas last summer and had paid a ridiculous amount of money to put his ass in that car. He showed that picture to people as often as he could. I didn't know where Van had found the picture, but it wouldn't surprise me if Wesley had it splashed all over the internet so strangers would admire him.

"Yes."

"Who is that? Is that who abducted you? Did you remember what happened?" Simon asked, peering closely at the image. "Is that his car?"

"That's my assistant manager, Wesley. The car isn't his."

"I'll call Simon if I think of anything else to ask. And please call if you remember anything more. Oh, and take that." Van motioned to the whistle. "We'll sort out what to do with it later. If we destroy it now, I don't know what it'll do to your bond. I don't think we should risk that until we talk to some mages."

Simon scooped the whistle from the table, then returned right back to my side and wrapped his arm around me. I'd already divested myself of the tool belt Van had given me, but he suggested I keep the tracking device for now. Just in case. After all, we still didn't know how I'd been abducted the first time.

"Let's go," I said. I was so ready to get out of here.

"I'll see you both tomorrow," Van said on our way out of the boardroom. "We might have more questions by then."

Simon wasted no time escorting me out of the station, but when we reached the sidewalk, he stopped and looked up and down the road as if he didn't know which way to turn.

"Simon? Talk to me."

His cheeks darkened. He really was the most adorable creature. "I'm not sure where to take you."

"Where do you want to take me?" I tried not to play into the innuendo. It was hard—ha, aren't I punny. But I must not have succeeded because my poor kitty cat made a strangled-sounding noise. How could anyone be so precious? I wanted to wrap him up in a fluffy blanket and hide him away from the world.

"I… I…" he stammered, and his cheeks reddened even more. Pretty soon, every bit of his blood would be in his face, and that wouldn't do. Not at all.

I cradled his heated cheeks in my hands and looked into his eyes. I was pleased to see my touch seemed to calm him. "Talk to me, Simon."

"I thought about taking you home, but it isn't very nice. You need nice things."

Aw. Wasn't he the sweetest?

"Your place sounds perfect," I said, then I pushed up on my tippy toes and brushed my lips over his cheek. It was a fleeting little kiss that did nothing to satisfy my need to taste my cat shifter, but it had to be enough for now. His nostrils flared as he inhaled my scent, and his hands caught on my hips. His fingers dug into me, and I was sure he wanted to tug me closer. I figured his inexperience kept him from following through. Well, and maybe the fact that we were still standing outside the police station.

Simon took my hand in his and led me away. The funny paper slippers Van had given me slapped sloppily against the concrete sidewalk as we walked down a few streets until we arrived at an older four-story apartment building.

Seeing the front door propped open with an old boot made me scowl. Anyone could waltz in and nab someone. With traffickers as close as Aspen Bay, it would be naïve to think Willow Lake was safe, especially when this place seemed like a haven for supes. The kidnappers could sweep in and have their pick of dozens of different supes. Although, their demon guardian might offer some protection. I hadn't lived anywhere with a guardian before, so I couldn't be sure.

When we entered the building, I kicked the boot aside. Simon nodded his understanding as he tugged the door firmly closed behind us.

His apartment was, thankfully, locked.

"Um, here it is," Simon said as he pushed the door open after unlocking it. Embarrassment poured off him as he looked at his feet and didn't move any farther inside.

"I'm sure I'm going to love it. It's going to smell like you and be filled with the things you love. I am happy you've brought me here."

"I... I..." He stammered.

"Come on, kitty cat. It's going to be okay. I promise."

With his shoulders rounded in defeat, he led me down the short corridor into his living room—his very bare and very empty living room. A long worn-out sofa lined one wall and a teensy tiny flatscreen television sitting on a couple of wooden crates sat against the opposite wall. And that was it. There were no side tables or lamps or pictures or knickknacks. Nothing.

"The space is great," I said. "Lots of room to move around. Clutter can be such a pain to dust and clean."

"Don't." Simon snorted. His cheeks were bright red. "I know it is bad. I keep meaning to buy some stuff, but I can't make up my mind."

"Never feel embarrassed about who you are." I patted his chest. "But if you want me to help you, I can do that."

"I would like that." His face turned so earnest that I

wanted to squeeze his adorable cheeks. Then his mouth twisted, and his forehead furrowed, and I knew he wasn't thinking about his apartment anymore. "I don't understand what happened. Tonight. Between us."

"I don't either," I confessed. "But we don't have to solve it tonight."

I closed the distance between us, drawn to him in a way I couldn't explain. Was this because of the magic that joined us? When we'd been standing in front of the police station, I'd wanted to kiss him. Soundly. Thoroughly. I still did.

It consumed my thoughts.

Because what if…?

What if we became lovers? What if we made this work? What if he didn't care about finding his fated mate either? Because our mutual attraction was undeniable. A lot of chosen mates made it work. My eyes darted to Simon's pretty pink mouth. I licked my lips and leaned forward. Except we shouldn't do this. Not tonight.

"Can I kiss you?" Simon asked.

"Oh, kitten, how you tempt me," I whispered.

"Is that a yes?"

I darted forward and swept my lips across his, then I pulled back. Any longer and I'd have succumbed to temptation and grabbed him and never let him go. That kiss, if you could call it that, had lasted only a tiny fraction of a second. I wanted more. I resisted.

The strange and intense blending of our magics had eased. Thank Magic for that. It almost felt… comfortable… now. What wasn't comfortable, though, were the ridiculous clothes I was wearing.

I brushed my hands over my borrowed clothes, inadvertently drawing Simon's attention to the bulge under those gray sweatpants. Oops. He had a similar bulge in his own pants. He was as interested as I was, but when I took him to my bed for the first time, I wanted to savor the experience. Tonight, I was too exhausted, and my mind too distracted to do what I wanted with him. When we came together, it would not be a quick, desperate fumble. We were not hooking up. We were... *something else*. What that *something else* was, well, that remained to be seen.

"It's been a long day, kitten," I said gently. "We should turn in. I'm sure Officer Hellhound will be around with more questions in the morning."

He growled softly, as if he didn't like me thinking about Van when my cock was hard.

"I'll sleep on the couch," I offered.

"There is room in my bed for both of us."

Did that sound like a cheesy line to get me in his bed? Yep. It did, but I liked it. I'm sure my eyes took on a wicked gleam at his invitation, but I shook my head and backed away. "Not tonight, kitty cat."

He frowned.

"Don't pout. I'll take care of you soon enough," I promised. "But a lot has already happened today. I think we should slow things down a bit."

"I know. You're right," he grudgingly admitted, "but that doesn't mean I won't be awake the entire night thinking about you. Fantasizing about you in those gray sweatpants. Obsessing about what you mean by taking care of me soon enough. Wondering what it'd be like to kiss you properly."

My pulse quickened at his words. Oh. My kitten had a wonderful imagination. Excellent. He dipped his head down. He coughed and shuffled his feet, as if embarrassed to have admitted so much to me. That wouldn't do. He needed to be rewarded for all that.

I rose on my toes and brushed my lips against his heated cheek. I lingered there, my lips pressing soft intimate kisses against his skin, until he turned his head and his lips met mine again. This time, I didn't duck away.

He moaned as our mouths met. He wrapped his arms around me and hauled me up against his chest. Yes. It was exactly as I'd imagined. Even with the fabric of our clothes separating us, every brush of our bodies against one another made me writhe and press closer. I craved his touch, but neither of us moved to strip off our clothes. Our tongues danced. Our breaths wove together. Our bodies rocked. It was sublime.

When the kiss ended, we were both panting. Simon's lips were deliciously plump and pink and wet. Oh, how easy it would be to take his hand and lead him to his bedroom and become lost exploring his body. I forced myself to step back.

"I'll be thinking about you too," I admitted. "But I still think we should try to get some sleep." A sudden yawn stole over me, as if to emphasize my point. "I don't know why I'm so tired. I don't normally go to bed this early, but it's been a crazy day."

"You like nights too?" He sounded surprised.

"I work until close every night, but I'm usually awake for hours after that."

Simon smiled, like our having this one thing in

common thrilled him. "I usually go into the woods at night, if I'm not working." Then his face turned serious. "But I won't leave the apartment tonight, not while you're here."

"If you want to go, please go. I know someone abducted me, but I'm really not an easy mark."

He didn't look convinced. "I'll stay close anyway. I don't know what I'd do if something happened, but my instincts are in control right now... and that's..."

"That's what?"

"It's strange. I'm not brave... My brothers call me a scaredy cat," he whispered, averting his eyes again. "I still have all my nine lives."

I didn't know much about cat shifters, although I sensed having all nine of his lives at his age was unusual. But I did know about bravery.

"You are brave," I said, brushing my fingers over his down-turned face.

He shook his head. "I was scared. So scared that you wanted to go back to that cage. I am happy you didn't go. But it's my fault all those people are still locked up now."

"Never. This is not your fault in any way. The only people to blame are the ones who put those supes in cages to begin with." I ducked so I could look into his down-turned eyes. "I was scared too. Being brave doesn't mean not being scared. I don't know you very well yet, but I can think of plenty of times just tonight where you were brave."

Simon's forehead crunched up in confusion. "You can?"

"I can." I nodded. "Like when you demanded the alpha

join the meeting. Or when I first had you wrapped in my coils, and you didn't pass out or piss yourself. Not many people can say that. Or when you brought me—a stranger —home. Bravery isn't about jumping into fights or rushing into situations or taking impulsive actions. Don't underestimate your own bravery, Simon. And if most cat shifters your age don't have their nine lives, but you do, I'd say you are pretty damn smart. And you might not have known what would happen when you blew on that whistle, but you are my savior. My hero."

Simon blushed.

"Now, go get some sleep. I think tomorrow will be another long day."

I had only just settled on his horribly lumpy couch, curled up under the stale smelling blankets he'd retrieved from a nearly empty hall closet, when Simon stomped out of his room. He didn't speak. He simply leaned over and scooped me up, blankets and all, and carried me to his room. Once there, he gently placed me on his bed. I noticed he positioned me on the side of the bed that was farthest from the door. Then he crawled up beside me and wrapped his arm around me and pulled me tight against his purring body. The gentle vibration was soothing, the soft sound lulling me to sleep like a lullaby.

"Simon?" I whispered. "Why am I here?"

"Couldn't sleep with you out there..." he mumbled.

Then he pressed his face into the back of my neck and drifted off to sleep. I snuggled against my kitty cat and let sleep claim me too.

Chapter Fourteen

OGDEN

Simon was into torture.

And not the fun, sexy kind.

He nudged me awake before dawn had even considered making an appearance. It'd taken a bit, but he finally realized I would not be leaving his bed to go to breakfast at his mother's house. Nope. Not happening.

I didn't care if she served Eggs Benedict with smoked salmon and capers.

Of course, as soon as Simon left—since apparently his attendance was not optional—I couldn't stop thinking about salmon. I'd never had a cat in my life before, but I seemed to recall hearing they liked fish. Maybe that was something else we could have in common. And... even better, maybe that would mean he had a tin of salmon kicking around, if only to replenish his magic. After using magic, every supe needed something to balance their energy. Most shifters needed protein, and I bet cats would prefer fish to steak. He didn't seem the type to keep fresh fish around, but canned would work. It wouldn't be as good as fresh or smoked or candied salmon, but it'd do in a pinch.

I rolled my ass out of the tangle of blankets and went exploring. His kitchen was sadly lacking. My cat was obviously not a cook.

That was okay. I could cook for both of us.

And it wouldn't require either of us getting up before sunrise. Although the way Simon spoke about his mother, with equal parts love and fear, I doubted I'd be breaking him away from his family's unnatural breakfast ritual any time soon.

My stomach grumbled.

When was the last time I ate? The kidnappers hadn't fed us while I was there. They must, though, because those other supes in the cages didn't look like they were starving.

And then, once Simon had summoned me, I'd become preoccupied with giving my statement to the police, making plans for my return to the cage, and getting to know the cute kitty cat. This wasn't the first time I'd forgotten to eat because I was distracted, but now I regretted not going with Simon to his family's place for breakfast.

I tidied up the bed, folding the extra blankets and returning them to the hall closet. Now what? It wasn't like Simon had a lot of stuff to snoop through. I glanced around the sparsely furnished living room. This space didn't work at all. He deserved to be surrounded by pretty things...

Soft things… Yeah, I needed to fix this. He was now mine to pamper and spoil.

I especially wanted to see him covered with jewels from my hoard.

There was so much to do.

Both our lives had been upended. But for me, I had a whole life to uproot and relocate to Willow Lake. The thought of taking Simon to Aspen Bay filled me with a wrongness I couldn't shake. And now that I'd felt the energy in Willow Lake, I wasn't sure I wanted to live without it. How this place wasn't fifty times larger and teeming with supes was beyond me.

Okay. I needed to make a list.

Normally I'd do that on my phone, but I didn't know where mine was. Had my kidnappers taken it? Or was it still sitting in my car where I'd left it when I'd gone for my swim?

I itched at my arm again. The bump hadn't gone down overnight. Maybe the hellhound was right. Maybe it wasn't natural. I frowned.

Those bastards could have done almost anything to me when I'd been unconscious.

Maybe my kidnappers' plan wasn't about trafficking, but something else? Yeah. I needed to go to that doctor, because now that the thought was in my head, I needed to know if they'd done any alien probing or whatever. Dragons were regal creatures. We were not supposed to be probed without our consent.

My stomach growled again. I tried to distract it by clawing through Simon's drawers, looking for a pen and paper, but he had the most anemic looking cupboards I'd ever seen. Where were the pens stolen from hotel rooms? Or the promotion pads of paper that businesses liked to give away? For fire's sake, he only owned two sets of mismatched cutlery.

The state of his cupboards made my eyebrow twitch. It was good he summoned me. He obviously needed my help. Unfortunately, though, without a pen and paper, my shopping list would need to wait.

With nothing else to do, I went to the bathroom and took a shower long enough to make the warm water turn icy cold. The cold water didn't bother me, but I doubted his neighbors would be happy when they jumped into a cold shower to get ready for work.

Oops.

In our new place, I'd make sure we had a big hot water tank and a big shower, because this one was inadequate. I needed space for everything I wanted to do to my little kitty.

What if he didn't want to live together?

My chest ached at the thought of being separated from Simon for too long. Was that another facet of our bond? My fingers tightened around the towel I'd been using to dry myself.

He would want us to live together, wouldn't he?

Given how our magics had merged, I didn't think I could go too long without having him close. The intensity of the connection made me wonder if our coming together like we did wasn't part of something bigger. Could the whistle have caused all of this, or was he maybe my fated mate too?

The link we'd formed through the whistle wasn't right

somehow. I'd heard a bond between mates was intense and beautiful and joyful. Our bond wasn't like that, but it also felt deeper than a transactional arrangement.

So what did that mean?

I pondered that question as I pulled the ugly necklace with the tracker over my head again. If this was going to be a long-term situation, I'd need to go to the jeweler. This pouch the hellhound had given me was hideous. That I wore it was a testament to how much waking up in that cage had rattled me. Seeing the pouch resting right over my heart made my situation impossible to ignore. I stared at it in the little mirror above the bathroom sink until my jaw ached from clenching my teeth. I would find out who had abducted me. I would. And when I did, I would help all those other supes. And then I'd destroy my enemies.

With renewed purpose and conviction, I straightened and lifted my chin. The bastards wouldn't know what hit them. I might prefer to sing songs about love and happiness, but I was still a dragon, and dragons were naturally badass. I was, of course, no exception. But sometimes, even badass dragons needed a reminder of that. There. Consider myself reminded.

First, though, I needed clothes.

I strutted naked through Simon's house to the bedroom. Earlier, I hadn't paid much attention, but this room was just as bare as his main living space. Its most redeemable quality was that it smelled like him. I inhaled deeply, drawing in his scent. It danced a seductive tango across my tongue. I wanted to taste him, every bit of him.

Wonderful. I shivered in delight.

Then I turned to his closet, which was the reason I'd come in here to begin with.

I rummaged through his meagre assortment of clothes. He didn't have nearly enough of those either. I sighed as I pushed the shirts around. And the colors? Why on earth did he have so many drab colors?

I itched for my phone again. I needed to find and hire a personal shopper. My sister Bridget had raved about her personal shopper at some point, if I remembered correctly. I'd never seen the need myself, but where I adored shopping, Bridget hated it. And I suspected Simon would be like Bridget. I doubted he would be comfortable bouncing from store to store to fill in the gaps in his wardrobe. Sure, he seemed amiable enough so far, but cats had a reputation for being headstrong for a reason.

After narrowing down the selection to the least offensive options, I finally settled on a blue shirt I found shoved into the back of his closet and paired it with dress pants. The faint chemical smell clinging to both pieces suggested he'd never worn them. Someone must have given them to him when he was a teen, because the sizes weren't too bad for me. I twisted to look in the dresser mirror at my ass. Not the best, but better than the sweatpants monstrosity I'd been forced to wear the night before. The blue shirt, though, complemented the color of my eyes, so at least that worked.

I'd just plucked out a pair of socks from Simon's drab underwear and sock drawer when someone knocked at the door.

Hmm… We probably should have talked about our situation before he left. What would Simon want to tell people about us? But we hadn't talked, so it was up to me, and I wanted everyone to know Simon was mine.

I strutted to the door and opened it like I belonged here. Standing in the hallway outside Simon's apartment were two big, muscular guys. Shit. I should have looked through the peephole first. For a heartbeat I wondered if my kidnappers had found me again, but then I got a sniff of the men and a look at their mischievous grins.

"Simon's littermates?"

"We're here to bring you to breakfast," the taller one said.

I opened my mouth to decline, but then my stomach took that opportunity to groan again.

"Sounds like we're just in time," the other guy said. "I'm Clive, by the way. And this is my brother Warren."

"I'm guessing you already know, but I'm Ogden." I held up a finger. "Just a minute. I need to go scavenging for something to wear on my feet." I refused to go all dragon-footed again. After slipping on the borrowed socks, I poked around in Simon's pile of shoes until I found a pair of canvas ones I hoped I could tighten enough that they wouldn't trip me up when I walked.

The brothers watched me. I could tell they were doing some sort of sibling communication, but I ignored it. I hadn't expected to be exposed—er, introduced—to Simon's family already, but I'd manage. People loved me. As they should.

I expected the two to pester me with questions, but they didn't.

"Give me the keys," Clive said, holding out his hand to his brother when we reached their car.

Warren scoffed. "No way. I'd like to get back to Mama's in one piece, thank you very much."

"I don't know what you're talking about..." Clive frowned, the picture of innocence.

Warren's face suggested Clive was full of shit.

"Ogden, you sit up front with me. Clive, get in the back."

Clive muttered under his breath and followed his brother around to the other side of the car. Then, without warning, he tackled Warren to the ground. They landed with a thud. There was a scuffle, much grunting, and some colorful cursing, but from the passenger side where I was standing, I couldn't see anything. Then Clive popped up, lifting the keys aloft in one hand.

"Got 'em," he shouted. "Get in the back, asshole."

Warren groaned, wiping at his now bloody forearm as he crawled into the back. I sat in the passenger seat. Given Warren's expression when Clive had originally suggested he wanted to drive, I buckled my seat belt. As a supe, specifically a very old dragon, I rarely worried about being injured, but it didn't hurt to be pre-emptive.

As Clive guided the car out of the parking lot, neither of them said anything. I expected cat shifters to be more curious. But if they didn't want to ask me anything, I was seizing the opportunity to ask my own questions.

"How big is your family? Is it just your parents and the three of you?" I said *just* like a family of five was common these days in the supe community, but it really wasn't.

"Nah, our litter was four boys and there was a litter of two more boys that came after us." Warren didn't look at me when he answered. He had his hands on the back of

Clive's seat as he peered over his brother's shoulder at the speedometer, which was shooting up now that we were on the main road. "Slow down."

Clive ignored him.

"Wow. There are six of you?" I couldn't imagine.

Dragon unions usually only produced one or two offspring over centuries. My sister was my clutch mate and my only sibling. Although my parents constantly talked about expanding the family, none of their other clutches had been viable. Finally, after centuries of trying, they'd given up and filled their home with animals of every description instead. Their place was more like a free-range petting zoo now, where the animals—the most spoiled assortment of creatures to ever exist—could do anything they pleased. After finding hens roosting in the bathtub, a herd of guinea pigs running around the kitchen, and a family of ferrets nesting in my bed during my last visit, I'd decided to stay in a hotel next time. But who was I to disparage another dragon's hoard?

My parents' clothing, though, that I could—and often did—criticize. It wasn't seemly for a pair of dragons to run about dressed in ratty and stained work clothes all the time. Where was their pride?

But, back to the cats…

Cat shifters, I knew, weren't usually as long-lived as dragons, so it made sense that their reproductive capabilities would be higher, but still… Having six children was unheard of for supes, particularly over the last century or so. And why have so many? I shuddered. There'd never be a moment of peace. "And all boys?"

Would Simon want a big family like that? Over the

years, I'd considered adopting—given the scarcity of supes, I'd even thought about taking in human children—so I was open to that possibility, but not too many. Only one to start. Then maybe another one a couple of decades or more later.

And there went my brain, treating us like a couple again.

Through the whistle, we'd forged a bond of sorts, but it differed from a mate bond. Would Simon's life expectancy grow to match mine? Or was that perk reserved for mates blessed by the Eternal Magic? My chest tightened at the thought of outliving Simon. I'd only known the cat shifter less than a day, but something had developed between us I wanted to explore. I could easily envision my exploration taking centuries.

"Yeah, Mama says she's waiting for the day we mate so there are more girls in the family to balance things out." Clive shot out around a slower vehicle—you know, one that was going the speed limit instead of trying to get their car to defy gravity and achieve lift off—and I grasped at the handle over the door. This guy was reckless. No wonder Warren wanted to drive.

"Oh?" I said, even though Simon was definitely not bringing home a girl. Ever.

"Except most of us are gay, so…" Clive shrugged as he sent us careening around a corner. He was looking at me instead of the road. I almost shouted at him to pay attention. Honestly, I'd never been afraid in a car before—even in the early years. As a shifter, my body was resilient, but Clive's driving was making me question if I'd survive if we crashed. Whoever had given him his driver's license was an idiot. "Mama's out of luck on that."

Warren grinned as he rocked to the side with the force of the turn. As much as he'd fought Clive for the right to drive, he appeared to be enjoying himself now. Were all cat shifters crazy? No. I couldn't imagine Simon liking this.

"She's pinned all her hopes on Justin, our other litter-mate," Warren said, "but I think he's like the rest of us. But we don't really know. He left right out of school and hasn't been back yet, so we can't confirm who he's been dating."

Clive spun the car into the driveway of a small suburban house that looked modest but well-cared for. The car lurched as he stomped on the brakes, and my seatbelt bit into my shoulder as I jolted forward.

"We're here," Warren said as he grinned and patted me on the shoulder. I half-expected him to hand me a framed certificate that said *Certified Survivor of Clive's Driving*.

I pried my fingers off the handle I'd been clutching. Note to self: Never let Clive drive again. And I was a little worried about Warren's state of mind too, given how relaxed he was after all that. I was definitely not feeling composed. I didn't like it.

It'd take just a moment to pull down the visor and check my hair in the mirror and see if I needed to pinch a bit of color into my cheeks, but I could see a middle-aged woman with her hands on her hips staring at us through a big picture window, so I refrained. It was showtime. I waved cheerily and got out of the car. As we approached the front step, another figure joined her in the window.

Simon.

He tilted his head in confusion as he eyed his brothers. Then he saw me. His mouth dropped open. I guess this was an unexpected turn of events for both of us.

When we stepped inside, Simon rushed to me.

"Surprise," I said. Some part of my brain decided this was the perfect moment for jazz hands, and I regretted it immediately. That gesture betrayed how frazzled I was. At least none of them knew me well enough to register that fact.

"What did they do to you?" Simon glared at his brothers.

Clive and Warren lifted their hands in a placating gesture.

"They didn't do anything," the woman, who had to be Simon's mother, said as she swatted the back of my kitty cat's head. "I heard all about your trip to the police station last night and then you came in here smelling like a stranger this morning. How could you not bring him? Are you ashamed of your family? Your brothers are good boys, though; they went and got him."

Simon's cheeks were bright red again, but I didn't find it adorable this time. His mother was making him uncomfortable because of me. This would never do.

"Mrs. Rivers, I presume? I'm Ogden Walsh," I said as I stepped between Simon and the rest of his family. "Your son was respecting my wishes this morning. He tried to wake me, but I'm afraid I'm not usually awake for another four hours or so. Simon has nothing to apologize for." I ended my explanation with a hard tone, and I did not offer any apologies. No one should apologize for not wanting to get up at this uncivilized hour.

Simon's littermates stared wide-eyed at me before their gazes darted over to their mother. Mrs. Rivers, for her part, narrowed her eyes. She looked me up and down as if cataloguing every piece of clothing I was wearing. Yes, I was wearing her son's clothes—we both knew it. I grinned at her and dared her to say something.

"You're not from here, are you? What is it you do, Mr. Walsh?"

"I'm a business owner in Aspen Bay."

She tilted her head, still assessing me. "What kind of business?"

Obviously, she was pondering how I could be a business owner when I didn't normally get out of bed until mid-morning.

"I own several, actually, but the only one I manage personally is called The Drunken Drake."

Warren and Clive hooted before they remembered they were standing with their mother. They slapped their hands over their mouths as their gazes bounced back to her. She blinked. Yep, she'd heard of it too. Simon was the only one who didn't look like he understood the significance of the name.

"The sleazy place with the strip club?" she managed to ask.

Warren and Clive looked like they were going to choke on their own spit as they tried to swallow down their laughter.

"It has changed under my management," I said. I was used to this conversation. The old reputation was the reason my lawyer had suggested I change the name when I bought it, but I rather liked the sound of The Drunken Drake.

"Quit interrogating the boy," a man boomed from deeper in the house. "My porridge is getting cold."

Everyone except Simon and me scurried away, presumably to the kitchen to be served cold porridge. I couldn't even pretend to find that idea appetizing. All I *could* do was try to keep my expression neutral. Maybe I could talk Simon into stopping at a diner for a second breakfast once we were released from his family's clutches. I was not usually a fan of the hobbit lifestyle, but I saw the merit in this situation.

"I'll explain everything," I said, taking his hand in mine and squeezing. "Don't worry. I'm not nearly as nefarious as that conversation suggested."

Simon's cheeks were still flushed, but he merely nodded, then dragged me down the hallway toward what was promising to be the most unusual breakfast experience of my life.

Chapter Fifteen

SIMON

If I was in my cat form, I would be manically licking my fur off about now. I'd never been so uncomfortable at a family breakfast before. Cleaning myself was the only soothing thing I could think of that might calm my nerves.

I wasn't sure what was worse: Warren and Clive collecting Ogden from my apartment, Mama talking about a strip club, or discovering Ogden owned that strip club. Now that I'd had a few minutes to replay the conversation, I realized I *had* heard of The Drunken Drake. I'd never been, but the rest of my brothers had—even the twins, who were three years younger than me.

But hadn't I heard it'd closed?

Of course, that's what Ogden had suggested, right? He said he was the new owner. But I still wanted to know what his role was there. Did he just own it and let others run it? Or was he more hands on—or clothes off, rather?

Claws pushed through the tips of my toes, ruining

another pair of socks, at the thought of my pretty dragon taking his clothing off in front of strangers. Okay, okay. It was Ogden's body; he could do what he liked with it. But... I still wanted to rip all those strangers apart for ogling him, getting aroused by him, getting off on memories of him. I might be the size of a house cat in my shifted form, but I grew up in a house with lots of aggressive siblings. When we were teenagers, with bodies suddenly pumped full of testosterone, the house had been the backdrop to our own personal *Hunger Games*. I might prefer to run and hide, but I knew how to fight dirty when I had to.

Being territorial was part of being a cat shifter, but people weren't property. I really needed to suffocate those asshole impulses and bury them in the back garden.

Warren and Clive were still snickering when Ogden and I made it to the table. As soon as we sat, everyone slipped into their usual roles. Mama scanned the table to make sure nothing was missing, like she did every morning. Clive and Warren fought over the cream for their porridge, spilling half of it on the table. The twins, Eli and Theo, were stuffing their faces and didn't look up to acknowledge us. And Pops merely passed a plate of bacon to Ogden before reaching for the syrup.

My parents, brothers, and I were all sitting in our usual spots, but it was strange to see Ogden sitting in Justin's place. Justin hadn't attended family breakfast in years and, apparently, I'd gotten used to seeing his spot sit empty. Mama always set a plate for him, though, just in case. None of us questioned her about it.

I wondered if she'd start adding another place setting after today or whether Mama would assign Justin's place to Ogden from here on out. Last I heard, our brother didn't have any plans to return to Willow Lake. Mama said every generation in her family had a tomcat like Justin, but that didn't mean he wouldn't find his way home again. None of us tried to change her mind about that either.

Mama was very much the ruler of our family.

That thought had my mind circling back to what'd happened when Ogden arrived. I hadn't known what to do when he had essentially told her off. Sure, he'd been polite, but we all knew that's what he was doing. And the weird thing was, she let him.

I didn't understand any of this.

Had I made a mistake in making a bond between us?

I didn't think so. Honestly, I'd kind of liked him trying to stand up for me, even if it was to my mama, who loved all of us kittens with an unwavering ferocity I had never once questioned. I didn't question her love now, either. She was worried about me and this stranger I'd invited into my life—well, not so much invited as summoned like an evil wizard.

I sighed. I wished I could see myself as Ogden's savior, like he suggested, but I didn't deserve the title. It'd been pure chance that I'd blown the whistle when I had. Dumb luck wasn't heroic. Another sharp urge to shift and clean myself swept over me. Since Mama would skin me alive if I did that at the breakfast table, I forced myself to eat instead.

This was the weirdest breakfast ever, even worse than when the power had gone out and Mama served us anchovies from a can. It wouldn't have been so bad if she'd left the fish alone, but occasionally Mama decided she was a culinary genius and did terrible things to food. Most of her creations weren't genius; they were diabolical.

That breakfast was the worst. She'd tried dressing up the anchovies with syrup—saying something about balancing the salty flavor with something sweet—except she'd grabbed the strawberry syrup instead of the maple syrup by mistake. It was awful, although I don't think it would have been much better with maple syrup. She'd been so upset when my brothers and I tried to make excuses to leave the table without eating a bite. Then Pops had given us a *look*, and we'd all done our best to choke down the fruity fish. I still gagged at the memory. The only good that'd come of that was Pops investing in an outdoor cooking station fueled by propane the following week.

As cutlery scraped and clinked against plates, Mama began her daily interrogations.

"Warren, why are you bleeding at the table?" Mama eyed his bloody forearm. It looked like he'd gone skidding along a gravel road. He must have gotten into a scuffle with Clive. The injury looked familiar. Ask me how I knew.

Clive shot a warning glance at Warren. Mama frowned.

"Clive, what did you do?"

"We'd agreed I was driving. I was just getting the keys back," Clive said. I knew exactly what that meant, and apparently, so did Mama.

"What have I told you about fighting with your brother? You aren't kittens anymore."

Clive's shoulders slumped under Mama's reprimand. But I knew he would do the same thing the next time he wanted something. He was a scrapper. I always wondered how he could be my littermate when we were so different. Then again, I wasn't like any of my brothers.

Then Mama interrogated Eli and Theo before going back to Warren and Clive. She skipped me—and well, Ogden too. That unnerved me more than if she'd tied me to a metal chair and shone a spotlight in my eyes until I spilled every single secret I had.

As soon as the plates were cleared and all the washing up was done, Mama sent my brothers out of the house. Ogden and I were told to wait in the living room. The dragon appeared amused by this. I was mortified.

Did I have enough time to shift and get in a few comforting licks before Mama and Pops joined us?

We sat on the couch, across from my parents' favorite chairs, and waited. Ogden settled right beside me. I suppressed the urge to lean into him. Canoodling with boyfriends wasn't the kind of thing you did in Mama's house. There were rules, and I was the epitome of a rule-follower. Although… was Ogden my boyfriend? And what exactly was canoodling anyway?

"It's going to be fine," Ogden whispered as he set his hand on the back of my neck and squeezed lightly.

Tingles cascaded over my body from where he touched me. Oh. That was nice. Yeah. That was almost as soothing as licking my fur.

"There you go, kitty cat," he soothed in my ear, and I relaxed a little more, well, at least until my parents walked in. Mama's face twitched like she was about to sprout her whiskers. Her irritation was building stronger and faster than a thunderstorm in July. Under her narrowed gaze, I pulled away from Ogden's touch.

I regretted it immediately.

"Alright." Pops leaned back in his chair and folded his hands over his paunchy stomach. "Here's what's going to happen. Your mama wants to know what's going on. So that's what you're going to tell her."

"Peter," Mama huffed as her fingers batted nervously at the fringe on one of her pillows. The pillow was new; those fringes would never have survived a house full of kittens. Although I wasn't sure they'd survive Mama's fidgeting now, either. "You want to know too."

He rolled his eyes at me but didn't disagree with her.

From the corner of my eye, I could see Ogden nod. "That is understandable. You are concerned about Simon."

Then he told my parents what he knew. The story hadn't changed from when I'd heard him give his statement to the police. When he got to the part about me and the whistle, Mama hissed out my name. I recognized the look on her face. She was ready to march across the room and swat me on the head again. Ogden leaned forward, like he was ready to jump between us if she made a move in my direction. I swallowed hard. Weird emotions bubbled up inside me.

Was I ashamed of what I'd done? Yes. Was I thrilled with how Ogden looked ready to protect me? Yes to that too. Was I happy that I'd ended up saving Ogden? Of course. Was I uncomfortable with how Ogden came to be trapped at my side? Absolutely.

My emotions were like a tangled ball of yarn.

Pops rested his hand on Mama's leg, effectively holding her down with the barest of touches. Ogden's body lost some of its tension. Then he continued with the story.

When he finished, both my parents turned their attention to me.

"Where did you get such a thing?" Mama pursed her lips and gripped the arms of her chair, like she needed to anchor herself in place. "You've had that whistle for a while, haven't you? I knew something was going on. Didn't I say so, Peter?"

My shoulders dropped. "I found it. I was out west of town, just doing my thing when I heard some wolves."

Mama gasped.

"It was back before the robbery at the inn." I wrung my hands together. I'd known Mama wouldn't be happy to hear I'd kept secrets from her for so long, but I couldn't do much about that now. "There were three of them, and they were talking about stealing from the inn." I shrugged. "I saw something drop out of their bags and when they left, I went to see what it was. That's when I found the whistle. I told the police about the wolves the next day."

"But you stole the whistle?" Mama's fingers twitched, like she was itching to pinch my ear and haul me over to the inn to give it back right now. "And what about the wolves? Who were they? Not Hayden, I'll bet."

I shook my head. "Nah. They were from up in the hills."

Mama's eyes bulged. "Did they scent you? Do they know you were there?" She grasped my father's hand and squeezed hard enough that he winced. "Oh, Peter... our baby..."

I grimaced. I wasn't a baby—I wasn't even the youngest in my family. In fact, I was the third oldest, according to our birth records. Just because I wanted to protect my nine lives didn't mean that I couldn't take care of myself.

Although perhaps no one would suspect that if they met me.

"They didn't know I was there. I waited until after they were gone to retrieve the whistle. Like I said, I went to the police station right away." Well, soon after, anyway. "Remember? I told you I'd reported those wolves to the police."

"You just told me you'd overheard something that the police needed to know about, not that you stole from them." Mama shuddered. Her hair looked a little bigger than it had earlier. If she was in her cat form, I was sure her tail would be puffed up. "What were you thinking?"

I winced then. Because, okay, that sounded stupid, even worse than her thinking I'd stolen the whistle from the inn. The wolves in the hills were rumored to be feral, even back before they went really crazy and set off bombs and all that.

"I told the police everything," I said.

"And what about this bond or whatever you call it? Do we need to hire you a lawyer to draw up terms?"

I sucked in a breath. "It's… uh… done."

"What do you mean it's done?" She leaned forward and sniffed in our direction. Her nose wiggled. "You've already bonded?"

I half expected Ogden to jump in and save me, but he didn't. "I… um… When we were talking about it last night, apparently my magic or whatever, yeah, it made Ogden's magic an offer it couldn't refuse."

"This isn't time for joking," Mama reprimanded.

"It isn't a joke, Daph," Pops said. "Look at them. This isn't just about the summoning. They have all the signs of being mates."

I jolted at that pronouncement. My gaze darted to Ogden, before shifting back to my father. "I don't think so. That's just the magic of the whistle. We haven't…" My cheeks heated to blistering temperatures. Holy Magic, was I going to talk about sex? With my mama in the room? "You know. Um… Done anything like what you do to… You know… Complete a bond like that."

"Oh, honey, are you still a virgin? I thought all my kittens had—"

"Mama!" I shouted to stop her from speaking. "That's not what I'm talking about."

Mama's forehead crunched in confusion, but at least she quit talking.

"There is more to being mates than sex, son." Pops laughed.

I wanted to die.

Mama stared at us. Her gaze darted over how close we were sitting and how Ogden was still leaning ever so slightly in front of me, like he was ready to protect me from anything that might pop up. Then she glanced at my neck and seemed to remember Ogden's hand had been resting there—a spot Pops had trained us to protect at all costs—when she and Pops had entered the living room. I'd been Pops' best pupil, and everyone knew I liked my nine. Letting a near stranger touch such a vulnerable spot was not like me at all.

She saw it all, and I knew the moment she came up with entirely the wrong answer. Her mouth dropped open.

Then her face lit up, and she clapped her hands. Then, before I knew what was happening, she'd rushed across the room. She yanked me out of my seat.

"Mama... Pops... No. This isn't—"

She hugged me so tightly I couldn't breathe, cutting off my protests. "My baby... Oh, my baby. He's found a mate. He's the first of my kittens to be blessed with a mate. I bet you've even been blessed my Mother Magic. You simply have to be fated. That's why this has happened so quickly. I always knew Mother Magic would smile on you. Always such a dutiful kitten. I can't wait to tell Vanessa. She went on and on when Alice started dating Buddy. But Buddy is only a mechanic. You've found your-self a successful business owner. She's going to be so jealous."

So suddenly The Drunken Drake was acceptable?

Then she let go of me and did the same with Ogden. "A mate for my baby. I know you'll take care of him. Fate will have chosen you with care for my special boy. I always hoped he would meet a nice older gentleman who could take care of him, and here you are."

"Your son is safe with me, Mrs. Rivers," Ogden promised. His words did weird things to my stomach. It felt a bit like I was being tickled from the inside. Did he mean it? Would he keep my nine lives safe? I wanted to promise him the same thing, but I didn't know what I could say that would be the equivalent for a dragon.

"Oh, none of this Mr. and Mrs. Rivers nonsense. Call us Daphne and Peter or Mama and Pops. That works too."

Ogden's wide-eyed gaze met mine over my mama's head while Pops patted him on the shoulder and welcomed him to the family. Obviously, any reservations about The Drunken Drake's lingering reputation were long gone now.

It was funny how the word *mate* seemed to fix everything, at least for my mama. She refused to listen to anything else.

A few minutes later, as Ogden and I were driving away from my parents' place, I caught a movement in the living room window. My parents were waltzing. They had taught us all to dance too, but I didn't think any of us kittens would make it look as easy as Mama and Pops. They might not be fated mates, but their love was right there for anyone to see. They made everything look easy. I'd always secretly wished for a love like theirs.

I wished Ogden and I could be like that someday too. Except it wasn't meant to be like that. Not for us. This bond wasn't real, not like a bond between mates. I gulped down a shaky breath. Besides, a worldly dragon like him would never want to be stuck with a simple homebody cat like me.

Chapter Sixteen

OGDEN

When we finally escaped my self-proclaimed new in-laws, I found myself humming "Be My Baby." Simon drove us a couple of blocks away before pulling over on the side of the street. He turned to me after parking the car.

"I'm so sorry about that." His cheeks pinked as he rubbed the back of his neck.

"About what, love?" I wasn't sure why he was apologizing. After we spent more time together, he'd understand The Ronettes were a positive sign. If I was upset, the song would be very different. I guessed there were a lot of things we needed to learn about one another.

"*Everything*." He groaned. "My brothers, my mother, the whole mate thing… I can't believe my dad suggested that."

I doubted Daphne and Peter were fated mates—not only had I not seen any visible markings, but fated mates were rare—so when they'd suggested we were mates, I was surprised she suggested we might be fated mates. Chosen mates were the norm. But, given how quickly Simon and I connected, I agreed with Daphne and wondered if we might not be more.

Fated mates sounded like a fairy tale to most supes, but I was old enough to remember when the Eternal Magic played matchmaker for almost everyone. Was I naïve for thinking that? Possibly. This might all be an artifice created by the magic in the whistle, but I kept thinking: What if it wasn't?

"I had already wondered if you might be my fated mate," I admitted.

"You did? But…" His words trailed off when he saw the serious look on my face.

I nodded. "Didn't you?"

"How could we be?" he whispered and averted his eyes, like he wasn't sure if he should admit that. "Isn't this all because of the whistle?"

"I wish we'd met under different circumstances, but what if this was the Eternal Magic's way of bringing us together?"

He glanced up at me, his face full of hope. "Yeah?"

"Yes, kitty cat. I think that's entirely possible," I said as I reached for him. I put my hand on the back of his neck and pulled him close. His breath quickened as my mouth neared his. He smelled of maple syrup and bacon and orange juice. And then his lips were on mine.

The kiss was torturous in that I couldn't hold him against me—the front seat of a car wasn't the best place for this—but I closed my eyes and savored the taste of him. His lips pressed the right amount of firmness against mine. His tongue was tantalizing when it slipped up against mine. His moans, though… Those made me want to haul him into the back seat and claim him.

A ringing noise interrupted the sweet music of our mingled panting breaths.

Simon groaned as he pulled away from me. I could have stopped him. I knew if I held him in place, he wouldn't fight me. But I let him settle back into his seat and pull out his phone.

"Hello?"

"Where are you?" It was the hellhound, Van. I could hear his question clearly in the quiet car.

"Uh…" Simon looked flustered as his gaze darted over the landmarks like he'd never seen the neighborhood before, although I was sure he'd grown up here.

"Is Walsh with you?"

"Yeah…"

"Take him over to Doc Roberts. I'll meet you there."

Then the hellhound was gone.

Right. With everything else that was going on, I'd forgotten about the bump on my arm.

Simon shook his head as if he was still boggled by my amazing kissing. I preened. Then he licked his lips and looked at me again. His gaze drifted down to my mouth before coming back to my eyes again. His pupils were dilated in a telltale sign that he liked what he saw.

"I didn't tell you earlier…" He hesitated and swallowed. His gaze darted away from mine. "But I like you in my clothes."

"Yeah?" I mimicked his one-word question from a minute ago with a smile.

"Yeah." He returned my smile with a shy one of his own when he glanced back at me.

Ugh, this kitty cat. He was so ridiculously adorable.

I rather liked being draped in his possessions too. And soon, I would drape him in mine. I had several gemstones that would complement his coloring. Perhaps I could buy enough peridots to line the walls of our bedroom with them. I was sure I could find the perfect color to match his cat's eyes.

I hadn't seen him shifted yet, but when his emotions ran high, his cat showed in his beautiful eyes. But perhaps when he took his cat form his eyes would reveal yet another color—Topaz? Emerald? Whatever it was, I would memorize it, then surround him with jewels selected just for him.

There were still so many things we needed to learn about one another.

Except, if he wanted me to wear his clothes often, we needed to expand his wardrobe. I didn't tell him that. Not today. I didn't want to burst this lovely feeling growing between us. But I needed color in my life.

Then again, if we were alone, we might not need many clothes... Hmm... I'd have to give that some thought.

Then Simon turned his attention to the road and guided the vehicle back on to the street again. I knew the hellhound was right to ask to have my bump checked out, but I didn't enjoy the interruption. And now that Simon was becoming more comfortable with being affectionate, I regretted it even more.

Soon, though, I was going to get him alone and show him how much I liked the idea that he could be my mate.

Instead of driving us to a clinic, Simon entered a residential neighborhood. The hellhound was waiting outside a stereotypical new build house with an ugly attached garage and concrete driveway in the front. Although perhaps it wasn't entirely stereotypical... the house was a lovely terracotta color, which clashed with the peacock teal house to one side and the flamingo pink one on the other. I'd never seen a neighborhood with such vibrant colors before. I loved it.

The hellhound waved us into the empty garage. As soon as Simon shut off the ignition, the door rolled down, enclosing us inside. I'd never had much to do with doctors —as a dragon, my body was tough—but I'd seen enough movies and TV shows to know this doctor's visit wasn't like anything in the human world.

"Doc? We're here," Van called out as he knocked on the door connecting the garage to the house. He ducked his head inside. "Doc? You here?"

"Take them into Two," came the reply from somewhere deeper in the house.

Van guided us down a narrow corridor to the right room. He knew this place well. Did he live here? I doubted it. Not with the way he knocked and called out to the doctor. But he moved through the place with a familiarity that suggested he spent a fair bit of time here.

We'd just settled into a small exam room—houses didn't normally have rooms like this, so the whole set up struck me as odd—when a man came in. With four men, the compact room was full. Too full.

The doctor's hair was a mess of untamed curls. His hair wasn't long enough to seem intentionally long, but more like he forgot to get it cut regularly. He reminded me of when I owned a lounge close to a university a few decades ago. He had the grad-student-who-survives-on-no-sleep-and-buckets-of-caffeine appearance, although the doctor was obviously well past his grad student era... He just hadn't moved on with his personal aesthetic. But the smile on his face when he spied Van made him almost handsome—if you were into the slightly unkempt type. Based on the mirroring smile on Van's face, that was exactly the hellhound's type.

"Why don't you take Simon and go to the waiting room?" The doctor set his hand on Van's forearm in an easy gesture that suggested he was used to touching the hellhound. Although, I doubted these two were lovers—and after watching people in my job for... well, forever... I had a pretty good sense of these things.

Van and Simon both looked at me. When I didn't protest, they shuffled out of the room.

"Hi. My name is Xander Roberts. Please call me Xander. I know Van always gets so formal about these things, but meh..." He waved his hand through the air. "And you're Ogden Walsh, correct?"

"Yes." I held up my arm and pointed at the bump. "Officer Hellhound thought you should look at this."

Xander's face lit up at my nickname for Van, but when he spotted the bump, his focus zeroed in on my arm. "Oh, how interesting... Can you tell me how you came to get this?"

I told him what I knew, which wasn't much.

He nodded and made curious noises as I spoke. When I

finished, he scratched his chin. His assessing gaze was intense.

"And how are you feeling after the summoning?"

The question made me squirm. I glanced at the door as a sudden urge to leave swept over me. I didn't think anyone here would use the information against me, but talking about my vulnerabilities with a strange supe was unsettling. But Van wouldn't have brought me here if he didn't trust this doctor. And Simon did too.

"Weak," I whispered. "I can shift, but nothing else. I can't access my fire or my electricity. I'm physically weaker than normal."

"Hmm…" Xander nodded. "I think we should do a full exam. Blood samples, the works. It is likely too late to identify what was used to incapacitate you—Van should have brought you here immediately—but we should try. I also think we should make sure you have nothing else wrong with you. Something that you might not have noticed yet."

I blinked at him. I glanced at the bump on my arm. That's all I'd expected the doctor to care about because we were supes. Supes rarely became ill. "Is that necessary?"

"Necessary? Perhaps not. But wouldn't you rather be sure?" He spoke gently and quietly. "You said it yourself. You can't be sure what happened while you were unconscious."

He was right, and now that the question had been asked, I needed to know the answer.

An hour later, Xander let me know my results were as they should be. No lingering drugs or magic. No other obvious violations. No other bumps.

"But don't push too hard to access your magic," Xander warned. "Shifting shouldn't do any damage, but don't strain yourself by trying to do more. Let yourself heal naturally. You'll be stronger for it."

I frowned. Sure, I was happy he thought this was temporary, but sitting back and doing nothing didn't sound appealing.

"Now, let's look at this," Xander said as he examined the bump. "Yes. Hmm... Interesting..."

"Doc?"

"Do you want something for the pain?"

"What pain?"

"When I extract the foreign object in your arm," he said, like it should be obvious.

"You found something in there?" I looked at my arm.

"Perhaps a local anesthetic?"

"Yes. That would be fine."

"Stay as still as you can. I will need to act quickly before your body absorbs and nullifies the drug."

I nodded.

He injected my arm with a clear liquid, then he grabbed a scalpel and sliced open my arm. I watched in horrified fascination as the doctor removed a tiny mechanical device from my arm. It reminded me of the tracker Van had given me the night before, except instead of being in a little pouch around my neck like the other one, this one had been stuck in my fucking arm.

Assholes.

The doctor dropped the offensive thing in an empty specimen bottle. The bloodied device landed with a click.

"Your arm should heal quickly now that it is out," the

doctor assured me as he wiped the incision clean and placed a bandage over it. I didn't think I needed the bandage, but Xander insisted.

When we opened the door, both Van and Simon were waiting in the hallway immediately outside the room.

"He didn't want to go too far," the hellhound said as he pointed at Simon. Simon ignored the teasing, although his face darkened to a charming pink. He looked lovely with a bit of color.

"You were in there a long time. Are you okay?" Simon asked. His attention was fixated on the bandage. What a sweet little kitty cat. All protective and such.

"I'm fine," I assured him.

"This was in his arm." Xander handed the bottle to Van.

"Thanks for not destroying it when you extracted it, Doc." Van held it up and examined it. Although if I could identify it, I knew he could too. He cocked his head to the side. "It's emitting a signal. I'm sure of it." The hellhound's smile would have been terrifying if he wasn't on my side. This was obviously a good lead.

How he knew about the signal, I didn't know. Could he hear something? Feel something? See something? I could have asked, but I didn't care. I didn't understand all the ins and outs of technology, only keeping up with the most popular trends. Tracking devices weren't a trend I'd ever needed to know about, even if they were all around me at the moment.

"Okay," Xander said with an easy smile, waving us away. "You all need to leave so I can see my next patient."

Van tucked the little jar into one of his pockets, then guided us down the hallway to the garage again.

"Do you think they've tracked Ogden here already?" Simon glanced around as if expecting someone to jump out and grab me.

"It's impossible to know," Van said.

Simon trembled a little and his ears shifted into his cat's ears. They swiveled, as if hunting for any sound that didn't belong. He was barely hanging on to his human form.

"But if they continue to follow the tracking device now, it'll take them to Officer Hellhound," I said, slipping my hand into Simon's and squeezing it. I looked at Van. "You should be prepared in case that happens."

A wicked grin spread over Van's face, and fire lit his eyes. "Oh, I'm prepared all right. I'd like to see them try to take me down."

I sighed and rolled my eyes. "I would have said the same thing a few days ago but look what happened."

Van dipped his head in acknowledgement, but I got the sense he thought he could take on my abductors and win. I hoped that wasn't hubris.

"But if they come to Willow Lake, they might still find Ogden." Simon's voice was shaky. Long, thin whiskers were poking through his cheeks now. "By now everyone in town knows about him being here."

And I suspected that was mostly because of his mother blabbing to everyone about how her baby had found his mate. But saying that wouldn't help anything.

"Gage's presence here should keep them back too," Van said quietly, as if finally realizing Simon needed some comforting words. His eyes met Simon's and held his gaze for a long moment, as if willing my kitty cat to feel the weight of his words. His calm confidence was working, or at least Simon didn't seem to be struggling to stay in his human form anymore.

"You think so?"

"Gage is a demon guardian. Few will want to take him on. His magic is tied to Willow Lake itself, and you are part of Willow Lake. You are under his protection, and now, by extension, so is Ogden. And it helps that Ogden was summoned. They may think the device malfunctioned when it suddenly showed him so far away from where they'd held him."

"I hope you're right," Simon muttered.

"I need to get back to the station and see what this little baby can tell me," the hellhound said, tapping the pocket where he'd hidden the jar. Van's eyes shone with the fire of his hellhound. His beast had to be close to the surface, perhaps eager to be on the hunt. "We need to act fast before they realize we're on to them."

"Will that little thing really help you track them?" Simon asked.

"Yep." He grinned as he walked us back to the garage.

"Let me know when you track the signal to a location. I want to go with you," I said. "I can help."

"Ogden…" Simon said my name like a plea as he spun to face me.

"I have to, sweetheart." My fingers brushed over his cheek. "I escaped, but I can't stop thinking about all those supes in there. I can help."

"But…"

"They may have nabbed me once, but now that I am aware of the threat, they won't catch me so easily again. And I could actually be quite useful."

"You know how to fight?" Van asked.

"Well, not recently, but I fought in the dragon wars…" I was smart enough not to oversell my abilities, but I wouldn't undersell them, either. The dragon wars happened centuries ago, but some things you didn't forget. "I may not have current fighting experience, but I am a water dragon. I have fire and electricity. All dragons are natural predators. And I do have a personal stake in this. I was the one they kidnapped."

I was counting on the doctor not having told anyone about my current problems. Not having access to my full abilities might be a bit of a liability, but it was only temporary. They would return. Soon. I was depending on them.

Van considered me for a moment. If I was a human victim talking to a human police officer, the officer would never entertain my request, but the supernatural community didn't work that way. After a moment, he nodded. "Okay, but you have to listen to me."

"Of course, Officer Hellhound."

He rolled his eyes and opened the garage door.

Instead of retreating to the driver's side like I expected, Simon stepped forward and stopped the hellhound from leaving. "If he's going, then so am I."

And just like that, the axis of my world tilted. Pain sliced across my chest. How could he not believe he was brave?

"Simon…" I whispered.

He crossed his arms over his chest and met my eyes

steadily. His cheeks were flushed, and his pulse raced, betraying his anxiety, but he didn't back down. Damn it. I wouldn't be able to stop him. Why did he have to discover his cat's inner stubbornness now?

Still, if the situation was reversed, I would never let him go without me, either.

But how was I going to keep him safe?

Chapter Seventeen

SIMON

I hadn't expected Van to call so soon.

I'd thought I'd have time to get to know Ogden a little better. To talk to him. To kiss him some more. To have him try on some more of my clothes.

Instead, Van called an hour after we'd left Doc Roberts and said he'd been able to pinpoint where the abductors were monitoring the tracking device. I suspected magic was involved, but Van didn't elaborate on how he knew all that. Less than thirty minutes after the call, we were on the road. And now, it wasn't even lunchtime, and we were already seeing signs for Aspen Bay.

When I'd heard my brothers talk about Aspen Bay—and The Drunken Drake strip joint, in particular—I'd imagined it was a long way from Willow Lake. I don't know why I thought that, since they could go there and be back in an evening. But, in my mind, I'd built it up as some place *other*.

Arriving at Aspen Bay not too long after leaving Willow Lake didn't seem right. Aspen Bay sounded exotic to me—like it should have a bunch of fancy hotels along the waterfront with fancy patio restaurants overlooking the water where fancy colorful drinks came with fancy little paper umbrellas. Instead, from the outskirts of town where we were, Aspen Bay looked a lot like Willow Lake, which looked a lot like every other small rural town. There was nothing inherently exotic about it at all.

I was a little disappointed, to be honest.

It was probably strange to feel happy about that disappointment, but it was nice to feel something other than my escalating anxiety. Because, seriously, what was I doing here? Why had I insisted on coming? And what the H E double hockey sticks could I do if something happened?

Not much, that's what.

This was not the behavior of someone who valued their nine. But I wondered if I was starting to value Ogden more. And wasn't that confusing? How could I have existed one way my entire life and have it all upended in such a short amount of time?

He was so… relaxed. If he could face his abductors with such calm, I could too, right?

Ha! What a bunch of lies.

Except I wanted to be there for Ogden. Protect him as best I could. Somehow. I didn't want to let him down. And that meant channeling big cat energy. Fake it until you make it, right?

Says the guy who is freaking out over holding someone's hand.

Because I didn't know what to think about Ogden

holding my hand the entire trip, either. I didn't hold hands with people. It was... weird. Not unpleasant, but not overly comfortable either. Although the discomfort had more to do with me worrying about my palms sweating or if I was squeezing too tightly or if I'd wreck the moment if I let go—just for a second—so I could change the angle of my hand.

Dillon was in the passenger seat, giving directions to Van, and coordinating with the local police department. I was in the back seat with Ogden, trying to pretend I wasn't losing my mind. We didn't go into the town. Instead, we turned down a gravel road just before the town boundary. Another couple of police vehicles turned down the road to follow us. Based on what Dillon was saying, those were the locals.

"We're almost there," Dillon said, watching a screen on the laptop he was holding.

Were they serious about trying to track the tracker right now without having any other discussion or planning or *anything*? Were they actually planning to—gulp—raid the place? Today? Right now? Shouldn't we wait for, I don't know, a SWAT team or something? The mere thought of it had my cat wanting to take over and hide under the seat.

"Close enough to be in my backyard," Ogden muttered. "The holding facility must be close too."

I scanned the landscape for a building that looked evil. Wait, could buildings look evil? Regardless, nothing I saw screamed "the bad guys live here."

"Slow down," Dillon said. "There."

He pointed to an old shack on the edge of a farmer's

field. The small wooden structure looked ready to collapse under the next big wind.

"Damn," Ogden said. "That's not where I was held. I should have known it wouldn't be that easy."

"Let's see what we find," Van said. He pulled the SUV to the side of the road. He and Dillon both hopped out. "Stay here."

I expected Ogden to argue, but he didn't. We watched in silence as Van, Dillon, and the local police officers stormed the building.

They came out empty-handed a minute later.

Ogden slipped his hand out of mine and jumped out of the vehicle before I could stop him. I raced after him, ready to pull him away if necessary. I clenched my hand, wishing it still held his. As much as I'd worried about it, it'd been nice to have that physical connection.

"What? What did you find?" Ogden demanded.

Both hellhounds' eyes blazed with fire. Dillon's nostrils flared. "It's a machine. Looks like it uploads information to the cloud."

"A dead-end?" Smoke and sparks spluttered out of Ogden's mouth and nose. He looked surprised at what he'd done, then he looked relieved. I wondered what that was about.

"It isn't the smoking gun we were hoping for, but we know more than we did," Van said. "Aspen Bay is collecting evidence. Hopefully we'll get some fingerprints. The equipment still has serial numbers, so we might get a lead there too. We'll pack up everything and send it to the SC. They have a hacker who might get more information from it, IP addresses and what not."

Ogden scowled at the shack, as if he could scare it into coughing up more clues.

"Hey, Van?" a local officer called out as he approached.

My first impulse was to look away and pretend I didn't see them. If I didn't look at them, maybe they wouldn't look at me. I knew it was stupid, but my mind did random stuff like that sometimes. Being surrounded by so many police officers made the back of my neck itch. Not that I'd ever done anything to get on the wrong side of the law—well, except for keeping the whistle, I guess. I shouldn't have done that. Oh, and then there was the inflatable tube man incident. I shouldn't have done that either.

Holy Magic, maybe I really was a criminal.

Mama would be so disappointed in me.

I swallowed. Hard. Maybe everyone would be so focused on the tracker and such that they wouldn't notice me. A cat could only hope.

I sniffed the air to get more information about the new arrival. He was a shifter. That was better than human police officers, so I relaxed... just a little. I mean, I still didn't like being surrounded by so many police officers, but at least everyone was a supe. Supes didn't look at petty crimes the same way that humans did, or at least that's what Clive and Warren always said. I hoped they were right.

But when the officers narrowed their eyes at me as they sniffed the air too, I was right back to maximum anxiety levels again. I swallowed hard and fought the urge to hide behind Van and Ogden.

"What's up?" Van asked.

"Since you drove all the way over here to Aspen Bay, do you want to come with us to The Drunken Drake?"

"You haven't been there yet, Norbert? What the fire and fury have you guys been doing?" Ogden demanded, swinging his scowl toward the officer, who he obviously knew. I guessed that made sense. Aspen Bay looked about the same size as Willow Lake and everyone in Willow Lake knew who Van was. Ogden set his hands on his hips in a way that reminded me of Mama when she got pissed at us kittens.

"Oh… Oggie. I didn't see you there." The officer grimaced.

Oggie? Really? Why did this guy have a nickname for my dragon?

"Why haven't you been there yet?" Ogden demanded.

"It was locked up tighter than dragon's hoard—uh, no offence," the officer said.

"Wesley was supposed to give you access."

The officer shook his head. "We haven't been able to find Wesley Scott since Van called us about him last night."

"Damn it," Ogden muttered. "Then we should definitely get over there."

A few minutes later, we were in downtown Aspen Bay. The place could easily have been mistaken for downtown Willow Lake.

"So this is it?" Van asked from the front seat once he'd parked.

"Yes." Ogden leaned forward in the back seat of Van's

SUV to peer up at the red brick building. I wished I could tell from his face what he was thinking. The uncertainty did nothing to abate my rampant anxiety.

I studied the building as if it could give me answers. The massive two-story structure had five storefronts facing the street, with The Drunken Drake taking up one end. I couldn't tell if the second floor held offices or apartments. Did Ogden own the whole place or just The Drunken Drake? Either way, it was impressive.

Van looked at us through the rearview mirror.

"You ready for this?" Van asked.

"Of course." Ogden nodded as he slipped out of the truck. He beckoned for me to follow. "Come on, kitty cat."

I was moving toward him before I even realized what I was doing, scrambling across the seats to go through his door and get to him as quickly as possible when I'd had my own door right beside me. Before I could overthink my actions, Ogden smiled at me like my eager response to his wish made him happy, and that made it all okay. Anything I could do to put a smile on his face right now was a win.

The officer who'd talked to us at the shack arrived next. He and a couple of other officers joined us on the sidewalk.

"We didn't introduce ourselves earlier," the officer said. "I'm Inspector Norbert. You can call me Peter. And this is Sergeant Glover and Constable Keats."

After a quick round of introductions, everyone looked at Ogden. Since the new officers didn't ask questions, I figured Van must have already briefed them.

"Shall we?" Van asked.

"Follow me," Ogden said with a nod.

Ogden had arrived in Willow Lake with none of his clothing or possessions. I hadn't thought about it until now, but how would we get in if he didn't have his keys?

He led us around the side of the building to a narrow walkway between The Drunken Drake and its neighboring building, which appeared to be a secondhand store of some kind. Toward the back of the building, there was a nondescript door painted the same color as the wall. At some point, it had probably been red, but was fading to a dull salmon pink now.

I glanced around for a welcome mat or a hollowed-out rock that might hide a key, but Odgen went straight to the door. He touched a nondescript brick beside the casing. I couldn't believe it when the face of the brick swung open to reveal a hidden compartment with some kind of high-tech security pad thing. I'd never seen anything like it outside of movies.

Of course, Ogden wouldn't have something as simple as a key.

After Ogden tapped in his code and swiped his finger over a shiny black square at the corner of the mechanism, a machine-like hum told me something was happening, which was followed by a small green light flashing on the pad. Something clicked.

"Good. Everything is as it should be." Ogden grinned as he twisted the door handle.

He beckoned everyone inside to a small landing. To the right was another door and in front of us was a steep set of stairs going up to the second floor.

"Let's go this way," Ogden said, opening the door. "My office is down here. We can collect the security footage first."

The door led to a dark narrow hallway with another couple of doors along its length. Ogden stopped at the first door. Once again, he tapped something into a pin pad and scanned his finger. As soon as the door opened, though, Ogden gasped.

Van shoved him aside, right into my arms. He and Dillon charged into the room, while the Aspen Bay police officers crowded around us in a protective stance. Unable to curb my curiosity, even though it warred with my carefully nurtured need to preserve my nine, I craned my neck to peer over the officers' shoulders so I could see what was going on. Someone had trashed the place. Furniture was tipped over, papers were strewn everywhere, and paintings were ripped from the walls. I may not have known Ogden long, but I knew this was not his doing. He was too particular to leave his office in a shambles like this.

"Clear," Van said a few seconds later. Their search hadn't taken long because the office wasn't much bigger than the galley kitchen in my tiny apartment. "Ogden, can you come in here?"

Ogden pushed through the others and stepped into the room. He pressed his hands to his chest as if it pained him. Scales rolled out over the backs of his hands and up his forearms, betraying how close to the surface his dragon was.

I followed at Ogden's heels, desperately wishing I could draw him into my arms and haul him out of here. Hadn't he been through enough? Except I knew he wouldn't want that. Not right now. He'd want to find whoever had made him a target.

"I take it you didn't leave the room looking like this?" Van asked.

"Of course not," Ogden snapped. A few sparks and a curl of smoke exploded from his mouth to punctuate his words. Then he muttered something in a language I didn't know and rushed to a painting on the floor. The canvas had a bunch of small holes, as if someone had repeatedly stabbed it with a pen.

"Don't touch anything," Van commanded.

Ogden stopped and spun around to face the hellhound. His scowl was fierce. Scales covered every bit of his exposed skin now. His eyes had transitioned to his beast's. He looked angrier than Mama had when Clive and Warren hitchhiked to the coast because they wanted to see if fish straight out of the ocean tasted better. They'd only been fourteen.

I ducked down to make myself a little smaller. Ogden wouldn't hurt me. I just knew he wouldn't. But I didn't want to get accidentally caught in the middle of something if my dragon went after the hellhound. Then I watched to see what would happen next.

Ogden was absolutely gorgeous like this. We'd been under the moonlight the last time I'd seen his scales, so I had paid little attention to them. Okay, so I'd also been convinced he was going to take one of my nine, so that'd been a bit distracting too. But they were beautiful—*he* was beautiful.

Most of his scales were blue, reminding me of the flowers in Mama's garden. She always called them Bachelor

Buttons. I remembered the name because I couldn't imagine anyone I knew—man or woman—wearing a button that looked like that. His scales had a slight ridge that caught the light and appeared to change color, making them switch from the darkest navy to the palest sky blue. They had a soft sheen that made them look like polished leather. Scales like that weren't for decoration; I bet they'd be nearly impenetrable, which might come in handy if he went for the hellhound.

"We'll see if we can get some prints off it," the hellhound said, not intimidated by Odgen's anger.

"That painting is worth more than your annual salary," Ogden said. "Keep that in mind when you do whatever you are going to do to it."

My eyebrows rose. What was something like that doing in this dingy office? And wasn't it destroyed now? By the look Ogden was leveling at Van, though, he seemed to think it could still be saved.

"Is anything missing?" Van asked.

Ogden huffed as he waved his hand at the mess. "I have no idea."

Van frowned but said nothing.

"The art pieces were the most valuable things in here," he said as he scanned the jumble on the floor. "There was this one and… Oh, there it is." He pointed to the corner of another gilt frame peeking out from under a bunch of paper. "There is the other. I don't know why someone would do all of this and not take the paintings."

"Unless they didn't know their worth," Van said.

"The security footage?" one of the Aspen Bay officers asked from the hallway. "You said that was in here too?"

Ogden pointed to the corner of the room. Van pulled on latex gloves, then started sifting through the mess in the corner to unearth the security system. It only took a moment to realize it wasn't there.

"So that's what they were after," Dillon said.

Van shook his head. "I don't think that was all, though. It would have been easy to come in and grab that without causing all this…" Van gestured to the room. "They were looking for something. The question is whether or not they found it."

"Or they were just angry," Dillon suggested quietly.

"Who has access to this room?" Van asked.

Ogden sucked in a deep breath. "Only me and Wesley."

One of the Aspen Bay officers—I couldn't remember which one was which—called his office to check if they'd found Wesley yet. They hadn't.

"We'll come back and process the office, but let's check out the rest of the building first."

On the ground floor, where the lounge was, everything looked like what I imagined any other pub or restaurant would look after hours. Chairs were up on the tables. Little stoppers were in the keg taps. Glasses and liquor bottles were all lined up on the shelves. Except for a guitar, mic, and amp, the stage area was empty. Seeing everything tidy and clean calmed Ogden. His scales slowly disappeared from his forearms.

Ogden kept an apartment upstairs, so after we checked The Drunken Drake, he led us up there. At first glance, it looked normal. But when he growled "that little fucker" and a puff of spark-filled smoke streamed out of his mouth, I knew he didn't agree.

"He's been up here," Odgen snarled. The scales were back. "In my home. Using my things."

"Let's not jump to conclusions," Van warned, but I didn't think Ogden heard him as he stomped through his apartment, going from space to space.

The apartment was enormous, a much larger footprint than The Drunken Drake. It took me a minute to figure out it must extend over all the businesses on the ground floor. Most of the living space was open and airy, with an industrial edge. A living room, although that label didn't seem quite right for a space like this, ran along the front of the building, with a kitchen and dining area toward the back. On the far side, there were a couple of doorways, which must lead to a bedroom and bathroom. Large windows faced the street and light streamed through them, making the space warm and cozy. Enticing squares of sunlight lit up the polished wood floors.

What a great place for a nap.

Except I wasn't here to nap.

I forced myself to look away from the sunlight. The exterior brick walls were all exposed, as were the shiny metal ducts overhead. An ornate spiral staircase in the corner led to the roof. And throughout the space were pieces of art I suspected were as expensive as the ones in Ogden's office. But instead of just paintings, there were sculptures and colorful glass pieces and bold tapestries and more in a profusion of color and texture and shapes and sizes of all kinds that I would never have thought would go together, but they did. The space was beautiful and chaotic and unexpectedly cozy all at once. And thankfully, none showed any damage.

I wanted to stop and look at everything—walk the perimeter of the room, maybe rub my scent on a couple of things—but Ogden wasn't stopping, and I needed to be with him. He marched through the living room and disappeared through a wide threshold. I darted after him, as did the officers.

It was his bedroom.

The bed linens were rumpled, but even in this state they looked expensive with fancy embroidered detailing and soft-looking fabrics—much nicer than the bed-in-a-bag set I had on my bed. I sniffed, expecting a rush of his scent, but getting a whiff of... a stranger and sex and... I growled and the tiny hairs on the back of my neck lifted.

Did Ogden have a lover? He would have said something, wouldn't he?

I looked to him for answers and found him fuming, literally, as he stared at his bed. His hands were fisted at his side and his skin rippled to show scales before receding back to human skin, only to ripple into scales again.

"Ogden," I whispered as I approached him. "We'll catch him."

I slowly reached out and wrapped my hands around his clenched one. His eyes snapped to mine.

"Wesley slept in my fucking bed, Simon. He fucked someone in my fucking bed." Smoky steam and sparks blasted out of his mouth with each word.

I swallowed. Should I tell him we could cover the bird shifter's scent with ours? Should I tell him we could burn the bed and bedding and forget this ever happened? Or should I drag him away from here and not stop until we were safely tucked in my bed, far away from this place? I didn't know, so I gave up on finding the right words and pulled him into my arms.

He vibrated against me, but he let me hold him. Then I did everything my mama always did for me when my brothers were jerks to me. I petted his back in long, smooth strokes. I rubbed my chin on the top of his head, coating him with my scent. I pushed myself to purr, to soothe away some of his anger.

Van and the others kept back and let me calm him. I supposed no one wanted an angry, out-of-control dragon on their hands.

When he finally leaned into me and pushed his face into my neck, I sighed with relief. We stood that way for a few minutes before Ogden patted me on the back, signaling he was ready to face everything again. I broke the hug, but I grabbed his hand in mine. He entwined our fingers, so I hoped that meant he was happy to have me there with him.

He didn't look at the bed again.

Instead, he pulled me toward an opening in the corner of the room. It led to his closet. The room was larger than my bedroom and lined with one of those expensive built-in closet organizers I thought only existed in show homes. When Ogden saw a small heap of clothing in the middle of the room, where it looked like clothes had been tried on and cast aside, he tightened his grip on my hand, but he didn't stop or comment on it.

When we reached the back wall, he glanced over his shoulder at Van and Dillon, who'd trailed after us.

"Give me a minute," he said. "I need to check my hoard."

They nodded and left us alone in the closet.

"Should I...?" I pointed to the door to the bedroom.

Ogden squeezed my hand to the point of pain, and I guessed that was my answer. I wasn't going anywhere. Then he pulled open a drawer filled with folded lacy underwear arranged in a rainbow of colors. My eyes bulged, and I glanced toward the bedroom. I moved to block the view just in case anyone snuck a peek inside. No way was anyone else seeing his underwear, not if I could help it.

Ogden reached inside the drawer with his free hand. I didn't know what he did, but another panel swung open. He fiddled with it to open another. And then another. Finally, whatever he'd done made something click on the corner cabinet. Ogden led me toward the corner.

"Sorry, kitty cat," he said as he pushed me against one cabinet and pressed his body flush against mine. "I designed this for one person, not two."

I was about to ask what he meant, but then we were spinning. When we stopped, I realized the cabinet had turned like a revolving door and dumped us into a vault full of, well, everything. Unobtrusive lights cast the windowless space in a warm glow. The room was massive, easily the size of my apartment. One wall alone was dedicated to wines, carefully stored in a fancy refrigerator type thing that looked like it belonged in an expensive restaurant. Another wall had floor-to-ceiling shelves filled with vinyl records. Artwork was stowed in beautifully crafted storage racks. But it was the jewels and coins that took my breath away. The only surface that didn't glitter with them was the floor. It was a room fit for a king... or a dragon.

I gaped.

Ogden narrowed his eyes and studied the room. The tension in his shoulders eased. "I don't think he found it. But can you give it a sniff, love? Just in case. Your nose is better than mine."

I nodded and did as he asked.

"I don't smell him in here."

"Thank the Eternal Magic for that," he muttered.

He dragged me to one of those long fancy couches you see in historical dramas and pushed me onto it. Then he crawled into my lap, straddling my legs with his. My arms came up automatically to hug him. He leaned forward and pressed his face into my neck again, as if breathing in my scent calmed him.

I hoped it did; I wanted to do that for him.

I didn't know how much time passed before he lifted his head. It seemed like hours, but if it'd been that long, I thought Van would have been pounding on the wall by now. Although maybe he was. This place looked like it could withstand almost anything, so maybe it was sound-proof too.

"I'd imagined you in my hoard."

"You did?"

"From the moment I met you." Ogden smiled. "I wish we could spend the rest of the day here. I want to drape you in jewels, cover you in gold, and then fuck you until we pass out."

My cock plumped at the image he painted. Ogden rolled his hips forward, and I realized he was hard too. I slid my hand to the back of his neck and drew him down until our mouths met. His lips and tongue and wet heat consumed me as we lost ourselves in the most erotic kiss of my life. Each time our lips joined, it got better and better. My other arm wrapped around him and pulled him even closer.

Chapter Eighteen

OGDEN

I wanted to consume my little kitty cat. Figuratively. Not like my former manager, who I could literally devour in my dragon form, then use his bones as toothpicks.

Simon was the only one keeping me sane right now.

His thick thighs between my legs and the pressure of the hard bulge in his pants against my own bulge were pretty effective at keeping my plots of revenge at bay. For the moment, at least. My cat shifter might be a touch on the naïve side, but he was quickly learning how to ignite a heat in me that only he could quench.

I wanted more.

His grip tightened on my ass, drawing my crotch right up against his. It was cheeky of him to try to control a dragon, but I would let him. For now. Because this was what I needed.

I ripped off my borrowed shirt, then went for him. My cat wasn't lean and muscular, but he wasn't overly round, either. He was the perfect softness, and I wanted to see more of him. I fumbled at his belt and jeans, wrenching them out of the way so I could dip my hands in his pants and finally touch him. As soon as my fingers grazed over the damp head of his cock, he groaned into my mouth.

"Ogden," he murmured and threw back his head as I wrapped my fingers around him.

Then his hands were pulling at my own pants, ripping them out of the way so he could touch me too. He freed my cock and jerked me. I grabbed the lube I had stashed in an ornate box beside the chaise longue. I opened the container and coated my fingers, then I pushed his hand out of the way so I could wrap my slick hand around both our lengths. His breath caught as I gripped us and thrust against him. His cock rubbed against mine with perfect, exquisite pressure and friction. His crown nudged my frenulum with each back and forth. So fucking good.

His cheeks were flushed, his lips were wet and red from my kisses, and his chest was heaving with each panting breath. He was stunning, easily the most breath-taking treasure in the room.

"Touch me," I demanded.

He obeyed immediately. His hands slid over me, down my sides to grasp my hips. Then one of his hands moved behind me. His thick fingers slipped beneath my under-wear to cup and squeeze my ass before sliding slowly down to my crack. I trembled at the sweet, tentative explo-ration. The heated look on his face as he swept his finger over my hole almost broke me.

"Yes," I encouraged him. "Keep going. More."

I slowed the roll of my hips so he could finger me

more easily, adjusting my grip to jerk our dicks instead. His finger tap-danced over my entrance. I pushed against his hand.

"Just like that, Simon…" I moaned. I leaned forward and licked the side of his neck. His pulse quivered beneath my tongue. I fought off the desire to bite. To mark him, even temporarily. It'd been so long since I exchanged energy with another supe. Most of my lovers were human. They were easier to manage than supes who either wanted to be dominated by someone stronger or wanted to have rough sex where they got to top someone stronger. It was about power, not pleasure. My kitty cat wasn't like that. Thank Magic.

"You are so beautiful," he whispered. "I can't believe you are letting me touch you like this."

I frowned. I would have to work on his self-esteem if he could think of such a thing at a time like this, but that was a later job. Right now, I wanted him to quit thinking altogether. I let go of my own cock and concentrated on him. I squeezed more lube onto my hand, then wrapped it around his hard and weeping length again.

"You feel so good," I said, gliding my hand along his shaft and then up and over the tip. "So hard. Just for me. Do you like this, kitty cat?"

He grunted, then hissed the word, "yes…"

I rubbed my thumb over his slit, loving the silky feel of his pre-cum on my skin. He writhed beneath me. Then I stopped. I waited until his eyes were on me again before I leisurely lifted my hand to my mouth and licked the taste of him from my hand. I tasted mostly lube, but he didn't know that. This was all part of my plan to drive him crazy. I grinned because it was working.

He shuddered under me. Both of his hands clenched brutally on my ass now.

"Now, be a good kitty," I whispered in his ear, "and push that nice thick finger deep inside me and make me come. Then, tonight, when we're all alone, I'm going to take my time with you until you're begging for me to push my cock inside you. Because good kitties get rewards."

His cock jerked and another spurt of pre-cum erupted from his tip. Then his fingers were back at my hole again. This time, he didn't hesitate. The broad tip of his finger pushed gently until it slipped inside. My breath caught, and I closed my eyes to savor the feeling. It'd been so long since I'd done this with anyone. I'd almost forgotten how different it felt to find pleasure with another person. I'd been in a dedicated relationship with my collection of dildoes for ages now. But this...

Fuck...

I rocked onto his hand in the same rhythm as I stroked his length. I lost myself in pleasure, listening to the music of his grunts and groans. He came first, shooting his load across our stomachs. His hot, wet cum splashing over me triggered my own release, and I came a moment later. Trembling, I clung to him until the last aftershocks of my orgasm faded.

I nuzzled his neck. I had no desire to move. The longer I waited, the more our combined scents would sink into our skin. I loved the idea of being marked like that.

When his breathing calmed, he began to purr. The

gentle vibration soothed me. We stayed curled against one another for several long minutes before he slipped his finger out of my ass. I wished we could stay locked in my hoard room for the rest of the day, but now that the heat of passion was cooling, I was suddenly very aware that five police officers were currently rummaging through my home and business unattended. I had nothing to hide, but I didn't relish the idea of them touching all my possessions either.

My most precious belongings were here in my hoard, but all my pieces were special to me.

I sat up and looked at my disheveled kitty cat.

The hellhounds wouldn't even have to sniff us to know what we'd been up to in here, not that they wouldn't have guessed already when we were taking so long to get back out there. But it'd only take one glance to see I'd thoroughly pleasured my little kitten while we were out of sight.

Good. That way, they'd know to keep their hands off him. I wouldn't tolerate someone touching my kitty cat. In fact, that would be even worse than someone touching my hoard.

What in the Eternal Magic had come over me?

Chapter Nineteen

SIMON

Was it a walk of shame when you stumbled out of a hidden vault and into a closet to find an annoyed hellhound leaning against the wall with his arms crossed? With one glance, Dillon knew what we'd been doing. Not that I thought it'd be a secret, but this made me squirm almost as much as when Mama and Pops had sat me and my litter-mates down and given us the "talk." No one wants to talk about sex with their parents. And I didn't want to talk about sex with a police officer, either.

Our pants had survived our make-out session in his hoard room, but our shirts hadn't. Ogden had destroyed them when he'd ripped them off our bodies. We'd used the ripped shirts to wipe away our mess, but I doubted we'd cleaned up everything. But that meant we weren't wearing shirts, and I didn't like another man's eyes on Ogden's body.

I stepped in front of him to block the hellhound's view of my... dragon.

I didn't even know what to call him. Some people didn't like labels, but I wasn't one of those people. I liked to know things and understand how everything worked together. It helped me figure out the rules for interacting with people. Was Ogden my boyfriend? I mean, we did just make out in the room where he kept his treasure. That seemed a step up from just friends.

We'd talked about being mates, but was it too soon? We'd only met like... Wow... Was it only yesterday?

"About time," Dillon muttered. He squished up his nose like the smell of sex offended him. He shook his head, as if he couldn't believe we'd stop to make out when we were in the middle of an investigation. The hellhound scowled at us, then spun around and marched out of the closet. "Glad to know you didn't run into any problems in there."

Ogden snickered. "Nope. No problems at all."

"Get your asses cleaned up. We're heading over to Wesley's place next."

My cheeks were scorching hot. I couldn't believe we'd just... done what we'd done... when we knew people were out here waiting for us. How would I ever face Van and Dillon again?

Holy Magic, I hoped Mama never found out about this.

"Come here, kitty cat," Ogden said as he tugged me deeper into his massive closet, distracting me from my spiraling thoughts. "Calm down. One step at a time. We have to get dressed first. Then we can think about all the rest."

At least Ogden's closet, with all its different textures and colors and types of clothes, was a distraction; I'd never seen anything like it. It boggled my mind. He'd arranged the clothes by color like a bright rainbow. I didn't know where he stashed his black, white, gray, and beige clothes, but I couldn't see any of them. He had to own them; everyone did. I looked around his closet again. Or maybe not. Everything on display was bright, bold, and vibrant.

Then Ogden pulled out various shirts and held them in front of me and I forgot all about black and gray and white and beige.

"This one will dry," I said, dangling the one I had clutched in my hand. I didn't relish the idea of wearing a ripped and cum-stained shirt for the rest of the day, but Ogden was smaller than me and he didn't seem the type to buy oversized or baggy clothes. I was sure nothing he owned would fit me.

"Here," he said as he thrust a lime green polo shirt into my hands. "Try this one."

I eyed the colorful shirt dubiously, trying to figure out how to say no without offending him, but he wasn't paying any attention to me. He'd already stripped off the clothes he'd borrowed from me and was digging in the drawer with his pretty underwear. The underwear he pulled out... They were teal. Was that the right word? They looked silky soft. When he'd wrapped his hand around me, his touch had been silky soft too.

I swallowed hard as my cock rallied again.

As he pulled on his underwear, I couldn't look away. The pretty fabric was beautiful against his skin. I glanced at the other colors in his underwear drawer. I bet they'd all be gorgeous.

Maybe someday he would model all of them for me.

But not now. Unfortunately.

We didn't have time to waste—not with Dillon and Van and the others waiting for us. I glanced back at the opening leading to his bedroom. He really needed a door on that. I wiped my plain gray T-shirt over my stomach where my skin still felt a little sticky.

Now what was I supposed to do with it?

"Just toss yours in the hamper. Maybe we can use it for rags or something," Ogden said without pausing as he sorted through his shirts.

I did as he suggested, thankful I hadn't worn one of my favorite shirts today.

Then I eyed the one he'd given me. It looked way too small. "I don't know about this. I don't want to wreck your clothes."

"It is stretchy. It'll be fine," Ogden said as he wiggled into some tight rusty red pants, hiding his silky teal underwear from view. I took a moment to appreciate the way his slim body moved. It reminded me of the way he'd undulated and writhed in his dragon form, all graceful and smooth, as he flew across the lake under the moonlight.

Then he tugged on a short-sleeved orange shirt, hiding his skin from me. I skipped shirts like that when I shopped because it looked like they'd need to be dry-cleaned, or at the very least, ironed. He smiled when he caught me watching him as his fingers danced over his buttons.

No one I knew wore bright clothes like that. Not in real

life. Every eye would be on him as soon as we walked out the door. I'd never ever be able to dress like that, but the clothes suited him.

"Go on," he said, nodding at the green shirt in my hand. "Try it."

I tugged on the fabric and sure enough, it stretched. Would it be enough? Only one way to find out. I slipped it over my head. By the time I pulled the hem down and adjusted the way the shirt stretched over my shoulders, I felt like a bit of sausage meat being shoved into a casing.

"Oh, that color is perfect for you," he enthused. "Brings out the color of your eyes."

He bounced over to me and smoothed his palms over my chest where the T-shirt molded to every dip and bulge, pausing only long enough to tweak my nipples. His eyes twinkled as his gaze danced over my body. He licked his lips as if he liked what he saw.

"A little snug, but so much better than what you were wearing," he said. "How do you like it?"

"I feel like if I take too big of a breath, the seams will burst."

He laughed like I'd told a joke, even though I was being serious. "It'll be fine. The shirt is quality. The seams will hold."

"Uh… okay… If you're sure… But I could just wear—"

"I'm sure," he said. "The color is divine on you, kitty cat."

Then, before I could come up with a better protest, Ogden pulled me out of the closet—ha! I'd been out of the closet for years—and through the apartment until we found the others.

"We're ready," Ogden announced to Dillon and the others when we found them all gathered downstairs in the office. "Let's go find Wesley and arrest that arsehole."

Chapter Twenty

OGDEN

The afternoon was a bust.

Wesley's mid-century bungalow was a jumble of partially filled boxes and packing paper. His favorite clothes were gone, and his neighbor said he'd left his budgie in its cage on her doorstep last night, begging her to adopt it.

In other words, the fucker had skipped town.

With each bit of news, more sparks and smoke streamed from my mouth. I was pleased to see my magic returning, but I would have preferred having Wesley in my coils.

"Son of a fire breather," I muttered as Simon steered me out of Wesley's house. As soon as we were clear of the door, he grasped my hand and tugged me over to Van's SUV. "I wanted to scare that bastard. Make him give up his cohorts."

To say I was irritated was an understatement. My

dragon was itching to break free and burn Wesley's house to the ground. Sparks flew from my mouth at the idea. One blast of dragon fire is all it'd take to get things started.

"I know," Simon soothed. He rubbed his hand over my scale-covered arm. His touch calmed my rage. Not completely, but enough.

"What a useless day," I growled.

"Van said they got some leads. We'll know more when the results come back from their experts."

I clenched my teeth. We weren't doing enough. Those other supes were stuck in those cages. They could be sold or moved or tortured or magic only knew what before we found that building.

Van and Dillon came out a few minutes later.

"Find anything?"

Van pursed his lips and shook his head. He was spewing almost as much smoke as I was. "Nothing obvious. Norbert's people are still in there, sorting through every little thing for a clue, and a mage from the SC who specializes in finding cloaking spells is arriving tomorrow. They might still find something."

We all looked at the house again. No one had jumped out to scream "aha" or "eureka" or whatever people shouted when they discovered something remarkable. What other leads were there that we could follow up on?

"Whatever happened with those questions Hayden was going to ask his former pack mates?"

Van grimaced. "They didn't know anything."

"They didn't know anything, or they weren't talking?"

"As alpha, Hayden's senses are pretty sharp. He can identify when someone is lying almost as well as a hellhound. If he says they didn't know anything, I believe him."

"Fuck." I thought that summed things up perfectly.

"Not much else for us to do right now," Van said, rubbing the back of his neck.

This was *not* how the day was supposed to go.

"Oh, and Norbert said they found your car. Right where you said you left it by the lake."

"I'm guessing they didn't find any clues in it either?"

I doubted Wesley or his accomplices had even gone inside the car. They wouldn't have needed to because I'd been out of the car getting ready for my swim when they'd captured me.

"Not yet." Van shook his head. "They want to keep it for a couple more days though. The SC is sending in a team to go through everything again."

I sighed.

"Norbert's posting someone outside The Drunken Drake. Maybe your manager will come back, and we'll nab him there."

The tone of his voice said what I already knew. No one expected my former manager to come back. I'd never pegged Wesley as being smart or ambitious. The idea that he could abduct me *and* evade being caught all on his own was ridiculous. He must be working for someone. Then another thought hit me.

"About my office at the bar," I said, "he'd been in that room enough times to know there weren't any hiding places or secrets stashed in there. I remember thinking that it was loud when he first answered my call and then went somewhere quieter. At the time, I'd assumed he'd gone into the office. I bet he trashed it right after that like a toddler having a tantrum."

"I'll let Norbert know Wesley may not have been looking for anything. And if that's the case, he might not return. Although we can't be sure of that until we find him." Van looked at me. "So, that leads me to my next question, what do you want to do? Stay here or come back to Willow Lake? I'll be honest with you. I don't think you should stay in Aspen Bay, even with the local guys watching over your place. But the choice is yours."

"You can't stay here. It is too dangerous." Simon squeezed my hand like he was scared I'd disappear. His face had turned ashen.

"It's okay, kitty cat," I said softly. "I'll go back to Willow Lake with you. But I need to pack some clothes first."

"Oh, thank Magic." Simon released a gusty exhale.

I hated how much this situation was frightening him. All because of Wesley. For Wesley's sake, I hoped his helpers had gotten him out of the country, because if I ever saw him again, I'd show him exactly how fierce dragons could be.

Chapter Twenty-One

SIMON

We'd only been on the road to Willow Lake for a few minutes when blue scales rippled up and down Ogden's arms again. As lost as he was in his own thoughts, he seemed unaware he was clenching my hand. Could someone squeeze a hand tight enough to pop another person's fingers off? I hoped not. I also hoped his talons wouldn't erupt from his hands. The last thing I wanted was to have his claws slice into me. An injury like that wouldn't claim one of my nine, but I bet it would hurt, and I didn't like pain.

For as small and delicate as he appeared to me, I was beginning to see how dragons had gotten their fierce reputation all those centuries ago when they'd battled ignoble knights.

"Damn Wesley." Ogden spat out his manager's name like a curse word. Smoke and sparks erupted from his mouth and nostrils a second later.

"Do I smell something burning? There better not be singe marks in my upholstery," Van warned from the front seat.

That jolted Ogden from his literal and figurative fuming. He patted the back of the seat to extinguish the spot where one of his sparks had landed and the fabric had ignited. It was little more than a glowing, smoldering circle, but... yeah... having the seats on fire would be problematic.

"Sorry, Officer Hellhound," Ogden apologized. "Send me the repair bill."

If that'd been me, I'd have been tempted to pretend the scorch mark had always been there. Van never sat in the backseat, so how would he know? My father had raised us to never admit we were at fault for anything—well, except where my mama was concerned. She got the truth. But anyone else? No way. Cats didn't apologize. They were never wrong.

Of course, that'd been a lesson I had a hard time learning. My brothers were pros at it, but not me. I couldn't even blame that personality defect on my desire to keep my nine. It was just who I was.

But my dragon wasn't like my brothers or my father. He had integrity. Honor. I kind of liked that about him.

"I can't believe that little weasel could escape so easily," Ogden said.

"Hopefully they'll find something when they finish going through his house." Dillon twisted around to look at Ogden. "And something still might turn up from that tracking device."

"Let me know what you discover," Ogden said. He

didn't ask. He just expected to be kept in the loop. His confident attitude was sexy.

"Of course," Van promised.

After that, everyone settled into their own thoughts. When Dillon faced forward again, it felt like I was alone with Ogden, even if we weren't alone at all. I wished we were sitting beside one another, but the middle spot on the bench seat didn't have any leg room. I doubted even Ogden with his shorter legs would be comfortable there. So I contented myself with petting the back of his hand. Slowly, his grip relaxed.

He shot me a rueful smile. "Sorry, kitty cat. I'll be in a better mood now."

"It is okay to be upset," I said. We may have only started this... uh... bonded situation or whatever we were calling it, but I didn't want us to wear masks around one another. If we started that way, it'd be hard to take them off later.

This time, his smile was easier. "Thank you. I just... I'm not one for brooding. Never have been. I don't know what's come over me."

"A lot has happened," I said. "Is that why you were singing when you were in that...?" Shoot. I shouldn't have brought up his abduction. What if I upset him again?

"In the cage?" He wasn't shooting out sparks or smoke again, so maybe it was okay to talk about it.

I nodded.

He shrugged. "It's hard to be sad when a good song is playing."

I'd never paid much attention to music. I rarely had the radio on and couldn't remember the last time I listened to anything on my phone app. But music was obviously important to Ogden. And if he wanted songs, I could get them for him.

"Van, can you put the radio on? Something happy?"

Van's jaw tightened, but he didn't protest when Dillon played with the radio until he found a station. As soon as "Sh-Boom Sh-Boom" started, Ogden sang along. By the third or fourth song, he was bopping and rocking in his seat. His entire mood had transformed. Light fizzy bubbles of happiness tickled my insides as I watched him losing himself in the music. This wasn't magic like I was used to, but it was still magic. He was magic.

I don't know how many songs we listened to on the way home, but even Van was tapping his steering wheel in time to the music when we arrived back at Willow Lake. Van took us straight to my apartment, where we unloaded Ogden's many, many suitcases.

As they drove away, I heard Dillon say to Van, "Can you imagine Jeremy and Ogden fighting over the jukebox at the pub? We'll never hear another new release."

I wasn't sure I was ready for Jeremy and Ogden to hang out together yet. I wanted to keep my dragon to myself. But I didn't have any food in the house, at least nothing I'd want to feed Ogden, so we might meet up with Jeremy sooner than I wanted. Ogden deserved so much better than canned spaghetti. Although... now that I thought about it, did I even have any of that left? I might have eaten the last can a couple of weeks ago.

Yeah. We'd need to either go out or order in.

"Let's get this stuff upstairs," I said.

I set everything inside the door, even though I wanted

to carry it straight through to my bedroom. After all the kissing and other stuff we'd done this afternoon, I had ideas—many, many ideas—for what else we could do, but was I being presumptuous?

Ogden eyed his luggage sitting in the empty dining room area, then looked at me. "I didn't last long on the couch last time. Do you want to try that again?"

"Uh… no."

"Then why aren't we taking my bags through to your bedroom?"

Why indeed?

My heart thudded hard in my chest as I moved the bags. I don't know why it took seeing his suitcases in my bedroom to make me realize how quickly all this was happening. But this was it. He was staying here. With me. In my bed.

I swallowed hard. My body heated as I remembered what had happened in his apartment. In his hoard room, specifically.

But instead of pushing him onto the bed like I wanted so we could continue where we'd left off, we moved back to my sparsely decorated living room. I detoured to the kitchen and grabbed a couple of glasses of water. Unfortunately, all I had to offer him was water, although I wished I could give him a fancy coffee or a soothing tea. I really needed groceries.

As soon as I sat beside him on the sofa, he swung around to face me. He didn't straddle me this time though. Instead he sat with his back against the armrest and his legs stretched over mine.

What was I supposed to do with my hands? Could I

touch him? Rest my hand on his thigh? Put my arm around his shoulders?

Since he wasn't straddling me and he'd accepted the glass of water, I didn't think this position was a precursor for sex… at least not immediately. I clutched my glass in one hand, and I made sure at least an inch of space separated my free hand and any part of his body.

He smiled at me, like I amused him, as he motioned for my hand. "Give it here," he said. "I want you to touch me."

"Oh… uh… right," I mumbled.

He placed my hand so my palm rested on his leg, just above his knee. Then he placed his own hand on top of it. He sipped his water and leaned into me. I exhaled slowly and felt the tension ease away.

"That's better," he said.

We sat in silence for a few minutes, and I relaxed more. I didn't remember ever sitting quietly with someone before and having it be so comfortable. My brothers were always arguing or teasing or being a-holes. My mama was always spreading advice or asking questions. And Pops was never without my mama, although I suspected he would like to sit quietly sometimes too, if given the chance.

But maybe I should take this time to get to know Ogden better.

"Your apartment is nicer than mine," I said.

"Thank you," he said, obviously used to compliments. "I think it'll be easy to sell."

"Sell?"

He nodded. "I'll have to set up a meeting with a real

estate agent soon. I want to get it on the market before fall."

"Why do you want to sell? Is it because of that Wesley guy? They're going to catch him, you know."

He nodded, then he cocked his head and looked at me. "Oh dear. With everything that's been going on, I guess I never talked to you about..." For the first time since meeting Ogden, his cheeks darkened.

"Are you blushing?" I reached up and traced my finger over his heated skin.

His cheeks darkened even more.

"Yes. Well," he said as he cleared his throat. He turned the glass in his hands and stared at the water as it swirled. "Since the summoning magic has linked us, I thought we should live closer together."

"You'd sell everything because of me?" I blinked.

"I can't see you living in Aspen Bay," he said with a casual shrug, as if him upending his life, which was way more complicated than mine, was no big deal.

If anyone should move, it should be me. He owned buildings and businesses and had employees. What did I have? An awful one-bedroom apartment and a security guard job for a place where nothing ever happened. I liked my job well enough, but there was nothing special about it. I could fit all my clothes in about one or two boxes and throw away everything else. It'd take me an afternoon at most to pack up and move.

But I didn't say any of those words because Ogden was right. I couldn't see myself living anywhere but Willow Lake. My brother Justin was the adventurous one in the family, not me. I enjoyed living in the town where I'd grown up, being surrounded by all the familiar faces and places and...

Ogden squeezed my hand. "Is it okay if I move to Willow Lake to be closer to you?"

I stuttered as I scrambled to find the right words.

"I've surprised you." He smiled and patted my hand.

"Where would you live?" Did that sound like I didn't want him here? I wasn't sure I did. I mean, even I didn't want to live here, but I put up with it because this was all I could afford. Ogden needed to live somewhere so much nicer.

"This is a big change for both of us. What would you think about me living here... with you?"

"Your hoard won't fit in my apartment," I blurted.

"No. I wouldn't bring my hoard to Willow Lake. Not yet. I'll arrange for it to be placed at a secure storage site." His gaze caught on mine, and my heart raced. "I love my place in Aspen Bay, it's true. I loved renovating it and making it mine, but it is time for a change and a new challenge. Until I figure out what that might be, I was hoping I could live with you."

"But..." I looked around my apartment. The drab one-bedroom place was nothing like his. At all.

"It feels... I don't know... Ever since our magics merged, I don't want to be separated from you," he said. He bit his bottom lip as his gaze caught on mine. "Is it different for you? Maybe it is just another factor of being summoned instead of being the summoner."

"No!" My emphatic shout startled us both. I licked my lips. "I mean. Yes, I've felt that too. But..." I gestured toward my apartment. "I'm not sure this is the best place."

"Well, perhaps we shouldn't stay in this apartment for too long," he agreed. "But I was hoping we could look for another place. Together."

"Are you offering to be my sugar daddy?"

Ogden burst out laughing. I loved that I had made him laugh, even if my question hadn't been intended as a joke. "I was thinking more about being your mate, but I will lavish you with everything your heart might desire, so perhaps your description isn't so far off. Even if we aren't fated, we could still see if we are compatible as chosen mates."

"Okay. Because I don't think I could call you Daddy."

Ogden was still smiling, but his laughter had faded. "Whatever you feel comfortable with, kitty cat. That's what we'll do."

Was it that simple? "And you too, right? We both need to be comfortable."

"Of course." He pressed a kiss to my cheek.

"I know we talked about that before. About us maybe being mates, I mean." I forced myself to look into his eyes. Since I'd met Ogden, there were moments when I felt sure and brave and confident, but my nature was to be cautious. There were also moments when I was convinced we were mates, but doubts kept popping up like dandelions. I usually liked dandelions, but right now, the ones in my head were big and full and ready to spread more doubts until that's all that existed. "Do you really think we are?"

He nodded as he set his glass down on the floor. Then he plucked the glass from my hand and set it beside his. When he turned back to me, he met my gaze again. "Yes, love, I really think we could be."

"I want us to be," I whispered as a light and fluttery sensation filled my chest.

The kiss was soft and gentle. And more of that light and fluttery feeling filled me until I was sure I could fly as high as Ogden had the first time I'd seen him. I liked it, which was weird, because cats don't fly.

"Now, kitty cat," Ogden said as he nipped at my earlobe and rearranged his legs, so he was straddling me just like he had when we were in his hoard room, "do you remember what I said about good kitties getting rewards?"

Chapter Twenty-Two

OGDEN

My kitty cat sucked in a sharp breath at my question.

"Rewards?" Simon asked. His eyes were wide, and his pupils were compressing into vertical slits, showing how close to the surface his shifter side was.

"Yes, love," I whispered in his ear. "I want to make you feel good, to be deep inside you when you fall apart."

"Yes." He gulped. "Yes. Let's do that."

"You're going to look so good on your hands and knees, waiting for my cock."

Simon slipped his hand behind my head and pulled me down to kiss him. Our mouths collided with the same fury as they had in my hoard room. We pulled at one another's clothing, throwing a shirt over my shoulder, dropping another behind the couch... The pants were challenging because neither of us wanted to separate, but we got it done. I tried to push off my underwear next, but Simon grabbed my hands.

"No." His voice was rough and deep. "Let me see."

Oh, my kitty cat liked my underwear. I grinned and wiggled my hips. He swallowed hard. It was a good thing I'd packed a lot more. Van and Dillon might have complained about all my suitcases, but they contained very important things… like two weeks' worth of silky and lacy undies in almost every color in the rainbow.

Simon's thick fingers slipped across the smooth fabric. His breath quickened as he traced the outline of my hard dick through the fabric. I braced my hands on his shoulders as I rose on my knees to give him more access. A wet spot stained the silk, and he rubbed his thumb across it. His tongue dipped out and slid along his top lip like he was imagining his mouth following the same route as his thumb. I shivered and moaned under his touch.

His gaze shot up to catch on mine. "You like that?"

"I think I'd like anything you did to me."

Emboldened by my words, he cupped my erection. The heat of his palm bled through the thin fabric. I was so hard now I thought the silk would rip under the pressure. With his other hand, he cradled my balls. His gentle touch almost undid me.

But I didn't want to come until he did.

I leaned forward and drew my lips across his neck, just like I'd done earlier. He tilted his head to the side to give me more access.

"I want to bite you," I murmured against his throat. I nipped at the taut skin. "Right here."

"Yes," he whispered as his hips rocked and his hands tightened on my cock and balls in the most delicious way.

"We should move to the bed."

He groaned his disappointment at the delay.

I expected him to release me so I could climb off him, but he wrapped his arms around me and somehow stood with me clinging to him. He carried me into his bedroom and sat down on the mattress, still holding me. I was stronger than most supes, but seeing his strength and ability to haul me around was a huge turn-on.

I pushed on his shoulders until his back hit the mattress.

"Good kitty cat," I murmured. "Now it's my turn to play. But if any of this is too much, tell me."

"I can handle you," he said, punctuating his words with a soft huff of breath and an eye roll. For as much as he called himself a scaredy cat, my kitty wasn't timid in bed. I liked it.

I started with kisses. I covered his face and his neck and shoulders with soft, teasing touches of my lips to his skin. Dropping a few on his temples and along his throat again and at the corner of his mouth. He turned to capture my mouth with his, but I didn't linger. I could get lost in his mouth, spend hours luxuriating in the gentle tug of his lips and the warm sweep of his tongue against mine. But we had a lifetime to kiss and make love.

Tonight, I wanted to get to know him, play his body until he created the sweetest sounds of want and need and pleasure. I wanted to discover what made his pulse quicken from allegro to vivace to presto, to rejoice in all the tones of his breaths and his moans as he gave himself over to pleasure, to explore how beautifully our bodies could harmonize...

Because we would harmonize, and it would be beautiful. There was no doubt in my mind.

With each brush of my fingers and sweep of my tongue, his body became my favorite instrument. Gorgeous. He wrapped his fingers in the sheets. Sweat coated his skin. His erection stood proud of his hips.

"Ogden, please," Simon begged.

I'd told him I wanted him to beg, but I hadn't intended to make him suffer.

"I got lost in your body, kitty cat," I whispered against his navel. "I won't make you wait much longer, I promise. Just let me get you ready." I looked around, but his bedside table didn't have any drawers. "Do you have lube?"

He muttered a curse, then he lifted me off his body. He raced to his dresser and pulled out... a box with a lock? Then he grabbed a pair of socks from another drawer, unfolded them, and dumped out a tiny key. He fumbled, trying to put the key in the lock. Finally, the two lined up and there was a click. He threw back the lid and wrapped his hand around a bottle of lube. He lifted it, brandishing it like a victor with his spoils.

"Simon, love, why is your lube in a locked box in your drawer?"

He looked at the box, then at the lube. "Uh... my brothers used to steal it. They always went through theirs faster than I did. They still do."

I squished up my nose. Families could share a lot of things, but I didn't think lube should be one of them. That was a discussion for another day. I would have a nice long chat with his brothers, all five of them, about personal boundaries. I took the lube from Simon and motioned him to come back to the bed. The lube was the cheapest brand available. It would work, I was sure, but that would be something else I'd need to change. My kitty cat deserved the best of everything, including lubricant.

"You go through that every time you want to touch yourself?"

He scratched the back of his head and bit his bottom lip.

"Simon?"

"I don't usually worry about lube. I mostly use spit, or if I'm in the shower, soap."

That would definitely be changing. If our relationship progressed as I suspected it might, we'd be getting naked a lot. Friction and discomfort were not part of the plan. Lube was one of the best inventions of the modern era. We would use it. A lot of it.

"I've dreamed of taking you from behind. You on your hands and knees. Do you want that?"

"Yes," Simon hissed. Then he tossed me the lube and crawled to the center of the bed. He raised his ass as if presenting it to me. He was beautiful like this, breathtaking really, with his thick thighs, his round smooth ass, and then there was his hole. Right there. Begging to be touched.

I dropped the bottle of lube on the mattress, needing to explore him a little more before we went any further. I spread my hands over his lower back and stroked up to his shoulders before drawing them down again to the base of his spine. His breath quickened as I did it again and again. Did he enjoy being petted like this?

When his legs started to shake, I let my touch skate lower to his ass. He whimpered. He was pure perfection. His skin was so soft. His ass was begging to be squeezed and spanked and bitten.

"Ogden, you said you wouldn't make me wait."

"Yes, yes," I said, as I reached for the lube. It was so damn easy to get distracted by his beautiful body. I coated my fingers. My heartbeats quickened as I pulled his ass cheeks apart to look at his tight hole. "So pretty."

I needed a quick taste first. As soon as I swept my tongue over him, he purred. I'd heard him purr before, but he usually tried to cover it up. He didn't this time. Maybe he didn't even know he was doing it. I licked and tongued him until I didn't think I could last much longer. The heady scent of his pre-cum told me Simon was right there with me.

My fingers slipped against him, and he shuddered. His purring grew louder.

"Ready?"

"So fucking—I mean freaking—ready," he mumbled.

I grinned. I'd never heard my kitty cat swear before. Not like that. I pressed the tip of my finger against his hole. He pushed back against it. Then my finger slipped into his perfect, tight heat. We both groaned.

"More," he demanded.

So I gave him more. When his entrance was slippery and prepped, I crawled over him. He was taller than me, but I was determined to make this an amazing experience for both of us. That meant biting.

Biting during sex wouldn't create a mating bond—as much as I wished it were true, human storytellers got that wrong—but it created an energy exchange that was exhilarating. As I released into him, I'd bite him and his blood would go into me, and if we were lucky, some magic might happen. Folklore said that if the energy exchange was particularly intense, it could be a sign you were with your fated mate. I expected our exchange would be nuclear.

"Can I bite you?"

He shivered and nodded.

"Words. I need words."

"Yes. Bite me. And hurry up."

I snickered, but I wasn't about to argue with him. We both wanted this. I reached for my cock. Fuck. I still had my damn underwear on. I shoved them down and positioned myself at his opening. My breath caught at the first brush of my tip against his crease.

This was so much better than being with a human. I was always so worried about hurting a human, but with a supe I could let go. And since supes couldn't transmit or contract sexual infections or diseases, we didn't need to use condoms. I would be with him, bare skin to bare skin. I almost came just from the thought of it.

And then I was pressing against him. Into him. Joining our bodies as closely as two bodies could be. He was beautiful perfection, exactly as I'd imagined.

His body harmonized with mine. His bubble butt cushioned my thrusts. His groans were the most beautiful sounds I'd ever heard. The air itself seemed to sing around us. And then a wild explosion of color exploded from me, originating in my chest where I'd always imagined my magic lived. The whirl of color encompassed every shade that made up my dragon's magic—the cobalt blue of water, the pale pastel blue of the sky, the vibrant yellow of fire. They flowed like ribbons from me, wrapping around the two of us like a cocoon.

"Ogden," Simon gasped, as another color—a verdant green—joined my magic. It was Simon's, and it was stunning.

I'd felt Simon's magic when our magics had connected during the summoning, but it was nothing like this. This was full, alive, powerful. Whatever magic the whistle contained, this was a thousand times stronger.

Our bodies moved in beautiful synchronicity, just like our magic. The tempo of our movements quickened, building to an explosive crescendo, chasing a beautiful bliss that could only be found with one another. My claws and teeth elongated as Simon twisted his head to the side, exposing the length of his neck to me. I bit down as euphoria grabbed me and threw me over the edge. Simon shook under me with his own orgasm. Everything erupted in a stunning display of color and magic and sweet ecstasy.

Simon collapsed beneath me, and I rolled us to our sides, not willing to separate our bodies yet. I wanted this connection to last forever and ever.

When our bodies cooled, and our breaths calmed, I reluctantly rolled away from Simon. I stumbled toward his bathroom and found a threadbare washcloth under the sink. I returned with the warm wet cloth to find Simon hadn't moved. His skin was flushed and sweaty. The red spot on his neck where I'd bitten him was already fading more quickly than I'd hoped. I wiped my spend and the lube from his body. I wished I had another cloth to wipe away his sweat too, but this was the only clean cloth I'd seen in his bathroom.

I nudged him until he rolled onto his back. His wide eyes watched me as I cleaned cum off his soft stomach with gentle strokes. His cheeks darkened with my actions, but he didn't turn away or avert his eyes. When I was done, I tossed the cloth toward the bathroom. It didn't make it that far, but we could get it later. Right now, all I wanted to do was to hold Simon, except our releases had soaked into the blanket, right in the middle of the bed. No one should have to deal with the wet spot.

"Roll to the side," I whispered. He did. Then I pushed the messy blanket off the bed. Damn it, I needed to get another one from the closet. I ran to the closet and grabbed one of the blankets he'd given me last night. I spread it out over him, then I crawled in beside him.

We faced one another.

"Are you okay, love?" I pushed his sweat slick hair off his forehead so I could see his beautiful green eyes.

"Did you see that? The magic… It… I've never…"

"Yeah. I saw it." I drew my fingers down his cheek. There was nothing sexual in what I was doing now, but I just… I couldn't stop touching him.

"Do you think that means we're fated mates?"

That's exactly what I thought, but I couldn't tell from his tone how he felt about it. He was cautious, my kitty cat. I didn't want to push him if he wasn't ready to admit it yet. I could be patient. "What do you think?"

"Yes, I think that's what it means," he said, much more decisively than I would have expected of him. His gaze held mine. "I think you are my fated mate."

I swallowed around a lump in my throat. "I think you might be right."

"Why wouldn't the Eternal Magic have blessed us then?" His gaze drifted up and down my body, not in a sexy way. He was searching for something. "We don't have matching marks that show us as fated mates, at least not that I can see."

"She is all knowing," I said after I'd given his question some thought. "Perhaps she doesn't feel we are ready yet."

"Willow Lake has a lot of fated mates. I heard someone say we now have more fated mate pairings than some big cities. But I... I never believed I'd find mine too." His eyes were glossy when he met my gaze. "Do you think she will bless us?"

"Absolutely. I don't doubt it for a moment."

His smile was beautiful as he scooted closer and wrapped his arms around me. We stayed like that, silently holding one another, for a long, long time.

In some ways, being fated mates wouldn't change much between us. We had connected through the summoning magic. Our relationship was already physical. And we'd agreed to live together.

Except... Once Wesley and the others discovered our bond, I expected them to try to exploit it. They'd chosen to abduct me for a reason. They'd even embedded a tracking device in my arm so they could find me if I escaped. I doubted they were done with me yet.

Suddenly I was even more determined to find Wesley and eliminate him and his cohorts, because our relationship put Simon at risk. I could handle them threatening me, but if they came for Simon to get to me, I couldn't deal with that. At all. Simon was more precious than anything in my hoard.

I had the urge to shift and coil around him, hold him tight and keep him safe from the rest of the world, but this was enough. For the moment.

Chapter Twenty-Three

OGDEN

Two mornings later, Van delivered my phone. Simon was still at work, and normally I would still be asleep at this time of day, but as soon as Van put the phone in my hand, I was wide awake.

I hadn't realized how much I'd missed having it until I held it. I plugged it in using Simon's cords and waited impatiently until it had charged enough to turn on. The first things I checked were my text messages and emails. As suspected, neither my sister nor my parents had noticed I was missing. Granted, I'd only been absent for less than a week, but still. I sent everyone a quick update before moving on to check on my employees.

My staff was shocked and upset by everything that'd happened. When they discovered I was moving, several asked if I was establishing a pub in Willow Lake, offering to follow me. I had to think about that. Willow Lake already had a local spot for supes to hang out, at least from what Simon said. I hadn't been there yet myself. I doubted a place the size of Willow Lake could sustain two similar businesses.

So what would I do here?

I started a list on my phone of possible new careers.

I checked on my investments next. Happily, Wesley hadn't gotten his filthy little hands on any of those. Not that I'd expected he could. Supe investment firms, like the one I used, took long-term investments seriously, since most of their clients lived much longer lives than humans. A lot of spells and wards protected the accounts, and nothing could be accessed or moved quickly or easily. Just to be sure, though, I changed all my passwords.

Then I moved on to more entertaining activities, like shopping.

My little kitty cat needed so much—clothes, dishes, cutlery, towels, bedding, personal hygiene products, groceries—it was difficult to decide where to turn my attention first. Oh, who was I kidding? Of course I started with clothes. At some point, I wanted to get Simon an appointment with my London tailor, but I didn't want to go abroad just now. Instead, I scrolled through the latest fashions in the best clothing boutiques I could find with an online shopping app. It would have been better to go to the shops in person, but we couldn't all have what we wanted. After the fourth website, I finally found clothes I thought my kitty cat would wear, except they were a thousand times nicer than anything he currently owned.

Simon arrived home just as I put another shirt in my digital shopping cart.

"Come, come," I said, waving him over. "I have so much to show you."

Simon kicked off his shoes, then warily approached the couch, which I'd been using as my personal office.

"Van stopped by to drop off my phone." I held it up, as if he could miss it.

"Okay…" Simon sat beside me.

I brushed a kiss across his cheek, then snuggled in close. I'd been an independent dragon for a lot of years, rarely inviting a prospective partner back to my place, but I loved cuddling with my kitty cat. He put his arm around my shoulders and tilted his head so it rested against mine.

"What did you want to show me?"

"I haven't purchased anything yet, but I would really like to get you a few new things."

"What kinds of things? Like for the apartment?"

I shook my head. "Clothes."

"I have clothes." He sounded confused.

"Everyone can always use more," I said, not bothering to point out how dismal his wardrobe currently was.

"You don't have to do that."

I turned and brushed another kiss against his cheek. "I want to."

"I… I…" He stammered.

"What is it, love?" This time, I sat up so I could face him.

"I can't dress like you and wear bright orange and fire engine red or vivid purple or lemon yellow or—"

I cut off his panicked words with a kiss. When we separated, I smiled at him. "Of course not."

"Okay, good." He sighed and relaxed.

"I found some beautiful blues that match my dragon scales because I love the idea of dressing you in my colors." I flashed the screen toward him. "And some lovely greens that complement your beautiful eyes." I scrolled down the many, many things in the shopping cart. "And some new jeans to hug your sexy bubble butt."

"I don't have a bubble butt."

"Of course, you do, and it is extremely biteable." I snapped my teeth at him.

His cheeks darkened. "Is that why I have a bruise on my bum today? Every time I sat down, I felt it."

I grinned at him. "I bet you thought of me every time."

"I think about you all the time anyway," he muttered.

"I think about you all the time too." Confessions like that were difficult for my kitty cat, so I rewarded him with another kiss. I didn't pull away until his lips were swollen, and his breaths changed to soft panting bursts. He looked wrecked, just the way I liked him. "Do you absolutely hate anything I selected?"

"Huh?" He blinked at me. Then he shook his head and dropped his gaze back to my phone. "Oh, you're talking about the clothes?"

I turned the screen to him again.

"You don't need to spend money on me. I have clothes."

"I want to spoil you. Sugar daddy, remember?" I grinned.

He groaned. "I wish you'd forget I said that."

"Okay, if you don't have any objections, I'm buying everything." I tapped the checkout button, checking to make sure I'd selected their expedited delivery. Then it was done.

"No, you shouldn't—"

"Already done," I said.

"Ogden…" He stretched my name out over several more syllables than it had as he flopped back on the couch.

"Simon…" I mimicked the way he'd said my name as I crawled onto his lap and tossed my phone aside. I was about to kiss him again when his phone rang. He groaned.

"That'll be my mother. She's called every twenty minutes for the last two hours to make sure I remember to bring you to breakfast this morning."

I sighed. Another Rivers family breakfast wasn't how I'd envisioned my morning going, but all relationships required compromise.

"I can tell her you are still sleeping," he said.

"It's fine, kitty cat. I'll go with you." Someday, maybe, we could establish some boundaries and new traditions, but for now, it looked like breakfast with the Rivers family was part of my new routine.

Breakfast at his parents' place was a more relaxing experience this time. Simon's father was much the same, but his mother was all smiles, and his brothers hadn't tried to scare me to death in a car. Perhaps things were improving. They'd all been shocked about what we'd found out in Aspen Bay. Clive, Warren, and the twins mouthed off about hunting down my abductors on their own, until their mother went around and pinched each of their ears. She didn't let go until they promised they wouldn't go looking for trouble.

My happiest moment, though, was when we were on

our way back out the door again. They were all nice enough people, but I wasn't used to having so many people knowing so much about me and my life. It would take some time to get used to.

As soon as we were back in Simon's apartment, we crawled into bed and kissed until we fell asleep again. We woke to Simon's phone ringing. For a shy guy, he had a lot of people calling him all the time.

"Hello?"

"Hi, Simon, did you get my text?" In the quiet of the bedroom, I could hear both sides of the conversation.

"Huh? Who is this?"

"It's Jeremy! Hey, you sound groggy. Did I wake you up? Sorry about that!" Jeremy sounded as full of energy as he had when I met him at the police station. "So, there's been a change of plans. We're going to postpone movie night. When I set it up, I forgot Saturdays were the busiest night of the week at the pub. We'll do it some other time."

"Uh. Okay."

A voice in the background on Jeremy's side rumbled something, but I couldn't make out the words.

"Yeah, yeah. I'm getting to it," Jeremy said to whoever he was with.

Another mumble.

"Anyway," he said loudly, and I figured he was talking to Simon again, "instead of movie night on the weekend, we're going to play board games tonight. Jake's never done that either, can you believe it? Everything starts at seven, so we'll see you then, okay? See you there."

He hung up before Simon could respond. Knowing Simon the way I did, he'd now feel obliged to go because he hadn't been able to say no. Jeremy was a sneaky bastard; I liked him.

Simon looked at me. "I… Uh…"

"I heard, kitty cat. It sounds like fun." I patted him on the chest. "I'd like to get to know your friends."

"They aren't really my friends," he said. "Jeremy started calling and texting me one day. I don't really encourage him, but he keeps doing it." Simon shrugged, like he didn't understand Jeremy's actions.

"Sounds like he thinks you are friends." Yep. I knew I liked that guy. "He has excellent taste in friends. Do you not like him?"

"No. He's okay. He's a little strange, but a lot of people in Willow Lake are weird."

"Perfect. Then let's go. I'd love to get to know him and the others. I thoroughly enjoy strange and weird people."

A few minutes before seven, we were sitting in Simon's car outside the Willow Lake Pub and Inn. I recognized the area. This was close to where Simon had been when he'd blown the whistle. Van's vehicle had been in this same lot that night. I hadn't paid much attention to anything but Simon at the time, but now I took it all in.

The old brick building was rundown, the type of place I'd been looking for when I found The Drunken Drake. It had character, but needed… well, I would say TLC, but a ruthless and critical approach would serve it better, along with lots and lots of money.

"Are you sure you want to do this?" Simon asked, making no move to get out. Whatever happy euphoria had clung to us since we'd made love had diminished during our trip to the pub.

"If you don't want to, we don't have to go, kitty cat," I reassured him. I brushed my hand over his arm. He liked it when I petted him, so I did it again.

"If you're really moving here..." He let his sentence hang between us uncompleted.

"I am." I nodded, not sure where he was going with his thought.

He sighed. "Then you should meet more people than my family."

He looked so apprehensive. I petted him some more.

"I can meet them anytime."

A knock at my window made us both jolt. How in the Magic had someone caught us both by surprise? I spun around to see Van leaning over and peering through the window at us.

"You coming in?" he asked. His question was muffled because I hadn't rolled down the window, but I heard him well enough. I waved him off. He laughed, but at least he left.

"I guess we have to go in now," Simon muttered. "They know we're here."

"We really don't." I didn't enjoy seeing my cat so agitated. "Do you not like the place?"

"I come here two or three times a week," he admitted.

"Oh?" Wait. "Are you embarrassed to be seen out with me?"

Simon's gaze leaped to mine. "Magic, no! That's not it at all. I just... You're you. You're going to meet all of them and wonder why Mother Magic stuck you with me. You're amazing. I'm just..." He shrugged. "Just Simon. Just a cat."

"Stop that," I snapped.

He cringed.

That was not what I'd intended. I hated hearing him talk about himself that way. And I hated he was parroting back the words I'd said that first night.

"Simon, I could never be disappointed with you. The Eternal Magic doesn't make mistakes. I guess it'll take some time for you to realize that, but I'm thrilled to have found you. I'd given up on finding my fated mate, and now here you are. Do you even know the last time I took someone to my bed?"

Simon growled.

"I'm not saying that to make you jealous," I said quickly. "I just... I'm saying this all wrong. What I'm trying to explain is that I chose you. Even before our magics put on their little show for us. I chose to be with you."

"It was the whistle."

"Of course it wasn't," I scoffed.

"You don't think so?"

"No."

"I don't want you to regret us. Regret me."

"Never."

He still didn't look convinced, but he looked more relaxed than he had. "Let's go inside."

"Only if you're sure."

He nodded.

It was a weeknight, so the pub had several empty tables. A song from the '80s that should have stayed in the '80s was blasting from the jukebox. The '80s weren't my favorite musical era.

Just inside the door to the right was a pool table. A large man, a bear shifter I thought, was leaning over to take a shot. His ass was almost as squeezable and bubble-esque as my Simon's. Almost.

Two sets of eyes peered out at us from what I assumed was the kitchen, based on the smells coming from that direction. As soon as they saw me, they started whispering to one another. I smiled at them. They ducked into the kitchen.

A woman was pouring pints behind the long counter. She smiled at Simon, then cast an assessing eye over me. I knew I looked good. My sweater, fuchsia with black leather detailing at the collar and cuffs, hugged my body perfectly, and my slim-fitting trousers in a gorgeous eggplant color complemented the top. I didn't normally dress in such understated clothes, but my kitty cat wasn't used to the attention my normal wardrobe would draw. Although, I supposed Willow Lake was small enough that people would stare at me no matter what I wore, just because I was the stranger who'd come in with one of their own.

"That's Alice. She's a brownie," Simon said. "Her mom and my mama are best friends. I think Mama always hoped one of us kittens would marry her."

I frowned and hooked my arm around Simon's. Simon was off the market. Everyone needed to know that. I steered him away from the bar and toward the group gathered on the far side of the room. They were standing around a few tables that had been pushed together. Someone had turned up the lights in this section too, although I doubted most of the supes would need the brighter light to play any of the games stacked on the tables.

Jeremy stood in the middle of them all, hugging a Scrabble box to his chest.

"Absolutely not." A small fire mage was shaking his head vehemently beside him. "I am not playing Scrabble with you. I told you the last time we played that I'd never do it again."

Jeremy frowned. "You're my BFF, Ash. Why are you being so mean? You know it's my favorite."

"Nope," Ash said, crossing his arms over his chest. "You read too much. Your vocabulary is…" He waved his hand through the air, like he couldn't find the right word. "Obscene."

"I can keep it PG." Jeremy pouted.

"Being PG isn't the issue. I'm not talking about the words themselves, Jer. I'm talking about the fact that you know and can spell damn near every word in the dictionary."

"We could make it fun. Like… Oh. I know. If you don't care about the words, we could do bonus points for anyone who can form the word fellatio or coitus or—"

The other man let out a groan. "This is what I'm talking about. You could have said blowjob or sex like a normal person, but you didn't."

"Blowjob and sex are easy. Someone could put down low, or blow, or job and someone else could build from it. And sex is only three letters long. Fellatio or coitus would take more work and planning. Although, I guess someone could put down the word fell…"

Ash turned to the others who'd gathered around the table. "Can someone else help me here?"

A centaur with long blond hair laughed. I remembered him from the meeting at the police station. I thought his name was Isaac. "I agree with Ash. The boss man here," he slapped Gage on the shoulder, "he's been around a long time. He knows too many obscure words and he'd probably try to throw in old English spelling or something."

Jeremy smiled eagerly at the demon. "Do you like Scrabble, Mr. Dimples? We should play some time."

"Does that mean you agree we aren't playing that tonight?"

"Fine. Yes." Jeremy rolled his eyes.

"Good," a calico cat said from where he was sitting beside the stack of games. "Because I can't play Scrabble."

That was no ordinary cat or cat shifter. Interesting. I hadn't expected to see him here. Willow Lake was just one surprise after another.

"You want to play too, Paws?" Ash asked. He looked at the games. "Uh... I guess we could play Hungry, Hungry Hippos."

I imagined the ancient being slapping his paw against a plastic hippo's butt, and it was spectacular. I scanned the pile of boxes. Did they have that game? Because I wouldn't mind recording that and sending it to my family. They'd laugh their asses off.

"That's for children!" the cat protested.

"Well, you don't have opposable thumbs. I don't know what else you could play. You can't hold cards. You can't pull pieces out from a Jenga stack. You can't hold a pencil to draw a picture for Pictionary. We can see about getting some devices to help with that in the future—I'm sure someone must have invented something that will work—but I don't know what we can do about tonight."

"These games suck," Paws said. His tail whipped back and forth in a vicious tempo. "And you're all assholes for bringing them here." Then he started cleaning his face with his paw.

Jeremy's shoulders slumped at Paws' proclamation. He looked around at the others, as if silently asking what they should do. That's when he spotted Simon and me.

"You came!" Jeremy shouted. "Awesome. We're deciding what game to play."

Simon cringed when everyone turned to look at us.

"Hello," I said, stepping forward, drawing everyone's eyes to me instead. "I'm Ogden."

"The dragon shifter," Jeremy added with a wide smile, like any of the supes in the room wouldn't have already known that. "You already know my sexy wolf man Adrian and his team of Super Supes." He waved toward Gage, Teague, Isaac, and Davina in one encompassing motion. "And Van, of course. You know him too. I haven't heard from Weston, Nelson, or Hayden yet, but I'm hoping they'll join us too."

"I think Weston said something about watching over the teenagers who were partying at the shore tonight. He hates it when they have bonfires by *his* lake," Ash said. He used air quotes around the word *his*.

"Oh, right," Jeremy said.

Jake averted his eyes. "And Nelson's… uh… *busy*."

"Are you making Nelson work tonight, Mr. Dimples?" Jeremy demanded.

"No, it's nothing like that…" Jake shifted from side to side. "He saw a *painting* I did, and I wish he hadn't. It is all he thinks about now."

"About him and the unicorn?" Van asked.

Jake looked up, startled. "How did you…?"

"I didn't, not really. You just confirmed my suspicions."

"I thought Nelson was interested in Carter," Isaac whispered to Teague.

Teague shrugged. "I guess not anymore."

Isaac stroked his chin and eyed the big bear shifter by the pool table. "I might go play pool for a bit."

"No, don't leave…" Jeremy said, but Isaac was already halfway across the room. Jeremy turned back to me. "Anyway, I don't think you've met Ash yet. He's my BFF forever and Dillon's mate." I'd already picked up on that based on the matching fire-like marks on their necks. "And this is Jake, our local oracle, aka Gage's mate, aka the owner of the pub. It's because of Jake that we're here tonight."

"It's nice to meet you all," I said with a nod.

"We haven't met yet," the calico cat said. "I'm Pawington the Third."

I studied the creature. "Are you sure we haven't met?"

Paws blinked. Everyone around us gaped. I leaned close to whisper in one of the cat's calico ears. When I was done, Paws shot a panicked look around the group.

"Don't worry. I won't tell anyone your secret." I winked at the powerful being.

The cat's tail jolted back and forth, then he raised one

of his paws and started cleaning his face. I laughed and ruffled the fur on the top of his head.

Jeremy's eyes bulged. He looked around at everyone at the table. "Isn't anyone going to ask?"

Jake shook his head at Jeremy. The movement made his collar shift a little, showing a bit of a mark that looked like the one on the demon. Those must be their mate marks.

No one asked me about the cat. I was surprised at their restraint, but it didn't matter because the cat's secret was safe with me.

"Don't blame this event on me," Jake said, taking the attention off Paws and looking at Jeremy. "This was all your idea."

"You said you'd never played a board game. You can't say that and think we won't do anything about it."

A massive wolf and a raven with matching mating marks in their hair were cuddling one another at the far end of the table. That meant the Eternal Magic had blessed four of the couples in this room alone. That was... well... unheard of. And based on the way they were together, they all seemed newly mated. Willow Lake was truly magical. The Eternal Magic seemed to draw mates here, and I was now even more convinced that Simon was my fated mate too. The raven wore a fabulous outfit that twinkled with his every movement. I caught the raven eying my clothes with a similarly covetous appreciation. How lovely to find a kindred spirit.

"That's Mercer and Oak," Simon said, nodding to the couple. Then he looked around the room. "Over there at the pool table, that's Carter rubbing chalk on his pool cue.

He's playing against Levi, who is a minotaur. Parker... that's the redheaded guy sitting at the table watching them... he's human. Doesn't know about supes, I don't think, so we probably shouldn't talk too loudly."

I nodded. Carter was the one with the nice ass I'd seen when we'd first come in, but Levi and Parker were the ones who caught my attention. I wasn't even a succubus, and I found the sexual tension pouring off them scrumptious. I had a whole set dedicated to helping people take those last few steps to admitting their love for one another. I might not have had many relationships myself, but I was a sucker for watching other people fall in love. Hmm... What would it take to get these two over that hurdle? If I was on stage watching this unfold, I'd go with my version of Alicia Keys' "Fallin'" and follow it up with James Blunt's "You're Beautiful" and then adapt what came next based on what they did.

"So, what'll it be?" Jeremy asked. "What are we playing?"

"What about Wits and Wagers?" Ash asked. "I think Paws could play that one."

Paws sniffed the box, then lifted his head quickly as if embarrassed at having done that. "Speaking of wagers, where is Hayden?" the cat asked, as if determined to turn everyone's attention away from him.

"Hasn't he been in?" Van asked.

"Not today." Jake shook his head. "He hasn't been in much at all lately."

"He told me..." Van's forehead furrowed. "Never mind."

"Finding out about what Robbie was doing seems to

have hit him hard," Mercer said. Oak wrapped his arms around Mercer and held him tight as soon as he said Hayden's brother's name. I wondered what Robbie had done to them, because there was obviously some trauma there. "Robbie was always a little asshole, and I for one am happy his pack of delinquents in the hills is gone. I never liked the guy, but even I never would have expected him to have people caged on his property. It must have been a real shock for Hayden."

"What wager is he talking about?" I asked Simon.

"There is a bet going on right now about how long it'll take him to accept he's the alpha. If you want to put your name down for a date, check with Paws. He's sort of in charge of it."

Willow Lake was a strange place.

I laughed more than I'd thought I would as we played. Simon even started to relax about half an hour in, and that made everything so much better. I was invited to their weekly community potluck on Sunday, which was being held in the parking lot until renovations to the inn were further along. Everyone—including Simon—warned me to steer clear of his mama's mystery casserole. I was half-tempted to try it at the next gathering because it seemed like a rite of passage.

A while later, I went to the bar to order a round of drinks. I'd always found that free drinks went over well when you were making new friends. As soon as I reached the counter, the two people who I had spotted peering out of the kitchen earlier rushed toward me. I hadn't looked too closely at them before, but I saw now that they were two young men. Since they were in the pub, presumably they were old enough to drink, but they couldn't have been much older than that. They were both supes.

The taller one was dragging the shorter one toward me. They obviously had something on their minds. This should be interesting.

"Hi," the taller one said as he pushed his long, dark hair back to reveal his smooth, golden-brown skin. This close, he looked even younger than I'd first thought. He was a kelpie. He was a long way from the ocean. How had he ended up here? "I'm Brodie. This is Dakota."

Dakota had earth magic of some kind; he had the energy of a druid or a green man. His tight black curls bounced around his face as he nodded at me. Perhaps it was the roundness of his brown cheeks, but Dakota appeared even younger than his friend.

"How can I help you?"

"What was it like?" Brodie blurted out the question like it'd been all he could think about the whole night.

I raised my eyebrows. "What was what like?"

Dakota leaned forward, although he kept a healthy distance between us, like he was scared to get too close. "They said you'd been in a cage. That you escaped from the trafficking ring," he whispered.

I nodded. "Yes. That's true."

"What was it like?" Brodie asked again.

"Why do you want to know?" I glanced down the bar to where Alice the bartender was filling pints. She was listening to the conversation but didn't seem alarmed or surprised by it.

"We were supposed to be sent there," Dakota said in another whisper. As he spoke, his face took on a green-ish tinge, and dark green vines wove through his dark hair.

Oh. These were the ones found on Robbie's property. I'd heard a bit about them from Van when we'd driven to Aspen Bay. I hadn't realized they were working for Jake now, although I remembered something about them living with Gage's team as part of a sanctuary they were starting.

Their faces were so young. So innocent. So scared. These two may have been safe here, but what they'd been through obviously still haunted them. They reminded me of Morgan, even though I was sure the unicorn was older than they were.

"You were lucky to have missed all that," I said. "But we're going to find everyone."

"But what was it like?" Brodie asked for the third time. "I can't stop thinking about it, imagining what it would be like. I just... I need to know."

He feared the unknown. I could understand that. Whatever had happened to him must have been terrible, but he knew those cages had been a gateway to something worse. In the mirror behind the bar, I could see Van and Gage approaching us. Simon was right behind them. The bar had gotten quiet. The laughter from the game tables had died down. The chatter by the pool table was gone. Everyone was listening.

Simon came right up and wrapped his arms around me. I was surprised. I hadn't expected my kitty cat to be much for public displays of affection, but his touch was exactly what I needed. I doubted these two were asking to be malicious, but this was certainly not a comfortable topic for me.

"Are you sure you want to know?" Van asked Brodie and Dakota.

"I need to know," Brodie said, lifting his chin in a defiant gesture that made him look even more like a teenager. Dakota simply nodded.

"I wish Hayden was here," Ash said. He'd spoken quietly from back at the table, but with no other sounds in the bar, his words carried. "He's good to have for discussions like this."

"That's because he's the alpha," Paws said loudly. There was no question in the cat's statement. He also didn't try to keep his voice down. He wasn't the kind of creature to worry much about what others might hear. If he said something, he'd stand by it.

As they spoke, Nelson joined us too. I hadn't seen him arrive, but he was here now, and he appeared keen to hear what I had to say. I wondered if his curiosity had something to do with his strange reaction to learning about the unicorn who'd been in that place with me.

Van looked at me. "Are you comfortable talking about it? You don't have to."

"What do you want to know?" I asked.

Brodie's shoulders relaxed. Dakota released a deep breath. Simon tightened his arms around me and nuzzled the back of my neck. He started purring. The soft sound was soothing, and the little vibrations reverberated along my back.

"Okay, so this is what happened to me…"

Then I described what it'd been like. I wasn't sure if they would sleep better knowing all this or if I was giving them new nightmares, but we were all survivors of the same thing. They deserved to be informed. They also deserved to know that I would do everything in my power to free the rest of those supes.

Chapter Twenty-Four

OGDEN

A week later, there were still no new leads. The Aspen Bay Police Department hadn't found anyone suspiciously skulking around The Drunken Drake. Wesley was still MIA. And being away from my hoard for so long under these circumstances was driving me bonkers.

The only good thing about the last seven days was spending time with Simon. In amongst watching a bunch of nature documentaries that Simon loved, there'd been a lot of online shopping, a lot of sexy fashion shows, and, of course, a lot of sex. Every time we came together, magic flowed around us like a warm updraft, lifting us higher and higher until all we could do was soar. I'd never experienced anything like it. It was addicting.

Maybe addicting wasn't the right word. It felt right. So, when Teague stopped by one day with Van and Gage and explained how he believed he could sever the bond between us, we'd asked for time to think about it. After they left, neither of us brought it up again.

Honestly, my current plan to return to Aspen Bay was leaving me feeling a little upside down. But it had to be done. The sooner I left to wrap things up there, the sooner I could return.

"I'll be back as soon as I can," I said to Simon.

"It isn't safe." Simon looked like he was trying not to hack up a hairball. His hand clasped something in his pocket, probably the whistle. He'd told me recently how he couldn't be without it after he found it, and now he didn't want to put it down anywhere it might get lost or stolen because it was connected to me. When we finally lived together, maybe he'd agree to put it in with my hoard—our hoard now.

"No one's seen Wesley in ages. And I won't take any longer than I have to. Just a quick trip." I hoped I wasn't being stupid. I hated it when I was stupid. At my age, stupidity wasn't becoming. "I have no desire to linger in Aspen Bay any longer than necessary."

That'd just be tempting fate.

But I had too many loose ends to tie up, and not everything could be organized over the phone. I needed to meet with the hoard movers, the furniture movers, the real estate agent, my employees, my tenants…

"Then I'm going with you." Simon folded his thick forearms over his chest in such a confident manner that it made my blood stir. Okay, well, it made my blood all rush south to my cock at any rate; it really wasn't stirring in any other direction.

"I will be perfectly safe," I said. "You don't need to

come with me. No one will trick me so easily again. I am a full-grown dragon, not a hatchling. I've been around for many centuries. I know how to take care of myself."

"I'm going with you," he said with more force. He ended his statement with a frown.

My little kitty had a stubborn streak. And how could I refuse when he seemed as reluctant to be away from me as I was to be away from him?

"If you come with me, you'll miss breakfast with your parents. Your mother won't be happy."

"I'll go pack," Simon said.

And that was that.

A few hours later, we were standing in my apartment in Aspen Bay. It looked and smelled the same as when we'd left it a week ago.

"What do we need to do?" Simon asked as he patrolled the perimeter of the main room, looking out each window as he passed it, as if expecting Wesley and his accomplices to storm the building at any minute.

"I've set up a meeting with the local realtor in the morning. And the hoard movers will be here after lunch. They may even start hauling my treasure to a local temporary storage facility by the end of the week."

"A storage facility?" He spun to face me, shocked. "That won't be safe."

"It's fine," I said, waving my hand through the air. "There are few people I would trust with my hoard, but my sister owns the company. Her entire business is securing hoards and treasures for her clients."

"I've never heard of anything like that."

"Well, they try to be discreet. It is an international company, catering to a very specific clientele."

"I suppose they would need to be secretive," he muttered, then resumed his route around the apartment. He brushed his hand over the furniture as he paced. I'm sure if he was in his cat form, his tail would be ticking back and forth, and his little ears would be twitching. Honestly, he was adorable.

And hot.

He was wearing one of the shirts I'd rush ordered for him. It looked delectable on him. I also loved him in the green shirt I'd given him to wear the first time we'd been here—the one that was so thin his nipples were on display. As soon as he'd pulled it on, I'd wanted to rub them to see if he'd squirm, and now, after having explored his body for a week, I knew he would.

We still had so many things to learn about one another, but I'd made significant progress in mapping out the most sensitive spots on his body. I'd discovered what made him arch and writhe against my touch. And I knew what would drive him to throw me down and strip off my clothes.

I shook my head. I wasn't meant to be thinking about sex right now. I eyed his shirt again. This blue one was a better fit than the one I'd loaned him. There was something scrumptiously sexy about a man wearing clothes that looked tailored for his body.

This one wasn't custom-made for him, but I had plans to add a few bespoke pieces to his wardrobe soon. I secretly wished I could toss everything in his wardrobe and start over, but that'd probably give my poor cat shifter a heart attack. Besides, he possessed a certain rugged appeal when he dressed in his worn jeans and faded T-shirts.

"Yes," I agreed, pushing away my distracting thoughts. I needed to get to work. "Announcing to too many people that they secured treasure would only make them a target."

"This is all expensive, isn't it?" Simon was studying a 15th century tapestry hanging at the far end of the drawing room.

When I'd moved into this building, I'd paid a mage a considerable sum to construct a protection ward around the tapestry, so I didn't have to hide it away in a dark, climate-controlled room. The mage's hefty fees had been worth it. I'd stared at it for hours, remembering the battle it depicted between my family and another powerful dragon family. It seemed impossible to imagine now that such a massive war between leagues of dragons had taken place, when there were so few of our kind remaining in the world. The Eternal Magic was much stronger back then. The very air had been vibrant and alive with it.

Willow Lake was the closest I'd come to feeling that type of power in centuries.

"What's the plan?" Simon asked, moving away from the tapestry.

"I suppose I should move the few treasures I have on display. Put them with the rest of the hoard."

One of the best things about living as long as I had was collecting amazing items along the way. Unlike newly turned vampires who aspired to live up to stereotypes about being wealthy, even if they were just turned a few decades ago, I did not need to plunder archaeological sites for beautiful, priceless artifacts. Most of my collection had been purchased as original works from the creators of the time. It was something I loved to do, even now. Sometimes the artist faded from collective memory, and sometimes they found fame. Either way, it didn't matter to me as long as I enjoyed the piece.

"I…" Simon's face paled, and he shook his head. "I don't think I should touch anything… uh… expensive."

"Whyever not?"

"What if I break something."

Oh, my darling kitty cat. He was such a worrier. "If it would make you more comfortable, why don't you pour us some wine? I can gather the art. Then we can decide about what to eat."

He nodded, but he didn't look any more comfortable with that.

"Or, if you prefer something else, dash downstairs. I'm sure I have something you'd like in the bar."

He worried his bottom lip between his teeth for a moment. "Will you be okay up here? By yourself?"

I lifted an eyebrow.

"Fine," he said. "Just… Don't do anything while I'm gone. I'll be right back."

"I'm sure I'll be fine, kitten." He was so adorable to worry about me. I turned away from him so he wouldn't see my grin.

I waited until I heard him open the door and scurry down the steps before I lifted a 16th century sculpture from its pedestal. I had lifted this piece countless times in the past. My sister couldn't understand why I moved my art and furniture around so often, but who wanted to live in the same space with the same things in the same places for months on end? How tedious.

But, as soon as I had it in my hands, I knew this time wouldn't be so easy. I grunted with the effort to balance the piece and haul it through the apartment. It'd never been this difficult. My arms ached by the time I set it on the floor in my closet. I shook them out, happy Simon wasn't here to see how difficult that'd been. He'd just worry even more than normal.

I slipped into my hoard room. The last time I was here, I'd just opened the smaller access door, which was the one I preferred, since the length of time my hoard was open and vulnerable was minimal. That wouldn't work this time. I needed the wider access.

From inside the room, using another series of secret levers that had to be triggered in a particular order, I opened a door that was almost the width and height of my closet wall. It made hauling the oversized pieces of my collection into the secured area so much easier. Each piece in my collection had a specific place to be housed in my hoard room.

I hadn't always been so meticulous—there was something marvelous about seeing heaps of jewels mounded all around you—but too many pieces became damaged that way. And no one enjoyed stepping on a gemstone in bare feet. That was almost as bad as LEGO pieces, or so I'd been told by my cousin. Her first hatchling, the only child in my family in a century, was about six years old now and had started stockpiling the little building blocks. It was their little one's first hoard, and my aunt and uncle were incredibly proud.

When the sculpture was in place, I heaved out a sigh and shook out my arms again. One down. Thankfully, none of the others were so heavy or awkward.

I heard Simon moving around in the other room, so I straightened my shoulders. I refused to show how weak I was in front of Simon. He'd blame himself for summoning me, even though he hadn't known what would happen. I would get stronger. I was already much stronger than I was when he'd first summoned me. My chest warmed with fire and electricity. Shooting sparks when I was angry was good too. Okay, it wasn't great that I was angry enough to lose control like that, but it meant my magic was healing. Another day or two and I should be at full strength again.

It couldn't come soon enough.

By the time I returned to the parlor, Simon was placing half a dozen beers in the fridge. The drinks people order could reveal a lot. The brand Simon had grabbed was a rather lackluster local beer, one that people who didn't really like the taste of beer usually drank.

"Is that your usual?"

Simon blushed prettily as he closed the fridge door. "Sometimes."

"Do you like it?"

"Sure."

I didn't want lies between us. I crossed the room to him. He looked surprised to see me so close. He took a step back, and I followed until his back was against the wall. "Tell me the truth. Do you like it?"

His cheeks darkened. "It is better than other things, I guess."

"Hmm…" I gently tugged his head down until I could whisper in his ear. His breath hitched as my breath cascaded over his skin. I loved how quickly he reacted to me; it was almost as fast as I reacted to him. "You know… I can make any drink you might like. I know at least twenty delicious cocktails made with cream."

He swallowed. Was it because I was pressed up against him, or did he really like the idea of a creamy cocktail? Ha! And just thinking about the words *creamy cocktail* had my mind dropping into a lovely and decadent gutter.

"Uh… This is fine."

"But is it what you like?"

"Uh…"

"Simon?"

He swallowed again and looked away.

"Don't be embarrassed by what you like, love. I thought we were past that," I said. "Whether it is a drink or something else. I only want to make you happy."

His gaze darted to mine before he looked away again. "I would like to try something like that. With cream," he said eventually. "But maybe not today? We have a lot to do, and I don't want to stay here any longer than necessary."

Always such a worrier.

"I'm going to fill your life with so many wonderful things. You'll see." I nipped at his earlobe, and he shivered.

I couldn't wait to be settled in Willow Lake with him. I wanted to spoil my little kitty. I wanted to give him everything, to ensure he knew he was safe with me, and to ease his worries and his self-doubt and his fears. He was already so much more confident and relaxed than he had been. I couldn't wait to see what he would be like in a year or twenty or a hundred.

Chapter Twenty-Five

OGDEN

"I feel like a lazy toad watching you work," Simon muttered from his perch on the edge of the sofa as I hauled another painting through the apartment. He looked ready to spring into action if I looked like I was struggling.

"Sit back and relax," I said. "That sofa was specifically chosen for comfort, but you're sitting on it like it's filled with rocks."

"Do you have anything that isn't priceless? I could move those things."

"There are only a few things left. It'll just take a jiffy to finish and then we can both relax."

"Huh," he said as he looked around the apartment. "I thought there were more things in here."

My living space was actually sparsely furnished. The large pieces of art had made it seem full because they took up so much visual space. As I removed the pieces, one by one, the apartment lost its personality, until it was just a large, empty, echoing room.

I'd expected to be hit with bittersweet nostalgia, but it hadn't come. I was too invested in what was going to come next for me. For Simon. For us.

Once I finished with the last of the artwork, I decided the movers could pack up everything else, except maybe the bed. I didn't want it anymore, which was a shame because it was the most comfortable bed I'd ever owned.

No. I refused to think about Wesley tonight. It was time to celebrate, and I knew just the thing to make the night special. I returned to Simon, carrying the bottle of red wine. "Would you like some wine?"

Simon squished up his forehead. "I'm not much of a wine drinker. My parents serve wine from a box for special occasions, but even then, I usually skip it."

Although the one in my hand was a thousand-dollar bottle, I wasn't a wine snob. I liked what I liked. Price didn't matter. I'd imbibed wine from a box and enjoyed it well enough. Sure, some of it was horrid, but I didn't enjoy every aged and corked vintage either.

Although not the priciest bottle in my collection, it held sentimental value, as it came from my favorite Italian vineyard. I'd been drinking their wine for over five hundred years. I'd tucked a case of this wine into my hoard several years ago, knowing there would come a time when I'd finally have something worthy to celebrate. Although I was excited to open the first bottle tonight, I'd never force my kitty cat to have something he didn't enjoy.

With deft movements, I uncorked the bottle before pouring a generous glass for myself and grabbing another beer for Simon. Normally, I might suggest retiring to the bedroom, but the thought of sleeping in my bed made my skin itch. Even after stripping the bedding, the mattress still reeked of strangers and traitors. Then inspiration struck.

"It's a warm night," I said. "Let's go to the roof. Making love under the stars is the perfect way to spend my last night here."

His breath caught. "Outside? Won't someone hear us?"

"Shifters will hear us whether we are outside or in," I pointed out.

Simon's eyes widened, as if he hadn't considered that before. But the people tasked with guarding us were supernatural; the only way they wouldn't hear us was if we were in my hoard room, but tonight I yearned for something else. I hadn't seen my kitty cat in his shifted form yet, and the only time he'd seen me was when I'd been threatening him after he'd blown that whistle. Although Simon would fit comfortably in my hoard room, my dragon was too big for the space. It was one of the few mistakes I'd made when designing it.

"Before we go up, do you have a charger I can use for my cell? I forgot to grab one. Mama will call in the morning. If I don't answer because the phone is dead, she'll probably call the local cops to do a wellness check."

"Of course." I bought a new phone every year, so I had almost every type of charger on the market.

Simon dug through my drawer of miscellaneous cords and chargers to find one that'd fit his older model. I kept my phone with me because I had plans for it later. Then Simon followed me to the roof.

Designing the rooftop garden had been delightful. This area would be one of the few things I would miss about this place. The finished space extended across the full expanse of the building, making it the same size as my apartment. Being open to the air and the sky, it seemed much larger. The same mage who'd protected my tapestry had created an illusion to hide the area from human eyes. It'd been worth the expense because it meant I could shift in comfort. I spent more time up here than anywhere else, even in the winter. But tonight, the weather didn't disappoint. Heat from the day had soaked into the materials and furnishings, so everything radiated enough residual warmth to keep even a vampire toasty.

I guided Simon to the end of the building so we could overlook the water. The view was stunning. Darkness hadn't fully claimed the day yet, so pastel pinks, moody purples, vivid oranges, and crisp yellows streaked across the sky, bouncing in a kaleidoscope of colors over the surface of the lake. The fragrant perfume of the flowers I'd grown in pots across the wide expanse of the roof filled the air, but when Simon wrapped his arms around me, pulling my back to his chest, all I smelled was him.

We stood at the railing in silence, sipping our drinks as we watched night conquer the day. As the darkness grew heavier around us, everything felt more intimate. I took his beer from his hands and set our drinks down.

Simon's mouth opened in anticipation of my kiss.

Our gazes met as the last rays of sunlight faded from the horizon. The ambient light from the streetlights below us provided enough of a glow to show me his handsome face. He was so young; I almost felt wicked even suggesting he might be my mate. His eyes shifted until they seemed to glow in the low light, and I knew he'd changed them to his cat's eyes so he could see me better.

I swayed against him, listening to the sweet melody of our hearts in the warm night. I fished out my phone and pulled up a playlist I didn't access very often. The songs were romantic and sensuous and just for the two of us. I wanted to share everything with Simon, even my love of music. The first song to play was "Coming Home" by Leon Bridges. The song was a lot newer than my usual preferences, but it was perfect for tonight.

Simon stumbled once, but by the end of the first verse, his muscles were relaxing under my hands. By the time the list played Ed Sheeran, Simon was leading me around like a dance instructor. His hands moved me wherever he wanted. I wasn't usually a follower, but I followed Simon. I was beginning to suspect I always would.

Anticipation for what would follow whirled through me with each gliding step, each brush of his body against mine, each ripple of his muscles beneath my hands. Foreplay with clothes, that's what this was. His smile was almost predatory as he spun me around before lowering me into a masterful dip. I was completely under his command, which was an unusual place for me, but I was surprisingly comfortable with it.

"Where did you learn to dance?"

"My parents taught all of us," Simon said as he pulled me snug against his body until we were touching from our chests to our hips. His arm cinched tight around my waist as he guided us around in another graceful turn. His thigh wedged between mine. "We grew up watching Pops spin

Mama around the kitchen or the living room or the back yard. Anywhere, really. It always looked so magical. Mama insisted we all learn, saying girls liked to dance with guys who knew what they were doing. I haven't danced with anyone in a long time. I'm surprised I remember how."

"No girls to dance with?" I teased.

"Never." His lips brushed my ear. A shiver of anticipation cascaded over me at the soft, warm touch. "No one, really, until you."

"I'll have to thank your mother," I whispered, because it *was* magical. I'd always suspected dancing under the stars would be nice, although few things lived up to the hype, but with Simon it did, and so much more. The stars sparkled above us. Below us, night had settled over the empty downtown streets. And all around us, the heat from the day still hung in the air.

Combine all that with the way he was dancing? I was thoroughly seduced.

"I want to be with you," he whispered against my neck.

"Anything you wish," I said and turned my head, needing to feel his lips against mine. Our lips met in a fleeting, teasing kiss. "That's what a good sugar daddy does, isn't it?"

He groaned. "Can we please forget I said that?"

"Never." I laughed as I tugged his face down so I could drop a kiss on his nose.

Then I took his hand in mine and led him across the roof to the space I used as a sun bed. The custom-made cushion, which was the size of four king-sized beds, was large enough to accommodate my dragon. One of my favorite ways to spend a sunny afternoon was to nap here in my dragon form, but tonight I had more *active* plans.

I pulled a few blankets and pillows from the water-proof chest beside the cushion. Then I dug a little deeper for the bottle of lube I knew was in there. As soon as everything was in place, I turned to Simon.

His eyes were riveted to me as he licked his lips. I always enjoyed it when people watched me, which was part of the reason I became an entertainer, but being the focus of Simon's attention excited me in a way I hadn't experienced before. I would never have guessed that it would be so different to be admired by my mate. It was exhilarating. The only feeling that seemed comparable was when I'd taken my first flight.

Under the weight of his gaze, I began to hum and dance as I slipped my fingers under the hem of my shirt. I rocked my hips slowly, rolling them in sensuous circles as I lifted my shirt to reveal my stomach. He swallowed hard. His breath quickened. I tugged my shirt higher before finally pulling it off and casting it aside. I let my hands drift down over my chest, tweaking my nipples until they hardened.

Simon moaned.

I spun slowly until I was facing away from him. I glanced over my shoulder to see him prowling closer. His fingers twitched as if he wanted to touch me. Then I loosened my pants and shimmied and pushed until my pants and underwear were down by my ankles.

"Damn it," I muttered.

I'd forgotten about my shoes.

I bent over to pull them off, stumbling forward to the soft surface of the cushions.

Simon's hot, firm hands grabbed my hips and stopped me from falling. It also meant that my bare ass was up against his clothed crotch.

"I've got you," he said in a voice deep, gravelly with emotion.

I loved hearing the effect I was having on him. I wiggled my ass against him as I pulled free of my shoes and clothing. Then his arms encircled me, and he tugged me upright again. His one arm banded around my waist, tugging me close, while the other snaked up to wrap loosely around my throat. I tipped my head under the pressure of his fingers and then his mouth was on the side of my neck. I wanted him to bite me. His sharp teeth scraped over me until I shivered and arched into him. Then he nipped at my skin until I trembled. I loved it. I loved how he was becoming so comfortable and confident with me.

"Yes, kitten." I purred. "Show me what you want."

He bit harder and my body jerked as unexpected pleasure jolted through me. I pulled his hand down to my cock. At the first touch of his hand, I rolled my head back to his shoulder and panted. He slid his palm roughly over the tip, coating it in my pre-cum.

"Feel what you do to me," I moaned. "I'm so close."

"Get on your hands and knees," Simon demanded, pushing me forward.

Without his arms to hold me up, I collapsed onto the cushions. I looked back to see him ripping off his clothing. Then he stalked toward me with his hard, thick cock swinging in front of him.

"You look so good like this," he said. "I want you so bad." Then he dropped to his knees behind me. His meaty hands gripped my ass cheeks and squeezed before pulling them apart to reveal my hole. "Can I do this?" His voice had dropped even deeper now. "Can I take you like this? Do you want this?"

During all the sex we'd had that week, I'd always been in control, and I'd always topped. Every time. It was the same with all my lovers. I enjoyed being in charge—more than one former lover complained about my need to take control in the bedroom, but I didn't want control right now. I didn't know what had come over me, but I wanted whatever Simon wanted to do to me.

Because I trust him. I want to please him. I would do anything for him.

"Yes," I whispered, whether in response to his questions or the voice in my head, I didn't know. I shuddered as he licked me. Then I couldn't speak. I couldn't do anything but feel as he set out to drive me crazy with his tongue.

When I didn't think I could take any more, Simon nipped my ass cheek as he pressed against my entrance. I didn't even know when he'd grabbed the lube, but his finger was slippery. It felt so damn good. I pushed back against his touch.

"You like that?" he asked as he thrust his fingers into me with the perfect amount of roughness to make me weak with want. "The things I want to do…"

"What? Tell me." I needed to know what he was thinking.

He pressed his forehead to my lower back like he was

trying to get control. His panting breaths fell across my skin in tantalizing bursts.

"Please, Simon... Tell me."

He groaned, and I felt the moment he decided to give in to me. "All I could think about all day was the first time we were here in your apartment, how you'd come on my finger in your hoard room. Every time we've been together, you always make sure I lose control before you. I want to watch you break this time. You did that to me. Made me dream about all the ways I wanted to have you. Do you think I can make you come again on my finger? Make you scream my name? Make you come without touching your cock?"

Yes, please. Fuck. Where had my kitten learned to talk like that? If he trusted me enough to share these deliciously dirty thoughts with me after this short amount of time together, I couldn't wait to hear what he'd say in another year or fifty.

"Now, Simon," I said, digging my claws into the cushions. "Need you now. Make me feel you."

Simon groaned, then he grabbed my hips, pulling me up. There was the squelch of the lube again, then he was there. Against me. Every inch of my body tingled with anticipation as the wet, blunt tip of his cock pressed into me. We groaned as he breached my hole and pushed inside with one hard stroke.

Once he was deep within me, our bodies joined as intimately as they could be, he draped his large body over mine. Covering me. Like he wanted to be between me and everything else in the world. One of his arms encircled my waist as he braced himself with his other. My entire body felt enveloped by his, consumed by it. Then he rocked his hips back, before plunging forward again. He shifted the angle of his hips with each stroke until he found the one that made me cry out in pleasure.

He grunted. Then he cursed.

"Need to see you." He pulled away from me, only long enough to flip me to my back. Then he was pushing inside me again. He stared into my eyes in a way that made me feel vulnerable and powerful all at once. I wanted to be vulnerable with him. But only him. He could have all of me. I didn't want to hold anything back from him.

"My mate," I whispered.

"Yes," he said. "I'm yours, and you're mine."

My magic stirred and swelled inside me with each thrust. When his magic reached for mine, mine flew out of me to join it. Every time we'd made love, our magics had done this, and every time was more potent than the last. The blues and yellows of my magic pushed and pulled at his green magic in time with the rhythm of our bodies.

"Bite me," I demanded.

But I hadn't needed to ask. His mouth was already there on the sweet spot where my shoulder met my neck. His teeth sank into my flesh and our magic exploded in a shimmer of light and love. When they came back together, they'd been remade into a new single color. A new united magic.

My breath caught.

That'd never happened before.

Then a primal urge welled inside me to claim this man as my mate. This was the stuff of fairy tales. This was magic. True, pure magic.

He really was my fated mate.

Satisfaction and joy and excitement flitted across Simon's face, and I knew he felt this too. The Eternal Magic was blessing us, joining us from this day forward in a way that only she could. Ancient words—even older than me—flowed from our mouths. The words were full of magic and promise and hope. I lost myself to the beauty of the vows I didn't know but still instinctually understood.

As soon as the words faded, Simon's mouth met mine in a hard, rough kiss. Our bodies rocked as we sought our release. The colors, a pure blend of our individual magics, pulsed in tempo with each thrust.

I shuddered in relief and joy as I came. Then Simon trembled and jerked his hips harder and faster until he found his own release deep inside me. Our magic wrapped around us, as if tying us together physically.

We collapsed onto the cushion in a heap of sweaty, tangled limbs.

"I made you come without touching your cock," he said smugly. He wrapped his arms around me as he rolled onto his back and carried me with him. Our bodies were still joined, and I wished we could stay this way forever.

"Yes, you did." I chuckled at his bragging as I tugged blankets over us. Then I snuggled against his chest. We were sticky and hot and sweaty, and I loved it.

"Did that really happen? Are we…?"

I lifted my head. That's when I noticed something about him had changed. His hand came up to brush through my hair, and I suspected I'd changed too. It was real.

"You have a green lock of hair at your temple," he whispered.

"You have one too."

His eyebrows squished together as he played with the strands of my hair. "Why is it green? Your magic is…"

"Blues and yellows, which merge to create green. And your magic is entirely green."

"Only fated mates have these," he said, looking away from my hair to meet my gaze. It didn't sound like a question, but I wasn't sure why he said that.

"Yes. Only fated mates," I agreed.

He blinked his eyes rapidly and a tear escaped out of the corner of his eye. "You're really my fated mate. I wanted to believe it, but when the Eternal Magic didn't mark us before…"

"Believe it, kitty cat. It is true," I whispered. "We're bonded now. Our lives are entwined."

"For the rest of our lives."

"Our very long lives," I amended.

"How old are you?"

"Older than anyone else in Willow Lake."

"Even Gage?" Simon sounded shocked, like he couldn't imagine anyone as old as that.

"Yes. Is that a problem?"

"No… I just… Wow."

"Just don't call me your Sugar Grandaddy," I teased.

I opened my mouth to tease him some more, but he cut off what I was going to say with a kiss. One kiss became two, and then more. We lost ourselves in one another until we were sated again.

"I'll be right back," Simon said when our bodies cooled and our breathing calmed.

He crawled out of the little nest of blankets and pillows. The beautiful sight of him walking naked through my rooftop garden mesmerized me. He disappeared down the steps to my apartment. I thought about following, but my body was still shattered from my last orgasm.

Then Simon was back, carrying a couple of bottles of water and a cloth. His smile was shy as he kneeled beside me.

"Here," he said as he set the water down, "let me clean you."

I blinked at him, but he didn't move until I nodded my okay. As he brushed the warm, wet cloth over my belly, I swallowed hard. I couldn't remember the last time anyone had taken the time to care for me like this. My past lovers had come—pun intended—and gone. Simon took his time, wiping away the cum from my stomach and then down over my cock and along my hole. Even with Simon, until tonight, I'd always been the one to tend to him. I loved caring for him like this, so I was surprised how much I enjoyed the reverse too.

As he worked, a soft purr rumbled from his chest, telling me he was enjoying doing this for me. His touch was gentle and sure, not meant to arouse me, but the intimacy of what he was doing made my eyes sting with emotion. When he was done, he tossed the cloth aside before grabbing a bottle of water and opening it.

"Here, this is for you," he said, passing one to me, while keeping one for himself.

"I thought I was the one who was supposed to spoil

you," I teased as I took the bottle, but my voice betrayed my emotions. I couldn't hide how much these little actions of his were unraveling me. Filled with a need to show him I appreciated his thoughtfulness, I drank down the water.

When we set the empty bottles aside, he stretched out beside me and wrapped his arm around me again. His fingers drew feather-light loops over my stomach.

"What if..." he said softly. "What if we spoil one another?"

"I love that idea."

"Good."

We lay beside one another, listening to the muted noises of a small town settling down for the night. A dog barked in the distance. A car drove past on the street below. A chorus of crickets sang their songs. I wanted to stay forever in this moment, wrapped in the warm embrace of my lover, my mate, listening to peaceful and familiar sounds. There was only one thing we had not done yet: shifted with one another.

"I would like to see your shifted form," I whispered. I wasn't worried about anyone else hearing me, but the intimacy of the moment begged for softly spoken words.

Simon lifted on his elbow so he could look into my eyes. "You want to see my cat?"

"Yes," I said. "But only if you want to show me."

"I am a boring house cat in my shifted form. I am not majestic like you."

I reached up to cradle his face in my hands. "Don't belittle yourself, kitty cat. I am interested in you, all of you. You could be the smallest mouse and I would still marvel at the privilege of seeing your animal half. I am a dragon by a twist of fate; there was nothing I did to achieve that. It is not an accomplishment; it is simply a fact. I am no more majestic than any other creature or shifter. But I would like to know everything about you. *You* are who I want to see because you are everything to me. I would be honored to see your cat form."

I could tell he wasn't sure if he believed me, but he would with time. I would show him every day that he was the most captivating person I'd ever known. Everything about him fascinated me, and I suspected it always would.

"If you want to see my cat form, I'll show you," he said. "But can I see your dragon again too? I was too preoccupied last time to truly appreciate your beauty."

"Of course. But you first."

The change slipped over him, transforming him from one form to another from one moment to the next.

"You are gorgeous," I murmured. I had to touch him. I sank my fingers into his long, glossy, midnight black fur, now interrupted by a splash of green, our mating mark. He purred as I stroked him from head to tail. Was it weird to find his six-toed paws ridiculously cute? "You're so soft."

His pale-yellow eyes blinked at me, then he nudged my chin with his head.

"Okay," I said with a laugh. "I'll change too."

I rolled away from him until I was far enough away that I wouldn't crush him with my larger dragon body. Then I let my transition flow over me. Unlike his under-stated transformation, my dragon washed over me in a flash of light. I didn't know why my kind's shift was so flashy, but dragons were a little different from most shifters, anyway. Dragon lore said we were the first shifters on earth, that all other shifters descended from us, so our shift was more closely connected to the Eternal Magic. I didn't know if that was true, but the look of awe in Simon's eyes when I achieved my dragon form made me preen.

Simon padded over to me. I'd known the size difference would be significant, but it was even more striking to see it. Scared of hurting him, I held myself still as he inspected me.

"Your scales, there is green in them now too. Not everywhere, just…" He hopped up on my back and rubbed his head against me, as if the visible mark wasn't enough and he needed his scent on my dragon too.

"Your fur shows our mating mark too," I said. I didn't move, scared of jostling him.

"Relax," he said as he kneaded my shoulders with his little paws. His purr grew louder.

"I don't want to hurt you," I said.

"You couldn't. We are mates. The Eternal Magic wouldn't have matched us if we weren't meant to be together like this."

"I know… It's just…"

Simon batted at the back of my head with his paw. Given our size difference, it felt like little more than a tap, but I got the message. I was being an idiot. I put my head down on the cushions and willed myself to relax.

"That's better," he said. Then he jumped down to lie beside me. He walked around my body, sniffing and licking, until he came to a stop by my front legs. He turned in a tight circle twice before settling down against me. I didn't miss how he curled up close to my heart. When he closed his eyes and let out a little huff of happiness, I relaxed a little more.

"I would like to go flying with you," I murmured.

Now it was his turn to be tense.

"I… Um… Maybe another time." *Or never*, was what I heard. But that was okay. We had a long life ahead of us. We'd both learn eventually that we wouldn't hurt one another. He would be safe with me, even miles above the earth.

I settled down beside him, not even looking up at the stars like I usually did. Instead, I curled my larger body around him, determined to keep him warm and safe all night long. After seeing the beauty of our combined magics coming together, I knew every other beauty the world could offer would be pale in comparison.

Chapter Twenty-Six

SIMON

I jolted awake. The back of my neck itched. Something was wrong.

"Shh..." Ogden whispered. "Something woke me. I thought something tickled my face, but now I swear some-one's watching."

Any lingering fatigue dropped away. The dark and quiet around us suggested it was either very late or very early, depending on how you looked at it. Luckily, I was still in my cat form, so my senses were sharper than if I'd shifted back to my human form. I scanned the shadows of the rooftop garden, but I couldn't see any threats. When I sniffed the air, though, a faint scent of brimstone, ozone, and something herbal irritated my nose. Someone was using magic, but where were they?

"There is magic in the air too," I said just as quietly. I pinned my ears back and tried to make myself as small as possible. "We need to tell the police."

"I don't think we'll have time," Odgen said.

I would be stronger in my shifted form, but if someone was coming here, I had to protect the whistle so they couldn't use it. My shift washed over me faster than it ever had before. I scrambled to dress as quickly as possible. The weight of the whistle in my pocket was a comfort. If I had it, no one else could get it.

"Shift, Ogden. Hurry."

But Ogden stayed in his dragon form. I saw the pouch with the tracking device Van had given him lying a few feet away with the rest of his clothing. Why hadn't we dressed again before we shifted? Then he'd have it with him. Just in case.

"Shift and grab the tracking device," I urged him.

But no one would take him again. They couldn't. We'd just found one another. We'd just mated. He was my everything.

We just needed to get out of here. Fast.

"I have a different idea," Ogden said. "The Aspen Bay PD are down on the street."

"Yes. Let's get to them. Then everything will be fine. Come on."

I grabbed Ogden's massive dragon's paw to pull him toward the stairs. He clenched it around my hand. As he moved, little bits of *something* cascaded off his face. It smelled like a plant. How did that get on him? Whatever. It didn't matter because he scooped me up and held me against his chest. My feet kicked at empty space.

"What are you doing?"

"It's time to fly, kitten," Odgen said.

Every muscle in my body froze at his words. He didn't

mean…? His wings swooshed open. Holy Magic, he meant *fly* fly, as in he was going to fly us off the roof. I braced myself, not sure if keeping my eyes open or closed would be better. Except we didn't lift off the roof. We didn't do anything. His body strained, but his wings showed only a shiver of movement.

"Fuck. They've done something… I can't…"

"What's the matter? Tell me what's going on." My gaze darted over the roof. How could they stop him—a powerful dragon—from moving?

"Hide," Ogden urged, letting go of me so quickly I stumbled. "Hide. Quickly."

"No." I shook my head and tried to take his paw in my hand again. The back of my neck tingled. We were taking too long. We could have been downstairs in his apartment by now. Then there'd only be one more set of stairs. "Shift. We can still get away."

"I… I can't." He gnashed his teeth as his muscles convulsed again. Still, nothing happened. "I can't shift. I can't move. Fuck… They must have used *Dracaena*…"

"The houseplant?" I knew they were toxic to cats —Mama had warned us all not to chew on those spiky leaves when we were growing up—but this reaction was something else. It impacted his magic. Why was I okay? It had to be something specific to dragon magic.

"You need to protect yourself so you can find me," Ogden continued. "The faster you can get help, the faster you can come get me."

His words felt like boulders crushing my chest. I panted, trying to catch my breath. He couldn't seriously mean he'd let himself be abducted again.

"You…" I couldn't get the words out. "You…"

"Whatever happens, hide," Ogden continued.

"No. I won't let them take you," I shouted, finally pushing the words out.

"Simon, something's happening. That magic has done something to my dragon," he whispered. He struggled, but no matter what he did, he couldn't move. "Can you get away? If you can, go. If not, hide and—"

Whatever else he might have said was interrupted by a sizzling sound. It reminded me of when Mama cooked too much bacon in her skillet. Ogden's massive dragon's paw pushed me toward the box that'd held the blankets and cushions.

"Please…"

Ogden's whispered plea undid me. I leaped into the box, shifting into my cat form as I did. Whatever magic had incapacitated Ogden had no effect on me. The lid slammed down, closing me inside.

"Begging already?" a stranger asked. I didn't recognize the deep, rumbling female voice. Was this the troll Ogden had mentioned?

I nudged the lid up a little with my head, lifting it so I could peer out. The only troll I knew was Old Thom, who liked to drink Witch's Milk down at the Willow Lake Pub. He wasn't the most personable guy, but he was a pretty harmless fixture in Willow Lake. From what I remembered, all trolls looked similar and spoke with a deep voice. This person was definitely a troll.

Although I sensed she was around my age, she had deep wrinkles and a wide, bulbous nose. Her forehead had a prominent slope, and her long straggly hair sprouted from her scalp about halfway back on the top of her head. She had one arm strapped to her chest. That must have been from the injury Ogden had given her. Good. I hoped it hurt.

Behind her, a strange shimmering circle glistened under the moonlight. An unnatural flame of yellow and orange blazed around the edge of the circle. Wow. That was a portal. I'd heard Jake's demon boyfriend could make portals, but I'd never seen one in person. The day of the bombing he'd made one and shoved half of Willow Lake through it, but I'd missed the whole thing. How was a troll able to do that?

"As if." Ogden laughed. "I don't remember inviting you over tonight. If you really wanted to hear the rest of 'Splish Splash,' you could have found it on YouTube rather than coming all the way here. If you want a private show, I'll need to check my calendar to see when I'm available."

"I don't know how you escaped, but I'm here to take you back," the troll sneered. "I would have preferred to kill you and strip your carcass of scales, but apparently you are too valuable." She was trying so hard to be tough, but she came across as whiny. In fact, she sounded a lot like Warren when Mama made him return something he'd stolen.

I stuck my paws through the gap I'd made between the lid and the box. I curled them over the edge and braced my hind legs. If I could leverage myself just right, I might be able to jump onto the troll. If I knocked her down, maybe Ogden could do something. His magic wasn't listening to him right now, but maybe he could flop on her and pin her down. His dragon was way bigger than she was.

Then a large dark being stepped through the portal. The being's power oozed across the rooftop. It looked a bit like Gage in his demonic form, except this supe was black instead of red. The dark creature—he had to be a demon—surveyed the scene and then nodded toward the portal.

Ogden struggled harder against whatever magic was pinning him to the cushions.

Then three other forms stepped through the portal. One was a mage, one a bear, and the last was... a human? It almost sounded like the start of a joke Clive would tell. Most of his weren't funny, and this one wasn't either. And why would a human be here?

"Good," the mage said with a satisfied nod. "You," he pointed at the demon, "go back and prepare the dragon's cage again. Obviously, you fucked up the magic on the last one and that's how he got free. Don't fuck up again." The *or else* was left unsaid.

The demon dipped his head in acquiescence, then stepped through the magical doorway, returning to wherever he'd come from. As soon as he was out of sight, the portal vanished. The remaining four supes rushed to Ogden. The scent of magic increased. Ogden groaned and thrashed, but he was no match against the powerful magic they wielded.

A giant shape descended from the sky, circling lower and lower until it landed in a flurry of feathers on the roof. The gigantic bird transformed to a man I recognized from the photo Van had shown Ogden. This was Wesley.

How difficult would it be to claw his eyes out? I didn't

think I could murder anyone—even him—but I could maim him.

"You have him again," the traitor said. "Give me my money."

The troll snorted.

"You wouldn't have known he was up here if I hadn't told you," Wesley argued. "And you wouldn't have been able to portal here without my help. I took the risk. I flew over and put those ground up leaves in his mouth while he was sleeping. You couldn't have done this without me."

Had he missed seeing me? I was a lot smaller than Ogden's dragon, even in my human form, so maybe he had. If he had seen me, I didn't doubt he would have turned me over to gain their favor.

"Look at the amount of crushed Dracaena on the ground. You wasted at least half of what we gave you. You couldn't even get that right." The mage turned away from Wesley.

"And we're the ones who have to do all the work to get him back where he belongs," the human complained.

"Wait…" The bear lifted his nose and his face distorted in a partial shift. "I smell another." He snarled at the traitorous bird shifter. "Is this a trap?"

"What?" Wesley's eyes bulged. "No. Of course not. I would never…"

"Gus, I am tired of his games," the mage said, sounding bored as he sent a significant look toward the bird.

The bear grinned at his new prey. His teeth elongated as he closed the distance between them. Wesley backed up.

"What are you…? No. Wait. I just want my money.

That's all…" Feathers erupted from his skin as he started to transition to his animal form.

The bear lunged for him and sank his teeth into Wesley's neck before the bird shifter could fully transition or utter another plea or protest. The sickening sound of breaking bones and the distinctive smell of blood gushed through the air. I choked back the bile that rushed up to my mouth. I'd wanted the traitor hurt, but…

But…

I hadn't been prepared for what that meant.

I hadn't been prepared for him to die.

The bear opened his mouth and Wesley's partially shifted body landed with a thud on the patio. He was a mess of feathers and distorted body parts. That's when I heard it… the gurgling breath. The wet, spluttering noise. The bird wasn't dead, like I'd thought. Not yet. But soon. Everyone knew it. A shifter could survive a lot of injuries, but not something like that.

Blood bubbled out of his mouth with each breath he struggled to take. His clothes looked like they were sinking into his skin. I'd never thought about what it meant to shift with our clothing on. It was just something we shifters did. And now I doubted I'd ever be able to shift again without remembering what Wesley looked like right now.

My future nightmares would feature Wesley's dying and mangled body, I just knew it. Trembling, I forced myself to look away. I couldn't help him, but I could still help Ogden. He was in trouble. But how would I do anything against someone who killed effortlessly and without remorse? I could kill a field mouse like nobody's business, but a person? No.

A pulse of light pulled my attention away from Wesley. When the glow faded, Ogden appeared in his human form, naked and vulnerable. I didn't know how they'd done it, but he was no longer struggling against them. He was eerily still. From what the intruders had said, I was confident they would keep him alive, but what if they hurt him? He was so vulnerable right now. They could do a lot of damage to him before his injuries would be dire enough to end his life.

"Why do we have to do this? Why can't we take him through a portal?" the human complained.

"Shut up, Edgar," the mage snapped.

"Portals do weird shit to some supes," the troll explained in a surprisingly nice tone to Edgar. "We can't take any chances that the portal will do something unexpected, like cleanse his body of the magic Teddy used to sedate him."

"You quit talking too, Vala," the mage snarled. "We need to get him out of here. Help me lift him."

The mage didn't seem like a Teddy. He was too mean to share a name with cuddly bears. As he beckoned the others forward, an ugly ring on his finger caught my eye. The gaudy mass of tarnished metal and uncut stones was not only hideous, it shimmered with magic. That was not a normal ring. Was that the ring Gage's team had been worried about?

Edgar made a face at Teddy but grabbed Ogden's arms. Teddy and Vala each grabbed one of his legs. Vala was almost useless since she only had one functioning arm, but somehow, they carried him toward the staircase without dropping him.

At the top of the steps, Vala frowned. "This won't work. We can't all fit down those stairs like this."

"Can we just push him and pick him up at the bottom?" The human peered down the steps. "He's a shifter, right? He'll be fine."

Teddy rolled his eyes. "And risk breaking his neck after all this? I don't think so."

Gus, the bear shifter who still had blood around his furry mouth, shifted and stomped over to them. He grabbed Ogden from them, hoisted my defenseless dragon up, and tossed him over his shoulder in a fireman's carry. Then the group descended the stairs and went out of sight.

How long before I could go after them? I didn't want to wait too long and risk losing them. If it was just about me, I'd have stayed hidden in that box for the next two days before venturing out. But those creeps had Ogden.

I held my breath and began counting. Why I was counting, I didn't know. But it was helping me stay calm while I waited to follow. Should I count to a thousand? Five thousand? Ten? What might be the best? If I followed them too soon, they would just capture me too… or worse.

At that thought, my gaze strayed to Wesley.

Blood pooled around him now. Although in the dark, it appeared to be a black stain. I didn't want to see what it would look like when the sun rose.

A clang resonated from somewhere in the building. Did that mean they'd gotten out? Already? I had to act. Losing one of my nine for Ogden would be worth it.

I shook my head to dislodge the thought of losing anything or anyone, then the shaking rolled over my whole body. That wasn't helping. Ogden needed me. I swallowed down my fear. Ogden thought I was brave. I could do this. For him.

In one motion, I pushed the lid off my hiding spot and leaped free. I detoured only long enough to snatch up the pouch with Ogden's tracker in my mouth, then I raced to the staircase. My phone was in the apartment, so I could grab it on the way through. I'd have to take a minute to shift to tuck it into my clothing, but I'd need to shift anyway in order to call Van and let him know what'd happened. The door leading into Ogden's apartment was ajar. I nudged it with my head to move it out of my way, more concerned with following the people who'd taken Ogden than anything else.

The door didn't swing open as I expected. I pushed harder.

Then the smell hit me. The sickening scent of blood in the air had distracted me so I hadn't noticed the lingering stink of bear. The door suddenly moved, and there, at the top of the stairs, was the bear shifter. He was in his human form—he wouldn't have fit in the stairwell otherwise—but blood still coated his human teeth, which gleamed menacingly from the shadows.

"Gotcha," he crowed triumphantly as he lunged for me.

I jumped away. The fur on my back and tail puffed out in surprise. I retreated, arching my back and hissing around the pouch, although pretending I could intimidate the deadly predator by making myself look fractionally larger was laughable. My head didn't even reach his knees, and after he shifted, I'd be no bigger than his massive paw. Not to understate the obvious, but this was bad.

"Come here, kitty kitty," Gus coaxed as he prowled

toward me. He even did the whole pspspsps thing, the a-hole. "Everything is going to be okay."

Hysterical laughter threatened to rip out of me, because really? Did that approach ever work to put his victims at ease?

I continued to back away. I couldn't let this beast catch me. He'd either kill me or kidnap me as a bonus prize from the night's endeavors, but either way, it'd mean I couldn't help Ogden. The bear stalked me across the roof. His teeth gleamed in the faint ambient light. His breath stank of blood and gore. His eyes glinted with predatory intent.

Then he shifted.

He was gigantic.

The bear lumbered forward on his enormous paws with their enormous claws, bringing his enormous mouth with its enormous teeth closer to me with every step. My heart was pounding so hard I feared it'd give out. But I focused on my one goal: Save Ogden.

When my tail hit the short parapet wall at the perimeter of the roof, I jumped in surprise. The bear laughed. Laughter should have been a reassuring and cheerful sound, but he embodied all the sick and demented joy he got from having his prey cornered.

I gulped.

It couldn't end like this.

I scanned the area, looking for an escape. There had to be a way to get out of this. But to get to the staircase, I'd need to get past the bear first. And even then, he'd be right on my tail. I was fast as a cat, but I doubted I could outmaneuver a seasoned predator.

What was left?

My gaze darted wildly over everything again until it landed on the short parapet wall.

And then I knew what I had to do.

I was a cat shifter, which meant I could do things cats did and that included surviving falls from great heights. The key to survival was to ensure the height wasn't too high and to stay in my cat form. I knew this. Of course, I could still die, but I had better odds of surviving than most, particularly since I still had all nine lives.

I sent out a short thank you to Clive for being an idiot and trying to leap like a flying squirrel when we were kids. And to Mama for teaching us what Clive did wrong that day.

This would take one of my nine lives.

I hoped it'd just be the one.

No, Mama wouldn't lie, not about something like this.

I'd even written that stupid paper about it.

But this was so much different. This was real.

Puke shot up to the back of my mouth, and my heart felt like it'd jumped into my throat right behind it. I trembled. I was seconds away from hyperventilating and passing out.

But Mama wouldn't lie. I had to trust that. I had to believe it. I had to—

The bear lunged at me.

I jumped.

Right over the short brick wall and into nothing.

I was flying.

Like Ogden.

Except… I really, really wasn't. I was hurtling through

the air. Fast. Right down to the ground a bazillion miles below me. What had I done?

I screeched in fear. The pouch, which I'd forgotten was in my mouth, dropped out of my mouth to free-fall with me. All I could do now was pray to the Eternal Magic that I'd survive.

Cats always land on their feet. Cats always land on their feet…

As the gravel alleyway got closer and closer, I forgot how to breathe. I forgot how to do anything at all. This was going to hurt. Real bad. And losing one of my nine? That'd hurt worse.

I wanted to close my eyes, but I couldn't. I wanted to cry for my mama, but my tongue wouldn't work. I wanted to shout out to Ogden that I… I… Holy Mother of Magic, I loved him.

I loved Ogden.

That was my last thought before I hit. Then everything disappeared under a wave of pain and darkness.

Chapter Twenty-Seven

SIMON

I groaned.

My head ached. My body ached. Everything ached.

But I was alive.

How long was I out? Was the bear still stalking me? Was Ogden already lost to me?

I lifted my head and tried to push up on my paws. The world tilted as my legs gave way under my weight. Nausea churned through me. It took everything I had to open my eyes and try again.

My front legs shook as I managed to lift my front half up off the jagged gravel lane. Then I tried to get my back legs to work. They didn't. I dragged them behind me, clawing forward. Needing to move. Needing to get help.

I collapsed again.

It took three tries before I could stand, but at least my back legs were under me this time. They wobbled, but they supported my weight.

How was I going to track Ogden in this condition? I was so screwed. No. I wouldn't give up. I couldn't. Ogden was counting on me. I needed to do better. I had no other choice.

I tottered forward one step. Then two. Then my limbs crumpled again.

I wanted to cry and scream and yowl, but none of that was going to help. The next time I tried to stand, it was easier and faster, and I even lurched forward five steps before falling. I stumbled over the pouch. The one Ogden was supposed to be wearing. I don't know why I bothered, but I picked it up in my mouth again. I clenched my teeth around the fabric and forced myself to move again. And again. Over and over until I finally reached the main street that skirted the front of the building.

The cop car was there.

Just seeing it filled me with rage. How could someone kidnap Ogden when the police officers were *right there*? They were supposed to protect us.

I staggered to the vehicle. They didn't even notice me. I yowled. I thought about jumping on their windshield so they couldn't ignore me any longer, but my body yelled *no way*. Instead, I opted to drag my claws down the driver's side door.

The door flung open, whacking me hard enough to send me sprawling. I lost the pouch again.

"Fu…dgesicle…" I groaned, almost letting out a swear word before I caught myself.

"What the fuck?" The officer apparently wasn't raised by someone like my mama. This woman had no problem cussing as she reached for her gun and sniffed the air. "It's the cat shifter. Simon."

Her partner darted around the car and fell to his knees beside me. I hissed half-heartedly as he reached for me.

"What happened?"

"Og…" I panted heavily. My lungs weren't working right. Each breath I took or word I tried to speak had pain exploding through me like fireworks. But I had to do this. Ogden was counting on me. "Gone. Taken." I groaned.

"Jesus…" the officer muttered.

The other one was on her radio, calling for backup and an ambulance. When she finished, she said, "Stay here with him, I'll go…"

"Greta, don't you dare go in there without backup. Greta? Fuck… Son of a… Fucking Fuck…" He looked torn between staying with me and following his partner.

"Go," I wheezed. "They… took… him… out… through… apartment… Find him…"

The guy nodded, then jumped up and followed Greta. I doubted they'd find anything. That stupid bear and his cohorts had obviously stashed a getaway car somewhere close, and I'd already been around the three sides of the building with roads and lanes and hadn't seen them. I must have been unconscious for a while after my jump.

My heart raced as every harrowing millisecond of my fall crashed over me again. But I was alive. And now people were looking for Ogden. I prayed it was enough. I lurched toward the stupid pouch with the tracker in it again. I don't know why, but it felt important to keep it close. I was probably wrong about that. After all, it hadn't helped yet—and Ogden was already gone, so what would I even do with it now?—but I couldn't shake the compulsion to take it with me.

A moment later, the two officers raced back to the vehicle.

"Grab him," Greta said.

"Shouldn't we—"

"He's a cat shifter. If he survived the fall, he'll be okay."

"I'm sorry if I hurt you," the officer said as he scooped me off the asphalt. Then we were in the car with sirens blaring.

So loud. It hurt my already aching head.

The officer had put me in his lap and was petting me. I wanted to protest. Ogden should be the only one to pet me. But it felt nice as he ran his fingers gently over my ribs and my legs and—Oh. Wait. He wasn't petting me, was he? He was checking for broken bones.

"How are you doing?" he asked. "Do you remember me? I'm Constable Keats, but you can call me Conrad, and this is Sergeant Glover. You probably heard me call her Greta. You wouldn't know it to look at us but we're cousins. You're Simon, right? You are going to be okay, Simon. You're safe now. Can you tell me how you feel?"

I huffed and opened my eyes just enough to look at Conrad. He seemed young to be a police officer, maybe even my age. He looked so sincere… and more than a little freaked out.

"Better," I said. "Getting better."

And amazingly, it was the truth.

With each minute, I felt stronger and less achy. I wasn't sure if that was my magic fixing me, or if my cat's innate ability to survive was at play. I prayed my magic wasn't stealing Ogden's. Still, I was sure I'd lost one of my nine lives. A hollowness had settled in my chest where my magic lived. Instinctively, I knew that feeling had nothing to do with the injuries I'd sustained when I'd smacked into the earth from the top of a tall two-story building. How had my brothers survived losing one of their lives so many times?

"Good. That's good, Simon," Conrad soothed. "Can you tell us what happened?"

Right. I needed to do that. Before I could start, we swung wildly to the left and Conrad grabbed me hard to stop me from flying off his lap. Greta cursed from the driver's seat and updated someone over the radio. Did that mean we were chasing after the a-holes who had Ogden? Yeah. That made sense. I should have figured that out when they picked me up and threw me in the car.

Huh. Maybe I hadn't been knocked out for as long as I thought.

My chest wasn't hurting quite as bad as it had earlier. And my breathing wasn't as labored. I could do this.

"We were on the rooftop," I whispered, because it wasn't as hard to push out words. "A demon... opened a portal. Mage, human, bear... and... and..." Why couldn't I remember who else was there? A mage, a human, a bear... It sounded like the start of a bad joke. Then I remembered I'd thought that when it'd happened. "And a troll came out. The bear killed..." What was his name again? "The bird."

"Wesley?"

"Yeah." I tried to nod. Pain ripped down my spine. Okay. Not doing that again for a while.

"Anything else?"

"Something was wrong with Ogden." Every word was a chore to push out, but I needed them to know what had happened. "Couldn't shift. Couldn't move. Made him sleep. I hid. Others took Ogden down the stairs. Bear tried to kill me. I jumped."

Conrad swallowed hard. "And the demon? Where was he? Why didn't he open another portal?"

"He opened the portal to get everyone on the roof." I'd said that already, hadn't I?

"Why didn't they use a portal to leave too?" Conrad asked.

"The mage said it was a risk. The demon left through the portal. Didn't see him again. The others stayed to move Ogden."

Greta cursed. "The van disappeared. Conrad, can you see it?"

Conrad's attention snapped to the road. "No."

"Damn it." Greta slammed her hands on the steering wheel. Then she called in their location, letting everyone know we'd lost the vehicle we'd been chasing. The car stopped abruptly and again Conrad had to hold me so I didn't go flying. Greta jumped out of the vehicle. Conrad shoved me off his lap and followed his partner. We were in the countryside now, although we couldn't be that far from Aspen Bay. They returned a few minutes later.

Neither of them jumped back inside to continue the chase.

"What?"

"We fucking lost them," Greta snapped. "I can't smell anything out there."

"Was it them? Are you sure?" I asked Conrad while Greta updated whoever was listening on the other end of her radio.

He nodded. "We followed their scent trail to the street over. Got there just as they were getting into the van."

"Ballsy move, carrying him so far," Greta said. "It's like they were taunting us."

"Probably thought no one would be out downtown to see them and normally they would have been right."

"We'll wait here for the others. Hopefully with more help we can pick up their trail."

I closed my eyes and let my head drop onto the seat. I wondered if even Mama would swear at a time like this.

Chapter Twenty-Eight

SIMON

I don't know how long we waited before a bunch of cars with sirens and flashing lights came racing down the rural road toward us and screeched to a halt in a billow of dust. I glanced at the clock, but it didn't tell me much. I did not know when those people had shown up on the rooftop. It had to have been a while ago, because the sun had risen pretty high in the east now.

On any other day, I would be making my way to Mama's house for breakfast about now. I missed it. I missed Ogden more.

Greta was telling their colleagues what she knew, but Conrad hadn't left my side yet.

"They'll take you to the hospital. They'll run some tests to make sure you are okay," he was saying.

I frowned at him. I wasn't sure that look would translate since I was still in my cat form, but I wasn't leaving. No way. Not until we found Ogden. If I pushed, I could probably shift, but my instincts were screaming at me not to—was I more injured than I thought? Shifting had never hurt before, but my body had never been so battered before, either. Whatever the reason my intuition had for warning me like this, I knew shifting wouldn't be easy and I didn't want any of these strangers to watch me fight my way into my human shape.

Pops always said cats were proud and noble creatures, and I was no different.

"At least let the paramedic look you over," the cop said.

"That's just a trick to get me in the ambulance, then they'll take off with me inside."

"I promise not to do that," the paramedic said.

I knew Ogden would want me to get checked over, but all that could wait. Besides, I was already feeling a lot better than when I'd first woken up after my jump.

The arrival of another convoy of vehicles saved me from answering. I'd never been so happy to see the Willow Lake Chief of Police, but when Van jumped out of the first vehicle, I could have hugged him—I probably would have if I wasn't still a cat. They couldn't have made that kind of time all the way from Willow Lake and still obeyed the speed limits. Even from here, I could see Van's eyes blazing with the fire of his hellhound and black smoke billowing from his mouth.

Right behind him was a bunch of other familiar faces too. Dillon was there, of course. But they weren't alone. Hayden, Ash, Gage, and the people who'd come to Willow Lake with the demon were all there too. Seeing them eased some of the aching worry crushing my chest. Before this moment, I never would have expected them to rush to help me. I was just Simon. Just a regular old cat shifter. Nothing special. But here they all were.

Van rushed over to me first, and Gage was right behind him—already in his shifted form—like a big red avenging angel. The dark horns on his head looked especially ominous and threatening under the bright early morning sun. His red, leathery wings snapped behind him when he saw me. The guy was badass, no doubt about it. And right now, he looked pissed. Power rolled off him in waves and even the Aspen Bay Police stopped to look at him as he passed.

"Teague," Gage called out to one of his people. "Over here."

I wanted to scurry away from the death mage, but I didn't have the energy. Van wouldn't let them do anything to me, would he?

Teague ran over. The paramedic scowled when Gage told them to get out of the way.

"Can I touch you?" Teague asked.

"Okay," I said with a yawn.

As soon as the mage's hands brushed my fur, his magic tingled through me. I squirmed but resisted the urge to hiss and bite. Gradually, the ache in my bones and my head eased.

"That's enough," I said.

"I haven't finished yet..." Teague argued, but the strange tingling sensation stopped abruptly.

"Am I going to die?"

"No, but—"

"Then that's enough. Save your energy in case…" I couldn't finish the sentence.

Teague frowned at me, then glanced up at Gage. Gage nodded. The mage pulled his hands away. "Come and find me if anything changes and you start to feel worse."

"Sure."

The hellhounds knew I lied when I agreed to do as the mage asked, but no one called me on it.

I shook out my fur and sighed in relief at how much easier I could breathe and move now. Would it last? I took a couple of steps by the side of the gravel road. My limbs all behaved as they were supposed to and none of them threatened to give out on me.

Success.

We'd wasted enough time. We needed to find Ogden.

As Teague backed away, Van and Gage closed in around me.

"Talk to me," Van said. "What happened?"

I groaned. Hadn't I already gone over all of this? Then shame flashed through me. Ogden was missing. The least I could do was tell anyone who'd listen what had happened. I just felt so weary.

Hayden pushed through the crowd of people surrounding me. Then he was crouching in front of me. He scowled at Van. "He's still hurt."

"He asked Teague to stop."

"Need to shift." I tried to force my body to change, but I was too weak. I looked at Hayden. "Help."

Hayden sucked in a breath. "It'll hurt."

"I need help," I argued.

The alpha cupped the back of my small skull in his

hand. The power of his touch washed through me. Then he leaned down until his mouth was right at my ear.

"Shift," he commanded.

My body responded to my alpha's wish. I groaned through the pain. Okay. So maybe I hadn't healed as much as I had thought. I ended up in my human form in a crouch position. I swayed and landed on my ass. Even though I was sitting, I was sure I was still swaying. Was I dizzy? I couldn't even tell, but something wasn't right with me.

Hayden dropped to his knees and grabbed me before I toppled over. He yanked me into his arms with one of his hands gripping the back of my neck again.

"Alpha," I murmured and pushed my face into his neck. His scent soothed me, even better than my mama's would have—but don't tell her that.

He smelled of grease and new tires and a strange bit like ash again, but under all that, he smelled of home and belonging. His gentle power wrapped around me, and I knew he would use that power to do anything and everything to protect me and my mate, because I was one of his. Even if he didn't aspire to be an alpha, he was still my alpha.

"I got you," Hayden said gruffly.

I relaxed into his embrace.

Then, from the safety of my alpha's arms, I told everyone what had happened up on that rooftop. When I got to the part about the demon, Gage cursed. When I told them about Wesley being killed, Ash muttered something about how he'd gotten what he deserved for betraying his friend like that. And when I described how I'd jumped from the roof to escape the bear, Hayden made a strange gasping noise.

Van and Gage had a few questions, but my answers weren't all that helpful.

"Okay, everyone," Davina, the woman who'd come with Gage, said as she clapped her hands. "Listen up."

She was wearing a fitted red leather jacket that flared at her hips, showing off her curves, and she had on the tallest heels I'd ever seen in real life. Her hairstyle was big —not big and crazy like people wore in the '80s, which I only knew from seeing photos of my mama, but big, smooth, and helmet-like. Was that from the '60s? Something like that. At any rate, the style was not current, but she was rocking it. And just as every single bit of hair was controlled and in its place, she'd also taken complete control of everyone who'd gathered here. A moment ago, she'd been listening to what'd happened, and now she was issuing commands.

"Okay, people. We're going to start our search here. You're being divided into teams. Each team is responsible for searching their assigned area and reporting back. If you notice anything or feel anything while you are walking around, let me know immediately. I don't care how small or inconsequential. You will report every damn thing. Suddenly have indigestion? Tell me. The urge to sneeze? Tell me. Shivers going down your back? That one you definitely better tell me about. You get the idea? Now, let's go find these fuckers."

No one from either police department questioned her authority as she started pointing at people and assigning them an area to search. With her ease at wrangling all those supernatural beings into obeying her, she reminded me of Mama, except Davina cussed a lot more.

Chapter Twenty-Nine

SIMON

"Are they gone?" Gage glanced at Davina.

"What do you think?" She put her hands on her hips and tapped her foot on the gravel like she couldn't believe he had to ask.

"Good." He nodded, making the sunlight ricochet off his dark horns.

"I have the whistle," I whispered to Gage. I hadn't wanted to say anything in front of the other officers. "Should I use it?"

"No." Gage's reply was loud and firm. "You are already bound to Ogden, so it won't work on him again. If you blow on it now, it'll pull another unbound supe to you. Probably a dragon, but if none are within range, it'll latch onto someone else."

A sharp pain sliced through my chest. "I thought... But..."

"Don't worry. We have a plan. Alright, Teague, let's do this." Gage beckoned the death mage over.

"What's going on?" I shivered.

Yes, I'd accepted Teague's help when I had to, but he was still a death mage, and I still didn't know what his magic could do. I'd already lost one life; I didn't want to lose another so soon. My eyebrows rose as Teague once again crouched next to me. Besides, he was supposed to be saving his energy to help Ogden.

"I can see your bond with Ogden. Congratulations on that, by the way."

"Thanks, I guess. But how does that help?"

The mage looked earnest as he smiled at me. Something about his unassuming good looks made me want to trust him, despite my misgivings about his magic. And he had already healed me, so that helped too. "We're going to use it to find him."

"Why did you send the others away?" Something was going on, and I wasn't keen on secrets. Secrets led to problems and problems put lives at risk. I only had eight left. I had to be careful.

"They'd be useless in fighting a demon," Gage, who was also a demon, said it like it was obvious.

"So we're going to find Ogden?"

Gage rolled his eyes like I was wasting his time with questions like that, but Teague smiled reassuringly and nodded.

I don't know why he thought we'd all be better off with half the people we could have, especially when I was pretty sure those police officers from Aspen Bay would be better at fighting a demon than I would, but whatever. The most important thing was getting Ogden back, and I trusted these people to do that. After that, I needed to make sure no one ever kidnapped him again.

"Okay. What do you need from me?" I asked.

"I'm going to put my hand here," Teague said as he rested his hand over my chest. "And then I'll work a short spell. It's as easy as that. Then we'll go and find your dragon."

I swallowed. "Okay. Do that."

As Teague mumbled his way through some kind of incantation, magic stirred through the air, making the fine hairs on the back of my neck stand on end. Then his eyes snapped open. They were glowing. I'd seen fire in Van's eyes showing his hellhound and I'd seen golden light flare in Hayden's showing his werewolf, but the mage's eyes were creepy as all get out. They were pitch black. No iris. No white. They looked robotic.

"That way," Teague said, pointing to the empty field behind me.

"How far? Can you tell?" Van asked.

"Not far." Then he stood and started walking across the ditch in the direction he'd pointed.

I scooped up the pouch with the tracking device from the front seat of the police vehicle I'd come in and shoved it in my pocket beside the whistle. As soon as I found Ogden, I would give it to him. I needed to know I could find him again. Easily. Even if the death mage wasn't around. Then I followed the mage, and everyone else did too. No one spoke.

Was I the only one wondering why we were walking into a wheat field? The tall seed heads nodded lazily at us as we trampled through the thigh-high plants, heading straight east. The early morning sun was low enough on the horizon that it made looking ahead difficult. I wished I had sunglasses like Van did because my eyes were burning and watering like crazy as I strained to see a building or Ogden or anything at all under the harsh, bright sunlight.

Nothing made a sound. There were no birds, no insects, no sounds of engines on the road, nor planes in the air overhead. It was eerie and unnatural. It took every ounce of the tiny amount of courage I had to press forward and keep up with the others.

Then Gage held up his hand and made a fist. Everyone froze. I'd only seen a gesture like that in military or cop shows. Apparently, shit was getting real.

And now I'd gone and sworn.

And I really wanted to swear a whole lot more, but I didn't think chanting *fuck, fuck, fuck, fuck, fuck* while hoping Ogden would miraculously appear was going to work. I'd performed one miracle the day I'd blown on that whistle. I was pretty sure that meant I'd already reached my lifetime's quota on miracles.

My heart was pounding frantically in my chest like it needed to beat its way out. Sweat poured down my face like I was standing under a faucet. And I desperately wanted to shift so I could hightail it out of there and hide.

Except Ogden needed me.

And… I still had eight of my nine lives left.

I'd be okay.

For Ogden, I could do this. And I could sacrifice

another life if it meant getting him back. The realization made me lightheaded, but it was true. I'd sacrifice all of them if it'd keep him safe.

Gage reached up with both hands, palms facing out, then he leaned forward as if bracing against something. The heavy feeling of magic rolled over me, nearly knocking me off my still unsteady feet. Gage grunted, and the scent of brimstone clogged the air. Then a crackling sound broke the oppressive silence.

Everything changed at that moment.

The wheat field disappeared, and suddenly we were standing before a concrete block building in what looked like an abandoned farmyard. No house was in sight, but there were a few other rundown shacks around the place. The concrete structure with its chipped paint and rusted metal roof looked newer than those little outbuildings, but it was still old.

Sounds of people crying and the stink of fear crashed over me. Not my fear. But someone else's... a lot of someones.

"Ogden!" I raced forward, shifting mid-stride into my cat form.

Van tried to stop me, but I ducked around him. Then Gage reached for me, and I evaded him too. I was a cat. I may not be a brave or big cat, but I was cat enough to get away from someone who tried to stop me.

Scrambling around the corner of the building, I looked for a door. Then it was there. Ajar. I darted inside without stopping to think about what I might find.

Large cages, stacked two and three high, crowded the interior of the long, narrow building.

Someone was running ahead of me. Was that the human who'd helped kidnap Ogden? He'd know where Ogden was. I surged forward, determined to catch him. I may not be the best runner in the family, but I could beat a simple human in a race any day. The human ran through the building. By the time he reached the large door at the far end of the building, I was snapping at his heels. All I needed to do was trip him and I'd have him.

"That noise! Did you hear it? They found us," the human—Edgar—shouted.

Then I realized he'd led me right to his cohorts. And I was alone. I skidded to a halt and scrambled back a couple of steps.

"Open the portal, demon. Troll, go get the dragon and the unicorn. Take your pet with you so he doesn't get in my way," Teddy the mage directed his underlings.

Vala the troll scurried off to do his bidding. The human followed. I guessed that was who Teddy called her pet. I didn't think trolls liked humans all that much. Was it a star-crossed lovers thing?

"Fuck," Teddy muttered. "We'll have to leave the rest of these. Start from scratch. Again." He huffed out a breath like this whole situation was an irritating inconvenience.

The demon growled but did as the mage said and opened a portal. How on earth was a mage controlling a demon? That was crazy. The demon didn't move or say anything else.

"Hello, kitty cat." The murderous bear shifter grinned at me as he waggled his fingers in the creepiest wave I'd ever seen. I hated that he called me by the same name Ogden used. "If only I had twisted your little neck when I found your broken body in that alley. I won't make that mistake again."

"We don't have time for that," Teddy snapped, stopping the bear's advance on me.

Meanwhile, Vala and Edgar had returned. They pushed a wheeled cage toward the portal. The cage was just as Ogden had described it, but this one didn't hold my dragon. The small man had shimmering curls, round cheeks, and big expressive eyes. I recognized him from the oracle's painting. This had to be the unicorn.

"Morgan!" I shouted, remembering at the last moment what Odgen had called him.

The man looked up at the sound of his name. He lifted his hand in a little wave; a small shy smile played over his face. I chased after them, hoping to stop the troll before she pushed the pretty man through the portal, but the bear swatted me with one of his massive paws. The impact sent me flying into the concrete wall. All my partly healed injuries screamed in agony. By the time I'd shaken off the hurt, the cage with the unicorn was gone.

The bear glanced at the mage to see if he was distracted, then he started stalking toward me again. He froze when a loud roar shook the building. The sound came from behind me. It had to be Gage and the others. The beast turned back and lumbered toward the mage. Obviously, he didn't consider me a threat, which was okay with me.

"Get back here, Gus. We have more important things to worry about than a little shifter like that." Teddy once again stopped the bear's advance on me. Then he scowled at the demon. "I thought you reinforced the ward this morning, Solon."

"I told you someone broke through already," the human muttered, crossing his arms over his chest. "Why does no one ever listen to me?"

"I listen to you, baby," the troll said softly.

The bear shifter ignored the exchange, and Solon didn't speak. The demon's face, though, betrayed how much he was hating this.

"How many are there?" the mage asked.

The demon closed his eyes and his magic pulsed. I didn't know how I knew this, but there was something wrong with it.

"Four. Two wolves, a medium, and a mage." Solon's eyes snapped open, and he looked at me. "Plus that one, the cat."

I barely registered that the demon had lied when everyone's head swiveled to look at me. I squeaked— and, no, I absolutely didn't sound like a mouse—and dove behind some boxes close to the shimmering portal. When no one pounced on me, I peeked over the boxes. I was sure that bear would be coming for me again, but Teddy snapped his fingers to get everyone's attention. Perfect.

Before I could second guess what I was doing, my shift flowed over me. This shift to my human form didn't hurt as much as when Hayden had forced my last one, but it wasn't as easy as usual. After using so much magic today, I was going to need a boatload of fish sticks to balance my magic. I crouched behind the boxes and prayed they would forget about me—I was just a little cat shifter, so I wasn't a threat, right? They wouldn't waste their time coming after little old me.

I pulled out the pouch with the tracking device.

"We need to do something," Edgar begged. "A cat is one thing; even I can handle a cat that size. But wolves? Jesus, Vala, we need to get the hell out of here." He tried to drag the troll toward the portal.

Everyone turned to stare at the panicking human. Good. It took their attention off me.

"Relax, Edgar. It'll be fine. Teddy knows what he's doing," Vala said. Then she pried her hand out of Edgar's and went scurrying back into the stacks of cages.

I peeked over the boxes again. The portal was right there. I squeezed the pouch. I could do this. A braver cat would jump through it, but my priority would always be Ogden. I could do this one thing, though, for that unicorn. My gaze darted to the group again. No one was watching me except the demon. He dipped his head a little, like he was encouraging me to act. I jumped up and hurled the pouch through the portal.

I ducked back down again and waited for the demon to cry out, letting everyone know what I'd done. He didn't.

"For fuck's sake." The mage huffed like this was all a terrible inconvenience. He polished the big gaudy ring he was wearing with the hem of his T-shirt. That ring was important. It had to be that Coven of One ring. Shoot. I'd forgotten to tell Van about that, hadn't I? Son of a tomcat, how had I forgotten about that? "If there are only five, we can take them. That way we won't lose all this inventory. Close the portal, demon."

The portal vanished.

"But the wolves…" the human complained, eyeing the spot where the portal had been.

"We've dealt with shifters before. We can do it again. Besides we can make good money if we sell them, even if there are so many of them around. Don't worry about taking the mage or the medium alive. Nobody wants them. Can't give them away."

That was ironic, right? Since it was a mage who said that? Ogden would know if that was irony. He was smarter than I was.

"Okay. Vala, you take—" the mage stopped and scowled. He cast his gaze around for the troll. "Where is she?"

A squeaky wheel, like something you'd hear at a supermarket, announced the troll's arrival. They were distracted, so I shifted to my cat form. It was time to sink away and find Ogden.

"What are you doing, troll?" Teddy demanded.

"You told me to get this one too," Vala said. She looked around and scratched her cheek. "Uh… Where is the portal?"

"Pay attention." The mage snapped his fingers at her. "We have to deal with the intruders first. Go secure the back door. It'll be better if we only have to defend from one side."

Vala scurried off to do as he wished. I didn't follow. I didn't care what she did because my entire focus was on the cage with the squeaky wheel that held my dragon. My Ogden.

He was alive!

"Gus, you deal with the cat. You've been bitching and

complaining about him ever since we retrieved the dragon."

Uh oh.

I didn't hear what order the mage gave to Edgar. My blood was pounding too loudly in my ears. The bear shifter's smirk had a downright evil twist to it as he stomped across the floor toward my hiding place. Fu—Fish bones! I should have moved while they were talking.

Ogden blinked. His head wobbled as if he wasn't fully awake yet. When his eyes caught on mine, he paled. We stared at one another for what seemed like an eternity, but had to have only been a second or two. Ogden shook himself, as if trying to shake off the lingering effects of whatever they'd used to incapacitate him.

"You won't get away this time," the bear promised.

Yeah. That didn't sound good. That was pretty much the opposite of good.

Ogden struggled to break the bars of his cage, but they didn't budge. Then I had to look away from my mate because the bear was closing in on me. My first instinct was to run and hide, but I fought it. I couldn't abandon Ogden to these people. What if the demon opened another portal and pushed Ogden through it to some faraway place? What if he was sent so far away Teague couldn't follow our connection?

No. I wasn't leaving Ogden.

I had to help him. I had to get him out. And if that didn't work, and they opened another portal, I'd follow Ogden through it. I would follow him anywhere. I still had eight lives. I could do this.

The bear's deep and menacing chuckle made me hiss. My back arched. I didn't know what I thought I was doing —no supe the size of this bear would be intimated by my puffed-up size or hisses—but my instincts had taken over and were doing whatever they wanted.

Before I could figure out what to do next, fire and electricity arced out of the cage and hit the bear. The massive supe shrieked in terror and pain. He spun wildly. The fire and electricity didn't stop. The smell of burnt flesh assaulted my nose, making me gag. The bear staggered one way, then the other, before falling with a thud to the ground. His skin was steaming and sizzling, but he didn't move.

"Simon! Run!" my dragon yelled at me from inside that cage. He'd saved me. Now I had to save him too.

"Ogden!" I rushed to the cage.

The troll snarled and snapped at me, blocking my path to Ogden. Where had she come from? It obviously hadn't taken her long to lock the back door. She kicked out at me, but I dodged her foot.

Then I was at the cage. Ogden was right there. After expending his magic, he had slumped against the bars, not moving except for the steady rise and fall of his chest. Throwing that electricity-charged shot at the bear had exhausted him. But he was safe and in one piece, and that's what mattered. He was right on the other side of those stupid magic-covered bars, and I would get him out. I clawed at the cage, but the door wouldn't budge. Of course it wouldn't. I knew that. Ogden had said as much when he'd talked about the stupid cages.

There had to be a key somewhere. I had to find it.

The troll shuffled sluggishly toward me. I was confident I could dodge her again. But what if I was mistaken, and she caught me under her foot? That'd be at least one more life gone.

But if she had the key…

I had five brothers. I hadn't done everything they'd done, but it would have been impossible not to pick up a few things from them over the years. They'd forced me to learn to climb trees when they chased me up them. They'd forced me to learn to steal back my belongings when they stole from me. They'd forced me to do things even when I didn't want to.

And right now, as I eyed that troll, I hoped I'd learned enough.

I had to get the timing right. She swayed with each step. Her arms swung. Everything was so predictable and rhythmic. Another shuffling step. Another swing. And… there! Go!

I jumped on the troll. I sank my claws into her pockets and pulled as hard as I could. My claws sliced through the fabric. Vala screamed, but like all trolls, she wasn't agile. I jumped away. I'd damaged her pockets, but they weren't open yet. I gritted my teeth.

I could do this.

I *had* to do this.

I did the same thing again. This time, the fabric gaped open to reveal… nothing.

Absolutely nothing dropped out of the troll's pockets. Not a thing. How did someone go through life with nothing in their pockets? Shouldn't she at least have a cellphone or a favorite pebble?

"I'll get you, you little bastard," the troll shouted. She spun away and stalked off. I didn't know where she was going, but I wasn't about to call her back.

I glanced around the room. The mage and the demon weren't there; all that remained were the bear, who still hadn't moved, and the human, aka the troll's pet, aka Edgar. Not that it mattered if I knew his name. We weren't destined to be friends.

I eyed him from top to bottom. He was an average height, an average build. He didn't appear athletic. I could handle him, right? He was a human. In my shifted form, I might only be a slightly chunky house cat, but I was still a supe.

"Fuck off," the human said, waving his hands at me like he was trying to shoo me away. "Go on."

His front pocket was bulging... and no, I wasn't checking out his junk. And if his junk was that lumpy and weird looking, he had a big problem. That bulge had to be keys. I bounded toward the human and clawed at his pocket. He batted at me, but I dug in and hung on. The fabric gave way. Amongst the coins were a fancy pock-etknife, a packet of gum, and a comb, but no keys.

I jumped away and shrieked my frustration.

Why couldn't this be easy?

And then, suddenly, it got worse.

The mage and demon were in the doorway. The light from the bright day made them look like dark and feature-less silhouettes as they raced inside. Well, the mage ran. The demon looked like he was just being dragged along by the mage.

"Seal the door, demon," the mage demanded. "We'll defend from here."

Solon's body took his demon form right in front of my eyes. Black wings sprouted from his back, his fingertips changed to black claws, and his eyes turned red. His skin wasn't black like I'd thought when I'd seen him on the roof, but a deep dark burgundy. It reminded me of dried blood. My tail puffed up as I hissed at the intimidating creature, but he wasn't looking at me. He was eyeing the mage.

His muscles bulged and rippled like he was fighting against a command.

Huh?

Oh!

This demon hadn't snapped. He wasn't one of those wild ones that inspired scary campfire stories. I'd bet anything the mage had trapped him in the same way the whistle could have done with Ogden. There had been another whistle missing, right? And when coupled with the Coven of One ring, the demon wouldn't have escaped.

He wasn't the instigator. He was an unwilling participant, a victim.

It was hurting him to fight the mage's order. My stomach rolled. How could anyone do that to another person? Was that what Ogden had thought I'd do to him when I summoned him? Bile shot up the back of my throat. I couldn't. I wouldn't. Never.

As if summoned by my thoughts, Gage, Van, and the others appeared from all directions. Some entered through the doorway that the mage and the demon were supposed to be defending. Others came from behind me, probably through the door that the troll had been tasked with locking. I knew she hadn't been gone long enough to do that.

I needed to tell them to leave the demon alone!

"You lied." The mage's accusation was low and full of menace as he glared at the demon. Then he did something with his hand, squeezing it into a fist. Solon's whole body trembled, and his limbs flailed.

"They... must... have... used... portal..." he lied.

Teddy's nostrils flared. The ring on his finger glowed an eerie lime green color. "Good fucking idea. Open a portal, now."

But Solon gritted his teeth and fought the order. His body convulsed and jerked under whatever power the mage wielded.

"Now, demon!"

No portal appeared.

"The demon isn't bad!" I shouted and prayed my deduction was right.

Gage scanned the room, taking in the whole situation.

"The mage is controlling the demon," I shouted again —you know, just in case the others, who were far smarter than me, hadn't figured it out yet.

Then everyone seemed to move at once. The human was running in one direction. The troll was waddling after him. The mage was still squeezing the life out of the demon. And all my... friends? Yes. I guess they were my friends after going through all this with me. My friends were all chasing down the bad guys or rushing to fight the mage.

But me?

I only had eyes for my dragon. His eyelids fluttered

like he was fighting to wake up. I suspected he still had drugs in his system and he'd spent his energy spewing his fiery electrical cocktail at the bear. Even seated as he was, he tilted to the side like a drunk at closing time.

"Ogden?"

He didn't respond.

"Ogden!"

Still nothing.

What had they done to him?

I eyed the bars of the cage. They weren't too close together... I brought my head up to the cage. The bars brushed my whiskers, but not uncomfortably so. I pushed forward, squeezing through the bars. Then I was in. I brushed up against my dragon, nudging my head against his hand. When he still didn't move, I nipped at his finger.

Ogden startled awake.

"Simon," he whispered. His voice sounded hoarse and scratchy. The scent of his fear grew stronger. "Run, kitty cat. You gotta get out of here."

"I'm not leaving you," I said. "We're going to get you out of here. Now cross your legs so I can sit in your lap. No one needs to see your..." The word wouldn't leave my mouth. It was bad enough that I'd sworn in my head earlier. I couldn't say the first word that came to mind. And now I couldn't think of what else to call... um, it.

Ogden's laugh sounded a bit like a sob as he picked me up with trembling arms and hugged me.

"I love you, my kitty cat," he said. He pushed his tear-dampened face into my fur. "I didn't think I'd get to tell you that."

"I love you too, Ogden." My words sounded odd and

rumbly, because I couldn't stop purring. I searched for the link that joined us. It wasn't as obvious to me as it might have been to Teague, but I found it. And when I did, I poured all the love and energy I could into it. "I was so scared we wouldn't find you in time and that I'd lost you."

"I wish you weren't in your cat form right now," Ogden whispered against my fur. "You don't know how badly I want to hug you and kiss you. But I don't think we'd both fit in here if you shifted now."

Chapter Thirty

OGDEN

I held tight to Simon's furry body, wishing I could get out of this damn cage. Having my mate close did miracles for me. I could actually feel my magic growing stronger and my energy levels rising as our magics entwined. It was crazy. I'd never heard of anything like that happening, although who would I have asked?

The drugs that had made me groggy a minute ago were draining quickly from my system. It had to be because of Simon. That was the only explanation.

And now I was ready to kick some asses.

"I need to find the keys," Simon said as he squirmed in my arms to get free. "Get you out of here."

"No." The single word came out more like a roar, my dragon adamant about not letting my mate risk himself again.

"Ogden." Simon peered up at me. His yellowy-green gaze met mine. "I don't take unnecessary risks, remember?

I like having my…" His words stopped abruptly. A flash of pain shot over his face.

"What? What happened?"

He shook his head.

"I don't take unnecessary risks," he repeated, leaving off whatever else he'd been about to say.

Something had happened. Someone had hurt my mate. My dragon thrashed for freedom, eager to devour my enemies. I didn't care if I had to swallow them whole. I wanted to destroy them. Some small rational part of me recognized it'd take a long time to digest something the size of a human, though, and I didn't want to be stuck in my dragon form that long. But if I got free, I wasn't sure my rational thoughts would have any sway over my desire for revenge and the need to protect my mate.

"Ogden, please…" Simon's soft paw touched my cheek. "I need you out of this cage."

I glanced through the bars of my cage at the fight going on around us. My mate's friends from Willow Lake were fighting my enemies, fighting for my life and my freedom, while all I could do was sit on my ass and watch. I hated it.

And if they lost…

I needed to be free so I could help. It could be the difference between winning or not. Between saving myself and all these other supes or living in a cage for the rest of my life.

I swallowed hard. With a shaky hand, I loosened my hold on Simon. I cupped his head in my hand, and he looked up to meet my eyes.

"You need to be careful. Be safe," I choked out. "If you need to run to protect yourself, then run."

"I promise." Simon swallowed hard. "Do you remember anything from when they brought you here?"

"I was unconscious. The first time I woke up was just as that bear went for you." I couldn't help him. It wasn't my fault, I knew that, but I still felt like a failure.

"I'll find them." Simon licked my hand with his rough tongue like he was trying to soothe me, then he darted out of the cage.

I gripped the bars, ignoring the zing of foreign magic, and watched my brave mate sprint through the room. I was determined to help him, if I could. The large bear shifter still hadn't moved from when I'd fried him earlier. Over the cacophony of noise, I couldn't hear if his heart was still beating or not. I hoped not. He'd threatened to kill my mate. He deserved death, but even if he survived, it would take him a long time to heal from the wounds I'd inflicted. Good. I hoped his burns got infected.

And I was ready to do the same to anyone else who came near me. My fires were slowly building up again. Normally my recovery period was quicker, but I was obviously still impacted by the summoning. They were coming though. Soon they would burn for release. My gaze darted from one of my captors to the next.

"Get back," the little bitch of a troll screeched.

Somewhere along the line, she'd armed herself with her favorite cattle prod, but I doubted it'd help her. She was trying to work it with her non-dominant hand, since her dominant one was still wrapped up and injured from when she'd gotten too close to me the first time we'd met.

"Put that down," Isaac demanded, keeping her attention on him and away from the wolf—I thought it was probably Adrian—who was stalking her from the other side.

Her back was against a line of cages. The imprisoned supes, showing a surprising amount of initiative compared to the last time I was here, clawed at her to hold her in place. She struggled against their grasping hands as she shifted into her alternate form, which would harden her skin, making it more difficult to penetrate. That was her only defense, though. Since she couldn't activate her cattle prod, her fight moves were limited to swinging the prod around wildly while cackling like a witch in a low-budget movie.

She smacked Isaac across the face. Before she could lift the prod again, Adrian had her arm clamped in his teeth. She thrashed her arm from side to side to dislodge him.

"Run, Edgar," she shouted.

But it was too late for the human. Davina and Teague had already cornered him. Good. He and his cohorts deserved to be at the mercy of a death mage.

"Don't hurt me!" The human lifted his hands in the air. His pants were shredded, and I wondered if that was my mate's work. "I surrender."

That was the first thing the human had done that showed he wasn't a complete idiot.

"Perfect. I'll take this one," Davina shouted to her teammates. She was laughing as she manhandled the man until he was belly down on the dirty concrete floor with his arms and legs spread out. She might only have been a medium, but the way she moved, I didn't doubt she could have taken down any of the supes. The human sobbed as Davina checked through his torn pockets.

She was a vision. If I'd been into women—and not happily mated to my kitty cat—she might even have tempted me. Her style was exquisite. Her flashy red leather jacket looked stunning on her. It had to be tailored. I'd definitely be asking her about it later.

Provided I ever got out of this blasted cage.

Within a few minutes, the human was cuffed and secured. The troll surrendered as soon as she saw the human was in custody. With those two down, there were only two more to go. *Only*. Ha. As if the demon wasn't the equivalent of an army on his own. I hoped Simon was right and the demon was working against the mage.

Actually, where was Simon?

I searched the area, sparing only a fleeting glance at the rest of Simon's motley group of friends who were working on the mage and the demon.

The bear shifter groaned. Damn it. I'd hoped he was dead. The asshole rolled.

And that's when I saw Simon. He was creeping over to the injured bear shifter. Couldn't he have done that when the guy was unconscious?

"Simon…" I whispered, whether in prayer or warning, I didn't know. His ears twitched, so I knew he heard me.

I held my breath as Simon's shift washed over him. He was so damn vulnerable in his human form. I clenched the bars, trying and failing to rip them apart. When Simon's hand slipped into the bear's pocket, I didn't blink.

A second later, he held a set of keys.

He did it. Holy Magic, he did it.

Simon raced toward me. His hands shook as he tried key after key. Then one slid into the lock. Magic shimmered along the cage.

Turn. Click. Freedom.

I burst out of the cage.

No cheerful song about innocence and first love suited this moment. I was free, and I was ready to destroy things. I usually preferred older songs, but that didn't mean I didn't know newer ones, and right now the chorus from "Bodies" by Drowning Pool was my personal soundtrack. I roared.

Everyone spun toward me, needing to assess the latest threat. The human, even though he'd already surrendered, pissed his pants. My dragon's roar hadn't scared my mate, though. Not at all. His flushed face and dilated pupils said it all. My display turned him on. Such a good mate. Every primitive atom in me wanted to bend him over, right now, right here, and reward him.

But first I needed to devour our enemies.

I yanked on my magic, urging my shift to flow over me.

It didn't work. My shift refused to come. Fire and electricity spewed from my mouth. At least I still had recovered enough to do that again. It arced across the room and slapped against the mage's shield. His ring caught my eye again. There was something about that ring. I'd bet anything that was the source of his unnatural power. It had to be the Coven of One ring Gage and his friends had said was missing. I hadn't believed it existed, yet here was proof.

I staggered toward the mage, not quite at one hundred percent yet, but determined to break through his shields and rip the ring from his finger. I didn't care if I had to bite off his hand to do it.

I made it three steps before my legs gave way. Blaze it all anyway. I thought Simon had fixed me, but whatever they'd drugged me with wasn't gone from my system yet.

"Fuck!" I screamed out my frustration.

"Teague, help Simon get the others out," Isaac shouted as he joined his teammates in a semi-circle around the mage and the demon. Adrian, still in his wolf form, was dragging the squirming troll across the floor to where Davina had the human tied up. She might have surrendered, but she wasn't happy about it.

"Come on," Teague shouted at Simon.

Simon lingered, staring at me like he didn't want to leave me.

"Go on," I urged. "I'll be fine."

He hesitated a few more seconds before following Teague to the caged supes.

I grasped at my magic again. Still, my body refused to obey me.

All I could do was watch and wait for the opportunity to blast my enemies.

"Get the mage's ring," I shouted at the others. Since they hadn't been drugged and weren't fighting through the drug's hazy aftereffects like me, I suspected they'd already concluded he was wearing the Coven of One ring, but it didn't hurt to say it.

Van and Dillon were both in their hellhound forms. It'd been centuries since I'd seen a shifted hellhound—they were magnificent, although not as magnificent as my beautiful mate. Fire dripped from their black, canine-like bodies. Touching that fire would scorch the mage, but they couldn't seem to get through the mage's shields to get to his body. They clawed at the shimmering cage but couldn't crack it.

Nelson was also in his ethereal, shadowy form, floating around the mage's shield like the guy's own personal black cloud. His wispy form opened only enough to allow the hellhounds through. At least if the mage couldn't see the others, it would hinder his attacks against them.

Gage, Hayden, and Isaac were fighting to free the enslaved demon. As soon as Adrian finished dragging the bear shifter over to Davina's pile of captured supes, he bounded toward the demon.

"We gotta get the demon away from here," Hayden shouted.

"On it." Gage grunted. His fatigue was showing. Since he was tethered to Willow Lake, he wouldn't be as strong outside his territory.

The trapped demon looked at Gage, as if begging for death. Instead, a portal opened behind Gage. Gage's team looked alarmed, so I hoped it was Gage's portal. Then Gage wrapped his arms around the other demon and dragged him through.

"Fuck," Hayden shouted as he lunged after them, only to have the portal snap shut before he could get there. "Gage took them to Willow Lake, didn't he?" Hayden shifted quickly and pulled out his phone from the back pocket of his torn and grease-stained jeans. A minute later, he was issuing orders to people to find Gage and help him subdue the strange demon. His fear for his people was palpable. He may not consider himself the alpha, but he was.

The mage was still fighting, but he was clearly weaker than he had been when the demon was there. He tried backing away but ended up tripping on the motionless bear, which sent him sprawling right to me. His magical shield faltered, just for a moment, but that was enough. I couldn't shift yet, but that didn't mean I was useless. My fires had ignited inside me again. I unleashed it and my fiery electricity flowed over the mage. My attack wasn't as strong as it had been against the bear, but my efforts were enough to stop the mage from creating another shield. I squeezed every bit of magic I could muster into my fire and electricity. It poured from me for a long moment before sputtering to an end. It was spent. *I* was spent. I had nothing left. I hoped it'd been enough.

Van—at least I was sure that one was Officer Hellhound—sprang forward and clamped his teeth around the mage's throat. I stared, waiting for him to rip through the tender flesh. He didn't. He simply held tight, as if waiting for the mage to surrender. I doubted that would happen.

The mage's ring pulsed. Putrid green energy surged around us.

Fuck.

The only way to stop this was to get that ring.

I wrapped my hand around the ring. The rising magic seared me. This was not a blessing of the Eternal Magic; she would never create something as twisted and dark as this. I cried out but didn't let go. My palm melted around it. The smell of burning flesh—*my* burning flesh— assaulted me. I had to get this ring away from the mage.

I tightened my grip and pulled as hard as I could. The ring came away... but so did the mage's hand. It came away like his limbs were no stronger than those of a paper doll.

Huh.

My dragon form and fires may have abandoned me now, but at least my strength hadn't faded again. If I'd been in my dragon form, I would have undoubtedly bitten his hand off. At least this way, I wouldn't have to digest any part of the guy.

Still... I hadn't planned to do that. Oops. As blood spurted from the ends of the limbs, I prayed that Simon hadn't seen what I'd done. I wished I could shoot a cleansing flame over my blood-splattered scales, but I couldn't even gather enough heat to form a smoke ring.

I dropped the hand.

A wild and defiant look fell across the mage's tear-stained face. His nostrils flared. Then he pushed his neck against the hellhound's fiery and razor-sharp teeth. He didn't even cry out as he severed his carotid artery on Van's canine.

Van gagged at the rush of blood in his mouth and dropped the mage, but it was too late. The mage was dead.

I looked away. There was a time in my life when the sight of blood and death didn't faze me, but it'd been a long time since I'd been a warrior. Peace and laughter and love were what I wanted in my life now. I was an entertainer for a reason; I enjoyed making people feel good.

I never wanted to see death and suffering again. This… I shuddered. This was not my life anymore.

Simon leaped into my arms, as if he sensed my turmoil and wanted to comfort me. I grabbed him tight and pressed his face against my chest. My innocent little kitten didn't need to see the blood pooling around the mage any more than I did.

Unfortunately, we could still smell the blood.

"It's deja-fucking-vu, isn't it?" Isaac said as he shifted and dropped to his ass beside us.

"We knew this was coming," Van said. He'd shifted too and was wiping his mouth on his sleeve. "Jake's vision told us this would happen."

"I'm going to need a fuck ton of apples to help heal that many people." Teague rubbed at his forehead as he rejoined us. It took me a minute to realize apples must be what he used to balance his magic. Each supe had something, usually a food, that helped them replenish their magic after they used it.

"Did you get them all out?" Van asked.

Teague shook his head. "Only a couple. We have the key, but none of them are opening as easily as Ogden's cage. I'm having to use a lot of magic, but at least with the key we don't need Gage's magic too, like we did last time."

"They mustn't have finished the spells on Ogden's cage after they abducted him again," Van said, eyeing the stacks of cages.

Some supes begged to be free, but some were quietly resigned to whatever might happen next. Those quiet ones worried me. How long had they been held in captivity that they assumed we were their new owners, and believed their situation wouldn't improve?

I'd only been in a cage for a short time, but I expected that helpless feeling would linger for a while. I never wanted to be trapped like that again. Ever. In fact, I wasn't all that keen on small rooms, either. Simon's place was okay for now, but I needed big. My hoard room alone needed to be at least four times the size of my current one. I needed room to shift. I needed room to cuddle with my mate.

I'd heard of some truly spectacular supernatural architects. When I got home—and wasn't it peculiar to call Simon's apartment home?—I would start reviewing their portfolios. And I'd need a real estate agent. We needed some land, preferably somewhere Simon's mother and her network of nosy locals couldn't spy on us.

"Police!" someone shouted from the door.

"We've already apprehended the suspects," Van shouted back. He heaved a sigh, then pushed to his feet to brief the other police officers. After a few terse commands, someone jogged toward us.

"Which one of you is Teague? I'm here to help you. I'm trained in supernatural medicine."

"You'll have to wait for me to open the cages, but you can tend to them once they are out," Teague said to the officer. "I can't manage both things."

I wanted to help, but now that we'd neutralized the threats, my energy was fading again. So I let Simon guide me to a sunny patch of grass. He left only long enough to unearth a blanket from somewhere. Then he settled beside me and draped it over my bare shoulders.

More paramedics arrived soon after. They came around handing out bottles of water and magic replenishing foods. Simon and I shared a couple of tins of tuna. Fresh fish would have been better, but we could make do. Being close to Simon was also helping to fix my magic. It must have had something to do with the whistle, because I normally needed a lot more to balance my magic. I worried he was pushing magic into me at his own expense, so I tricked him into eating a larger portion of fish.

As we ate, Simon described all the things that had happened while we were apart.

I had mixed feelings about Wesley's death and knew I'd have to sit with it for a while. I'd thought he was my friend, but he'd betrayed me. He'd almost cost me my freedom. Was it over money? Or had something else driven him to that extreme? Should I have seen it coming? Could I have prevented this if I'd given him a raise or full management of The Drunken Drake?

Thoughts like that were futile, but feelings of guilt, warranted or not, lingered. And when Simon told me about jumping off the building? I'd hyperventilated so severely the paramedics rushed over, put a paper bag over my mouth, and told me to breathe slowly. For the record, holding a paper bag over a dragon's mouth when they're upset is a shitty plan, because then there was a fire to deal with on top of everything else.

Simon didn't say anything more after that. He pulled me onto his lap and rocked me back and forth. Slowly, the area filled with all the other naked former prisoners. More blankets were procured and distributed.

When it appeared the last of the prisoners had been

released and no one new had emerged from the building for a few minutes, I struggled to my feet. I gripped the blanket around my hips and staggered toward the door.

"Ogden? Where are you going?"

"I haven't seen Morgan yet. I want to check on him…"

Simon made a soft noise. I stopped and looked at him.

"What?"

"Morgan isn't here, Ogden. He was pushed through a portal. He's gone."

"No… That can't be…"

"I'm sorry. I tried to stop them." Simon's eyes were glossy as he clasped his hands in front of his chest.

"He was just here…" I stared at the building.

"Wait… I threw the tracking device in after him." Simon scrambled to his feet and dashed toward Officer Hellhound. "Van!"

Simon explained what'd happened, and Van made a call. Before the call ended, I knew it wasn't good news.

"They can't find the fucking signal," Van said. His eyes showed the fire of his hellhound.

"What does that mean?"

"Either something is blocking the signal or it's been destroyed." The hellhound clenched his teeth.

"Could it be out of range?"

He shook his head. "The magic and the technology combined should make it traceable anywhere."

Simon's shoulders drooped. "I should have jumped in after him. I should have…"

"This wasn't your fault, kitty cat." I wrapped my arms around him. "And if you went after him, I might have lost you too."

After that, we waited impatiently for the bear, the troll, and the human to be questioned. Van, being a hellhound, could tell when someone was lying, so I trusted him when he said those three didn't know where the unicorn had ended up. That meant we needed to talk to the demon Gage had hauled away. As if reading my thoughts, Van was already on his phone again.

"Damn it," Van snarled after a brief conversation.

"What? What happened?" Hayden demanded.

"The demon is gone." Van frowned.

"He escaped?" Hayden looked ready to shift and run all the way back to Willow Lake to hunt for the demon.

"No." Van shook his head. "Apparently when we killed the mage, the demon started convulsing. They tried to save him, but... He's dead. Gage suspects it was part of the mage's curse to keep the demon under his control."

Dread pooled in my stomach. "So how are we going to find Morgan?"

"What if he's with someone who is hurting him right now?" Simon paled. "Or... What if he is all alone and trapped in that cage with no one to care for him or release him?"

Van grimaced. "Unicorns have more magic than most supes. He can survive a long time, even if he is trapped without food or water."

"But it'd be torture..." I whispered.

Nelson emerged from the shadows at the side of the building. He looked me square in the eye. "I'll find him. I can promise you that."

His promise calmed me. I didn't need to be a hellhound

to trust Nelson was telling me the truth. I believed him. I had to trust he'd find Morgan.

"Thank you," I said, tugging the austere-looking man into my arms. "He is sweetness personified. He doesn't deserve this."

Behind me, Simon growled. Then he pulled me away from Nelson and pressed his face into my neck.

"It's okay, kitty cat. I'm all yours."

"Don't like you hugging people where you are half naked," he muttered as he tightened his arms around me.

"I know. I'm sorry." I patted him. Being in his arms gave me a sense of peace I feared I'd lost when I first woke in that stupid cage again.

It took another few hours before we could leave. This time, when we climbed into Van's SUV, I pulled Simon into the back seat and crawled into his lap. Then I cuddled close to my mate and hummed "We are the Champions" all the way back to Willow Lake.

I couldn't believe they'd all come to help us... to help me. I was thankful for every one of them and I would never forget what they had done today.

It would take a long time to pay off this debt to them.

Few younger supes observed ancient traditions like life debts. But I was ancient myself, so I did. I would use all my power to give each and every one of these people whatever they desired until my dragon believed they had been properly compensated for coming to my mate's aid when I couldn't.

Chapter Thirty-One

SIMON

For two full days, we didn't answer our phones or the door to my apartment. But by the third day, I knew Mama would take an axe to my door if we didn't surface soon. We probably should have gone to see her when we returned from Aspen Bay, but I'd just wanted to hold Ogden and never let him go.

We'd spent a lot of time in bed during those two days, just like we had during the week before, but we'd also talked a lot. We also watched a lot of shows. Ogden said I was addicted to nature documentaries, joking about how he now knew more about flamingoes, sea cucumbers, and tamarin monkeys than he'd ever wanted to. Then I'd tease him about his musicals and talent shows. And somehow it all worked.

Now that the Eternal Magic had blessed our union, everything was better. We had better conversations. Better sex. Just better *everything*.

Ogden told me about the many, many things he'd done throughout his long life, his family, and his plans to build a home for us in Willow Lake. I didn't have nearly as many stories to tell, but he seemed to find them interesting anyway.

And he'd also used that time to try to convince me his money was my money. I didn't fall for it right away, but his arguments were increasingly difficult to resist, particularly when he talked about the custom-designed home he envisioned for us. And, let's face it, Ogden deserved a life of luxury. I refused to live apart from him, so it looked like I'd have those luxuries too.

He could be relentlessly persuasive when he was naked... and I was naked... and we were doing naked things together.

And to make his point, he'd bought heaps more of *everything* from online stores. I'd thought after last week he wouldn't need to buy anything more for me. I was wrong. Since our mating, his current obsession was finding clothes and furnishings that matched the green of our mating mark.

Given Ogden's love of buying things, we'd need to move soon. There was almost too much stuff in the one-bedroom apartment already. Considering how little there'd been in my place before Ogden moved in, that said a lot about how much he'd ordered.

Surprisingly, I didn't mind wearing the clothing he bought me at home or even at work, but now that I was standing in front of the door to the Willow Lake Pub, I was tempted to go back home and change. By wearing such different and colorful clothing, I was just asking for people to look at me and talk about me. I mean, I already expected people to talk to us and about us, given what happened in Aspen Bay, but I didn't see the reason to give them even more things to talk about.

Ogden tightened his grip on my hand and hauled me inside. For a smaller guy, he was really strong.

As soon as we stepped inside, cheers went up around us. Mama rushed over and hugged me. Then she broke away and started patting my arms and chest as if to check that all my parts were still where they were supposed to be. When she finished fussing over me, Pops grabbed me and tugged me close.

"We were worried, son," he said. "But we're so proud of you. You did good."

My eyes burned by the time he let me go.

Then my brothers all came over and slapped me on the back. Even Justin was there. I hadn't seen him in a long time, so I was surprised when he hugged me almost as long as Mama and Pops had.

"I hope you don't plan on fighting any more bad guys," he whispered.

"Nope. I'm done," I said.

"Good. You aren't meant to do that. You need to leave that shit to…" He paused, his arms tightening around me. "Well, just leave that to other people," he finished.

Something about the way he said it made me wonder what he'd been doing since he left Willow Lake.

"Get your asses over here," Van called from one of the tables, "so I can buy you a drink."

Mama's eyes went wide when she realized the hellhound was calling me over to sit with him, Gage, and the others. She shooed me over, then pulled Pops and my brothers over too. She wouldn't miss out on an opportunity to be seen with the demon guardian. This kind of social currency would keep her going for weeks, maybe even months.

I glanced around the room. Almost every supe in town was here tonight, with two notable exceptions.

"Where is Hayden?" I asked after we'd pushed a few tables together and sat down.

Van pursed his lips and glanced at Gage. The two of them exchanged a long look before they both nodded. The silent communication thing was impressive, but it worried me. Van heaved a sigh, then looked at the people sitting around the table. Gage nudged Isaac, who was sitting closest to my family at the other end of the table. He leaned forward and boisterously regaled my parents and siblings with some story about when some wolf shifters had captured him and tried to ride him like a horse. His animated tale captivated everyone except Justin, who was watching my end of the table with keen interest.

"This can't go any further, but we've been meaning to bring you into the loop. Any extra eyes on the situation would be welcome."

I swallowed. I shouldn't be brought into any loop. I liked living loopless.

Then I paused and thought about that. That seemed like *old me* talking. *New me* wasn't all that different from *old me*, but if Hayden and the others needed me, I would go. I might not have in the past, but I would now. They'd been there for me when I needed them most, and I would be there for them in return, not out of obligation or debt, but because these people were my friends. My family. I wanted them to be safe and happy.

"We'll help any way we can," Ogden said, echoing my thoughts.

Van rubbed the back of his neck. "We think he's searching for Robbie."

"Alone?" I asked.

"Yep." Van nodded. "The asshole. He keeps forgetting how a pack works. Thinks he isn't the alpha, even though he is absolutely the alpha. Thinks he doesn't have a pack, even though he does. And now he thinks we'll let him go all lone fucking wolf."

"What do you need?" Ogden asked.

"Just… I don't know. Keep an eye out or something. If you see him skulking around, see if you can figure out where he's going."

"Why now? Why go after his brother after all this time?" Normally I'd never ask a question in a setting like this, but everyone else seemed to know about Hayden's nocturnal activities already, so Jeremy, Ash, and the others weren't asking the questions I'd have expected of them.

"I think it started when we found Brodie and Dakota out on Robbie's pack lands, but we haven't seen him in two days. Not since we got back from Aspen Bay." Van leaned forward. "I guess we haven't told you yet, but Norbert and his team found evidence that Robbie was working with that mage."

"Fuck," I muttered.

Mama might not have heard anything else we were saying, but she heard me swear. Her head swiveled in my direction so fast it was creepy. Her disapproving gaze locked on mine. I cringed.

"Sorry, Mama."

She nodded and returned her attention to Isaac, but I expected she'd corner me about my bad language before the end of the night. The tips of my ears were already stinging where I knew she'd pinch them.

"And what about Nelson? Any word from him yet?" Ogden asked.

He might not have known the unicorn for long, but my mate found Morgan's continued absence a heavy burden. If Gage hadn't agreed with Nelson that Ogden would slow him down, my dragon would have joined the search efforts. It was killing him to be sidelined.

"No." Gage frowned. "He's still following leads, but this might take some time."

"I understand." Ogden pinched his lips together. "Let me know when I can help." Not *if*, but *when*. I didn't want Ogden anywhere near the trafficking investigation because what if we hadn't stopped it all? What if getting involved put another target on his back? But if Ogden needed to do this, I would be at his side, even if I was quivering.

A few minutes later, Jake and Alice came over, balancing two full trays of drinks.

"Here's a round for the heroes of the day," he said as he gave everyone their drink. "On the house."

The freaky cat Paws jumped into the middle of the table and poked his nose into everyone's glass to sniff at them. When he realized none of them were for him, he sat down and scowled at Jake. His tail swished back and forth.

"Hey, where is mine?" Paws demanded.

Jake ignored him as he set my drink in front of me.

My hand curled around the pocket with the whistle. I supposed I should return it to Jake, but I still couldn't part with it. It'd brought Ogden into my life, and I couldn't imagine my life without him now. I owed everything to those three mangy wolves who'd dropped the whistle on the ground all those months ago.

Ogden turned to smile at me, as if guessing my thoughts. And then he was all I could see. It was as if the entire pub full of people disappeared and it was only the two of us.

"I love you, my kitty cat," he said.

"I love you too, Ogden."

When we kissed, I didn't even care about how my brothers were whistling or how my mama was ah-ing or how the whole pub seemed to have stopped what they were doing to watch us. I was with my dragon and from here on out, I was going to live my eight remaining lives to their fullest.

Epilogue

SIMON

When I'd decided to live my remaining eight lives to their fullest, I'd never meant for this to happen. Not that my eight lives meant anything anymore, since apparently when Ogden and I had been bound by the Eternal Magic, our life spans had merged somehow. The idea still seemed fantastical, no matter how many people told me otherwise. And what if they were wrong? Because I was sure I felt the difference when I lost my one life, even if everyone did their best to convince me I was mistaken. They said between worrying about Ogden and being so badly injured, it'd just felt like I'd lost one of my nine.

I wasn't convinced.

But it didn't matter. After a lifetime of preserving my lives, I wasn't about to become a daredevil overnight just to find out if all those people were telling me the truth. So how had I ended up here?

I stared at my beautiful mate. His shifted form was

gorgeous. His long, lean body shimmered under the fading sunlight. His small but powerful black wings twitched on his back. The tip of his tail had curled toward me, to nudge me closer to him.

"Come on, Simon love," Ogden coaxed. I loved the way his long, forked tongue moved when he said my name, but I didn't love what he was trying to talk me into.

"I don't know…" I glanced over my shoulder toward the tree line, which was hard to do with the helmet on my head. If I shifted and ran, I could put this off for another night, maybe longer.

"I won't let anything happen to you. You know I won't."

I mean, I did trust him.

He'd been horrified to learn about my jump off his rooftop garden the night of the attack. Since then, he'd woken up sweaty and panting from nightmares about it on several nights. The only thing that calmed him was assuring him I was still alive and at his side. So I knew he'd never put me at risk.

Except…

"What if someone sees—"

"Simon," Ogden interrupted me. His vibrant blue eyes stared at me until I met his gaze.

"Yes?"

"It's a new moon so the sky is dark and we're going to fly toward the mountains, away from all the towns and houses. No one will see us. It is the perfect night to fly. I want to share this with you. Please come with me, kitty cat."

He wasn't playing fair. He knew I'd give him anything he asked. Just... Why did he have to ask for this?

"Are you sure this contraption is going to work?" I tugged at the collar of the strange bodysuit he'd found for me online. It had fabric sewn between the legs and under my arms. When I spread my arms and legs, I looked like the flying squirrel Clive had tried to emulate all those years ago.

"Of course." Ogden's tone was patient, but sure. "And remember, it is only a third failsafe, nothing more. The first and most important safety measure is that I won't do anything to make you fall, and then we have the harness. It's cinched tight across my belly and isn't going anywhere. The wingsuit is only an extra precaution. You've been practicing your position all week. If you somehow get separated from me, you're going to hold your arms and legs away from your body like a starfish and slow yourself down. But even without your wingsuit, you know I would catch you. This is just to give you a little more peace of mind."

"Right. I know. Okay." I huffed out a couple of quick breaths and jumped up and down.

"Okay?"

"Yes."

"Then, come over and climb aboard."

I scrambled onto my dragon and slid into the harness before I could talk myself out of this. Again. This was the third time this week that Ogden had tried to get me into the air. This was the first time I'd made it as far as getting into the harness. The harness was custom-made for Ogden's body and was essentially a bucket seat that was secured to Ogden with thick straps wrapped around his torso.

"Okay now, buckle up."

With trembling hands,I tugged the safety harness over my shoulders and across my chest. The buckles were the hardest to snap into place—my fingers didn't want to work. When everything finally clicked into place, I was ready to throw up all over him.

"Done?"

I gulped. "Uh… I…"

"Simon? Are you strapped into the harness?"

I nodded. Of course, he couldn't see that. "I… yes. I—"

His wings flapped. His body undulated. I screamed.

Then we were in the air. My fingers shifted to my cat's claws as I clung to the harness. I wanted to grab onto Ogden, but what if I hurt him? I didn't want to hurt him. And I didn't want to distract him.

But I might puke on him.

There was like a ninety percent chance.

I closed my eyes and pretended I was on a wobbly carnival ride. Or a horse. Yeah. That probably made more sense. I was on the back of a horse. Yep. This was me, moseying along like a cowboy. Down a trail. On the ground.

"Do you see it, Simon? Do you see how beautiful it is up here?"

My imaginary horse evaporated.

"Simon?"

"Mmhmm?"

"Do you have your eyes closed?"

"Uh… maybe?"

Ogden laughed. "Open your eyes, baby. Look around. I promise, I've got you."

I forced my eyes open.

"Oh, fuck." I slammed my hand over my mouth.

Ogden laughed harder. "It's okay. I won't tell anyone you swore."

I kicked him softly with my foot. I didn't appreciate him laughing at me. He turned his head until he could see me from the corner of his eye.

"I love you, kitty cat. You're doing great."

I let out a shaky breath and flashed him a tremulous thumbs up. It was false bravado. I knew it. He knew it. I got the impression he was still laughing at me, but at least he wasn't teasing me about it. Then I made myself look beyond Ogden to the darkening sky overhead and the world below.

"Wow…" I murmured.

I'd never imagined the world would look so different from above. Willow Lake, with its twinkling streetlights and tidy little streets, was unexpectedly pretty. But my eyes were drawn to the sun setting in the west. The last remnants of twilight clung to the horizon and shimmered across the lake.

"It reminds me of that night we shared on your rooftop."

A lot happened that night and not all of it had been bad. That was the night the Eternal Magic had blessed us as fated mates, so that part of the night, at least, would always be special. I often pretended, if only in my head, the rest of the night—Ogden's abduction, my leap off the roof, and seeing someone murdered right in front of me— was some other night. That probably wasn't the healthiest way to deal with everything that'd happened, but Ogden was still trying to find a therapist we both trusted, so for now that's how I coped.

"Do you remember how we danced under the starlight?" he asked.

I smiled. "Of course."

Then he hummed the same song we'd danced to that night. I loved hearing him sing and hum. Well, okay, I loved everything about him. I leaned back in the harness. Tension eased away and I let myself marvel at the beauty all around me, but mostly, I looked at my dragon.

I understood now why he'd pushed so hard to get me up here. This was a part of him, and he wanted to share it with me. He wanted to share everything with me, just like I wanted to share everything with him. We were bound through the magic of the summoning and then as mates. We were destined to be together like this. Always.

"Thank you, love," I said, leaning forward to brush my hand along his long neck. "Thank you for sharing this with me. I used to think I was a scaredy cat and nothing more, but now, with you, I am simply yours. Your love. Your mate. Yours. And together we can do anything, even fly."

THE END

Want to see what happens when Ogden tries to convince Simon to go flying with him? Sign up for my newsletter and download the bonus scene:

www.loriames.com/newsletter

———

Interested in seeing Hayden finally get his happily-ever-after with his fated mate? Alphas Never Hide, *the last book in the new Willow Lake Supernaturals series, is now available!*

A Note from the Author

Hi!

Yay! You've made it to the end of Simon and Ogden's book!

I hadn't originally planned for Simon's book to come at this point in the series. I mean, I love Simon, but he doesn't show himself at his best in the first few books. And, even now that he's found his inner lion and is now happily mated with no need to worry about protecting his nine lives anymore (even if Simon isn't convinced), I still expect he will be hiding under furniture again at some point. But, Simon kept whispering in my head that he'd found something amazing—having voices in your head when you're a writer is okay, right? Anyway, I couldn't ignore him. So I hope you enjoyed their story!

I'm such a softie when it comes to these guys! It broke my heart when Simon jumped off the building, but I was so proud of him too. Ha! Listen to me. I talk about these characters like they are real. But sometimes it feels that way after living with their stories for so long.

I finished the first draft of Simon's book in March 2023 and began revising it after Jake and Gage's book was released. I'd expected to finish it quickly, but I hadn't anticipated that the book would almost double during the revision stage so it took a little longer than I'd anticipated. I hadn't started the editing stage planning for such a massive expansion, but I'm happy that I put in the extra time. Simon and Ogden deserved it! And with the help of some amazing people, I am super happy with how it all came together.

Thank you to my beta readers Kirk Waite (Rare Bird Beta Reading) and Courtney Bassett. You have both been amazing help as I finished Simon's story, especially since it was a little rough in spots when you got a look at it. Thank you also to my editor June, who is a calm and steady rock in my process. I'd be lost without her. You have all helped me so much as I worked through the final steps on this book. But, as always, if any errors have survived to the final version, that's on me. If you spot any typos or oddities, feel free to email me (lori@lori ames.com), rather than reporting the book.

One last thing... Did you figure out who finds their happily-ever-after next? It is Hayden! Yay! Finally! He deserves it, right? I've started writing his book already and I'm so excited about it! I don't have a timeline on a release date for it yet, but if you join my newsletter, you'll receive all the latest news, including an email when my next book is available at Amazon.

Okay, I think that's all I have for now! Wishing you a never ending supply of books you love! <3

Cheers,
Lori

PS… Reviews help other readers decide if a book might be something they want to read, so please consider writing a review of *Cats Never Fly*. That would be wonderful. I'm sure even Jeremy and Ogden would want to serenade you with a duet. Well, they would have to agree on a song first… '50s vs. '80s? I'm not sure who would win.

About the Lori

Lori Ames writes MM romance with touch of magic! When Lori was in elementary school, she wrote a very compelling story about a girl with a prickly personality who turned into a rose. (Sounds amazing, right? She knew you'd agree.) Then she discovered romances in her teens and, well, she knew she wanted to write romances. It took her a little longer to find MM romances, but once she did, she was addicted. She lives in a small town in Alberta with her husband and an elderly black cat.

You can find out more here:

- Patreon: patreon.com/c/LoriAmes
- Facebook Group: facebook.com/groups/LoriAmesReaders
- Facebook Page: facebook.com/LoriAmesAuthor
- Website: loriames.com
- Newsletter Sign Up: loriames.com/newsletter
- Bluesky: bsky.app/profile/loriames.bsky.social
- MM Wire: themmwire.circle.so/c/lori-ames/

I also have a store with fun merchandise now! Find a link to it on my website: loriames.com